C0-ATL-662

Annette Cappelli

THE
GHOST OF
AFRICA

ALSO BY DON BROBST

Thirteen Months: The True Story of One Couple's
Journey of Passion, Life, and Undying Love

THE GHOST OF AFRICA

DON BROBST

Waterfall
PRESS

This is a work of fiction. Names, characters, organizations, places, events, and incidents are either products of the author's imagination or are used fictitiously.

Text copyright © 2016 by Don Brobst
All rights reserved.

No part of this book may be reproduced, or stored in a retrieval system, or transmitted in any form or by any means, electronic, mechanical, photocopying, recording, or otherwise, without express written permission of the publisher.

Published by Waterfall Press, Grand Haven, MI

www.brilliancepublishing.com

Amazon, the Amazon logo, and Waterfall Press are trademarks of Amazon.com, Inc., or its affiliates.

ISBN-13: 9781503933224
ISBN-10: 1503933229

Cover design by Cyanotype Book Architects

Printed in the United States of America

This book is dedicated to the precious children of Africa, struggling to survive each day in the face of tyranny and famine, and to the village chiefs in South Sudan who shared their lives with us.

PROLOGUE

Twelve men lay motionless on their beds in the makeshift barrack. Charles Manning stood in the doorway in disbelief as the stench closed his nostrils. But it wasn't death he smelled. It was the chemicals and vomit. He turned in disgust to leave the room, but Quinn's massive frame blocked his exit.

"You didn't come to Africa to leave so quickly. So tell me, Doctor . . . how many of these men do you think are still alive?" Quinn gripped Manning's shoulders with his enormous hands and spun him to face the test subjects that lay before him. "How many?"

Quinn's calm voice forced a chill down Manning's spine as nausea urged him to close his eyes and swallow hard. He rubbed his sweaty palms against his slacks as beads of perspiration dripped from his brow.

"See what you've done, Doctor? This, after only fifteen hours of exposure." Quinn squeezed harder on Manning's shoulders, radiating pain across his back and chest. Manning imagined Quinn could crush him with his grip alone. "Tell me how your work is coming now. Is your experiment a success?" Quinn pushed Manning into the room with such force that he fell to the dirt floor.

From there he saw puddles beside each bed. When one of the men moved, Manning forced himself to stand. He hurried to the man's side and reached for his pulse. It was faint.

"He's alive, Quinn! This man's alive."

Quinn walked to the bed unhurried, as if he didn't care, and looked at the man. "What are you feeling right now?" he asked him.

Instead of answering, the man turned to Manning. "Help me."

Manning attempted to take the man's hand.

"Don't—you'll catch what I have." He glanced around the room, then back up at Manning. "Water . . . I'm so thirsty."

Quinn shook the man's leg. "I asked you a question. What are you feeling right now?"

Manning fidgeted with the stethoscope that hung around his neck as he waited for the man to answer. His heart pounded, and he felt short of breath, anticipating what was about to happen. The man's pupils constricted and he wheezed. Manning stepped back from the bed.

Quinn seemed to notice and let go of the ill man's leg just as a seizure shook him violently. Less than a minute later, he stopped moving. Quinn motioned for Manning to check him.

"He's dead."

Quinn punched the support post beside the bed and shook his head. "You promised me."

Manning did his best to control the panic rising in his chest. "You have to understand, Quinn—we're experimenting. We don't have all the answers yet. I don't have a photographic memory like . . ." He caught himself and fell silent.

"I've paid you a great deal of money for this formula, and you have immeasurable riches to gain from its success, Dr. Manning. You told me you could deliver it in three months—it has been six. Instead of riches, dead men surround me." Quinn swept his hand through the air as he turned in a circle, emphasizing the carnage in the room. "Explain this to me!" He walked from bed to bed, glancing briefly at each man before turning back to Manning. "My time is running out. That means your time is running out. Do you understand?"

Manning's head throbbed, and he used his shirtsleeve to wipe his brow. "There's no need for threats."

Quinn grabbed Manning by the neck and pulled him within centimeters of his face, drew his sidearm from its holster, and placed the cold steel against Manning's temple. "Don't take my promise as a threat, my friend."

Manning struggled to breathe. "I can do this." He could barely force the words out. "Let me. I can do it."

Quinn released Manning's neck and shoved his pistol into its holster. Manning gasped for air.

"You have one more chance to prove yourself to me, Doctor. Go back to your lab in New York." Quinn flailed his hands in the air as he turned away. "Find the papers, steal the papers, ask your partner—I don't care. Whatever it takes, get me that formula or don't come back. I'll send someone for you instead—to finish this."

Manning nodded nervously. "Understood. You won't be disappointed again. I'll get it right this time." He stammered, "I'm sorry for all these men who died."

Quinn shook his head. "These men who died?" He walked to the door of the barrack and pushed it open. "Take a closer look, Dr. Manning. Please. I insist. Come and see your work."

As Manning squinted to see in the fading light of day, he couldn't believe the scene that stretched before him. He shook his head. "No . . ."

Everywhere he turned, bodies lay scattered on the ground—men, women, children. Some struggled, most lay motionless.

"You have two months, Dr. Manning."

The village was silent.

CHAPTER ONE

The shrill cockpit perimeter alarm jolted Dr. Paul Branson from sleep. "Sorry about that, Paul, just a little turbulence." The voice of his brother-in-law, Jim, crackled over Paul's headphones. "I wasn't expecting a radar sweep." Paul reached into his backpack for binoculars—being a good companion in South Sudanese airspace meant acting as a copilot and lookout rather than just a mere passenger. "I guess we flew too close to the North Sudan border, but I think we're a little more invisible at this altitude. I wish we didn't have to take this route at all. It's out of our way, but if we fly straight to Mundri we'll be over rebel territory. I have no desire to be chased by a shoulder-fired missile today."

North Sudan's incursions into the South were increasing in frequency. Paul turned and scanned the interior of the twelve-seater Cessna turboprop. Half the seats had been removed to accommodate his medical supplies, which were strapped to the floor with cargo nets. He adjusted his headphones and glanced again at the radar. After he spent a few minutes scanning an empty horizon, a pit formed in his stomach. "Hey, Jim, that's our problem right there."

"Yep, I got 'em." Jim tapped his finger on the blip entering the edge of the screen. "Can you record the new parameters for me?"

"Sure." Paul reached for the keyboard and entered his password into the computer. The temperature in the cockpit rose ten degrees as they descended sharply. "Out my window—four o'clock," he said.

Jim craned his neck. "I don't . . . hold on . . . I see it. What kind of plane is it?"

"Can't tell yet. It's too far away. You fly. I'll keep an eye on it."

"Right." Jim shifted in his seat.

Paul attempted to ignore his nervousness as the single speck became two, closing the distance rapidly. He studied the approaching aircraft for warning signs and didn't like what he saw—something hung from the undercarriage on each one.

"Jim, there are actually two. They're headed straight for us, and they're belly-heavy."

Jim leaned forward to look out the copilot window past Paul's broad shoulders. He shook his head. "Not good. Belly-heavy can mean only one thing out here. They're packing."

Paul looked again. "If those are missiles suspended from the fuselage, they may be military aircraft. We'll find out soon. They're making good time. Can you give me a better vantage point?"

Jim banked the Cessna into a right turn. "Is that better?"

Paul focused on the approaching aircraft. "Pull back on course, Jim. They're coming fast on our right."

"Hang on." The plane banked hard left as Jim fought the controls to the original heading. Within seconds, North Sudanese helicopter gunships flanked them, armed with thirty-caliber machine gun turrets and fifty-caliber automatic weapons mounted on the sides. Missiles suspended from their underbellies unfolded into launch position. The gray, camouflaged tails of the giant choppers bore the North Sudanese identifying marks.

Jim looked to his left, then his right. "Military?"

Paul put the binoculars down and sat straight in his seat. "Yeah, and they mean business." He stared at the machine guns aimed directly at their cockpit. "What are North Sudanese gunships doing in South Sudanese airspace?"

Jim adjusted the settings on the radio as if he hadn't heard the question. "Come in, North Sudan military escort. Come in, escort." He changed frequencies and repeated the call in English and Arabic.

Without warning, one gunship suddenly closed the sixty meters that separated them to fifteen meters. A soldier appeared in the doorway beside the machine gun.

"They're manning the fifty-cals. We need to do something, Jim!"

"Use your hands and signal."

"Signal what?"

"I don't know, but do it fast!"

Paul turned to the chopper on the passenger side, threw up his arms, and shrugged his shoulders as if to say, "What do you want us to do?"

The soldier manning the machine gun pointed to the ground and moved his hand up and down.

"He wants you to land."

"What?" Jim looked out his window, scouring the terrain. "You sure? That's easier said than done out here."

Paul felt his chest tighten as a sudden wave of apprehension swept over him. "I'm sure. They want us on the ground right now."

"Give them a thumbs-up. We'll set it down—over there." Jim pointed to a small clearing. "We should be able to pull that off. Maybe." He gave Paul an unnerving grimace.

Paul signaled the gunships, causing them to back away, although they continued to follow close. He turned to Jim. "What do you need from me?"

"Keep an eye on the gauges. I'm gonna have all I can do to keep us upright on that uneven terrain."

The choppers hovered dangerously near as they forced the Cessna down. Jim maneuvered the plane past a few broken trees and approached the short rough clearing. The gunships gave them some space—just enough to land.

"This is going to be bumpy."

Paul nodded tensely. "That's an understatement."

They touched down, and the plane rattled as if it were pulling apart at the rivets. They skidded to the right and stopped, just before reaching a massive rock jutting from the ground.

Engulfed in the sandstorm of the landing choppers, the plane trembled. Before the dust cleared, soldiers circled the aircraft with assault weapons trained on the cockpit.

"Don't move yet." Jim spoke calmly as he shut the engine down. "Wait till they tell us. I've heard too many stories. These guys don't play."

A tall officer wearing fatigues, a sidearm, and an imposing knife on his belt approached the plane. "Come out. Hands over your heads. If you have weapons—we shoot." His English was crude but understandable.

Paul and Jim exited the craft, and four North Sudanese guards pushed them against the tail to search them while several others climbed on board, pulled out their duffels, and tossed them on the ground. The body odor of the soldiers, mixed with the arid air and settling dust, nauseated Paul. He leaned against the plane.

"Turn around. Keep your hands up."

Paul took a deep breath to steady himself before he and Jim turned to face the commander.

"Passports," he said impatiently.

Paul pulled out his papers, and the commander snatched them from him, then motioned for them both to put their hands over their heads again. He flipped through Paul's passport, reviewing every page. "You checked in to have your documents stamped in Arua this morning?"

"Yes. We usually stop in Arua. It's—"

"You are Dr. Paul Branson?"

Paul looked at the man quizzically. "Yes. I work in the villages of South Sudan. But my passport doesn't say I'm a doctor. How did you—?"

"Why you do not help our people in North Sudan?"

"I'm not welcomed in North Sudan."

The commander looked back at Paul's passport, then showed it to another officer. They spoke quietly in Arabic. Paul listened intently, but only picked up the words "tell him right away." As the second officer hurried back to the nearest chopper, Paul glanced at Jim, who shook his head, indicating that he hadn't made out what they were saying either.

The commander turned back to Paul. "Where do you go in South Sudan?" He scrutinized the pages again from the front, as if starting over.

"Flying into Mundri."

"You will stay there?"

"Well, no—just passing through."

"Where do you go? Where do you stay?" The commander seemed agitated.

"Matta. I'll be living in Matta for the next three months." The soldier studied the markings on one page. "Can I put my hands down now?" Paul asked.

"No."

"I'm unarmed. I think we've proven that."

"I said no." The commander threw the passport on the ground at Paul's feet, turned to Jim, and grabbed his papers. "You are the pilot?" He skimmed through Jim's documents.

"Yes, well, we're both pilots. I mean—I flew today, but he also . . . never mind. Yes. I'm the pilot."

"Stay away from North Sudan." He thrust the papers into Jim's hands.

"Yes, sir."

The commander turned his attention back to Paul. "Pick up your passport."

The moment Paul retrieved it, the commander stepped closer. "Put your hands over your head again." Paul complied reluctantly.

"If you come near the border again, we shoot you. This is your warning." He moved within centimeters of Paul's face, stared at him, then turned and spat on the ground.

The soldiers pulled boxes from the main passenger compartment and took them to the choppers.

Paul lowered his hands. "Those are my medical supplies."

The commander pulled his pistol from its holster, and Paul quickly raised his hands over his head again. He eyed Paul as he held the gun at his side. "You care about North Sudan also, do you not?"

Paul didn't answer.

"You will donate these supplies," he demanded sardonically and stabbed the barrel of his pistol against Paul's chest. Paul didn't flinch. He knew they would probably sell the goods on the black market, but the cold steel against his ribs reminded him who had the upper hand. He watched in silence while the soldiers transferred case after case from the plane to their gunships.

As they boarded the choppers, the commander holstered his pistol. "When do you go to Matta?"

"I don't understand. What difference does that make?"

"You fool. You will stay here until you answer." He waved at one of the soldiers on the closest gunship.

The unmistakable sound of the chambering of the fifty-caliber machine gun caught Paul's attention. The gunner took aim at the airplane engine.

"Wait—tonight! Late tonight I arrive in Matta—if you let us leave now."

The commander grinned and waved for the gunner to stand down. "Why does it matter when I'm to arrive?"

"I ask the questions," the man said before signaling with his hand for the pilots to start the choppers. He turned, walked to his gunship, and climbed aboard moments before it lifted from the ground.

Paul and Jim covered their faces as the massive helicopters rose together and disappeared in a thick whirlwind of swirling sand, making it nearly impossible to breathe. As the cyclone settled, they coughed and rubbed their eyes.

Paul walked back to the plane and glanced inside at the empty cargo area. "My actual medical supplies, bottled water, and filters are still safe in the underbelly, right?"

Jim opened the lower compartment to check. "Right. Everything's still in the smuggler's bay. They just stole three hundred pounds of Clif Bars and Imodium."

Paul nodded his approval. "Next time, a little warning like 'we may get grounded by some gunships today' would be nice."

"Well, if it had ever happened before, maybe I would have included it in my preflight briefing. But, you know, not my fault, dude. They said almost nothing to me. *You* obviously looked suspicious." Jim closed and latched the underbelly compartment.

"I wonder why they forced us down. And how did he know I was a doctor?"

"Not sure, but these guys had an agenda." Jim checked his watch. "Speaking of agendas, we need to move." He bent to inspect the landing gear for damage. "Paul, can you walk the field and look for rocks or ruts I need to avoid? I don't want to bend a strut and get us stranded. Landing on a dime is one thing—taking off on one is another."

Paul set off across the field. "I got this. You check the plane. We still have a long day ahead."

"Remember, we're in black mamba territory, so keep your eyes open."

◆ ◆ ◆

Within an hour the plane roared down the makeshift runway, back on course to Mundri.

Paul rested his head against the seat and gazed out the window. Far below, tufts of trees appeared as tiny islands in a sea of dry grass interrupted by a single watering hole. Elephants gathered on its muddy banks while gazelles, frightened by the drone of the plane, ran toward the foothills. He caught himself smiling.

The midmorning sun stretched its brilliant fingers across the flatlands, reaching over the Imatong Mountains and bathing the clouds in a deep pink hue.

"Doesn't seem like six months."

Jim turned to him. "What's that?"

"It's been six months since I was last here."

Jim shook his head. "That's hard to believe, but I guess it has."

"I've missed it, but . . ."

Jim quickly filled the silence. "But it's going to be good. Different, that's for sure, but good. Why don't you take a nap? I'll wake you when we're close. There's nothing to see for the next three hours but elephants and grass."

Paul could always count on Jim to help him temporarily move past what he'd never get over. He had to admit he was tired even though it was only midmorning.

"I'll wake you when we're ten minutes out." Jim tapped the temperature gauge in the instrument cluster. "You know this is the coolest you're going to be for a few months. It's thirty degrees hotter on the ground. So sleep while it's somewhat comfortable. You're gonna need your energy."

Paul gave him an affirming glance, laid his head back, and stared out the window. It didn't take long for his mind to focus on the empty seat behind him. Africa had been Nicki's dream, and now it was his job to live it for her.

CHAPTER TWO

Almost two hours later, Jim tapped Paul's shoulder and pointed to a vacant swath carved into the woodlands. "There she is—Mundri landing field. Last stop before Matta, your home away from home."

Paul gazed out the forward window as he tightened his seat belt harness and scanned the landscape. "That runway looks shorter every time we land here."

"Yeah. No joke," Jim said under his breath.

After circling the field, they began their approach. Below them they could see villagers hurrying into the area to remove debris from the landing site. The region, unspoiled by modern civilization, provided no place to land except a rocky path bordered by trees.

Paul always kept the details of their arrivals quiet. A year earlier two pilots had been killed on this airstrip when terrorists overran their plane.

After the expected rough landing, they taxied to the end of the field. Fifty or sixty villagers ran to meet them as the engine powered down.

Jim pointed to the grinning crowd. "Your family awaits."

In this part of Africa, people were convinced that they'd been forgotten by the rest of the world. But they weren't. Not by Paul and not by Jim.

Paul opened the copilot door and climbed down the folding ladder as the growing crowd clapped and danced.

He did his best to feel festive, but all he could picture in his mind was Nicki, twirling the children around and singing with the women whenever the plane landed. Occasionally she'd even dance with them. Without her, the event was strikingly different, and Paul struggled with the change. But Africa was where she'd want him to be. These people needed him, and he needed them.

"Hey, you want to give me a hand?" Paul turned and saw Jim struggling with the cargo. He hurried to the bay and grabbed a box.

"Sorry, man. Zoned out for a minute."

As Paul reached into the plane to pull his gear out, a firm hand gripped his shoulder from behind, causing him to drop the backpack. Emeka, one of the leaders in Matta, engulfed Paul's hand in his and shook it hard. His grip was so strong Paul almost winced.

"Hello, Dr. Paul!" Emeka grinned from ear to ear. His bright smile and excited eyes reminded Paul of a child on Christmas morning. Emeka couldn't do enough for Paul and certainly wasn't about to let him carry his own bags. With his giant arm, he gently pushed Paul aside to keep him from retrieving anything from the bay, then called to the men in the crowd for help. Within moments they were all carrying supplies from the plane to the jeeps as they'd done countless times before.

Although English was the official language of South Sudan, the local dialect was Dinka. Paul spoke Dinka and some Arabic, and many of the villagers, including Emeka, spoke English. Between them, they understood each other well.

Emeka looked at him. "I want to tell you something. I'll do what I can to help." Paul knew that he meant more than just helping with the boxes of medicines. Emeka glanced at the ground briefly, then back at Paul. "There isn't much I can do to make up for Nicki not being here," he continued, "but I can lift, and I can carry, and I can be your friend. No matter what, a day alive is a good day."

Paul cleared his throat, in awe of this man standing in the heat of the African sun, offering all he could—all he had. "I remember someone else saying that to me every morning for twenty years."

Emeka grinned as he grabbed another box and headed for the jeep.

Paul leaned into the cargo bay to retrieve the next item as another voice came from behind him. "Doctor, it's good to see you." Buru, a village elder, spiritual leader, and their most skilled hunter, stood tall before him, his bow and quiver slung over his left shoulder.

"And it's good to see you, Buru." Paul shook his hand.

Buru had made the three-hour drive to the airstrip with Emeka so they would have two jeeps to help transport all of Paul's supplies and to protect him on the trip back to Matta. Bandits were known to be active along the roads, and Paul was glad to have Buru along. As the final supplies were unloaded from the plane, Buru and Paul walked to the vehicles to supervise.

A woman approached Paul with a worn plastic cup filled to the brim with fresh mango juice. Mango juice was his favorite, and he couldn't help but snatch the cup eagerly from her hand. He gave her an apologetic look for doing so, an apology she seemed to accept, offering him a knowing smile. A long sip of the sweet, fragrant orange drink satisfied him to his toes.

"I thought I could smell those sweet blossoms in the air."

Buru laughed. "The mangos are in season. You came just in time."

Paul took another sip of the rich drink. "How's Leza?"

"She . . . is stronger, and waiting for you." Buru paused, then added, "She speaks of nothing but your return. Emeka and I wondered if you would come back—alone."

Paul looked into the distance. "It's been a struggle. But I knew I had to. I wanted to." He paused for a moment. "Did you receive the medicine I sent Leza last month?"

"Yes. But she needs you more than medicine." Buru tilted his head. "Are you sure you're ready to be here?"

Paul leaned against the jeep and folded his arms. Things would never be the same without Nicki, but he was here, and there was work to do. He nodded. "Yeah. I'm ready."

The village children gathered around Paul, and he welcomed the distraction. As he selected a box from the pile and tore off the top, the children began to dance and shout with anticipation. Paul always brought them something fun. When he lifted out a deflated soccer ball, their excitement turned to disappointment. He grinned as he searched inside the box, finally removing a small hand pump. He inserted the nozzle into the flat white-and-black ball and slowly inflated it. The children shrieked when it transformed into a perfectly round globe.

Paul waved his hand, signaling the kids to "go long." Kicking it high in the air, he watched with a smile as they scrambled to catch it. Paul had taught them to play soccer a year earlier, but they insisted on catching the ball and running with it like a football.

As Buru supervised the men packing the jeeps, Paul returned to the plane and helped Jim secure the cargo bay. Then his brother-in-law turned and shook his hand.

"I need to get in the air. It's a long flight to Entebbe, and I have to be on the ground before dark." Jim climbed the short folding metal ladder to the cockpit, and Paul helped him flip it up and secure it. Jim moved his seat forward into position and checked his gauges.

"You have your instructions memorized, right?" Paul asked.

Jim strapped himself in. "Of course. I'll see you right here in a week with the new chemo doses for Leza. We should have the shipment a day in advance, packed in dry ice. I'll deliver it the following morning still frozen."

"Jim. One more thing. If anything goes wrong—"

"What? No, nothing's—"

Paul held up his hand. "Hear me out. If anything goes wrong, I want you to be the one to tell my daughter. She misses her mom. This is a struggle for her—my leaving for Africa again. And even though she insisted I come back before it's too late for Leza, she's uncertain about, well, everything. If anything happens to me, you're the only family she has. My sisters will always be there for her, but they live so far away."

Jim paused, then gave a quick nod. "You have my word." He closed the door and lifted his hand in a swirling motion. Paul responded with the same gesture, indicating the propeller was clear and it was safe to start the engine.

Minutes later, the small craft roared down the dirt field. Paul stood waving as the villagers cheered. Then it lifted and disappeared in the distance.

Paul watched long after it was out of sight. Collecting his thoughts, he turned to Emeka. "It's good to be back. We should leave for Matta so we can make it there before dark."

Emeka nodded. "We must be careful. The roads are filled with robbers and thieves. Times are hard for the people. Hunger has made them desperate."

Paul checked his watch. "We'll take the old road. We should have time." He'd traveled it before. No more than a path barely wide enough for a vehicle, it was rarely used. If anyone intended to ambush him, it was the last road they'd expect him to take.

Paul climbed behind the wheel of one of the two jeeps. He leaned back in the seat and closed his eyes for a minute, savoring the squeals and laughter of excited children playing with their new soccer ball. His nostrils filled with the scent of nearby elephant dung and the sweet fragrance of mango blossoms—only in Africa. He leaned forward, stretching to reach the backpack he'd purposely placed on the passenger floorboard. He hadn't wanted it buried with the rest of the duffels as the men were packing. As he lifted it to move it to the seat behind him, he saw a corner of his ragged Bible protruding from the pocket. He paused and lifted it from the pouch, instinctively rubbing his fingers across the smooth, familiar surface. The engraved leather felt like home. He carefully secured it in the backpack and tossed it onto the backseat.

Buru approached the passenger side of the jeep and unstrapped his bow from his shoulder. He carefully laid it on the floor behind the seat as if it were a priceless heirloom, then positioned the quiver of arrows beside it. Grabbing the handle above the door frame, he pulled himself into the dusty passenger seat.

He leaned toward Paul. "I told Emeka to find a few detours to be certain we're not ambushed." He gave Paul a grin. "Try to keep up."

Paul cranked the old but faithful engine. "Yeah, he told me about the robbers on the main roads." He dropped the jeep into first gear. "This is not my first rodeo, my friend."

Buru offered a blank stare.

"Sorry. That means I've done this before."

Buru nodded, and Paul noticed a faint grin on his face as they followed Emeka's jeep onto the narrow path to Matta.

As he maneuvered the rough road, Paul thought about his new village home. Even by Sudanese standards, Matta was small, with just five hundred people, though the surrounding settlements utilized a common clean water supply, which added several thousand more. Providing clean well water had been one of Paul's passions from the beginning. Without fresh water, no amount of medicine could keep people healthy.

Matta was Buru's and Emeka's tribe, Leza's home, and the place where Paul felt called to go. He'd thought about moving there permanently to provide full-time care to the villagers, but Nicki's cancer diagnosis had changed everything.

"How have things been, Buru? I mean in general. Are the wells working, the cattle surviving—any new threats?"

"The panther is back. For the past two weeks, many of our people have seen a black panther in the vicinity of the village near dusk. It's not a common occurrence. At the same time, a panther has attacked men in the villages of Wiroh and Witto, killing to eat. This is something to be feared. There's no escape if you're the panther's prey."

"Okay, in by dark. Got it."

"I'm serious, Dr. Paul. The black panther is the shadow of death. We call it the Ghost of Africa, and for a reason. Its presence means something evil is about to happen or that someone is going to die. If the panther enters the village while there is food in the fields, as there is now, he is there for a reason. He brings a message. The panther carries great power among the people of our nation."

"That's very superstitious, Buru. Do you? Believe this, I mean?"

Buru paused. "The spirits can speak to us as they wish. They choose who lives—who dies. If it's time to die, they send the panther. If the panther comes and does not devour the one he stalks, he brings a message from the spirits."

"I think Chief Chima tolerates me because I'm a doctor. He sure doesn't like me talking about God."

Buru smiled. "We believe in the spirits, and they are different from your God. But he thinks highly of you just the same—as do I."

Paul didn't speak for a moment as he attempted to gather his thoughts. The eerie quietness drove a tense wedge further between them with every turn in the road.

"Buru, I have to confess I feel uneasy this time around. I can't quite put my finger on it, but something doesn't feel right. In fact, it feels wrong."

"You're a man who's been wounded deeply."

As Paul tried to wrap his mind around Buru's comment, Buru added, "You're a man of faith and a doctor. The forces of evil will attack you, but you will be used for a special purpose. You will have what you need, but not until you need it."

"The forces of evil? If you're trying to comfort me, Buru, you missed your mark."

"A wise man once told me that if you take a stand for good, you should expect to be attacked from every direction." Buru gave Paul a knowing look. "Have you ever heard that?"

Paul smiled. "Yes, but I didn't mean me."

CHAPTER THREE

For two hours Paul chased Emeka's jeep down bends and curves, bouncing along dirt roads and through meadows where no road existed. Occasionally they would blaze across an empty field with tall grass reaching the windows.

Every rut the jeep hit jarred Paul's spine as he maneuvered over the rocky terrain, following the vehicle in front of him. Emeka's eleven years as a safari driver provided him with the unique advantage of knowing every aspect of the mountains for hundreds of kilometers. He was the most experienced wilderness driver Paul knew.

"He's taking no chances, is he?" Paul shouted over the engine. "I told him we'd take the old road, but this is no road at all."

Buru gripped the handle on his door. "This is what we call 'chasing the cheetah.' The driver in front doesn't decide which way to go until the last moment so it's a random choice. No one can follow us or tell where we'll be in ten or fifteen minutes. It's the safest way. It kept the soldiers from finding us during the war."

Paul followed by only several car lengths. Thieves were prepared to overcome one vehicle. Two made a successful attack unlikely. A second jeep provided a formidable deterrent.

But in spite of the dangers and discomfort, Paul looked forward to the bumpy ride—it helped him remember where he was and, most of all, why.

Until he'd established the clinic in Matta, treatment for malaria and typhoid required a two-hundred-kilometer journey to Juba. It took Paul a year to convince the village chiefs that mosquito netting would decrease malaria outbreaks. When someone was injured or a surgical emergency arose, Paul was their only hope. But cancer treatment had become his passion, especially for Leza. With Paul's groundbreaking formulas designed to withstand the heat and humidity, and the new dry ice–packaged medications Jim would begin flying into Mundri every week, there was now hope where none had ever been. In the sweltering heat and absence of electricity, cancer had been a death sentence in the African bush—but no more.

For a short time Paul followed Emeka on the Juba highway, a nine-hundred-kilometer pothole-infested dirt road. Twenty-four hours a day, trucks transported goods from Juba to North Sudan and the Congo on its rough, rocky surface. Villages located near the road were accustomed to the nonstop stream of vehicles.

Before long, Emeka steered back off the road onto rocky terrain through tall grass. Paul followed as close as he dared.

An hour later a young boy stood beside the tree line waving and shouting "hallo" in Dinka. They were nearing Matta. Paul spotted several more children appearing from the dry shrubbery along the road. His heart pounded with anticipation. Suddenly a tree frond landed on the hood of the jeep and drifted off. Another and another fell as the villagers tossed the delicate branches in honor of Paul's return, welcoming him home. Paul couldn't ignore the lump in his throat each time one hit the hood and brushed against the windshield before falling off.

By the time they arrived in Matta, Emeka had pulled far ahead. Drums in the distance grew louder as Paul approached the village square, and women on the path started their melodic chanting. So many people lined the road waving branches and brushing them against the sides of Paul's jeep that he was forced to slow to a crawl to avoid hitting anyone. He stopped when he reached the clearing and shut the noisy engine down.

Children clambered onto the running boards and reached through the open window, grabbing any part of Paul they could. He carefully pushed the door open and crawled from under the pile of skinny, squirming arms and legs. His knees buckled under the strain as he dragged a few of them on his feet for a ride. The chaotic greeting from the kids had become a custom reserved for Paul's arrivals. Nicki had been the original instigator, shouting to the crowd of gathering young-sters one day, "He has candy in his pockets! Get him!"

Paul walked past many friends who greeted him along the way to one small hut in a circle of many, depositing giggling children as he went. He poked his head inside.

"Babatunde!" eight-year-old Leza called from her bed as Paul hur-ried to her side. He swept her into his arms. "I've been waiting for you, Baba."

"And I missed you, little girl." Paul remembered fondly the new name she had given him. *Baba* meant father; *Babatunde* denoted a father who faithfully returned.

For two years Paul had done everything he could to treat Leza's leukemia. The past ten months, filled with tests and treatments in Juba, had robbed her of most of her energy. He'd arranged for the lab work to be performed in the United States and obtained permission for his special chemotherapy to be administered in Juba. When the doctors there refused to continue treating a child they considered terminally ill, Paul had to make other plans. Having worked on government research in the past opened new doors for him to accomplish what he needed now. Leza was back in Matta and there was a new plan—weekly chemo treatments delivered by Jim in addition to Paul's proprietary chemo, which required no refrigeration.

"I missed you too, Baba." Leza's smile was radiant despite her circumstances. Her short hair never detracted from her natural softness and beauty, even at her young age.

Paul sat on the edge of the bed and took her hand. He said quietly, "You know she's not coming back, don't you?"

Leza never looked away as her eyes filled with tears. "Yes, Baba. Buru explained this to me."

"She wanted to. She loved you."

Leza nodded. "I will miss her, Baba. I know you will too."

As they shared a hug, Leza's mother, Orma, hurried in to greet him. "Dr. Paul! It's good to see you!"

"Same here, Orma." Paul stood and took her hand, clasping it briefly between his own in customary fashion.

"Will you stay for a while?"

"I'll be here for a few months at least." Paul sat back on the bed and squeezed Leza. "Okay, sweetie. I have to go to the clinic for a little bit, but let me take a look at you."

Paul pulled his stethoscope from his backpack and listened to Leza's heart and lungs. He checked her reflexes and examined her muscle tone.

"You've lost a little more weight, young lady. We've talked about this. You have to eat."

Leza looked sheepishly at him. "I know. It's just that sometimes I can't. Even the thought of it makes me feel sick."

"I understand, but to increase your chemo, we need you to be strong. You have to try."

Leza nodded. "Okay, Baba."

"Good. I'll come back to check on you tonight."

Paul lowered her onto the pillow as Orma sat down next to her and held a cup for her to sip. This was why he was here—why his daughter, Jessica, had told him to come back before it was too late for this precious little girl. When he returned to the jeep to gather his things, Emeka was already busy unloading supplies into Paul's hut.

"Go. You have patients to see. This is my job. Remember? I can carry things." Emeka grinned as his huge arms grabbed duffels from the jeep, four at a time.

"Thank you, my friend."

Paul checked his watch. He had about an hour before dark. He turned and walked the short distance to the clinic—a bamboo lean-to with a sloping thatched grass roof. Nothing fancy, but it worked and allowed a breeze to keep him cooler in the oppressive heat. Villagers gathered in the fading light of day, patiently waiting for their chance to visit the doctor.

Paul saw one patient after another with similar problems: upset stomach, fever, diarrhea, loss of appetite. It was the same every trip. Dysentery and malaria plagued the region.

"Multaka, how have you been? It's good to see you again." Paul shook the thin man's thickly callused hand.

"I am good, but now I am not. There is much pain here." He placed his hand on his abdomen.

As Paul examined Multaka's bare belly, others sat patiently on logs arranged in rows like pews in a church. Paul suddenly had the strange sensation he'd never left this place—as if no time had passed. But it had.

"Are you okay, Dr. Paul?"

Paul realized his mind had drifted. "Yes, Multaka. Tell me, has your family been well? Your children?"

Multaka grinned proudly. "Yes, my wife is much better from the medicine you gave her. The malaria—it is gone, and she is pregnant again."

Paul shook his hand. "Congratulations. I'm happy for you. Bring her to me soon so I can check her. I want to be sure she has everything she needs. And tell her she must use the mosquito netting over her bed. It's what stops the malaria." He continued his examination. "Have you had a fever or any other problems?"

Multaka shook his head. "No, nothing like some of the others. But my brother is sick—too sick to come today. He lives in Witto."

"What kind of sickness? Is it just he who is ill or are there others?"

"Many have been ill with something we've never seen. They have fever and chills, then tremors before they pass out. They don't move for a while, as if they had died. Afterward, they get better for a while. But we are afraid that someone will not get better."

"How long has it been since it started?"

"About two weeks."

"Well, I'll figure it out. We'll get to the bottom of it, whatever it is." Paul handed Multaka a small bottle of pills. "For now, take this medicine, and the pain in your stomach should go away. It sounds like the normal dysentery you get from drinking polluted water. Haven't you been drinking from the well?"

"Not always. Sometimes I drink from the standing water in the ponds. I know that I shouldn't, but it looks clean and I'm thirsty."

"No, you shouldn't. It makes you sick like this. The medicine should stop it, but tell me if it gets worse or it's not gone in a day or two. I'll try to get to Witto and see what I can do to help. I'll visit your brother there."

"Thank you, Dr. Paul." Multaka paused for a moment. "It's good to have you here again."

"Thank you. It's good to be back."

Multaka waved and left with his medication. Paul sat for a moment, fatigue nagging at him. The sun was slowly fading, and he checked his watch. It was time to quit for the day. He stood to address the people who still waited.

"I'm sorry, but I have to stop for tonight. I'll be back in the morning."

One of the men spoke as he stood. "Get some rest, Dr. Paul. We'll return with the sun."

Paul packed his instruments and headed toward his hut. Remembering Buru's warning about the panther, he quickened his pace to reach it before nightfall.

Walking through the clearing as dogs barked in the distance and the sun settled over the mountain ridge, bathing the countryside in brilliant colors, Paul was reminded of the many times he'd done this before. Strapping his headlamp in place so that it would be ready when darkness fell, he made his way to the familiar little hut that would be his home for the next three months. Several villagers tried to walk with him, but he smiled and assured them he was fine on his own. He tossed his backpack inside his hut, then took a brief right turn to Leza's house. Orma sat outside using the last of the daylight to sew a tear in a skirt.

She smiled. "You can go in, but she's asleep, Dr. Paul."

"I won't disturb her. I'll just check on her, if that's okay."

"It's okay. She's a good sleeper."

Paul stepped through the doorway into the dark room and switched on his headlamp. The light glowed off Leza's short hair as she lay in her bed fast asleep. Quietly he walked to her side, lifted the mosquito net suspended over her from the ceiling, and reached under it to take her hand. The warmth of her skin reminded him why he was there. If he hadn't fought for her and battled to keep her chemo going, she'd be gone too. Her breathing as she slept stirred his heart. He forced himself to let go of her hand and tuck it back under the netting, then carefully left the tiny hut.

As he pulled the door curtain closed he noticed Orma quietly sobbing.

"She's going to make it, Orma. I'm going to do all I can to get her through this."

Orma nodded. "I believe you, Dr. Paul. She's just so weak, and there's only so much anyone can do—even you."

Paul sat. "I know. But we've made great progress, and the best is yet to come. You'll see when I go pick up the medicine Jim flies into

Mundri. It will start working right away." He put his arm around her briefly. "I promise."

Orma smiled through her tears. "Thank you for saving my baby."

Paul took his arm from her shoulders. "Believe me, it has been my honor."

"Good night, Dr. Paul. Don't give up on her."

Paul grinned. "Never. Good night, Orma."

He stood and walked back to his hut, scuffing his feet along the sandy ground as he focused the headlamp on his path. When he arrived moments later, he reached for the drape that clung to the doorway, but then he stood motionless, remembering sweeping this very curtain out of the way countless times before, allowing Nicki to enter as she carried her toothbrush, hand towel, and bottle of water. She'd always pause and lean toward him for a brief kiss—or sometimes not so brief.

This had been their home, but the nights would no longer be filled with her laughter. There would be no giggles to brighten the dark mud-walled room. Memories—wonderful, sweet memories—suddenly overwhelmed Paul.

As he stood in the doorway, doubts filled his mind. He'd trusted God, but the most difficult thing he'd ever done—continuing on without Nicki—loomed before him like a mountain he couldn't climb. The sun disappeared, and darkness settled over the countryside. For the first time since leaving home, Paul was alone—truly alone. In the silent blackness of the African night, the weight of it seemed more than he could bear.

He finally moved the curtain aside and glanced around the room, his headlamp illuminating the shadows. His duffels, neatly stacked near his bed, waited to be unpacked. He looked at the floor and slowly stretched his foot across the threshold as if he was entering a forbidden world—a world where none of the old rules applied.

Exhausted, he pushed the mosquito net around his bed out of the way and sat down on the paper-thin mattress. A quick scan of the room did little to comfort him. The dried mud walls with a single window opening were mercilessly unchanged from his last visit.

Grabbing a bottle of water from his backpack, Paul placed it beside his pillow under the netting, an act that had become routine after many visits to Africa. Forcing his stiff muscles to cooperate, he unlaced his boots and pulled his stocking feet onto the bed. With his last ounce of energy, he lowered the mosquito net around him, turned off the headlamp, and laid it beside his pillow.

The morning sun woke Paul abruptly, and he suddenly felt someone's presence in the hut. Instinctively his head turned quickly to the left. Leza stood over him, clapping her hands and shrieking.

Paul jumped, shoved the netting aside, and hopped out of bed. "What's the matter? Are you in pain?"

Leza wrapped her arms around him. "You're here! I thought I'd dreamt it all. I'm so glad you're really here."

Paul hugged her, then peeked at his watch—6:00 a.m. The roosters crowing in the village reminded him it would be pointless to fall back asleep.

"Leza!" Orma's voice in the clearing sounded desperate.

"She's in here, Orma!" Paul called. He let go of the little girl. "Let's go back to your hut. I need to examine you."

Paul slipped on his boots, and they took the short walk to her tiny home, where Orma stood outside with her hands on her hips. "You scared me, Leza. You should never leave without telling me."

"I'm sorry, Mama. I just had to know if Baba was really here. You were asleep, and I didn't want to wake you." Leza sat on the bed, ready to be examined. She was used to this.

Orma shook her head and turned to her work. "Silly girl," she laughed.

Using his stethoscope, Paul listened to Leza's heart and lungs. Then he pressed on her abdomen. She whimpered slightly.

"Does that hurt?"

"Not much."

"Is she okay?" Orma anxiously wrung her hands.

Paul eased Leza back onto the pillow. "She is, but she's so thin I can feel her spleen. She has to stop losing weight. It's important for her to be strong for the new chemo."

Paul squeezed Leza's hand. "I have to give you some medicine, and it needs to go through here." He pushed on her arm with his finger, indicating an IV was necessary. Leza shrugged her shoulders and cringed a little, but she had become accustomed to it. He opened a box Emeka had delivered to Orma's hut and took out everything he needed, except the chemo treatment, which he'd brought in his backpack. As he started the IV, Leza confessed, "I guess I don't eat as much as I should."

"I know there are times you don't feel like eating since your appetite is gone, but you have to. You need your strength."

Leza's eyes started to close. Then she popped them open. "Can you stay with me a little while? I feel like sleeping even though I just woke up."

"The IV medicine is making you tired. I'll be right here." Paul pulled a chair next to the bed and sat.

Leza snuggled into the sheet, laid her head on her pillow, and closed her eyes. "Thank you, Baba."

"You're welcome, little girl. Get some rest."

Paul watched as she drifted off, and he felt Orma's hand on his shoulder. "Could we talk outside for a moment, Dr. Paul?" she whispered, then turned and headed for the door.

Paul followed her into the clearing in front of the hut.

"Dr. Paul, I know we talked last night, but I need to know . . . is Leza really going to live?"

"If I have anything to say about it, she will."

Orma smiled politely.

"Okay, Orma. That wasn't an answer. Here's the truth . . . Leza needs her medications—her chemo. If all goes well with that, I believe she'll be okay. But it will take months of treatment. I'm dedicated to that and will do all I can to make sure it happens."

Orma squirmed a little. "She's been having bad dreams lately."

Paul knew the villagers' superstitions often collided with his own beliefs. "I don't think her bad dreams mean anything, Orma. She just doesn't feel good."

"I want her to be okay. I want her to get better, and what if you have to leave again?"

"Okay, Orma. Know this . . . I will stay until she doesn't need me anymore, and then some."

Orma hugged him briefly. "Thank you, Dr. Paul." She hurried inside.

Paul had never been more determined. He was going to get this little girl well if it was the last thing he did.

CHAPTER FOUR

"What do you mean they forced you down?" Jarrod Vincent, Jim's boss and fellow pilot, scanned the threatening clouds gathering over Lake Victoria as he stood in the hangar. Most of his experience came from the military, but Jarrod was a civilian now and had left a very good job in the United States to work in Uganda flying relief teams into Sudan. Due to the number of flying hours he had logged and his experience in the US Marines, he was placed in charge of the small airport. His reputation for speaking his mind and protecting his pilots had gained him respect, and Jim had a great deal of esteem for this man even though they'd only met six months earlier.

Jarrod's deep voice had a hint of a Chicago accent. "North Sudan has no jurisdiction in the South. They have no right to make you land in the middle of God knows where." He abruptly turned from the hangar door and walked toward Jim's plane. It barely fit inside, but with a storm approaching, it would be safer under shelter. Jarrod flung a partially folded map onto the table as he sized Jim up. "You serious about this? You did nothing to provoke them?"

"We weren't even in the gray zone." Jim walked to the table, rotated the map, and placed his finger on the spot. "There. Right there. They did this in South Sudanese airspace twenty kilometers from their own border in broad daylight, guns locked and loaded—literally." Jim leaned against the wing strut and lowered his voice. "They knew we were coming, Jarrod."

Jarrod cocked his head and cast a cynical eye at Jim. "You mean they were expecting an airplane full of medical supplies to pass near enough to chase it down? Why would they do that, Jim? You told me yourself they took nothing of value and didn't even search the plane that well."

Jim shook his head. "That's just it. This wasn't random. They weren't looting valuables. That was for show. They were looking for us—or, more precisely, they were looking for Paul."

Jarrod sat on the landing gear beside the strut. "What aren't you telling me?"

"The commanding officer was no flunky. He knew what to look for in Paul's passport. His eyes lit up when he saw something on one of the pages, but I don't know what it was. Once he questioned Paul about when he'd arrive in Matta, I knew something was wrong. When Paul refused to answer, things got tense."

"What could he have possibly seen in Paul's passport?" Jarrod seemed strangely curious.

Jim shifted his weight and shrugged uneasily. He was caught off guard and knew he hadn't responded well to Jarrod's previous question. Jarrod must have spotted his protective posturing. "Spill it, Jim."

"It's just that—Paul performed some government research in the past and has a few Iraqi stamps in his passport."

"Iraq? What kind of research would take him to Iraq?"

"I really don't know, Jarrod. But remember that Paul's a chemistry genius. If the Department of Defense was involved, I suspect it had something to do with chemical warfare."

"The DOD? Seriously?"

Jim sighed. "Seriously. But honest to God, I don't know what."

Jarrod nodded slowly and stared at the crinkled map as if deep in thought.

"What's on your mind, Jarrod? Your wheels are turning, but your mouth isn't moving."

"No, I . . . It's just . . . Sorry. My thoughts wandered. This is a lot to take in. You know, Iraq and all."

"I don't know if that was it. I just know Paul hates having those stamps in his passport. He gets flack everywhere he travels."

"Well, there was no way for them to know he was on that plane. Couldn't you just be overthinking this?"

"They locked their fifty-cal onto the engine of the plane—my plane—just because Paul wouldn't tell them what they wanted to know."

"Maybe this guy was trying to scare you. I doubt they'd have opened fire."

"This guy was going to blow our plane halfway to Juba to make a point. I know the difference between a bluff and a man holding all the cards."

"I suppose anything can happen in this country, but it doesn't add up."

Jim's satellite phone buzzed on his belt. He took it from its holster and glanced at the screen, then hit the cancel button. "Sorry. It's Paul's daughter, Jessica. I'll text her later." Jim clipped the phone back on his belt and faced Jarrod. "Anyway, yeah, this guy kept pushing Paul, but Paul stayed calm."

"Well, we need to be sure not to cause problems near the border, so keep your distance until we get this sorted out."

"Do you want me to write it up?"

"No. It's better if it comes from me."

"Got it—and I'll keep my distance."

"I think that's best. I'll get to the bottom of it, Jim. Don't worry."

Jim nodded. "Thanks, man."

"Hey. I got your back."

"And I appreciate it."

Jarrod walked toward the hangar office, grabbing the tattered map from the table on his way, making no attempt to fold it.

Jim gave his plane one more walk around, then closed the hangar door. As he left the building, he tapped on the glass window partition to the office and yelled so Jarrod could hear him. "I'm out. You got the lights?"

Jarrod looked up, nodded, and then turned his attention back to the computer screen.

The trail to Jim's apartment took him down a narrow but neatly groomed, well-lit cobblestone path with steps every three meters or so. His mind spun with details of the day, and the warning flags were difficult to ignore. It was one of the strangest days he'd experienced since being in Africa—and that was an accomplishment.

When Jim reached his apartment overlooking Lake Victoria, he sat on the brick wall of the patio, pulled out the satellite phone, and typed in Jessica's number.

"Uncle Jim?"

"Hi, Jess. Sorry I couldn't take your call earlier. I was talking to my boss. You okay?"

"Yes, I'm fine. Just getting ready for a run before my three o'clock class. It's ten p.m. there, right?"

"Right. Eight hours."

"Is he okay, Uncle Jim?"

"Yeah. He's just, you know, struggling without your mom beside him." Jim stopped and thumped his forehead. "I'm sorry. I didn't mean he should be over her, Jess. I just—"

"It's okay. I know what you mean. But otherwise, did everything go okay with his return to the front lines today?"

Jim's pause stretched into a long silence as he tried to think of what to say.

"What do you need to tell me?" Jessica pressed.

Jim cleared his throat.

"Be straight with me, Uncle Jim. You paused when you were talking—for way too long. What's going on? Did you guys have problems?"

Jim took a deep breath. "Well, while we were on our way to Mundri, a couple of choppers forced us to land. We had to answer a few questions, and they checked our passports. That's it."

"Uh-huh—a couple of choppers. Like sightseeing choppers, I suppose? Where were they from? Did they point guns at you?"

Jim knew another pause would scream "guilty!" "Lots of people carry guns here."

"Stop it. It's dangerous over there. You pretend it's not in order to protect me. And you didn't answer me. Where were they from?"

"The North."

"The North? As in North Sudan?"

"Yes, sort of. I mean it was . . . yes."

"When you hide stuff, it makes me afraid to trust you."

"I'm sorry, Jessica." The awkward silence between them made Jim uneasy. "Look, your dad's worried about you, and so am I. You mean the world to us, and if we could, we'd keep you from all the bad things in life, like muggers and pestilence and . . . flies."

"Flies?"

"Just . . . c'mon, give me a break here. Flies are bad. You know what I mean."

"You stink at this, Uncle Jim."

"I know. Your mom told me that many times while we were growing up."

"Okay. So I accept your desire to keep me from the evils of . . . flies, but when my dad is in danger, I want details. It makes me worry less when I know you're giving me the ugly, frightening specifics of everything that happens. That's how I can trust you. That's how I sleep at night. I'm a woman. Don't try to figure this out, just trust me."

Jim sighed. "Okay. I'll do better."

"Thank you."

"But keep in mind, Jessica—your dad has training from his rough years in high school. He can fight better than most. I wouldn't want to get into the ring with him."

"I know, but still . . ." Jessica paused. "Okay, speaking of Dad's past, now it's my turn to confess something. Two agents from the FBI came to the apartment and asked questions about Daddy's research."

"What do you mean? His college research?"

"Yeah. A year ago the project he'd started in college came back to life somehow through a guy named Charles Manning. I don't know what the grant was for back when Dad was working on it. He took his top secret clearance seriously, so we didn't know much. Do you, Uncle Jim?"

"From what I remember, Jess, he stumbled onto something, and the government buried it. The scientists working with him referred to it as an incredible breakthrough, especially Manning, but not for long."

"I'll never forget when Dad came home one night all upset. The grant had been pulled. It was over."

"What then?"

"Dad said they sealed the research, but I don't know what that means. He wouldn't talk to us about it—not even to Mom."

"What did the FBI want from you?"

"They wanted to know if Dad had ever spoken of Charles Manning or if they were still friends."

"What did you tell them?"

"The truth. He didn't—not that I knew about. I was no help at all. Then they asked when he'd be home."

"This doesn't feel right, Jess. Let me know if they come back."

"You're scaring me."

"I just want you to be cautious. You're my niece—my sister's daughter—and I love you. Tell me if they make contact again, agreed?"

"Agreed. I'd better let you go. I love you, Uncle Jim."

"I'll talk to you soon. Love you too." As he ended the call, Jim wondered what the FBI was up to. And why they would bring up Paul's research after all these years.

He unlocked the door of his apartment, sat down at his MacBook Pro, and pulled a Google Earth map of Africa onto the screen. When he scanned the landing area where they had been forced down, there was nothing there but dirt. The only thing unusual was that it was the only place for a hundred and sixty kilometers where he could have landed. Is that why they had chased them to that spot?

Jim thought back to the helicopters and what the commander had said. Something bothered him, but he couldn't quite put his finger on it. He wished he could reach Paul to talk things through with him, but it would have to wait until he saw him next week.

When Paul promised Multaka he'd visit his sick brother in Witto, he'd expected a quick stop in the village. But it was taking longer than he'd anticipated. Almost everyone had similar symptoms—weakness, fever, cough, chest tightness with difficulty breathing, blurred vision, confusion, abdominal pain, and—for some—convulsions and seizures. The only differences involved the severity of symptoms.

Paul finished drawing blood from the last patient of the day, a young boy who'd been lethargic and running a fever for a week. Paul addressed his parents. "We should have results on the lab work from Juba in a few days. In the meantime, he'll need some medication to help with the fever, and I'll treat him for malaria until we receive results."

Paul grabbed a bottle of water. The climate exhausted him. It always had. His fatigue from sleeping poorly in the heat in addition to his travel lag made him feel worse.

Chief Chima had driven his own jeep to meet Paul in Witto. He ducked his head under the edge of the lean-to. "Dr. Paul, I remember this day. It is the anniversary of my daughter's marriage. That means it is also Nicki's day of birth. Do I remember correctly?"

Paul smiled. "You're right, Chief. I'm going to take a little time later today to honor her, and . . . you know, just remember."

"I understand. I wanted you to know that I didn't forget." Chima paused, then abruptly changed the subject. "Why are the people here sick and not the villagers of Matta?"

"I don't know, Chief. It doesn't make sense. I can't find a common thread to tie it together. Usually when I come to the villages, we have the same problems in each one—dysentery from contaminated water and malaria from the mosquitoes. But this . . . this is different."

Chima nodded. "To make matters worse, the panther has been ravaging this village, and others too . . . everywhere except Matta. It has killed men in Witto, Lanyi, and Wiroh."

Paul shook his head. "That's horrible. Do we need to take precautions in Matta?"

"The more important question to ask is what the panther is doing here and in other villages and why it has spared Matta. For a reason I don't understand, the Ghost of Africa is attacking."

"Well, it's hungry, right? From what Buru said, if the panther can't find food in the hills or plains, it comes into the village to eat."

Chima stared into Paul's eyes.

"What?"

"It's not that simple."

"I'm confused, Chief. It seems simple. Does it have to be superstitious for you to believe it?"

The chief stared at Paul.

"Sorry, Chief. I don't mean to be disrespectful. I just don't understand."

"To keep the panther from attacking people, the villagers tie a goat to a tree in the clearing to give it an easy meal. The panther is passing the goat, going deeper into the village, and attacking men instead."

Paul shrugged his shoulders. "Why would it do that if it wasn't hungry?"

Chima stared again.

"You need to tell me what you're thinking, Chief. I'm missing it."

"The panther started killing just before you arrived this time, although you have been here before. Until now, that's never happened." Chima paused as if carefully considering his next words. "I know that you struggle with our traditions."

"Pardon me, Chief," Paul said quickly, "I honor your traditions. It's your superstitions that conflict with my personal beliefs. And that's okay, because we all—"

Chima interrupted while nodding. "Yes. I know you respect our traditions. In fact, Nicki adopted many of them."

Paul chuckled, remembering her attempt to perform a ceremonial wedding dance for Chima's daughter while wearing a traditional, and very ornate, Sudanese dress.

Chima added, "At least she tried. You're right, Dr. Paul. It's not the traditions—it's our beliefs that you refer to as superstitions. These beliefs are important to us. They make us who we are, determine how we react, and sometimes they even protect us."

"Are you speaking of the Ghost of Africa again?"

Chima gave Paul a quick nod. "In part, yes. We know the spirits send the panther to us. He comes to kill." Chima took Paul's arm, and they walked to the edge of the clearing away from the other villagers.

"The spirits send the panther when we have angered them. Many men have died recently."

"Okay. Let's assume that's true. How have you angered the spirits?"

Chima took a deep breath and sighed. "At first I thought you might have brought this upon us with your failure to believe."

Paul remained silent. He didn't want to blurt out what he was thinking.

"But then I thought, why now and not before?"

Paul nodded but still didn't speak.

"When I realized Matta was the only village spared by the panther, I wondered more about your beliefs."

"Wondered what?"

"What if the panther has spared us because of you?"

Chima's comment surprised Paul. "So what's your conclusion, Chief? Are you blaming me for the deaths of these people and the illnesses? Or are you thanking me for saving your village?"

"I'm not blaming you, no, but—"

"But nothing, Chief. There are no spirits, angry because I don't believe in them, who have started killing innocent people in this village."

"You do not understand our ways. You're a good man, but you don't understand."

Paul looked away in frustration. "Where do we go from here?"

"I don't know, Dr. Paul. What is stronger? Your beliefs or our spirits?"

"Chima, no one is sending death panthers to your villages. They're hungry wild animals, and we're food."

"I know it is not you killing our people. It is the Ghost of Africa, driven by the spirits."

Paul paused and then said, "There is no ghost, Chima."

"Perhaps we should look deeper."

Paul walked from the clearing back to the lean-to, grabbed his stethoscope and instruments, shoved them into his backpack, and tossed the straps over his shoulder. "Chima. I'm not the man I used to be—not since Nicki died. Something's going on here, and it's not angry spirits killing your people. It's a hungry wild animal in search of food. Now, like it or not, I'm here for a reason, and unless you're going to force me out, you're stuck with me. You got a problem with that?"

Paul didn't wait for Chima to respond. He turned, left the lean-to, climbed into the jeep, and drove toward Matta. Chima could follow in his own jeep if he felt like it. It had been a tough day physically and emotionally, and there was something Paul still needed to do that would drain him even more.

A half hour later Paul pulled into Matta and parked the jeep near Buru's hut. Grabbing his gear from the backseat, he slipped past the dead oak tree, pushed his way through the thick, tall grass, and began his short hike to the foothills.

Why did you do that, Paul? Chima's your friend.

He grabbed a branch and pulled himself up a steep spot on the trail. He had wanted today to be special, but his encounter with the chief had destroyed that possibility. He promised himself he would apologize to Chima when he got back to camp.

Paul climbed the last few meters to his favorite spot—the rock ledge overlooking the mountain range and valley. Nicki had loved coming here to look at the scenery below. They'd spent her last birthday in this spot, and Paul had brought along a small biscuit one of the village women had made for a birthday cake. Paul had even brought a candle for Nicki to blow out, but he'd forgotten matches.

As he sat on the ledge and looked beyond the mango grove, he found it hard to believe that it was Nicki's birthday again. He determined to set aside the hardships of the day to reflect on her and on the strength she used to give him—and still did.

When Paul had first seen her, she'd been sixteen and he seventeen, and they'd been preparing for a medical trip to Africa with a local church group. He'd noticed how her long blond hair had flowed softly across her brow and onto her shoulders and how her blue dress had hugged her perfect figure as she'd gracefully crossed the meeting room. He'd been mesmerized. It was strange how a girl he hadn't even met had such power over him. He'd finally mustered up the courage to introduce himself, and the rest was history.

As the sun slowly disappeared behind him, casting its glow on the Imatong Mountains, Paul realized he didn't have long before nightfall. He'd promised Buru to be inside before dark.

He climbed down from the ledge, crossed through the mango grove and the field of tall grass, and finally entered the clearing near his hut.

The moment he did, he knew something was wrong. He stopped. A chill ran up his spine. He slowly turned to face a huge black panther staring at him from six meters away.

CHAPTER FIVE

Paul took a shallow breath. The panther's icy stare bored into him. Paul couldn't look away. At any moment this sleek black cat could be on top of him, tearing the flesh from his bones.

The panther gave a deep, guttural growl.

Buru stepped from his hut holding his spear high. He moved to the edge of the clearing and stopped.

The panther grunted and took two steps closer to Paul.

Buru stood five meters to Paul's right and one meter in front of him, creating a triangle: two men, one panther. Buru held his spear poised to strike.

The growls of the beast had drawn the village elders from their huts—all of them seasoned hunters. Now they took positions to Paul's left. Each readied his weapon and stood like a statue, waiting. Paul knew these men were the best hunters in the region, but the panther didn't seem to notice them—only Paul.

As he stared into its dark eyes, Paul's muscles tightened. For a moment he thought about running or backing away. Slowly he slid his foot to one side. The cat crouched, and Paul froze.

Buru whispered, "Do not move. Do not look away. He is the Ghost of Africa. He comes for a purpose."

From the corner of his eye, Paul saw Buru lower his spear and lay it on the ground. The other elders followed his lead. Paul's breath quickened.

The panther slowly closed the gap, stopping barely a meter in front of Paul. Its sleek black fur rippled over powerful muscles as it moved.

Paul calmed the panic welling inside. The panther studied him, mouth closed and ears pinned back.

Slowly, as if guided by an unseen force, Paul squatted on the ground in front of the Ghost of Africa. The black cat towered above him. Paul's heart pounded harder. He knew he was at this animal's mercy. The panther growled and lowered its head, moving within centimeters of Paul, who saw nothing but dark, piercing eyes as the cat's hot breath burned his face. He refused to break the gaze.

Suddenly the panther took a single step back and screamed loud enough to make Paul's ears ring. Crouching as if to pounce, it suddenly leapt over Paul and disappeared into the tall grass.

At first Paul couldn't move. Slowly, a sigh of relief escaped.

Buru grabbed his spear and hurried to him. He reached out his hand and helped Paul to his feet.

Chief Chima entered the clearing. He held Paul's face between his hands almost ceremoniously. "Look at me." He studied Paul. "The Dark One has spoken to us—to you. I saw it. The Ghost of Africa has not come to this village for many years. The last time was to warn us of marauders who raided our people in the night and took our children." Chima's expression changed. Paul wondered what horror he was remembering.

"He entered the village and approached a little girl. The next night, raiders came and ravaged our village. They took every child but her." The chief shook his head. "They walked past her as if she wasn't there."

"Who was she, Chief?"

"Orma, Leza's mother—just a child then."

"I had no idea," Paul said. "The panther didn't speak, Chief. It stared into my eyes."

"You don't understand. There was a reason for the panther's visit—a message in its coming."

Paul's frustration continued to build, but he tried to remain calm. "Chima, are you trying to say the panther is a god?"

"You listen when your heart speaks in your ways. We listen to the spirits when they speak in our ways." Chima gestured toward the gathering crowd of villagers. "Our people heed the panther who speaks and does not devour the prey before it. They understand it. It is you who question."

Paul pondered what Chima was saying. In a way it made sense. He tried to wrap his mind around it.

Chima continued. "This is a warning to us. You have been spared as few men have. Evil is coming." Chima turned and walked toward his hut. He spoke without facing Paul. "From now on, I will call you Abdu. You have been chosen."

"Chosen? For what? What are you saying, Chima?"

"I'm saying you are The Chosen."

"To do what?"

"To save us."

"From what? Evil that's coming?"

"Chosen to do what must be done, Abdu. Come, we must prepare. We have been warned. The spirits have been faithful. Show me what that means."

Paul welcomed the next morning, especially since he'd tossed and turned all night. His mind wouldn't slow down as he thought of the preparations that he, Chima, and Buru had begun the night before to move the children from Matta to Mundri for safety. Chima had contacted the captain of the local military unit and used their shortwave radio to request trucks from Mundri to move their precious young ones. The trucks would arrive tomorrow morning with armed military escorts; while they didn't want another massacre any more than Chima did, tomorrow was the soonest they could gather enough trucks and personnel. Understandably, Chima was concerned. He took the panther's visit seriously.

Paul pushed the mosquito net aside, glanced instinctively at the floor to check for spiders or snakes, and crawled out of bed. He shook out his shoes and slipped them on, threw one strap of his backpack of supplies onto his left shoulder, then crossed the small clearing to Leza's hut where Orma waited in a chair beside Leza's bed.

"Did you sleep, Dr. Paul?"

"Not well, Orma. I'm trying to figure out how to move Leza. I'd like to keep her IV going during the transport in the truck." He stepped into her hut.

Leza stopped eating when she saw him. "I dreamed the panther came back." She shuddered.

"I'm glad you weren't there last night to see it. I've never been so scared." Paul gave a little shudder of his own.

"You could never be afraid, Baba. You're too brave."

Paul patted Leza's leg and turned to Orma. "The chief told me you had a similar experience with a panther when you were a child. Can you tell me what happened?"

Orma squirmed, and Paul sensed he had opened a deep wound.

"Mama, you never told me."

"It was a long time ago—a time I would like to forget."

"I'm sorry, Orma. I shouldn't have asked."

"It's okay, Dr. Paul. Your encounter last night made me realize I should tell you. I was just a girl when I stood in front of the panther that came into this village. I thought I was going to die. My father stood by helplessly watching as the panther walked up to me and growled. I was so afraid." Orma unconsciously wrung her hands as she relived the memory.

"You don't need to tell me."

"Yes, I do." She seemed to be collecting her thoughts. Paul gave her time. "I remember I stood in the clearing unable to move, and how terrified I was of the panther."

"What happened?"

"I reached out my chubby little hand and touched his head." Orma smiled with tears in her eyes. "When I did, I knew he wasn't there to hurt me. His purpose was to warn us that evil was coming—and it did the next day."

"What about the panther, Mama? How did you get away?"

"I didn't. He put his head down, jumped over me into the bushes, and disappeared."

A chill ran through Paul's veins as he remembered this same experience the night before. "How did you know the raiders were coming?" Paul asked.

"I didn't at first. But that night I had trouble calming down to sleep. When I finally did, I dreamt of men, horrible men, coming into our camp, taking my friends, and killing everyone who tried to stop them." Orma paused. Her expression was one of horror, as if being drawn back to that moment. Slowly she appeared to gather her thoughts. "It seemed so real. I woke up crying and ran to the chief's hut. My father jumped out of bed and chased after me. At first he was angry that I woke the chief in the middle of the night, but when I told Chief Chima the dream, he believed it." She looked out the window as if thinking what to say next. Her hands trembled, and she clasped them to keep them from shaking.

"Just tell me what you need to, Orma."

She searched Paul's eyes. "Hold this in your heart and be willing to listen when the panther returns."

"Returns?"

"This is the beginning, Dr. Paul. The Ghost of Africa is not finished. He has chosen you."

"I keep hearing that, but I don't know what it means. Did he come back for you?"

"He was finished with me. He is not finished with you."

"Forgive me, Orma, but how can you know that? I can't base my decisions on ancient legends."

"These are not legends. They're true experiences with real people, and it doesn't happen often. It is an honor to be chosen." Orma stood and walked to the doorway, visibly upset.

"I'm sorry, Orma. I've been insensitive and disrespectful. Forgive me."

She turned to Paul and offered a tearful smile. "It's okay. But I want you to understand. We believe the Ghost of Africa is the instrument of the spirits. They did not choose a child this time to deliver a message. They chose a man to do something more. If so, they will make it clear to you."

"Orma, when you told the chief what the panther was warning you about that day in the dream, what did he do?"

She dabbed her eyes with her apron. "Chief Chima was a young man at the time—a warrior. He had his men ready to fight, but they were not able to protect the village." She shook her head as she remembered. "We had bows and spears—they had guns. The raiders killed and kidnapped many, but they didn't touch me. I stood in the village square, paralyzed by fear. But they ran past me as if they didn't see me, carrying my screaming friends and family, shooting the men and women who got in the way. I expected to be next." She sobbed briefly. "My best friend grabbed my arm, and I tried to pull her away from the man dragging her to the truck. But he was too strong. Worst of all, they didn't take me. I should have been thrown onto one of the trucks too. When I wasn't, I knew I would never see any of them again." She paused and took a deep breath. "It sounds strange, but it feels good—it feels right for you to know this. The spirits wanted me to tell you."

"Thank you, Orma. All these years, I had no idea. It makes me realize that I know almost nothing of what you and the others in the village have been through."

"Dr. Paul, there is one more thing. I don't know if you are protected by the Ghost of Africa the way I was."

"Protected?"

"The bad men ran past as if they couldn't see me, but the spirits may have protected me because I was a child. You are a man. I don't know if the panther will protect you the same way. The Ghost of Africa cannot be predicted."

Paul's mind spun as he tried to make sense of his thoughts. What on earth did this mean? His comments to Buru in the jeep ran through his mind—the feeling that the world was about to cave in on him. Now the encounter with the panther. What was he supposed to do?

He took a long breath, smiled at Leza, and kissed her forehead. "I'll see you in a few minutes. I need to help with the preparations."

She curled onto her side as he dropped the mosquito netting around her, gave her a wink, and then left the mud building. Orma followed him outside.

"Dr. Paul, since we are going to Mundri, how will Leza receive chemo treatments?"

"She needs the chemo for six to nine months, depending on how she responds to it. We can do this in Mundri. I'll take her to Juba for more tests three months from now. That will help me decide how long the chemo will be needed."

"How do we move her?"

"The South Sudan military still has the refugee camp in Mundri they used in 2011, and they'll transport her by a personnel vehicle lying down. They'll allow us to stay there until it's safe to return to Matta and will send a military escort to protect us on the roads. The government doesn't want another massacre like when the South separated from the North. I'll set Leza up in the infirmary to start with. It isn't very big, but you can stay there with her. It has a refrigerator we can use if we can get gasoline for the generator. I'll ask Jim to help with that when I see him in a few days."

Orma squeezed his hands. "Thank you for all you are doing, Dr. Paul."

Paul offered a weak smile. "We'll get through this. It'll take time, but we can do it." He knew they had to go, but in his heart Paul wondered if they were making the right choice. Something deep inside told him otherwise, but he didn't know why.

Jarrod walked out of the hangar office and approached Jim as he busily reinstalled the seats in his Cessna.

"Well, no surprise, Jim. The airbase in Khartoum said there were no choppers deployed near the border of South Sudan, and no reports have been filed regarding airspace invasion in the past month."

"I didn't imagine it, Jarrod. The gunships were real, the soldiers were real, and the weapons—they were very real."

"I'm not questioning you. I just don't understand what it is you did to bring these guys chugging across the border."

Jim threw a wrench into the toolbox—hard. He turned to Jarrod. "Nothing. I did nothing to cause them to come 'chugging' after us."

"Well, just mind yourself up there this time. Stay away from—"

"Jarrod, I stayed away last time. You're not listening. Do you honestly think I would risk my life or Paul's by doing a flyby near the North Sudan border? You need to get that through your head, and you don't seem to be."

"Look, I'm on your side. For that reason I filed a different flight plan for you this time. I want you to land in Juba, get your passport stamped, and head to Mundri. You drop that medicine off and hightail it back here before dark. Understood?"

Jim stared at Jarrod.

"Don't look at me like that. It's safer, Jim. Much safer than checking in at Arua like you guys did last time. They nailed you twenty minutes after you left there. If they're looking for you, let's throw them off their game."

"So you believe me?"

Jarrod pulled up a work stool and sat beside the folding stairs of the plane. "What on earth would make you ask that? Of course I believe you. I want Paul to get his supplies, Leza to get her medicine, and you to come back here safe and in one piece—with my plane," he added with a grin.

Jim nodded. "Okay, Jarrod." He continued to close the lock downs on the seat frames.

"Seriously, Jim, I don't know what's going on between North and South Sudan, but I don't like it. They lied to me on the phone about the gunships, and I know it. They forced you guys out of the sky for a reason we don't understand, and they can't be trusted. I'm tempted to fly this mission myself."

Jim stopped and turned. "It isn't a mission. This isn't the military."

"I know. That's just the way I think, especially when somebody's pointing guns at my pilots."

Jim finished the seat installations and loaded Leza's chemo supplies on the plane. "I'll be fine, and I'll go through Juba instead of Arua. Okay?"

"Thank you. I appreciate it. It makes me feel better."

As Jarrod walked back to the office, Jim watched him take out his cell phone.

"I wish it made me feel better," Jim said under his breath.

Paul tossed and turned for hours in the humid night air. He knew the mosquito net surrounding him was necessary to prevent malaria, but it seemed to collect his body heat like an oven. Finally he drifted off with thoughts of the panther in his head, its eyes boring into him.

As he slept restlessly, he dreamed that he was standing in the doorway of his hut, watching men approach the village from every direction and run toward the villagers as they scattered. Finally, one of the men spotted Paul. As Paul turned and fled, every man chased him as if he were an animal, yelling, firing their guns in the air. He sensed them right behind him, their body heat so close he could feel it. Then, suddenly, they were on top of him.

Paul sat up in bed, covered in sweat. It was morning already, and he could hear a few voices outside in the clearing. He placed his hand on his chest—his heart raced, and he was a little short of breath. The dream had seemed so real.

He got dressed and left his hut. Stepping into the clearing, he scanned the dwellings around him. It seemed quieter than usual. When he arrived at Orma's little house, Leza was sleeping peacefully, the IV line in place. Once Paul started the chemo drip, she stirred a little and stretched. Her eyes opened.

"Hi, Baba."

"Good morning, little girl." Paul changed the batteries on the IV pump and adjusted the settings, then looked back at her. "I need to tell you something."

He lifted the mosquito net and took her hand. "A lot of things are happening around here. Sometimes they're hard to understand. But today we need to move you and the other children to Mundri for safety."

Leza's grip on his hand tightened.

"It will be okay. It will be safe there."

She gave a tiny nod.

"I had a dream last night that showed me it's important for us to move from here."

Leza stared intently at him. Silent tears welled up, then trickled down her cheeks and dripped onto Paul's hand as he held hers.

Paul sighed. "It'll be okay, Leza."

She leaned forward and hugged him. He held her for a minute, maybe longer, until she asked, "I'm dying, aren't I, Baba?"

"What do you mean? Where did that come from?"

"I have the same thing Miss Nicki had, and she died. We prayed for her, but she died."

"Nicki did have cancer, but hers was a different kind. There was nothing we could do to help her. We tried. If we do everything right, you're going to be fine." Paul laid her back on the pillow.

"Right now, we need to get ready. The trucks should be here from Mundri in an hour or two." He glanced out the window.

"You don't believe in the panther, do you, Baba?"

"I do believe in the panther, Leza. I don't understand what it means, but there's no doubt in my mind that it's important. And many years ago, your mom went through the same thing I did. That's not a coincidence."

"The elders in our village said that death was coming to take those who offended the spirits. Are the evil spirits coming, Baba?"

Paul had heard the same comments from others. "It's not evil spirits coming, it's evil men."

"Chima talked to Mama. They say you are The Chosen One to help us—that you are Abdu. The panther, the Ghost of Africa, has spared you and chosen you. They believe the spirits sent you to us. Have they sent you to us?"

Paul stared at Leza in disbelief. How could they see him as their savior? He was just a man full of doubts and misgivings. He sat on the edge of her bed, careful not to pinch the IV line for the chemo drip. "I've never considered myself a special messenger. Now I want you to rest while we finish the chemo. As soon as the trucks get here, we'll leave. Jim will meet us today in Mundri with your new medicine. You'll like your new home."

"I'll be ready."

"I'm going outside to find Buru and make sure everything is going as planned."

Paul left the hut, and as he scanned the clearing for Buru, he thought about what Leza said. What was he, The Chosen One, supposed to do next?

In the distance, a flock of birds suddenly took flight from the treetops. Paul knew it could mean a predator was approaching. Then he remembered the trucks coming to transport the villagers—kids first, then the others. Maybe they were early, which was good. They could get the children loaded and to safety with daylight to spare.

Screeching chimpanzees at the tree line startled him as they scurried into the branches. Paul glanced at them. "What's spooking you fellas?" he mumbled as he looked at his watch. Really, it was too early for the trucks. They'd have to have left at dawn. He turned and noticed Buru outside his hut, twenty meters away, staring in the same direction.

"Buru! Are our trucks coming already?"

Buru continued to look intently toward the tall grass as if he didn't hear Paul.

The faint sound of truck engines broke the silence, and Paul enjoyed a brief moment of relief that disappeared when he heard screams from the outer circle of the village. He knew at once that it wasn't their rescue trucks. Around him, villagers scurried for cover.

He turned and ran back into Leza's hut. "Leza, get up. We have to get you out of here."

She stared at him. "What's the matter, Baba?"

Orma ran in from the back room. "No. It can't be. Not again."

The roaring engines grew louder. Paul stepped out the door for a better look. Four jeeps burst through the tall grass and into the village center fifty meters away. Women grabbed their children and scattered.

Dust flew from the jeeps as they skidded to a halt. They were filled with soldiers, but they were not dressed in Sudanese military garb. Paul rushed back to Leza and disconnected the IV. As he did so, he heard gunfire.

"Orma, let's go. We have to get out of here." Leza began to sob as Paul scooped her into his arms. Orma stood beside the bed, unable to move.

"Orma!"

She looked at Paul with fear-filled eyes.

"Let's go!"

Orma followed Paul out the door.

"Leza. It'll be okay." Just as Paul said it, a firm hand grabbed his arm. He turned to see Emeka behind him.

"Put her down. Go back inside and put her in bed. You must leave, Dr. Paul."

"We have to get her to safety, Emeka."

"They're not here for her. They're here for you."

"What do you mean?" But he thought of the dream. Deep inside, he knew.

"Just go, Dr. Paul."

Paul ran back through the doorway and laid Leza on her bed. "I'll be back for you."

Emeka pushed Paul out the door and behind Paul's hut. Emeka peered around the corner as more gunfire erupted.

A voice on a megaphone echoed from the clearing. "Dr. Branson, come out now, and no one will be harmed."

"Emeka, who was that? How do they know my name?"

"They're going from hut to hut looking for you. Asking for you by name."

Emeka dragged him behind another hut near the tall grass. Paul glanced around the corner of the building. The soldiers were running toward them.

"Who are these guys?"

Emeka didn't respond. He took Paul's arm, and they ran into the grass that reached well over their heads.

Emeka shoved Paul deeper into the dense greenery. He pushed him so hard that Paul almost fell. "Go now!"

"Dr. Paul Branson from America. Come out, or I will kill this girl. Her name is Leza. I give you five seconds. One—"

Paul turned and ran past Emeka toward the clearing.

"No, Dr. Paul!" Emeka tried to grab his arm.

"Two—"

Furiously Paul thrashed through the thick stalks with his arms.

"Three—"

He reached the edge. A soldier held a pistol against Leza's head.

"Four—"

"No! I'm here!" Paul sprinted into the clearing. "Don't hurt her. Let her go. I'm here." He held his hands over his head.

"You are the doctor?" The booming voice came from a man standing in a jeep to Paul's right. Tall and muscular, he wore blue army fatigues and a beret.

"I'm Dr. Paul Branson, and I said let her go."

Several soldiers circled Paul with their rifles trained on him. Leza sobbed as the first soldier continued to hold his gun to her head. Paul tried to give her an encouraging smile, but then something struck his head, and everything went black.

CHAPTER SIX

Paul's head pounded as the vehicle bounced him from side to side on the rough road. Something warm ran down his neck, making his shirt stick to his skin. Blood?

He opened his eyes and blinked, but could only make out a dim glow. The thick, tainted air around his face smelled of sweat, probably his. He realized a hood had been pulled over his head—a thick baglike cloth cinched around his neck and filled with stale air that made it difficult to breathe. Panic tightened his throat, and he struggled to control it. He couldn't remember what had brought him here—or why. He started to reach up and pull the head covering off but realized his hands were bound to the seat. *Think.*

A gust of wind pressed the hood against Paul's face. The hot air surrounding him and his overheated skin made him suspect it was midday. From the rushing air and the sound of a tired engine, he knew the vehicle had no roof or doors.

When it turned abruptly, the chassis creaked, and the bindings on Paul's hands and feet cut into his skin. He tried to work free, but it was no use—his bindings were too strong.

As they raced along the uneven road, something whipped against Paul's right arm, tearing his shirt and slicing into his flesh. He gritted his teeth and clamped his arms against his sides to protect himself from the jagged branches that lined most of the roadways in the region.

His stomach twisted as its contents searched for a way out. He fought down the gorge and tried not to imagine what it would be like to vomit with a hood over his head.

Then suddenly, in the darkness, a face danced before his eyes—Nicki. He could almost hear her say, "Take a deep breath and let it out slow, just like you taught me when I was in labor, remember?" Her voice echoed in his head as if she were there. He took a deep breath. It seemed to help a little. "Take another one. Go ahead. A nice, long, deep breath."

Paul did it and concentrated on Nicki. He could picture her face for a few more seconds, then he was alone again.

Voices floated back to him. Male voices—angry, excited conversation from the seat in front of him. Paul cocked his head and tried to listen, but could make out only bits and pieces of Arabic over the noise of the engine and the wind. Desperate to hear, he leaned forward as far as he could. Maybe he could catch a phrase or a word, or—

A hand seized his shirt collar and yanked him down. "Sit back if you want to live!" a man shouted in Arabic.

A loud voice in the front seat called to someone. For the first time, Paul noticed the sound of another vehicle pulling alongside them; no, two—one on each side.

Their vehicle dropped several meters as they plunged down a slope. For a moment Paul hung suspended, held to the seat only by the restraints on his wrists and ankles. Then the vehicle hit the bottom with enough force to send pain up his spine. His head thrust forward with a snap. The force of the impact squeezed the air from his lungs, and he gasped. The stagnant air inside the hood did little to quench his thirst for oxygen.

A fragment of a memory surfaced: jeeps coming into the village and a soldier holding a gun on Leza, but he couldn't remember anything after that—until now. Why would anyone want to harm her? And what could they want with him? Most importantly, who were they?

The vehicle slowed, and a cacophony of men's voices assaulted Paul's ears. His heart pounded so hard he wondered if they could see it through his shirt. The voices surrounded him now, shouting at each other—and cursing the doctor from America in Arabic.

Paul clenched his fists in anticipation of what might come next, his fighting instinct surfacing. He did his best to calm himself. Took several more deep breaths. Escape would be impossible if he lost his nerve. He had to stay on top of this.

"Our friend is awake, I see," boomed a deep voice in English. Rough hands untied the hood and snatched it off his head.

Paul's eyes took a moment to adjust to the glaring light. A man towered above him with massive, muscular arms and dark, leathery skin. He wore blue camo and a matching beret. The forty-five-caliber semiautomatic pistol holstered to his belt assured Paul he meant business. Paul remembered seeing this man in the village. He had asked Paul his name.

"I'm Quinn, leader of this division of the Lord's Resistance Army. You are here because I want you here. You will do what I say, or there will be consequences." His intimidating voice matched his cold face. He threw the hood into the back of the jeep.

"You have a strange way of welcoming your guests," Paul mumbled. The man seated beside him struck him in the ribs with the butt of his rifle. Paul groaned as the searing pain tore through his chest. He turned and glared at his assailant. "Untie me and try that again."

Quinn held up his hand, halting the man from taking further action. He turned back to Paul. "My friend Miju doesn't like you. I don't like you, and you're not my guest—you're my prisoner. Would you like to speak again?"

Paul narrowed his eyes but didn't respond.

Quinn didn't smile. "Very good."

Miju cut Paul's ropes with a knife that he pulled from his belt.

Quinn glanced at his men before turning back to Paul. "Come. See why you are here, doctor from America." He turned and walked away.

Miju grabbed Paul's arm, shoved him out of the jeep, and motioned for him to follow Quinn. Paul's stiff legs buckled, and he stumbled from the dizziness and pounding in his head. When he touched the back of his throbbing scalp, his bloody hand confirmed that he had been struck from behind.

Miju tried to push him forward, but Paul snatched his arm away. "I can walk. Keep your hands off me."

A woman clanging cooking pots at a nearby campfire drew his attention. The icy stares of young boys dressed in military fatigues who hovered around her forced him to focus on the path.

Quinn's broad stride required Paul to quicken his pace. A scream in the distance caused him to stop and turn—an action that earned him another poke in the ribs from Miju's rifle.

"Mind your own business," Miju barked in a gravelly voice.

They arrived at a mud hut in the center of the village. Quinn entered, stooping to clear the low-hanging thatched roof. Paul ducked and passed through into a room of decent size.

Miju lit a kerosene lantern hanging from the bamboo pole at the center of the hut. In the glowing light, Paul saw a beautiful young woman lying on a makeshift bed, writhing in pain. Her green eyes, sunken and desperate, pierced him. Her chestnut skin was sallow, her thick brown hair damp with sweat. Paul finally knew why he'd been brought there.

"This is Adanna, my wife. She's been ill four days." Quinn placed his hand on her forehead. "Her skin is hot."

A young woman entered the hut and placed a wet compress on Adanna's forehead. Her skin was fairer than most of the women Paul had seen in the camp so far, even lighter than Adanna's. Her eyes were a glistening blue, and she gave him a faint, shy smile. She was beautiful.

Paul turned back to Quinn, his anger at his abduction fading as the doctor in him kicked in. "Does your wife speak English?"

"Yes, very well. But she is weak right now. I will tell you what you need to know."

"Has she been eating?"

"No. She cannot."

"Is she able to walk?"

"Not for two days. The pain in her stomach is worse today than ever before. She can't even stand."

Paul knelt on the ground near the woman's bed. "Does it hurt her if I push here?" He pressed against the sides of her chest.

Adanna shook her head as she spoke. "No. It does not."

Her voice, filled with kindness, surprised Paul. He leaned closer as she spoke faintly. "The pain—it is lower."

He gently pressed her left abdomen. "Here?"

"No, but it hurts on the right when you push on the left." She reached toward the young woman. "Hanna, take my hand."

Paul waited for Hanna to move to Adanna's side, then he pressed on her right lower abdomen. "Here?" She drew up her knees and screamed.

Quinn grabbed Paul's arm, lifted him to his feet, and shoved him against the wall so hard it took his breath. "What did you do?"

Paul gasped, "You want my help." He coughed. "I'm examining her, not trying to hurt her. I needed to know."

Quinn glared at him.

Paul tried to speak calmly. "Your wife has appendicitis. She'll die unless we get her to a hospital today. She needs surgery."

Quinn shook his head. "There can be no hospital for her—for any of us." He moved to her bedside, then pointed at Paul. "You must do the surgery."

Paul's heart sank. "I can't operate on her here. She'll die." He looked around the room. "Unless we have anesthesia, surgical instruments, IV fluids . . . No, there's no way. She'll be in shock in a matter of hours—then it's over. We have to get her to a hospital."

Paul detected a flicker of fear in Quinn's eyes—fear followed by anger. "No. You must and you will. The closest hospital is three hundred kilometers away, and the Sudanese army and the United Nations—thanks to your president—are looking for us. They're getting close, and we can't break camp with her in this condition. We don't have time, and she has no choice. Neither do you."

Paul turned to Adanna, who was weeping and holding Hanna's hand as she knelt beside the bed.

"Please help me," she begged through her sobs, then turned to Quinn and spoke something quietly in Moru.

Paul waited for a translation, but it didn't come. "What did she say?"

"She says the panther comes for her tonight." Quinn seized Paul's shirt and balled it in his fist. "You must stop him, doctor from America. You are her hope, and you will do this."

"Think about what you're saying. You want me to operate without surgical instruments and barely enough light to see."

Quinn's eyes bored into Paul's as he pulled him closer. "You will help her. You will do this." The determination on his face was unmistakable. There would be no reasoning. Paul turned to Adanna. Her tears touched him. Hanna's eyes were filled with compassion.

Paul pulled away from Quinn's grasp and walked to Adanna's side. "I'll do all I can for you." He choked on his own words.

"Thank you, doctor from America." She tried to smile but couldn't.

Paul turned back to Quinn. "Do you have any IV bags or surgical equipment here? Is there anyone who can help me with the surgery?"

"Whatever we have is yours to use. Hanna will be your right hand. She has much experience with . . . this sort of thing."

Paul turned to the young woman they referred to as Hanna. As she walked toward him past the window, the sun cast a striking reddish light that glanced off her hair.

"I'm Hanna. I will help you."

Quinn put his hand on Miju's shoulder. "Find the women Hanna tells you she'll need. Hurry. And gather the supplies from my jeep."

As Quinn turned back to Adanna, Miju slung his rifle over his shoulder and ducked his head to clear the low doorway of the hut. Hanna followed close behind.

"She cannot die. You can save her, and you must." Quinn sat on the edge of Adanna's bed as he spoke to Paul. "And we do have IV bags. They are from your village. You will use them for her."

"You took IVs from a little girl with cancer?"

Quinn sprang to his feet and moved within centimeters of Paul. "You question me? You believe you can judge me? You will do as I say and not oppose me. Do you understand?"

"I understand you're a monster. That's what I understand."

"What did you say?"

"You heard me."

Quinn backed up and stared at Paul. "If you desire to see your little friend again, do as I say." He paused. "Understand this—if my wife dies, your Leza dies."

Paul's fists clenched and his temples throbbed as his mind raced. But Nicki's voice echoed in his head: "The bigger man speaks gently. The bigger man stands down. The man I love walks away." He closed his eyes briefly as he remembered her gentle yet wise words that had worked so often. He unclenched his angry fists and stared at the woman before him. She needed him, and maybe, just maybe, he could help.

He nodded at Quinn. "Understood."

As Paul began preparations for surgery, Quinn assigned one of his men, Cijen, to guard him closely. He was never to leave Paul's side.

When Paul exited Adanna's hut and walked to the clearing by the fire, Cijen followed close behind, holding his assault rifle trained on Paul's back. Miju joined them and sat on the other side of the fire, skillfully swiping a knife blade on a honing stone, sharpening the glistening steel to perfection.

Paul checked the pot of water they were heating by the fire. Sterilizing the instruments would involve boiling Miju's pocketknife and some hemostats Hanna had provided. She also had suture material on hand for repairing bullet wounds. Cijen stood next to Paul as he squatted by the fire. This man seemed different from the others. He didn't give Paul icy stares or make threatening comments. His quiet, calm demeanor seemed out of place.

While Paul stirred the water, he studied this new captor, taking inventory of every weapon visible. Cijen carried an assault rifle. His belt holstered a semiautomatic pistol on the right with extra ammo. It looked like a nine-millimeter. A second pistol, a forty-five-caliber semiautomatic, was strapped to his left hip. To complete the ensemble, a ribbon of assault ammo was draped from his right shoulder to the left side of his waist.

"Cijen, could you hand me that ladle, please? I need to scoop some water out of this pot." Paul pointed to the one he needed. Without hesitation Cijen picked it up and handed it to him.

"What are you doing?" Miju snapped in Arabic. "You're his guard, not his servant."

Paul gave Cijen a reassuring smile as he ladled out some of the water that was boiling over. He didn't want to reveal that he understood Arabic, which would remove any chance that the two men might speak Arabic or Dinka in front of him, not realizing he could comprehend what they said.

Miju must have noticed the smile. "You have your work cut out for you, Doctor. Stick to that, and don't try making friends here." He went back to work with the honing stone. "I told you before to mind your own business."

Paul glanced at Miju's pocketknife. "How sharp can you get that?" Paul continued to ladle water from the pot, peering in to see if it was the right amount.

"Sharp enough to cut a man's throat with one stroke." Miju held the knife to his own neck for effect.

Paul tried to ignore the threat but knew better than to dismiss it. "When it's ready, drop it in here." Miju didn't acknowledge the instruction.

Paul's thoughts shifted to what lay ahead. In an hour he would perform an impossible surgery on a woman who had virtually no chance of survival, and Leza's life depended on the outcome.

He'd performed many surgical procedures in his career—some of them under extreme circumstances. But this time there would be no anesthesia, proper instruments, or lights—just a pocketknife sharpened on a whetstone by a radical terrorist by a campfire in the middle of . . . somewhere.

Paul reached into his pocket and pulled out a quarter. Holding his hand flat, palm down, he began flipping the coin from his thumb across the backs of his knuckles. When he got to the pinky, he turned his hand over without dropping the quarter and flipped it through his fingers with his palm up. He repeated this each time the coin reached the edge of his hand, over and over, with the coin moving fluidly from finger to finger in a shiny wave.

"How are you doing that?" Cijen broke Paul's concentration, but he didn't drop the coin.

Paul responded without looking up from his hand. "It's an exercise to keep my fingers limber before I perform surgery. It improves my coordination and helps me focus. Want to try?"

He handed the coin to Cijen.

"Pinch it between your thumb and index finger first, then roll it across your index finger knuckle and grab it with the next two fingers. Once you do that, pass it to the next finger and then the next."

Cijen struggled over and over to roll the coin, but he couldn't move it past the first knuckle without dropping it. He smiled sheepishly. Paul took the coin back.

"I've been doing this for years. It takes practice—lots of practice." He effortlessly rolled the coin across his fingers again as he looked into the boiling pot.

"Where did you learn that?" It was the first question Miju asked without shouting.

Paul grinned. "From a pickpocket in New York City."

Miju laughed out loud. It was strange to see him anything but angry and violent.

Paul added, "I can steal wallets too."

Miju laughed harder.

Quinn came out of his wife's hut and stood over Paul. Miju quickly stopped laughing as Quinn spoke. "How much longer?"

"Not long." Paul could hear her sobs inside the tiny hut. "We just need to sterilize the knife," he said as Miju reached over and dropped it into the water.

While the knife boiled, Paul had Cijen break off a truck mirror to use to focus sunlight from the window onto the bed. It would serve as a surgical lamp. Paul went into the hut and started the IV from the supplies they had stolen from Leza, but the problem of anesthesia remained.

"We'll have to start in a few minutes, Quinn." Paul paused. "We don't have any way to numb this pain, and I have to cut open her abdomen." Quinn looked at Adanna and then took her hand.

Paul had to find a way to minimize her suffering. He grasped at straws. "Do you have any alcohol we could give her?"

Quinn didn't hesitate. "Miju. Get my whiskey—and a glass." Miju ran out, returning moments later with a half-filled bottle of Jack Daniel's.

Quinn poured some into the glass and held it up for Adanna. She pinched her nose and drank, sputtering and choking.

"More," he insisted. She repeated the process until she had drunk half a glass.

"No more," she begged. "I can't."

He laid her back on the pillow.

Paul approached Quinn and whispered, "I need to talk to you outside." Paul saw the hesitation in his eyes. "It's important."

Paul followed Quinn out the door. As the two stood in the clearing by the fire, Paul cut to the chase. "The whiskey will help, but when I make the incision, it's going to hurt her more than you can imagine. I'm sorry. I'll be cutting into her flesh all the way to her intestines. She'll eventually pass out from the pain, but it takes a minute or two." He waited for Quinn to respond and then added, "If you get angry and kill me when she screams, she'll die."

"Then I can't stay. I don't trust myself." Quinn turned and walked back into the hut with Paul behind him.

Quinn sat on the edge of the bed and took Adanna's hand. He spoke tenderly to her, kissed her forehead, stood, and faced Paul. "I'm leaving you with Miju. Remember what I told you. If she dies . . ."

"I get it. But I'm going to do my best to help your wife for *her*, not because you've threatened me. I love Leza and don't doubt you'll kill her if Adanna dies. But if I can save your wife, it's because I'm doing everything I can for her."

"I hope for Leza's sake you are up to the task."

"For Adanna's sake, I pray that I am."

Paul watched from the doorway as Quinn climbed into his jeep and drove away. Then he whispered to Miju, "This is going to be horrible, and I need your help if she's going to survive."

Three women from the camp entered the hut together. Adanna sobbed inconsolably. She knew they were there to hold her down. Hanna ducked through the doorway behind them, carrying a tattered leather bag.

Miju noticed Paul looking at the satchel. "She is skilled at removing bullets and sewing us when we get cut. She will assist you well."

"How's your English, Hanna?"

"Very good."

"Excellent. Can you start a second IV on her other arm? We'll need two to keep her blood pressure up if she bleeds much, and the IV fluid will do that. And I need you across from me when we begin. You can assist me from there."

"As you wish." Hanna gave a single nod and offered Paul a brief moment of eye contact.

Miju took his place next to Paul and handed him pieces of cloth that had been sterilized in boiling water. Paul prepared the area of Adanna's abdomen for the incision and scrubbed his hands with some of the Jack Daniel's. Hanna did the same. Paul picked up Miju's knife from the table and nodded to Cijen at the window.

Cijen took his cue and held the mirror to reflect the sunlight from the window to the incision site while two of the women grabbed Adanna's legs and arms and held her down on the bed. The third woman stood at her head and gently placed a twisted cloth into her mouth to bite on.

Paul addressed the woman at the head of the bed. "Do you know how to check her pulse?" She stared at him blankly.

Miju spoke to her in Dinka and then translated her reply. "She says she can."

"Are you ready, Hanna?"

"The IV is in place. I'm ready."

"Open the IV saline all the way. She's going to lose fluids, and I must keep her pressure up."

Hanna nodded and opened the valve fully.

Tears trickled down Adanna's delicate face, her eyes heavy from the alcohol. Her silent sobs broke Paul's heart. He closed his eyes and took a deep breath, letting it out slowly. He turned his attention back to her, and their gazes met. "I'm sorry, Adanna." He placed his hand on her abdomen and touched the knife to her soft skin. She quivered and stiffened as the women pushed her against the bed.

The sharpened knife sliced easily into Adanna's tender flesh. Her screams, muffled by the cloth clenched in her teeth, filled the tiny room. Paul swallowed hard and continued to cut into her abdomen.

Adanna arched her back and bent her knees to break free. Paul drew back on the knife to keep from cutting into her bowels when she squirmed. One of the women sat on her legs as she writhed in pain and attempted to twist away from the blade. She bit down hard on the rag and groaned with every breath as beads of sweat covered her face. Then, finally, she passed out.

Paul slowly made his way to the bloated, inflamed appendix. "Hanna, hand me that ligature there—the purple package. It's absorbable suture material. I need to tie this appendix off before it ruptures." Hanna handed it to him and without hesitation held the incision open for him with her bloody hands. Paul tied off the appendix and removed it. There, it was out.

"I need to get the incision closed before she wakes up. We're almost there—wait. What's this?"

"What? Is something wrong?" Hanna leaned in to see where Paul was looking.

Just then, the woman at Adanna's head shouted in Dinka, "She's not breathing!"

Hanna translated, "She said she's not breathing!"

Paul looked at Adanna's face—her eyes were partly open, her chest wasn't moving, and she was no longer biting on the rag. "Does she have a pulse?"

Hanna checked her wrist. "I can't feel one."

Paul reached up and placed his fingers on Adanna's neck. "There isn't one." He inspected her abdomen. The appendix was out, the bowel was tied off, and there was no bleeding. He reached across and opened the other IV all the way, wiped his hands on the rag they used for a surgical drape, and moved to Adanna's head. He examined her eyes and listened to her heart. A thready, faint heartbeat was all she had left.

"She's in shock. Help me, Hanna."

"Help you what?"

"Watch me. I'll need you in a minute."

Paul tilted Adanna's head back, took a deep breath, and placed his lips on hers.

"What are you doing?" Miju questioned.

Paul didn't acknowledge him as he pinched Adanna's nose and blew deep and strong into her mouth, causing her chest to rise. When he moved from her lips, her chest fell.

"What . . ." Miju stood with his mouth open, but Hanna nodded as if she understood.

Paul realized they'd probably never seen such a thing. He did it again, and a third time, and then shifted to Adanna's chest. As he compressed it, he saw fear in Miju's face for the first time. "Hanna, come over and put your hands right here. Just like this. It's easy. Got it?" Paul did four more compressions, then took Adanna's face in his hands, placed his lips on hers, and breathed into her lungs again. Hanna waited.

"Okay, go," Paul instructed.

Hanna began chest compressions between Paul's breaths. They worked side by side for several minutes.

Adanna lay motionless, her frail body overwhelmed. She was too tired to fight.

Miju grabbed Paul's arm. "She's gone."

Paul looked at him sternly. "She's gone when I say she's gone."

CHAPTER SEVEN

Orma stared out the window at the distant hills and wept. Two years earlier she had thought that nothing could help her sick little girl. Paul and Nicki had brought hope—a chance for Leza to survive. But now . . .

"Mama, what are you doing?" Leza's soft voice interrupted Orma's thoughts.

She dried her eyes before turning to face her daughter. "Just watching the children play outside."

"Mama, you haven't been sleeping much. You need rest."

"I can't stop thinking about him."

"You have to believe. He'll come back. He's Abdu."

"I know. But I'm worried. Your medicine is useless since they took your IVs. And even though Jim brought your chemo treatment to Mundri, by the time the men drove to meet him and bring it back here to Matta, Paul was already gone. It is of no use without him."

Leza was quiet for a moment. "How long?"

"What do you mean?"

"How long do I have . . . if he doesn't come back?"

Orma blotted her eyes again. "I don't know."

"Yes, you do."

"You're too smart for your own good, my little one."

"Tell me, Mama. I need to know."

"Dr. Paul said eight to ten weeks without the chemo."

Leza was silent for a moment. "You think he's dead, don't you, Mama?"

"No. They're horrible men, but Dr. Paul is strong." Orma swallowed a sob. "He has to come back. He promised."

Leza swung her legs over the side of the bed.

"No, Leza. You're too weak."

"It's okay. I can walk. I feel good today." Leza stood and wrapped her arms around her mother's waist. "We can hope, Mama. I believe in Abdu—in his power. He has been called."

"I want to believe. How do I?"

"Just accept it. If the Ghost of Africa is real, he is being used by one who is in control, and Abdu is his master."

Orma smiled. "I know the panther is real, and I believe in Abdu. I'll do my best, little one. Dr. Paul has tried to tell me many times to believe."

Jim threw his hands up in frustration and shook his head.

Jarrod pulled up a chair and straddled it. "I just find it hard to believe that you've had another encounter with authorities in a seven-day period without a reason. They had no cause to detain you, unless . . ."

"Unless what, Jarrod?"

"Unless you violated protocol, and they say you did."

"I landed in Juba like I've done a hundred times. They looked at my passport like they have a hundred times, then they disappeared for an hour. I have no idea what they were doing. It took another hour to get clearance for takeoff, even though I was the only aircraft on the ground. It cost me almost two hours between landing and takeoff."

"I'm sorry, Jim. I know this is upsetting, but you have to follow protocol. You're in a third world nation, and that means—"

"Upsetting? Seriously? That's what you call it? My brother-in-law, my best friend in the world, was kidnapped. If I hadn't been delayed, I would have landed in Mundri and driven to Matta in time to help. Instead, I was detained in Juba for no reason whatsoever."

"You never would have been there in time. It was early morning when they showed up."

"How do you even know that? How did you arrive at that conclusion? You know what? I don't care. It's like an unseen force prevented me from getting there."

"Well, it's not like that type of delay hasn't happened before."

"You mean my friend being kidnapped? No, it hasn't. And being the only aircraft on the ground that's being detained? No, that hasn't happened either. And having no one to talk to even at the tourist counter in Juba? Nope. Not that one either. I even stood there taking pictures with my cell phone since they normally arrest people doing that, but nobody came, nobody protested, nobody took my phone or came to the window or did anything! You don't see a problem with that, Jarrod? That doesn't seem out of the norm to you?"

"You know what I mean—the delays at the airport. It happens. And we have no control if and when it occurs. There's no telling why. No predicting."

Jim paced to the front of his plane and leaned against the prop. "He's gone, Jarrod. They have him. The LRA has Paul. Where on earth are they taking him—and why? Why in God's name would they kidnap Paul Branson?"

Jarrod shook his head. "Beats me. Don't know what to say. It's weird, I'll give you that."

"Tell me you care then. Tell me something, because it seems like you don't. Just another day in Africa, right? Someone disappears, and that's too bad just as long as it isn't someone who matters to you. I need to believe this matters to you, right now."

"Take it easy, Jim. I care. I'm just saying I wouldn't know where to start to try and find him."

"Start by calling Arua and Juba. Ask them who told them to look the other way."

"Jim, that's crazy talk, and you know it. We'll get ourselves arrested before we find out what happened. There's nothing we can do right now but wait. I'll make calls, but it has to be subtle."

Jim walked to the bulletin board and pulled off the Sudan relief map. "I need to try."

"How are you going to do that? You have no idea where they've taken him."

Jim rolled up the stiff map. "I know. But I have to try. First I need to talk to Jessica. I promised Paul I would, and I'm going to keep that promise. Then I need to look for him. I don't know how, but I'll figure it out." He sat down on the landing gear of his plane and stared at the satellite phone in his hand. He'd never imagined he'd have to make good on that promise.

Paul washed his hands in a basin beside Adanna's bed as Quinn's jeep pulled into the compound. Even though it was only five o'clock, Paul's mind raced from the events of the day, and he wondered how Quinn would respond to what he had to tell him. He dried his hands on a small towel.

"Doctor!" The shout startled Paul even though he had been expecting to hear Quinn any moment. He looked out the window and saw Quinn standing in the front seat of the jeep. "Dr. Branson!"

Paul tossed the towel onto a nearby table and ducked through the doorway to face his captor. Cijen followed close on his heels, poking

Paul's back with the rifle barrel. Quinn stepped from the jeep, his broad stride quickly closing the gap between them. "Is she alive?"

Quinn's question was an accusation, and he hovered so close to Paul that it forced him back a step against Cijen's rifle barrel. "If she's dead, you've left me no choice. I warned you your Leza would die as well." Quinn's voice quavered as he prepared to pronounce judgment. "Did you let her die?" His hand rested on his holster.

"No, I didn't."

Quinn's expression changed to a mixture of anger and disbelief. "Don't lie to me."

"She's alive, Quinn. Alive and doing well."

Quinn glanced toward the hut, then back at Paul. "The surgery . . . ?"

"It's done. Her appendix is out. As I suspected, it was infected and ready to burst. She would never have lived until tomorrow. It was difficult and painful for her, but she'll be okay. You saved her."

Quinn stood in frozen silence as if, for the first time, he didn't know what to do. Paul realized he'd expected to return to find Adanna dead and had already planned to kill Paul and Leza. Quinn's hand remained on the pistol holstered at his side.

"Quinn?" Adanna's faint voice came from the hut. He turned to where Miju waited in the doorway.

"There's something else, Quinn. She's going to have a baby. Adanna's pregnant."

Quinn looked back at Paul, and a crooked, puzzled grin broke through. "She's . . . are you sure?"

"Yes. Her uterus was enlarged, so I looked a little closer. From what I can tell, they're both strong. They'll be fine. The little bit of Jack Daniel's won't cause any problems." Quinn didn't move, obviously stunned. Paul gestured toward the hut. "She's waiting for you."

Quinn snapped out of his trance, hurried to the doorway, and disappeared into the square mud building. For the first time Paul saw hope in Quinn. Could this man be human after all? He actually seemed capable of compassion, at least for his wife. That was a start.

Paul smiled at Cijen and pointed toward the area of tall grass they'd designated as a latrine. "Hey, do you mind?"

"No. But I must come with you. I have my orders." Cijen nodded and waved his rifle, indicating that Paul could go.

"Cijen, how long have you—?"

"Cij."

"Pardon me?"

"They call me Cij. You can call me that too, if you want."

"Cij. I like that. Very cool name."

"Thank you." He grinned.

"Cij, how long have you been here? With Quinn, I mean?"

"About eight years. Quinn took me from my village when I was twelve. He taught me how to fight. At first I hated him, but now I owe him everything. I know it was for the best."

"What happened to your family?"

"They died in the battle, but Quinn had no choice. If he had not killed them, they would have killed him."

They walked for a minute in silence as Paul pondered what Cijen had told him. How could a man believe that allowing Quinn to kill his own family made sense?

"You can go back there behind the tall grass. I will wait here, but please do not try to run. Quinn will punish me if you escape, and there is nowhere for you to go anyway."

Until now, no one had treated Paul like a human being, except Hanna and Adanna. He went around the wall of tall grass woven together as a privacy fence for the latrine.

When he didn't come out for several minutes, Cijen called, "Doctor." Paul didn't answer. Cijen shouted, "Doctor!"

Paul remained silent as he peeked through the grass at him, waiting until Cijen pulled up his rifle and ran toward the latrine. When he did, Paul rushed around the corner from the opposite direction and purposely collided with him. The impact knocked them both to the ground with Paul on top of his captor.

Paul scrambled off him, picked up Cijen's rifle from the ground, and handed it to him butt end first.

"Sorry, Cij. Thought I saw a snake. It freaked me out."

Cijen appeared surprised, then took the rifle from Paul.

"I'm not your enemy, Cij."

Paul turned and walked toward the huts with his hand under his shirt, holding his ribs and a stolen pistol he'd tucked into his belt. He prayed that Cijen wouldn't notice the empty holster.

"Are you okay, Doctor?"

"I just bruised a rib. I'm fine."

Cijen followed Paul back to camp, holding him at gunpoint.

As they neared the hut, Cijen motioned with his rifle to a log by the fire. "Sit there." Cijen took a seat on Paul's left. Moments later Quinn exited Adanna's hut and sat next to Paul on his right. Six men gathered across the fire from them and glared at Paul.

"Miju told me Adanna died and you breathed air into her." Paul stared at the fire but didn't speak. "He says you pushed on her chest and brought her back to life."

Paul leaned down, picked up a stick, and threw it on the fire.

"And he told me you demanded the surgery to be finished by the time she woke up so that her suffering was less." Quinn waited. Paul nodded.

"Are you afraid of me? Is that why you aren't speaking?"

Paul was surprised to hear Quinn ask. "Anyone would be afraid of you. You have the power to kill, and I don't think you'd hesitate. But your boys over there creep me out more." Paul pointed at the glaring men on the other side of the fire and suddenly stood. "What's your problem?" he shouted at them. They seemed surprised at his boldness.

Quinn waved them off. "Watch the borders, men. Get up. No one told you to rest." He pulled Paul's arm to make him sit.

The men stood and walked a short distance, talking among themselves.

"Go!" Quinn ordered.

The men separated, quickened their pace, and moved to their guard positions.

Miju was the last to exit Adanna's hut and sat on the other side of Quinn.

"Well, you don't seem as afraid as other men we've brought into camp," Quinn said.

"Are those men dead?"

Quinn thought for a moment and offered a quick nod. "All but one."

"What about him?"

"He listened to me. He was reasonable and did what I needed him to do."

"I'm not afraid to die. Don't get me wrong, I'm not trying to die, and I have no desire to die today. I have things to do, like taking care of a little girl who's counting on me to come back to the village where you found me." Paul never looked up from the fire.

"I am God's right hand." Quinn sat straight and proud.

"You're what?"

"My power comes from God."

Paul turned from the fire and looked Quinn in the eye. "Seriously, you believe this?"

"The LRA is the Lord's Resistance Army. That's God, is it not?" Quinn looked at Miju, then at Paul.

Paul made no attempt to hide his disdain.

"But I'm His right hand," Quinn boasted. "He's the boss, but I do the work. That means I get the spoils."

"Spoils?"

"Spoils of battle. Money, food, trucks, jeeps—anything I want, including women."

Paul shook his head in disbelief. "Is that what it's about for you?"

Miju jumped in. "Quinn is the hand of God. If it were not so, I wouldn't follow him."

Quinn spoke as if Miju had said nothing. "No. That is not what it's all about. I have much greater ambitions than you could ever imagine. And one day soon, I will be as great as Kony."

"You take what you want and throw away the rest. That's not being a leader."

"So you don't believe what I believe," Quinn snapped.

A long pause interrupted their conversation, then Quinn spoke bluntly. "I know you saved Adanna, but I can't let you go. I have plans for you, Dr. Branson, plans that will change Sudan forever. You're an important part of that change, which I hope you will embrace."

"What?" Paul turned to Quinn. "What plans? You kidnapped me to help your wife. I did that. What more can I do?"

Quinn glanced briefly at Cijen, then Miju, and then back at Paul. "Her illness made it necessary to bring you here sooner than we had planned. But we were coming for you anyway."

The hair bristled on Paul's neck.

"You see, Dr. Branson, it's my business to know every intruder who enters my world. I discovered something very important. I learned that the man I needed to help me was in my own country. When your wife died, I worried that perhaps you might never return to Sudan and that I had missed my opportunity. But here you are." Quinn grinned. "We planned to come for you in several weeks when our preparations were complete. I knew you intended to stay in Matta for three months. But when my wife fell ill, I needed you sooner than expected."

"What use could you possibly have for me? I'm only a physician, and I did what you wanted." Paul paused for a moment as something nagged at him. "And how did you know I'd be in Matta for three months?"

Quinn smiled smugly. "You're the key to my plan. The commander of the gunships that brought you down at the border of North Sudan informed me you would be in Matta that same day and remain for three months. I have loyal men in places you can't imagine."

Paul's fears welled like an erupting volcano. "How could you possibly have that much control?"

"Money breeds friends. I don't expect you to understand. All you need to know is that you will not go back to Leza today—or tomorrow. Perhaps someday . . ."

Paul suppressed the irrational desire to pull the pistol from under his shirt and kill Quinn, but that would be the last thing he ever did. Leza would die. And his daughter, Jessica, would never discover what happened to him.

"I require your assistance, Dr. Branson. You must understand, I—"

"In the trees!" A voice in Arabic from the lookout tower two hundred meters away interrupted Quinn.

Quinn stood and studied the mango grove adjacent to the tower, which was surrounded by a field of tall grass.

"Miju. My binoculars."

Miju quickly retrieved the field glasses from Quinn's jeep and handed them to him. Quinn held them to his eyes and scoured the terrain as he spoke in English. "There are men in the trees. I see four, but there are probably more."

Quinn lowered the binoculars and spoke in Arabic. "Ready the men, Miju. Move Adanna to the rear huts, and—"

"Near the foothills! In the grass! Fifteen! Twenty!" the lookout shouted.

Paul could see men moving through the tall grass.

"Miju, come back. It's too late to move her. They're upon us."

Quinn pushed Paul down. "Stay low." He spoke in English when addressing Paul.

A single gunshot echoed in the trees, and the guard dropped to the ground.

"Formations, men!" Quinn ordered in Arabic. "Take your positions! They're on the north perimeter! Take cover!" He grabbed Paul's arm, pulled him up, and pushed him toward his vehicle. "Get behind the jeep, and keep your head down!"

The men ran to their positions. The first burst of semiautomatic gunfire scattered lead across the compound, striking three of the men before they could raise their weapons. They fell a few meters from Paul.

He peered over the fender to see the LRA returning fire into the trees with AK-47s. The men in the mango grove responded with a hail of hot lead, showering the clearing where Quinn's men huddled behind vehicles, rocks, and trees.

The soldiers who had been near the fire with Paul moments before unleashed a barrage of gunfire into the trees. Paul watched as Quinn emptied his pistol into the tall grass and reloaded with another clip from his belt. A cloud of bullets followed from the direction of the foothills.

The powerful rounds slapped into the trees beside Paul and into the jeep. He crouched and hugged the tire as the dirt exploded around him from bullets that missed their marks. He pulled the pistol from his belt and moved to the back of the vehicle, wondering if the people shooting at them were Quinn's enemies or his own friends.

He peered over the edge of the bumper. Quinn and Miju had their backs to him. Cijen was farther away, fighting bravely with the other men.

Paul glanced behind him. No one guarded the rear perimeter. This was his chance. In the chaos, he could shoot Quinn and Miju and escape undetected. With all the gunfire, no one would know he'd killed them, and it would be hours before they realized he'd escaped. But escape to where? He might be able to make it to the foothills before nightfall, but then what? What if the men attacking them were even worse than Quinn? He looked at the loaded pistol in his hand. His mind raced.

Adanna's scream snapped him back to reality. He glanced toward the hut where she lay trapped in bed, an easy target. He glanced from the protection of the bumper to see if Quinn had heard her. If he had, he didn't react to his wife's voice.

Paul chambered a round and placed his finger on the trigger. He aimed at Quinn. It would take one shot to kill him, and Miju, only a few meters away, would be an easy second. He rested his arm on the back bumper and took a deep breath to calm his hand—

"Help!" Adanna's weak voice somehow broke through the chaos and noise.

Paul ignored it. He closed his mind to her plea and concentrated on Quinn. That's what he had to do. There would be no second chance. He took another deep breath and then lowered the pistol.

He couldn't shoot a man in the back—not even Quinn. And he couldn't leave Adanna at the mercy of whoever was attacking them. No matter what, she didn't deserve that. Paul eased the hammer down with his thumb and tucked the pistol into the back of his belt.

Quinn's soldiers fired at the assailants, but the dense foliage made it difficult to spot the men in the trees. They fired from their hiding places with only an occasional muzzle flash alerting the LRA to where the snipers were.

The windshield of the jeep Paul hid behind splintered into tiny fragments as the bullets passed through. Bark exploded off the trees as the thud of hot metal split their trunks.

Pure adrenaline coursed through Paul's veins. His reflexes were brisk, his mind sharp, and his strength unsurpassed. He bolted across the clearing to Adanna's hut and dove through the narrow doorway as a high-velocity round exploded into the wall, spraying fragments of dirt and wood into his path. Debris fell from the walls and ceiling as he crashed to the floor.

Adanna screamed and reached for the table to pull herself from the bed, but it was too far away. Another bullet whistled past the doorpost, missing Paul by millimeters. Undaunted, he crawled toward her, the air thick with dust.

"Adanna. Stay down!"

As the assault bullets pelted the tiny hut, they were unable to penetrate the dense mud, but with each thud, the walls weakened. Paul knew they would soon crumble and that he was running out of time. The next bullet exploded through the window frame, creating a hole the size of a baseball and scattering painful projectiles across the room.

"Help me!" Adanna pleaded.

Paul forced his way past the debris, scooped her into his arms, and pulled her to the floor as a shot burst through the back wall, barely missing her. She screamed and grabbed her abdomen.

"Did I hurt you? Are you shot?"

"No. It's the incision." She pressed her hand against it and cried, "I'm sorry."

Covering her body with his, Paul pointed toward the far wall. "We need to move over there. Wrap your arm around my neck, and press your other hand on your abdomen."

Adanna pulled herself against him with her right arm.

"Hold on tight."

She nodded, squeezed her eyes shut, and pressed her cheek against his as he held her close and carried her to the safety of the wall. Carefully he laid her on the ground and covered her body with his.

She held onto him and sobbed, "Don't leave me. Please don't go. I don't want to lose my baby. I don't want to die."

"I'm not going anywhere. I promise."

As Paul spoke, a bullet erupted through the side wall and pierced his left shoulder, forcing him to let go of Adanna and fall backward.

It felt as if he'd been struck with a hammer. He grabbed his arm and scrambled to cover her again.

"What happened? Are you okay?"

Blood oozed between Paul's fingers as he gripped the wound, and an involuntary grunt escaped his lips.

"You've been shot!"

"Stay down." Paul gritted his teeth, pushed Adanna lower, and tried to focus as the scorching pain in his shoulder gripped his chest too. He closed his eyes and took a breath. "It'll be okay. Just stay down. It went all the way through."

Paul pushed Adanna behind him, pulled the gun from his belt, and aimed it at the doorway with his bloody hand. "I won't let them get you. I swear I won't." He pulled back the hammer, waiting for the intruders to show their faces, ready to fire. He didn't care who they were. They weren't going to kill this woman in cold blood.

The next bullet seemed to bore through the damaged wall in slow motion amid a cloud of dirt and debris. It splintered through the table and pierced Paul's left upper chest, slamming him against Adanna.

Searing pain exploded through his body as the bullet embedded itself deep inside. Paul struggled to inhale, but the air wouldn't come. He opened his mouth, but he couldn't speak—couldn't breathe. His strength abandoned him as if it were being poured out on the floor. As the room darkened, he turned to the door, rolled to his side, and was still.

CHAPTER EIGHT

"Oh dear God." Adanna leaned over Paul as he lay bleeding on the floor. Relentless gunfire pinned her down behind him, but slowly she turned him onto his back. The blood from his chest formed a growing puddle at his side. She pressed her left hand into the soaking hole in his shirt. With her right she held her abdomen. Several more bullets pelted the hard mud facade but didn't find their way through.

"Please, don't die." She cringed when the next bullet hit the dirt wall.

Then, as suddenly as it started, the shooting stopped. Paul's shallow, coarse breathing filled the silence.

Adanna gently stroked his hair and struggled to lift his head onto her lap, but the sutures pulled against her tender skin, and the ache in the pit of her stomach nauseated her. Pain, radiating from her belly to her chest, accompanied every movement.

Men barked orders in the courtyard. An occasional shout in the distance reminded Adanna of the chaos outside. She tried to call for help, but before she could, Quinn rushed through the doorway with his pistol drawn and spotted her on the floor. He dropped to his knees and holstered his weapon.

"Are you okay? Your wound—it's bleeding." He began to check her incision.

"No. It's not my blood. Don't move my hand. He's been shot, Quinn."

When Quinn saw the pool of blood oozing between her fingers from the wound in Paul's chest, his eyes widened and his expression changed. "No! This can't happen."

He tore Paul's shirt open. The wound was bleeding heavily despite Adanna's efforts to stanch it. Quinn ripped a piece of cloth from Paul's shirt, wadded it into a ball, and pressed it into the wound.

Adanna brushed the hair from Paul's face with her bloodstained hand. "Help him, Quinn."

As he held the bandage firmly, Quinn spotted the gun in Paul's hand. "Where did he get that?"

"I don't know, but he used it to protect me. He saved me—again."

Quinn took the pistol from Paul's hand and tucked it into his belt, still holding the bandage in place.

"If he hadn't come in, it would be me lying in a pool of blood," Adanna said.

"Miju!" Quinn shouted. "Come quickly! Adanna's hut!"

Seconds later, Miju stood in the doorway with his pistol ready. When he saw Paul on the floor, he holstered it and ran to Quinn's side.

"He's been shot twice, Miju. This one in his chest is bad."

Adanna continued to stroke Paul's hair. "Is he going to die?"

"Hanna!" Quinn shouted, ignoring the question. "Miju, find Hanna." He turned back to Paul. "You cannot die. Not now." He straightened Paul's legs with his free hand and with his foot shoved a box under his legs to elevate them.

Miju burst through the door followed by Hanna.

Quinn pointed to the medical supplies in the corner. "Start an IV on him. He's losing blood."

Hanna stood motionless as she stared at Paul.

"Hanna! The IV!"

She snapped out of her trance, grabbed the bags and IV tubing kits, and knelt next to Quinn. She paused as she looked at Paul. "No. He's bleeding out," she told Quinn. "Here. Push here." Hanna grabbed his hand. "You must stop the bleeding, or else the IV won't help." She pushed Quinn's hand into the artery that was spouting blood. "Good. Hold it there. If it spurts, press harder. I need to put a stitch in that artery."

Hanna turned, pulled the supplies from her bag, and began working on Paul. Quinn continued to push against the bloody opening in Paul's chest.

Adanna leaned against the wall. "I don't feel well."

Quinn turned his attention to her. "What's wrong? Are you sure you're not bleeding?"

"No. I just feel weak and dizzy. And sick to my stomach."

Still pressing on Paul's wound, Quinn helped her lie down. "We'll be leaving soon. Rest for now." He took her hand. "Listen to me. I love you, and I brought the doctor here to save you. But there's more that I can't tell you. I was going to bring him here anyway. That's why we risked a trip to Sudan right now—we had to find him. But when you were suddenly so ill, we had to abduct him sooner than planned."

Adanna looked at Paul's pale, graying face. *Sooner than planned?* "What if he dies? What if he bleeds to death?"

Quinn responded quickly, "He can't die."

He turned to Miju. "Gather the men. We move to the base tonight. The Sudanese army will be back with reinforcements. We don't have much time—maybe a day. We can launch our plan now that he's with us. We'll speed up the clock."

Adanna, confused, grabbed Quinn's wrist. "I don't understand. What plan?"

"You'll see in time. I'll keep him alive, but he's not your friend. I don't know why he came in here, but he's not your friend."

Quinn turned to Miju. "Go. You have your orders."

Miju hurried out. Within an hour, flames consumed every hut in the village, and the loaded trucks awaited Quinn's orders. He peered into the back of the transport vehicle. Paul lay on the floor of the truck bed with an IV hanging from the wall support and sutures closing the bullet hole in his chest, thanks to Hanna. She sat next to him and checked his pulse regularly.

Adanna leaned against the bulkhead a meter away with a pillow propped behind her. Quinn climbed into the cab of the truck, and the driver started the engine. One by one the other trucks did the same and pulled onto the path, following Quinn.

The personnel transport vehicles bounced across the terrain, jostling Adanna from side to side, causing her incision to feel as if it were going to burst. She pressed her hand against her abdomen to ease the pain, then moved it over to where her baby was growing. "I'm sorry for what Quinn has gotten you into, doctor from America. But thank you for saving me and my baby."

Taking Paul's hand in hers, she held it tightly. Hanna wrapped her arm around Adanna's shoulders until she fell asleep.

◆ ◆ ◆

Paul continued to dream.

He felt Nicki's soft, warm hand squeeze his as they strolled through the woods along a path lined with gardenias, and the first drops of rain found their way through the branches above. The path opened onto a pasture where a towering oak beckoned. They huddled beneath its limbs.

The gentle patter of rain on the leaves quietly hushed the cares of the world as Nicki stood on her tiptoes and wrapped her arms around Paul's neck. She closed her eyes and pressed her soft cheek against his face.

He whispered, "I love you, Nicki."

"I love you."

He pulled her close and touched his lips to hers in a deep, warm kiss. He would be hers forever.

Paul's eyes popped open. It took a moment to focus. The ceiling wasn't mud or thatched grass. He lifted his pounding head and stiff neck to discover he was lying on a narrow bed with an IV in his left arm and his wrists and ankles zip-tied to the metal frame. He glanced around the room, blinking sweat from his burning eyes. Nothing looked familiar. No mud walls, no dirt floors. He lay back for a minute to let the pain in his head and chest subside, then gritted his teeth and looked up again.

The bamboo walls were a marked difference from those of the hut where he'd performed Adanna's surgery. The wall on his left had two large window openings. He looked to his right. Three meters away the dead bolt on the door confirmed his status as a prisoner—as if he needed reminding.

He tried to sit up far enough to see out the window, but searing chest pain forced him back down. He took a deep breath, but it felt as if a hot poker had been shoved between his ribs, preventing him from doing more than taking shallow sips of air.

Memories returned in fragments. He recalled running to help Adanna, and then . . . then someone shot him. Twice.

Reluctantly, he looked down. A crude, bloody bandage covered the wound on his bare chest, but the pain reached through to his back and radiated to the left side of his neck. He tried to remember if Adanna was okay or if . . .

Men's voices speaking Dinka drifted into his room from somewhere, but they were too far away to understand.

Every movement Paul attempted rewarded him with pain. He would have to be content to lie flat on his back for now. He wiggled his left arm but couldn't free his wrist from the zip tie holding him to the bed frame. The pain in his left shoulder throbbed. He twisted his right wrist. It was secured to the bed rail even tighter than the left.

"God, help me." He spoke the words but made almost no sound. He didn't know where he was or how long he'd been there. He had no idea what he was supposed to do or what would happen next.

A loud clank of metal on metal from the door startled him. Seconds later, Quinn towered over his bedside. "Why were you mumbling? Were you praying that someone would save you?"

Paul didn't respond.

Quinn leaned down to his ear. "I don't know if you remember what happened, but the Sudanese army sent twenty-eight men to attack us. They're dead. They're all dead." Paul stiffened. "They didn't come to save you, they came to kill me." Quinn looked at Paul for a reaction. He didn't have one.

"We're partners, Dr. Branson, like it or not. You will make me rich and powerful. And if you wish, you can be part of my dream. Considering your current position, this is a generous offer."

"What are you talking about?" The weakness of his own voice surprised Paul.

"We'll discuss it when you're feeling better. There is much to do."

Paul closed his eyes again.

Quinn paced slowly around the bed. "You'll do what I tell you, or I'll kill your Leza and every man in her village, take the young women to do with as I please, and burn everything to the ground."

Paul turned to him and opened his eyes. Quinn stood proudly with his hands on his hips, as if posing for a magazine cover.

"Good. I have your attention." Quinn laughed briefly, then his expression turned serious. "I know I can't threaten you with death, but you will do as I say, or that little girl will die."

"Why are you doing this? I saw hope in you, Quinn. With your wife you showed compassion."

Quinn walked to the door, stopping at the last moment to look back. "When it comes to Adanna, my heart has a tiny soft spot." He emphasized the word "tiny." "Don't mistake that for compassion."

The door slammed behind him. Paul took a shallow breath. It was the best he could do.

Jessica returned from a run in Central Park in time to shower and get ready for class at Columbia. She had always hoped to attend law school but had never expected to be accepted by such a fine institution. Her dad had encouraged her to apply, and now she was attending her first semester.

Her phone buzzed on her hip. "Hi, Uncle Jim. Everything okay?"

The pause on the line sent a chill through her body. When Jim finally spoke, his voice quavered, and Jessica's knees grew weak.

"I promised your dad I would call if anything went wrong," Jim stammered.

Jessica eased into a chair at the kitchen counter. She couldn't breathe. Her heart pounded harder and harder as she waited for Jim to collect himself and speak. She couldn't ask what was wrong. She couldn't move. Finally, through her sobs, she formed a question. "He's dead, isn't he?"

She heard her uncle struggling to compose himself. His voice cracked as he spoke. "I don't know, Jess. We . . . I don't know. But it's bad."

Paul woke in the dark. He needed a deep breath, but the burning in his lungs stopped him. A shallow breath, released slowly, offered a moment of relief.

The reality of where he was numbed his brain. It was too surreal to grasp no matter how hard he tried. But as Paul lay in bed contemplating his fate and all that had happened, the only thing that made sense was that Quinn was holding him for ransom. That must be his big plan to get rich—by holding him for a nice payoff. That would also mean they'd be contacting Jessica, and then the FBI would be involved. The thought of his daughter dealing with Quinn turned Paul's stomach.

His legs cramped, and when he moved, a sharp pain radiated from his shoulder to his back. He gasped. He had little doubt that the bullet wound in his chest was infected. Holding his head high enough to see the IV bag was a challenge. From the moonlight glowing through the window he was able to see the label on the fluid bag. It read "Vancomycin."

When Paul attempted another deep breath, the torn muscles in his chest gripped him like a giant hand pinning him to the bed. Searing pain shot into his neck. He held what air he had until the grip on him waned, and then he sighed. A hot sensation several centimeters below the bullet wound gained his attention.

Paul closed his eyes. "Not that, God. Please. Not a pneumothorax." If his lung were partly collapsed, he would die without treatment. But who could help him? He was a prisoner tied to a bed in the middle of . . . the jungle?

As Paul surveyed the bamboo walls and tin roof of his new confines, the sound of two sets of footsteps coming up the stairs gave him something new to worry about. He counted fourteen steps to the doorway and wondered if his room was on the second floor of a building. The door opened, and the light flipped on. A young girl accompanied by a soldier entered the room.

Paul raised his head just enough to look at the girl and then at the soldier. "Do you speak English?"

No response.

The young girl approached him and tore the dressings from his chest.

Paul winced but refused to cry out, then glanced at the wound. "It's infected." There was no indication the girl understood him, but the guard leaned closer.

"How do you know?"

"You speak English. Good. The green skin on the edges should be pink. Green is bad." The soldier listened. "The area around that is red and hard. You can tell by the way it—"

The soldier pushed firmly against the wound without warning.

"Stop!" Paul yelled.

"You do not give orders," the guard grunted.

"Then don't do that again unless you want pus dripping from your chin. And you'd better wash your hands if you ever want to eat again."

The guard looked at his fingers and spread them.

"That's infection right there, my friend. You wanna die? Be my guest. I'm a doctor. I can see the bacteria from here."

The guard grabbed the girl, pulled her aside, and told her in Dinka, before quickly leaving Paul's cell, that he needed to get Quinn. Paul looked at the girl, who appeared petrified. He smiled.

"I hope you actually speak English, because I would love to tell you something. I was just messing with his head."

The girl giggled and relaxed.

Paul nodded. "I thought so. Don't worry. You're not really in danger. Just wash your hands when you get a chance."

At that moment the guard returned with Quinn and Miju. As they came in, Quinn motioned to the young girl, and she left.

Quinn sauntered to the edge of the bed and placed his hand on Paul's forehead. "You have a fever, and this is infected." He reached down and almost pushed on Paul's wound like the guard had, but hesitated and withdrew his hand.

"Quinn, did Hanna remove the bullet while I was unconscious?"

"No, she tried, but the bleeding was heavy, and she couldn't find it."

Paul sighed. "Well, that's bad. Sometimes a bullet can be left in, but not this one. It's infected, probably because of the mud wall it went through before it reached me. Then it punctured my lung. Hanna probably couldn't find it because it traveled downward when it hit the sternum—the breastbone. I can feel where it is when I breathe."

"Tell me what you need," was Quinn's curt response.

"You're not listening. The bullet punched a hole in my lung and caused infection, and that will kill me. Hanna already tried to remove it and couldn't. You want me alive, right?"

"Yes, as I said before. Now tell me what you need."

"Quinn . . . this is going to require surgery. My guess is I'm the only surgeon around, so I'm going to need a hospital and another surgeon who can do this. I can't pull a bullet out of my own chest, let alone fix the hole in my lung, right?"

Quinn glanced at Miju, then back at Paul. "I have told you before, Doctor, no hospitals. You are in the middle of the Congo, a three-day drive or two hours by plane from any hospital." He leaned toward Paul. "You can do this, Dr. Branson. I will get you whatever you need to make you well, but there is no way to get you to a hospital."

Paul stared in disbelief. "Congo? How long?"

"Four days. You've been very ill. I thought you were going to die, but you're like a cat with many lives."

"I saved your wife. That's why I have a bullet in my chest. I remember that part."

Quinn gave Paul a crooked smile. "Thank you for saving my wife, but for all I know, you were planning to kill me with that gun you found. As for the rest, well . . . I will keep you alive because, as I told you, I have plans for you that you will understand in good time. For now, it is important to make you better so that you can cooperate, which you will do." Quinn turned to the soldier next to him. "Get a pen and paper to write down his instructions."

The man felt through his pockets but had no paper. He looked around the room—nothing. Miju handed Quinn a pen as the man launched a drastic search for paper.

"There's a small piece of paper in my pocket, but my hands are tied to this bed, so . . ."

Miju gave Paul a despising look.

"It's in my shirt pocket. The right one."

Miju pulled a bloodstained scrap of paper from Paul's shirt pocket and held it gingerly.

"Seriously? You just shot half the South Sudanese army and you're holding a bloody piece of paper like it's going to bite you?"

"You have infection," Miju snapped.

"Oh yeah. Good point. Better wash your hands."

Miju dropped the paper on the floor as if he were holding a snake.

Quinn angrily snatched the paper from the floor and thrust it into the soldier's hand. "Write!"

Paul sighed. "I'll need a sixty-cc syringe, a long needle for it—fourteen gauge—four centimeters long." The soldier wrote down the supplies as Paul named them. "More IV tubing, curved hemostats, and a scalpel. Lidocaine with a ten-cc syringe and a twenty-five-gauge needle would help numb this, and I would really appreciate that."

"Anything else?" Quinn made no attempt to conceal his impatience.

"More clindamycin or vancomycin—antibiotics to fight the infection. Like you're already doing." Paul glanced at the IV bag. "My feet and legs are swelling. That probably means my kidneys aren't working properly because the infection is taking over. We need to take this bullet out soon."

Quinn turned to the soldier. "Get those supplies. If we don't have them, gather them. Do it quickly."

The soldier and Miju left the room.

Quinn studied Paul, who could only stare back, wondering what evil plan lurked in the man's mind. Quinn strolled slowly to the door and turned to Paul.

"There are many ways to motivate men, Dr. Branson." He turned off the light and stepped out, pulling the door closed behind him.

"I don't know what to do for her," Orma sobbed. Chima sat in a chair facing Leza's mother. "She's strong now, but how much longer will her energy last? She'll become weak the longer we go without medicine." She shook her head.

"I think we should ask Jim to take Leza back with him to Entebbe for care, Orma."

"She can't go, Chief. She doesn't have a passport."

"Maybe we should have evacuated to Mundri like Abdu planned."

Orma sighed. "Once Dr. Paul was kidnapped and the danger was gone, no one wanted to leave, including me."

Chima glanced at Leza, who was sitting outside the hut on a rock Paul often used as a chair. She was watching the other kids kick a soccer ball Paul had brought with him, occasionally cheering and clapping her hands.

Chima turned back to Orma. "We must find him somehow. I have news from the captain of the guard in Lui. He told me their battalion took heavy fire from the Lord's Resistance Army near their camp by the mountains. Twenty-eight of the thirty soldiers who fought the LRA were killed. Paul may have been there, Orma. He may have been in their camp."

"Is he still alive?"

"The battle consumed the compound with heavy gunfire for fifteen minutes. If Paul hadn't left yet, he may have been killed. By the time the battalion returned with reinforcements the next day, the LRA had disappeared. They burned the village to the ground before they left."

"If he's dead, Leza will die too," Orma said quietly. "Dr. Paul said she only has eight to ten weeks to live if we don't get the chemo finished, and he's the only one who knows what to give her. Even if we could find another doctor for her, we can't afford it. The hospital in Juba said she's terminal and won't treat her anymore. She's strong enough right now, but she'll grow worse each day she's without treatment." Orma looked up at the sky. "Where are you, Dr. Paul?"

The morning sunlight pressed through the cracks in the bamboo walls, creating thin slices of glistening dust in the air. Paul raised his head to scan the room. The coppery taste of blood filled his mouth, and he spat a clot onto the floor. Breathing was difficult, like a weight on his chest, and a stabbing pain in his ribs accompanied every breath. He glanced at the blood-soaked bandages taped to his chest and shivered feverishly despite the intense heat of morning.

Exhausted from the attempt to see his wounds, Paul flopped his head onto the crumpled shirt he used as a pillow. He was weaker than the night before, and edema stretched the skin of his feet so much he thought they would burst.

The sound of a vehicle skidding to a halt in the loose gravel outside startled him. Moments later, he recognized the voices of Quinn and Miju. Their footsteps on the stairs gave him a tiny bit of hope that they might have brought help.

The bolt on the door clanked, and the door swung open to reveal Miju in the entrance.

"I don't feel well, Miju."

Miju walked to Paul's bed. "You have a bullet in your chest. Of course you don't."

Paul saw Quinn standing outside the door, talking to the guard. "Here are your supplies." Miju placed a bag on the bed.

"I'm going to need help. I can't pull this bullet out by myself."

"I know. Hanna's coming."

"Hanna? How is she going to help?"

"I'll come back with her." Miju slammed the door as he joined Quinn outside.

"This is too much," Paul mumbled to himself.

He waited for what seemed a long time for Miju to return, but finally he dozed off. The dead bolt interrupted his nap, and he looked up to see Miju enter, followed by Hanna carrying a dirty leather satchel, and the guard toting a stool. Hanna walked without smiling, keeping her eyes on the floor even though Paul stared at her, hoping to grab her attention. He just needed a friend. If not a friend, a smile would do. Just . . . something.

Wearing a long green dress and a red scarf on her head, Hanna took a seat on the stool the guard had placed beside Paul's bed. The guard left the room without a word.

"Hanna's here to help remove the bullet from your chest," Miju said. "She has done this many times for our men—even for me. She tried on you but failed for reasons you probably understand. You can help her. Tell her what to do."

"Hanna, are you a doctor?" Paul asked. He recalled how well she had performed during Adanna's surgery.

Hanna laughed. Then, just as quickly, her smile vanished, but a hint lingered in her eyes as she glanced at Paul. "No, I'm not a doctor, but I only had a semester left before I received my medical license. I studied at Makerere in Uganda for three and a half years. So I'm almost a doctor."

"Why didn't you finish?"

"Enough," Miju interrupted. "She is here to get the bullet out—not for you to chat with. Just tell her what she needs to know."

Hanna pulled the leather bag to her side and began digging through an assortment of surgical instruments. Methodically she laid them on the bed beside Paul.

"First, when you push in the hemostat," Paul said, "use that pair right there."

She pointed to one.

"No, the one on the left. It's longer and opens wider at the tip. When you push it into the wound, you'll have to find the bullet's path and follow it downward. That's why you couldn't reach it before. The bullet hit the bone, my sternum, and traveled down it."

Hanna nodded. "Okay."

"There's another problem, Hanna—it's not just the bullet that's stuck in my chest."

She stopped her sorting and looked at him. "What do you mean?" The softness of her voice took him off guard.

"I'm sure I have a partly collapsed lung. It will need to be reinflated once the bullet is removed."

Hanna glanced nervously at Miju.

"We talked about this, Hanna. He'll tell you what to do. He's a doctor—you're a doctor . . . almost. He knows."

Paul drew her attention back to him. "Since I have a collapsed lung, once you take out the bullet, air may leak in between the lung and the inside of the chest cavity where it doesn't belong. If that happens, you will take that needle . . . Miju, can you cut my right hand loose?" Paul raised his right hand as far as it could go with the bindings holding it to the bed frame. "There's nothing I can do anyway. I'm too weak, and my other hand and legs are tied. I'll die without this surgery, and she needs my help."

Miju grabbed the knife from his belt and sliced through the nylon tie.

With his hand free, Paul realized how stiff it had become, as if it weighed a hundred pounds. He reached across his chest and pulled off the new bandages they had applied only hours earlier. The macerated flesh burned like fire when exposed to the air. He forced himself not to wince.

"Hand me that," he said to Hanna as he pointed to the bag of supplies Miju had brought. He fumbled through it until he found the item he was looking for.

"Take the large syringe and put this fourteen-gauge needle on it." He handed it to her, and she secured it in place on the hub of the syringe. "If the air leaks in, I won't be able to breathe. You'll know. If that happens, push the needle into my chest, right here—all the way in." With his finger, Paul pushed between two of his ribs to show Hanna the exact location. "You'll have to do it quick. You won't have much time. Once it's in, draw back on the plunger to pull the air out. If you don't, the trapped air will compress my lung, and I won't be able to breathe." Her eyes grew wide. "Then I'll die."

Hanna shook her head and again glanced at Miju.

Miju reached out and briefly grabbed her arm. "You're going to do fine. I'll be here."

"You can do this, Hanna." Paul took her hand. It was warm and soft. He pushed her index finger into the spot where she needed to place the needle. "You will put it in right there, all the way in, as far as it will go. Then pull the plunger of the syringe out."

She stared at him as he held her hand in place.

"Hanna, if you don't do this . . ."

She swallowed. "Okay." She turned to Miju. "I have no anesthesia for him. They brought no lidocaine to numb him with." Her eyes filled with compassion. "Do we have any whiskey?"

Miju pulled a silver flask from his hip pocket and removed the cap. "This is all I have." He lifted Paul's head and then paused. "If you hadn't done this for Adanna, I wouldn't do it for you." He held the flask to Paul's lips and poured the contents in his mouth. Paul gagged but swallowed. Miju grinned. "Not a whiskey man, huh?" He poured more, and Paul held his breath while he drank. He coughed and sputtered, but managed to get it down. "That's all I have."

Paul nodded through a final cough. "Thank you."

Hanna handed Miju a cloth twisted into knots. Paul recognized the biting rag from Adanna's surgery. He took a deep breath and let it out slowly.

Hanna touched Paul's face as she softly said, "It's time. I'm sorry." She turned to Miju. "Hold him." She picked up the large pair of hemostats and took a deep breath. After a brief hesitation, she pushed them into the bullet wound and downward as Paul had instructed.

The cold steel pierced the wall of his chest, and even though he knew it was coming, Paul bit down on the rag as hard as he could. He wanted to scream, but he refused. Miju pinned Paul's shoulders to the bed as he arched his back involuntarily. The hemostat scraped against the bullet lodged in the bone, and Hanna spread the tip of the instrument to enlarge the opening. Intense nausea swept over Paul, and he broke into a cold sweat.

When Hanna found the edge of the bullet, the hemostat inadvertently clamped on the bone ridge, and Paul groaned. He couldn't help it.

Hanna stopped. "Let him breathe, Miju." She wiped the sweat from her brow with her free hand. "I need him conscious so he can help me when the bullet comes out."

Miju pulled the rag from his mouth, and Paul gasped for air. "Oh God!"

"Try to focus on something else. We must do this. Are you ready?" Hanna didn't wait for Paul's answer. "Take a deep breath."

Paul did as he was told.

"Let it out and take another," she insisted.

Paul inhaled as deeply as possible, the pain in his chest limiting him. He took in all the air he could before Miju stuffed the rag back in his mouth.

Hanna pushed the hemostat deeper into the wound. The searing pain in Paul's chest pierced his neck and back. She clamped the instrument onto the bullet and pulled, but it was so embedded in the muscle and rib that it wouldn't budge. Paul grabbed the side of the bed and clenched the mattress with his fists. He bit hard into the rag and panted.

Every important moment in Paul's life flashed through his mind: Nicki saying "I do," the moment his daughter, Jessica, came into the world, the morning he realized he was supposed to go to Africa, and the last five minutes before Nicki died.

Paul tried to control himself, but his muffled screams echoed off the bamboo walls. "God!" he groaned through the rag, but his plea sounded as if it came from someone else.

Hanna pulled harder, and the bullet shifted but remained lodged. Paul's nausea came in tsunami-like waves, and his vision narrowed as if looking through a tunnel. He gazed into Hanna's eyes.

Do this. Don't let me die, Hanna.

Miju stood to hold Paul's broad shoulders down. Paul watched as Hanna grasped the hemostat in one hand and a scalpel in the other.

"I have to cut the bullet loose."

With his eyes closed and his teeth clamped on the cloth, Paul nodded. When the scalpel cut through the ligament that held the bullet against his rib, his head spun and his vision vanished. As if she were somewhere in the distance, he heard her say, "I think I have it. Just a little more."

Strangely, he no longer felt pain, but his ears rang, and he couldn't move his arms or legs. As his mind drifted, he struggled to focus. *You can't pass out now. You have to breathe. Your brain needs oxygen.*

"We're going to lose him, Miju. His lips are blue!"

Paul could barely hear Hanna. He couldn't tell if he was breathing, but his heart beat rapidly and his head throbbed. An odd sensation came over him, as if something warm poured over his chest and spread to his abdomen. He was losing this fight.

Faintly, he felt something strange. Soft, warm lips touched his and blew air into his lungs. He felt it. There—again—another breath. It burned, but the oxygen helped. One more time her soft lips closed on his, and sweet air entered his lungs. He heard noises, then the pain in his chest returned. Her lips left his, and she was back at his side.

"I have it!" Paul heard Hanna exclaim when she broke the huge metal fragment free. Suddenly he was awake—and suffocating.

"Can't . . . breathe." He gasped and pointed to the large syringe beside Hanna and pressed his skin with his finger to show her again where to place it. His strength was gone. "Do it—"

Paul's mind shut down, and the ringing in his ears returned. It was up to Hanna now. He couldn't help anymore. The warmth of her delicate hands on his chest comforted him as her fingers tenderly felt for the spot to insert the needle. *That's it . . . right there . . . right there . . .*

He turned his head toward her and watched as she fumbled nervously with the syringe. He couldn't help it. He barely felt the sting against his skin as she pushed the long needle between his ribs, deeper and deeper. The moment the tip reached the air pocket, the pressure trapped between his lung and chest wall pushed the plunger partway out, filling half of the huge syringe with a fine, blood-tinged mist.

Paul felt immediate relief and tried exhaling to push the air out of his chest, but the pressure still sat on top of him.

"Plunger . . . pull," Paul mumbled. Hanna pulled the plunger out, and as the lung reinflated, he felt the sweet oxygen pouring in. "Hold it there. Don't move." Breathing slowly and deeply, he felt as if he'd been deep underwater and finally reached the surface.

After several minutes, Paul heard Hanna's voice again. "His lips are pink." She laughed nervously as she removed the syringe and sealed the opening with her finger. "Press here, Miju, until I can close it."

Paul felt Miju's big, rough hands replace Hanna's soft, tiny fingers as she sutured the bullet wound and needle puncture. Every stitch sent a painful signal to his brain, but it was nothing compared to what he had just been through.

"Hanna," Paul said weakly.

She stopped suturing and looked at him. "Yes?"

"Did you . . . were your lips on mine?" He turned his head to her.

She blushed noticeably. "Yes. You taught me when Adanna was dying, and I had to. You were dying, and . . ."

"Thank you."

She smiled and began suturing again. "You're welcome."

Exhausted, Paul closed his eyes as he heard her packing her surgical instruments into her bag.

"I think he passed out again," Hanna whispered.

"He'll be okay. He's been through a lot."

"Miju . . . who is this man?"

Paul felt Miju tying his right hand back to the bed frame.

"You don't want to know."

"Please?"

"Quinn says he's the key to our future, that's all I can say."

"I think he's more."

"What do you mean?"

"I don't know. I just . . . I don't know."

"Regardless, Hanna—you should be proud of yourself. You did a great job. This was your toughest case ever. You can say what you want, but you're already a doctor in my mind. You saved his life, and I'll make sure Quinn knows. He'll be very pleased."

"Thank you, Miju."

"I'll meet you outside. I need to tell Quinn it's done and that our man is alive."

Miju closed the door behind him as he left, and even though Paul's chest burned, his legs cramped, and the pounding in his head wouldn't stop, he felt soft, tender lips kiss his cheek as he drifted off.

CHAPTER NINE

Usually Orma slept well despite the thick, humid air, but tonight every noise made her restless. A barking dog interrupted the quiet—then another, and a third. When they finally fell silent, she dozed off.

"Mama!"

Orma jolted awake. "Leza?"

Orma lifted the edge of her mosquito net and swung her feet to the floor. "Leza?" she whispered. No answer. She slowly made her way in the dark to the doorway separating her room from Leza's. A tall, shadowy figure stood in the middle of the hut.

Orma froze, unable to move, unable to breathe.

"Mama . . ." Leza faintly whispered through a sob.

As Orma turned toward her daughter's voice, a blow to the head drove her to the floor. Her mind spun and her heart sank when she felt the cold steel of a knife blade against her throat.

"Silence." The coarse, deep voice sounded like Satan himself.

"Mama . . . help me." Leza's voice trembled.

Please, Orma said silently, *let this be quick.* She never felt what happened next.

The moon cast a warm glow on the trees across the courtyard from Paul's window. If he pushed up on his elbows, he could see the highest branches.

After the bullet removal and five days of antibiotics, his strength was finally returning. He twisted his neck from side to side to work out the stiffness. Lying in the same position for so long made his joints hurt and his back ache. Still, with the fever gone and his lungs filled with air, he felt like he could handle anything.

He gazed at the trees swaying in the warm, gentle breeze. The brilliant canopy of stars cast a faint glow on the lilting branches and illuminated the dark sky. The distant sound of an engine interrupted the peaceful night. But it wasn't a truck engine. It sounded more like . . . an airplane?

Paul struggled to raise himself higher without cutting his wrists on the ties and peered through the window. As the sound drew closer, floodlights pierced the trees from the opposite direction.

Landing lights? A runway?

Moments later the beacon of an airplane appeared in the distance, but as it approached the landing site, dense jungle overgrowth obscured it from view. Before long, Paul heard the engine slow as if for landing, then taxiing, and then it stopped. The runway lights went out, and a quiet darkness infused the room once more.

Paul lay back but couldn't sleep. Instead, he stared at the ceiling as the pain from his healing lung reminded him of a time in his past he'd tried to forget. Being in the wrong place at the wrong time had made him an easy target during junior high. The bullies had found what they wanted in him—an easy target with a few dollars in his pocket. Paul had spent three weeks in the hospital with broken ribs and a punctured lung. His body had healed, but the invisible scars had changed him.

After that he'd lived in constant fear—fear that the next time his attackers would kill him. To overcome his vulnerability, he'd sought training from a martial arts expert. Over time, the paralyzing fear that had controlled him turned into confidence and arrogance, and he had soon secured the title of "tough guy" by fighting anyone, anywhere. He'd liked his new tag. No one would hurt him that badly ever again. Heading down the wrong path full steam, he hadn't counted on Nicki. If it hadn't been for her . . .

Paul's mental wheels slowed down and finally stopped turning as exhaustion took over, and he drifted off to sleep.

Jessica folded her legs under her as she sat anxiously on the sofa watching CNN. A now-tepid cup of coffee remained untouched on the table beside her. News coverage portrayed her father's situation as a tragic turn of events in a politically troubled area of Sudan. According to the report, escalating tensions had resulted in the senseless kidnapping of a wealthy American physician for ransom. But Jessica knew no ransom demands had been made and that the LRA had never before abducted an international figure for money. A typical case of media incompetence—or perhaps a government cover-up?

The banner across the bottom of the screen read: "Authorities are hopeful for a peaceful resolution of the escalating situation." But Jessica knew there had been no contact, and no one knew the whereabouts of her father, Dr. Paul Branson.

Jessica turned to Special Agent David Kensing. "I'm going to take a shower." Surrounded by laptops and the portable command center the FBI had established in Jessica's living room, Kensing nodded. He had been with the government for twelve years, the last three with the Department of Homeland Security, and he now coordinated with the FBI to investigate international ransoms and kidnappings involving government interests. He'd given Jessica a rundown of his experience when he first set up shop. She guessed the information was intended to give her hope.

"Yes, ma'am. If anyone calls, Andrea will come and get you. But remember, we'll be leaving for the safe house as soon as it's been cleared."

Agent Andrea Cummings smiled from her position at the dinette table as she looked up from her briefing folders. "Please leave your bedroom door unlocked, Ms. Branson, so I can get in if I need you. If anyone calls, you've got to be the one to answer the phone."

Jessica understood, but she didn't have much hope that anyone would call—not after so many days. She glanced at the TV screen one more time before heading down the hallway.

"Dr. Paul Branson, prominent New York City physician and research pioneer in preventing chemical warfare, is still missing," the announcer was saying. "Dr. Branson's studies were designed to determine weaknesses in chemical substances believed to be a potential threat to national security and develop new antidotes to save countless lives."

Jessica shook her head. "This is wrong. He wasn't a research pioneer—he was just a doctor. His patients love him." She looked at Agent Cummings. "And why is a safe house necessary? Why would I ever be in danger?" She turned back to the TV.

The photo of her father on the screen showed him standing with his arm around fellow researcher Charles Manning. Manning, the announcer said, was being sought for questioning but his whereabouts were unknown.

Jessica looked at Agent Kensing. "Unknown? Wait—I know that man. I've met him. I think Dad introduced me to him once a long time ago. But what does any of this have to do with chemical warfare?"

"Manning was . . . Manning is a person of interest to the US government. Unfortunately, he's missing."

"What do you mean 'missing'? Missing as in dead?"

Kensing stood. "No, just missing. It will make sense in time, Ms. Branson. For now, please trust us, and remember—keep your cell phone turned off."

The clank of the dead bolt jarred Paul. After nearly a week, he still wasn't used to its interruptions. Outside, the sun shone brightly, and the birds squawked in the acacia trees. Miju entered.

"Get up. Quinn wants to talk."

Paul lifted his wrists as far as he could. Miju cut the ties on his ankles with the knife he pulled from his belt, then moved to free him of his wrist restraints.

"Let's go. Quinn's not a patient man." Miju pulled Paul to a sitting position. Swinging his stiff legs over the edge of the bed and slowly standing, Paul's left hand instinctively clasped his ribs to ease the pain. He paused, short of breath. Lying flat for days except when they let him use the bucket beside his bed as a toilet had made his muscles shaky and weak. The stench from the bucket nauseated him, but the guard only emptied it once a day.

"Give me a second, Miju." Paul's feet tingled from the blood rushing into them, and the room spun. He lowered his head to give his circulation a chance to catch up with his brain. He imagined he was still several units shy of a full blood supply.

"We need to go."

"I'm coming." Paul's feet were swollen and his knees weak, but he managed to walk hunched over at first. The pain in his chest caused him to take shallow breaths, but he pushed on. Miju waited impatiently by the door.

"Do you need me to drag you?"

"I'm stiff, but I'm coming." Paul took small steps, but every movement stabbed his chest and burned his legs.

When he walked onto the porch, the sun on his face and the wind in his hair were exhilarating. It was his first breath of fresh air since he'd arrived. He squinted, allowing his eyes to adjust. Glancing around the compound, he noticed many huts similar to his scattered among the trees. He counted ten from where he stood. From the distant sound of barking dogs, he assumed there might be more dwellings beyond the dense overgrowth. The huts were built on platforms supported by posts that ranged from two to three meters in height.

"Miju, why are the huts on stilts?"

Miju looked back at Paul as if trying to decide whether to answer, but he did. "Keeps the water out in the rainy season and the snakes out in the dry season. Let's go."

"I'm working on it."

As Paul moved toward the stairs, he scanned the huts closely. The walls, constructed of sturdy bamboo poles, gained their strength from tightly woven vines binding them together. Tin roofs covered most of them, but some still bore the traditional thatched grass.

Soldiers in fatigues carrying automatic weapons stood guard around the periphery of the compound, which was about half the size of a football field. Paul counted seven guards. Three of them appeared to be younger than teenagers.

Voices drifting from above drew his attention to a makeshift building resembling a toolshed located high in the trees overlooking the compound. Secured at the corners to four sturdy branches, the design gave the guards a 360-degree view but left a blind spot immediately below. Camouflage made the shed difficult to spot from the ground.

The dense brush and taller trees helped distinguish the Congo from Sudan. A strong breeze provided relief from the thick, humid air. And the lush green vegetation indicated it rained more here too. This compound made the settlement where Quinn had originally brought Paul seem tiny in comparison. It not only boasted more buildings but also consisted of permanent, sturdier structures.

"Don't get any ideas." Miju started down the stairs.

The armed guard outside Paul's door looked at him sternly, rifle pointed at his chest. Paul's first step down the stairs made his legs wobble and buckled his knees. He grabbed the wood railing with both hands.

"Let's go." By the look on Miju's face, Paul thought he might reach up and pull him down the stairs. He gathered his strength and forced his feet to take one step at a time. The moment he reached the bottom, Cijen appeared.

"Cij—good to see you." Paul grinned.

Cijen didn't smile back. "I'm your guard. Don't attempt to escape."

Paul wiped the smile from his face and nodded. "Understood." Still, he winked at Cijen when no one was looking.

Maneuvering over the rough terrain posed a challenge for Paul's weak legs, but he quickened his pace to keep up with Miju.

After walking a hundred meters, they reached a clearing surrounded by larger multiroom buildings. These structures were built at ground level in contrast to the smaller huts on their elevated platforms. Wood plank walls rather than woven bamboo made the buildings look more secure but hotter. Although the windows were open, they were fitted with steel shutters that could be bolted shut.

They passed the first building, and as Miju walked up the two steps of the second one, something about the warehouse behind it caught Paul's eye. He leaned to the side to get a better look. The structure of interest stood beyond the tree line.

"What are you doing?" Miju's voice snatched Paul back to reality.

"Just looking around. I've been indoors for a long time."

"Never mind that. Stay close and don't wander off—even in your head. Got that?"

"Got it."

"Keep an eye on him, Cij." Miju opened the door and went inside, leaving Paul and Cijen on the steps.

Paul moved to the side and quickly snuck another peek. He could make out a building with three guards. All of the shutters were closed in the middle of the day. Strange. That would prevent circulation. It must be like an oven in there.

Paul felt something poke his back and turned to see Cijen shaking his head as he held the rifle barrel to Paul's spine.

"Just looking, Cij."

Miju stepped out and motioned for Paul to come in. "Let's go."

Paul reached for the wall to support himself and stepped inside. A blast of hot air struck him the moment he walked through the door. The dark interior caused him to stumble against a chair. He grabbed it and eased himself into it.

"This is your new clinic, Doctor." As Paul's eyes adjusted to the dark, he recognized Quinn's huge figure across the room.

"Clinic?"

"Yes. Your new home." Quinn held his arms up as if presenting it as a gift. "We have many sick men in this compound."

Paul's stomach twisted into a knot. This must be a joke. Had Quinn kept him alive to care for his sick men? All this time he'd expected a ransom demand. But if there was no ransom, he would never go free.

"I see you're speechless. Good. I prefer speechless." Quinn stepped to the window, pushed the shutter open, and clasped his hands behind his back as he stared outside. "I'm a businessman, an adventurer, an entrepreneur, and a man of mystery." He turned and sauntered toward Paul. "So are you, Doctor."

Paul didn't speak.

"At this very moment, CNN is broadcasting something I already knew. They have discovered the research on chemical warfare you performed during your graduate years. It has become a matter of interest to the world."

The hair on Paul's neck bristled and his mind raced.

Quinn began to pace. "They know you received a government grant but never completed the work."

"What are you talking about?"

"I'm talking about the research you performed for the United States government on chemical warfare with Dr. Charles Manning."

Paul stiffened. "How do you know Manning?"

"Charles Manning, your trusted research colleague, was my first choice, and I was very hopeful since he was so . . . malleable. He wanted to be a part of this so badly, but he couldn't figure out what you did when you performed the same research."

"I was a chemist. And that research was a dead end—"

"And they shut down the project," Quinn interrupted.

"They didn't shut it down. They took our funding. We failed—they cut us off. End of story."

"Hardly. They confiscated and sealed your research papers because you failed? Is that what you would have me believe?" Quinn continued to pace as he spoke, appearing to carefully select his words. "Dr. Manning was afforded every opportunity to figure out the chemical formula I need—the formula I must have. He was highly motivated by money, and if he'd been able to deliver, you wouldn't even be here." Quinn paused briefly to look out the window as if he'd seen something of interest. Then he continued, "In our conversations, he spoke of you on numerous occasions. He warned me that you're a man of integrity, that you'd never compromise your principles, that you would never cooperate with me, and most importantly—that you have a photographic memory."

Paul gripped the edges of his chair.

"You were onto something, Branson. You made a discovery of epic proportions, and they needed it secured—permanently."

The bile rose in Paul's throat. "That's ridiculous. There hasn't been a word spoken about it since then."

"That isn't true. Is it, Doctor? They asked you to review your findings a year ago, did they not?"

Paul was stunned and speechless. How could Quinn know this? Manning, of course. That fool. Paul slid to the edge of the chair.

"We both know why nothing has been said about the research, don't we, Doctor?"

"I don't know what you mean."

Quinn pounded one fist into his other hand. "Yes, you do! They took your research from you and sealed it. Why would they do that if you'd failed? You were experimenting with chemicals, and I need those formulas. Manning couldn't reproduce them from his memory, and the records are no longer available."

"That's true. They're locked away in a government warehouse somewhere. I don't even know where."

Quinn faced Paul with a devilish grin. "They're locked away in a warehouse—and in your brain."

Paul's heart skipped a beat. He had a strange feeling in his chest and instinctively pushed his hand against his wound.

"You, dear Dr. Branson, were experimenting with how to neutralize chemical agents dispersed in an aerosol form. You're correct that those experiments failed, but according to Manning, your research uncovered a secret about the chemicals you were investigating. You learned something important, something deadly, and that's why they sealed everything and made you swear not to talk to anyone. You signed a document of secrecy. Now do you remember?"

Paul looked around the room for something he could use as a weapon. He was in deeper than he'd ever imagined. It all made sense now. Manning had always been looking for an angle.

"Where is Manning? I want to talk to him. Is he working with you? Is he here?"

Quinn slowly shook his head. "Dr. Manning is no longer . . . how should I put this—participating in our plan."

"You killed him?"

"What does it matter? You're missing the point," Quinn scolded. "You signed documents in which you swore you would never divulge your work, your findings, the products you were using, or your government clearance, didn't you?"

"If I had done that, I wouldn't be able to tell you—"

"Yes or no!" Quinn's face distorted with anger.

"Yes." Paul spoke in barely a whisper.

"Good. The truth. You'll tell me what I need to know, Dr. Branson." Quinn spoke with the confidence of a man who held all the cards.

Paul turned to him. "It was a graduate research project requiring that level of confidentiality. There was no top secret work going on. I'm not a spy."

"You had government clearance, did you not?"

"For advanced chemical handling, I had to. The government needed to know I had no terrorist ties."

"What level?"

"What do you mean?"

"Of clearance. What level?"

Paul hesitated, but he knew Quinn already knew. "Top secret."

Quinn nodded and looked at Miju then back at Paul. "I need to know what you know."

"I don't know anything. This is a mistake. There is nothing from that research that would benefit you. We were researching airborne chemical warfare with forbidden substances that are impossible to obtain, and it was shut down. How on earth could you ever have imagined otherwise?"

Quinn walked to the window and stared into the courtyard. He sighed.

Paul decided to break the silence. "Quinn, is that the reason you brought me here?"

Quinn turned to face Paul but remained by the window. "Yes. My wife's unexpected appendicitis caused us to move up the clock. We had hoped to obtain this information from Manning, but his attempts were failures—horrible failures. Then he told me, quite accidentally, about your photographic memory—your ability to recall every detail of your research. When we discovered that you were coming to Africa, we couldn't risk you refusing to be involved, so we brought you here."

Paul shook his head. "And what made you think I'd cooperate with terrorists?"

Quinn looked at the floor with his hands still clasped behind his back. "Do you feel pain, Doctor?"

"What do you mean?"

"Right now, are you in pain?"

"A little. Why?" Paul's body tensed.

Quinn turned from the window, strutted to Paul, and then twisted his fist into the wound in his chest. "How about now?"

Paul crumpled to the floor, grinding his teeth to keep from crying out.

"You will do as I say. I don't tolerate arrogance." Quinn leaned down, wrapped his huge fingers around Paul's neck, and lifted him to his feet.

The little air Paul had in his lungs vanished. He gasped for more, but it wouldn't come. Suspended by Quinn's massive arms, his ribs felt like they were being pulled from his body. Then the fighter in him escaped. He used a right jab and struck Quinn's throat. Quinn dropped him and bent over, gasping for air. As Paul scrambled to his feet, Miju swung his fist into Paul's abdomen, pushing the air from his lungs and the food from his stomach onto Quinn's shirt.

Paul grabbed the chair and pulled himself to his knees to catch his breath. Miju hovered like a vulture while Quinn cursed and tried to wipe the vomit from his chest.

"Stand up," Quinn demanded.

Paul managed to stand.

"You're going to kill him!" Cijen yelled.

Miju responded, "Shut up, Cij. Stay out of this."

Miju stepped in and swung hard at Paul's chest, but Paul blocked him with his arm, throwing Miju off balance. Before Miju could turn back for another attempt, Paul planted his right foot into Miju's right knee. The cartilage exploded when it dislocated, and Miju dropped to the floor. Paul didn't hesitate to drive his heel squarely into Miju's jaw, forcing him against the wall.

Paul dropped to his knees. He had nothing left. Quinn grabbed Paul's shirt, pulled him to his feet, and dropped him back in the chair. He walked to the window again while Miju glared at Paul, holding his knee with one hand and his jaw with the other.

Quinn stood at the window. His muscles bulged across his back and shoulders, and his arms rippled with strength. "You surprised me. You can fight. I am not often surprised by anything."

Paul didn't respond. He was too busy pressing his hands against his chest and breathing.

"I know what you're thinking." Quinn slowly circled Paul's chair. "You're thinking my threats are empty. You know I don't want you dead. It's to my disadvantage that you know this."

Quinn stepped to Paul's side and loomed over him. "I've told you before that I know you don't fear death. But I do know the way to make you cooperate—the way to your heart."

Quinn grabbed another chair and straddled it backward to face Paul. "You're a man of integrity, as Manning said. You risked your life to save my wife—of course you are." Quinn paused, obviously for effect.

"I understand men, Dr. Branson—all men. I know what makes them happy, what makes them angry. I understand what they need to survive, what they need to kill, and what they fear more than anything in the world." Quinn leaned closer to him.

"For some, it's easy. The fear of death is all that matters. For others, like you, it matters very little, knowing that you believe you will see your dead wife when you die."

Paul stopped breathing for a moment.

Quinn scooted the chair closer to him. "But that's where I stand above all others. That's my specialty. I understand what it takes to make men do what I want them to do." Quinn stood, walked behind Paul with eerie calmness, and placed his hands on Paul's shoulders.

"I know how to motivate you even though you don't care about death or pain."

The rancid statement hung in the air like decaying meat.

"I have a secret," Quinn whispered as if he could barely contain himself. "I know you love Leza."

Paul closed his eyes.

"You love her as your own daughter."

The sweat trickled down Paul's back.

"And what is your daughter's name? Oh yes—Jessica."

Paul tried to stand, but Quinn shoved him down. He squirmed, but Quinn didn't yield.

"You see, you'll tell me what I need to know about those experiments, or I'll bring Leza here and kill her in front of you." Quinn chuckled like a demon. "Just the thought of it pleases me. And then there's Jessica."

"Quinn. Don't." Paul coughed, and blood filled his mouth. He spat on the floor. "This is between me and you. Leave them out of it."

"A moment ago you fought me. You injured Miju. Now you want to make a deal? How am I to trust you?" Quinn bent to his ear. "You will never doubt me again, Paul Branson."

"Baba?"

Paul's head spun toward the tiny voice in the doorway, and he struggled to focus. Leza stood in a torn, dirty dress with a rope around her neck like an animal on a leash. The guard held her by her shoulders as tears streamed down her sweet, precious face.

"I have your dog. I own you."

Chief Chima sat at the end of a room not much larger than one of the village's mud huts. It was used as a gathering place for town meetings. Humid air, thick with smoke, drifted in from nearby campfires. Chima knew the men were accustomed to worse. The tin roof, metal door, and battery-operated lantern suspended from the ceiling were the only signs of modern civilization.

Chima's anxious demeanor was out of character. He didn't like calling meetings, especially when he didn't have good news.

Chiefs from four other villages were in attendance, along with a representative from the Sudan People's Liberation Army. Each man paused in the doorway and nodded in respect to Chima before taking a seat in the circle of chairs.

Commander Toru of the South Sudanese Special Regiment Detail, the SRD, entered last. Tall and distinguished, he was dressed in full military uniform. It was no secret the commander was obsessed with accomplishing his mission: finding Joseph Kony and Jason Quinn. He took a seat next to Chima.

Chima stood and spoke in Moru. "Thank you, my friends, for being here tonight. We have unpleasant business to discuss and decisions to make. Our people are in danger." He glanced around the circle. "All of you know me, and you chiefs know each other. But not everyone here knows Commander Toru. He is our guest."

Each man nodded once at Toru.

Chima continued, "As everyone knows, Dr. Paul Branson, our mission doctor and friend, kidnapped from my village, has yet to be found. Two days ago, a very sick little girl named Leza was also taken. The kidnappers murdered her mother in typical LRA fashion." He paused for a moment. "The man responsible we know as Jason Quinn, who has brought terror to our villages, murdered our wives, and raped our daughters."

The men appeared deeply moved. Several of them looked at each other, while others covered their eyes—a symbolic gesture of respect for the dead.

Chima paused to regain control of his emotions, remembering Quinn's men carrying away their screaming children. "Commander Toru of the South Sudanese Army has worked for ten months with the United States to capture Joseph Kony and put an end to the LRA. I have asked you to come because the commander's men have uncovered something that affects us all. I will let him explain."

Toru stood. Chima sat. "Thank you for being here, men." Toru's deep voice and position commanded their respect. "You are the leaders of South Sudan. Your people admire you because you care for them. They follow because you lead." Toru looked around the room. He had everyone's attention. "I want you men to know that I attempted to invite leaders of North Sudan to this meeting. I received no response to my request. This was expected since they are believed to have formed an alliance with Quinn."

No one seemed surprised.

"This murderer, thief, rapist, terrorist, slave trader, drug lord, and, above all, madman will stop at nothing to get what he wants. Even Joseph Kony, the only man he respects, is no more horrible.

"In the past six months, Quinn purchased potentially dangerous chemicals from six locations around the world. They were not controlled substances, and no one put it all together until our team compiled the lists and cross-matched the items with missing and stolen products internationally."

Toru pulled a map from his briefcase and spread it on the floor in front of the men. He pointed to specific areas on the map as he spoke.

"Five months ago, a freighter from Iran sank here in the Persian Gulf following an explosion on board. Among other things, the vessel carried sensitive but undisclosed chemicals destined for Saudi Arabia. The ship, tracked and escorted by the United States for that reason, sank without warning or an SOS call. Intel tagged the cargo as a potential threat to US and global security, depending on the final destination and buyer. For that reason, United States Army Special Forces were to accompany the shipment to its final destination." Toru paused. "We are not certain exactly what these substances were, but chemical weaponry is of primary US concern. None of the Special Forces troops were recovered from the wreckage."

Chima glanced around the room. The men appeared confused. "Commander Toru, tell them what you have found."

Toru nodded. "At the time the ship went down, Jason Quinn had business in Qatar." Toru tapped the location on the map with his finger. "We tracked him there in an attempt to close in on him. The first and only time he has been in Qatar is when that ship went down. Two days later, we approached his suspected location, but he had disappeared. By the time we discovered that the ship had sunk and began to fit the pieces together, it was too late."

After a brief silence, Chief Majo from the village of Wiroh was the first to speak. "What does that have to do with our villages? Why are we in danger?"

Toru drew a circle on the map. "Qatar is here. When Quinn surfaced again, he had rented a plane in Djibouti over here. He loaded six fifty-five-gallon drums onto a twelve-seater airplane with only two men on board. He filed a flight plan to Dubai, but the plane disappeared from radar thirty minutes after takeoff. He must have known we would be waiting for him in Dubai."

The men looked at each other. Several still appeared confused.

"We fear he is planning a strike on African soil, probably South Sudan. He has been buying thousands of acres of land surrounding your villages and has negotiated with North Sudan to sell them rights to the oil, circumventing the peace treaty and separation between the North and South. The question is why would he do that?"

Toru looked around the room. "Gentlemen, it is not yet public knowledge, but recent studies have indicated that there may in fact be significant oil deposits farther south in Sudan than originally believed, including the regions where your villages are located. If Quinn owns this land, he can drill oil wells wherever he wants and sell to the highest bidder. His power will be unopposed.

"But he can only accomplish his goal if South Sudan is not able to stand in his way. The North is rich with oil. The South needs to harvest it just to survive. If Quinn gains control over the oil, without a single gunshot, the North and South will be one again, and many in South Sudan . . . will be dead. There will be no declared war. There will be no reason for outside governments to send in troops or intervene." Toru paused as the chiefs looked at each other. "Quinn will have the power and the wealth. Tyranny will reign."

Chima spoke. "How do you know so much about Quinn but not where he is?"

"We don't know for certain where and when he is planning to attack, nor do we know how. But we must be prepared for him regardless. With a little luck, we can stop him."

Chima stood and looked around the room at his fellow leaders. "Gentlemen, we have already been warned by the Ghost of Africa. I did not understand at the time. He spoke to Abdu, then Abdu was taken. This was a sign to us. We must prepare. The Ghost of Africa will return."

Toru walked to the center of the room and gathered his map from the floor. "Gentlemen, there is something you should know. Abdu . . . is very much alive."

CHAPTER TEN

Men surrounded Paul's cot in the dark room and removed his bindings.

"What's going on?"

One of the guards shined a flashlight in Paul's eyes, but no one answered.

"Someone tell me what's happening."

Paul's legs wobbled when they pulled him from the bed. With a man on each side holding his arms, he stumbled out the door and down the stairs. He almost fell, but they held him, pushed him into the back of a jeep, and tied his arms and legs to the seat frame. Paul was beginning to get used to this.

He scanned the darkness but could see only the jeep parked next to his. If he could spot some clue that would help him understand his hostile awakening . . .

Someone whisked a hood over his head and cinched it at his neck.

"Relax, Doctor. This is not the day you die—unless you give me reason." Just hearing Quinn's voice aggravated Paul. "We're going for a ride. There is something you need to see."

◆ ◆ ◆

Paul's head bobbed up and down, back and forth in a futile attempt to sleep—exhaustion plagued him and he dreamed of a soft bed and fluffy pillow.

"Wake up!" Someone slapped Paul on the back of his head. "You have slept enough." It wasn't Quinn's voice this time. It was Miju's.

The drive along the roughly hewn path pounded the jeep for what seemed an eternity. Paul's head throbbed, but concentrating on breathing kept the nausea at bay.

"Miju."

"What?"

"For what it's worth, I'm sorry about your leg."

"It's worth nothing. We're not finished."

Paul rode in silence for another half hour. "Hey, Miju."

"What do you want?"

"When I said 'I'm sorry about your leg,' I didn't mean the one I smashed with my foot."

"What?"

"I mean I'm sorry I left you with a good one."

"Who do you think—?" Miju's response was cut short.

"Silence. We are entering the village. No more talking," Quinn demanded.

Paul began to hear loud voices on the trail beside the jeep. He was used to the villagers running to meet him wherever he went, but it sounded as if these people were screaming and running away.

The jeeps skidded to a halt.

Miju untied the hood, snatched it off Paul's head, and gave him a menacing glare, but Paul turned the other way as if he didn't notice.

The hot, humid air had never felt as good as it did the moment the hood was removed. Paul inhaled deeply, then gagged. The stench of decaying flesh filled his lungs. He recognized the smell from his time in New Orleans when he had worked as a relief surgeon during the floods of Hurricane Katrina. It was the only other time he had smelled the scent of death so powerfully.

The village consisted of a clearing surrounded by twenty mud huts of varying sizes, but Paul could see many more humble buildings behind the dense overgrowth.

Quinn explained, "This is Botan. The people here are very ill. Many have died. Their sickness is different than anything I have ever seen."

Paul slipped from the vehicle and walked a short distance behind Quinn and Miju. An armed guard followed close on his heels but slung his rifle across his shoulder instead of pointing it at him.

"I don't know what's wrong with these people, so I brought you here. It's spreading from one village to another, but this is the worst."

They entered one of the larger huts, which was filled with men, women, and children. These villagers lay in different stages of illness, from looking as though they felt poorly to appearing close to death. Paul walked among them, speaking English that Miju translated to Dinka or Arabic. Keeping Quinn in the dark about his ability to speak their language gave Paul an advantage. Examining the villagers, Paul noted that some had pupil constriction and diarrhea but others displayed dilated pupils and were unresponsive. Most suffered from confusion, headaches, rapid breathing, and severe cough.

The most advanced cases vomited and complained of blurred vision before seizures set in. Paul questioned those who were still able to speak and learned that the disease often progressed within less than a day to a sudden, agonizing death.

After an hour of interviews and inconclusive examinations, Paul turned to Quinn. "I don't know what's wrong with these people."

"What do you see?"

"The symptoms don't fit any one disease."

While Paul spoke, a woman lying on a cot beside him touched his arm. Her frail voice whispered, "Are you a doctor?"

"Yes."

"Please . . ." She swallowed and struggled to talk. He leaned close but barely understood her. "That's my father over there. I'm dying, but . . . help him." Paul turned to see an elderly man staring at them from a cot across the room. "If I die, he will have no one."

"I don't know if there's anything I can do, but I'll—" Before Paul could finish his sentence, the woman's body stiffened and her eyes rolled back. He tilted her head to open her airway and held her down as she convulsed.

At once, those surrounding her bed backed away in fear, except Quinn, Miju, and Paul. The other women in the hut wailed and tore their clothing. Paul prevented the woman from falling off the bed as the seizure worsened. "Hand me that, Miju." Miju didn't move and gave Paul an arrogant glance. Paul reached for the spoon himself and held the woman's tongue down as she seized violently.

He searched her face, her eyes, her skin—but there was nothing, no clue as to what could be causing this horrible illness that spread like a plague.

Her father across the room rose from his bed, knelt on the floor, and prayed. When the convulsions stopped, her breathing did as well.

Paul checked her eyes again. Her fixed, dilated pupils didn't surprise him. He listened to her heart by putting his ear on her chest, then started CPR. Every compression sent bolts of pain through his battered body. Every breath he delivered into her mouth made his lungs burn. But she didn't respond. He felt for a pulse, but there was none. She was gone.

The old man screamed and began shouting in Dinka. Quinn and the guard turned to him.

"Be quiet, old man!" Quinn barked in the man's language as he stepped toward him.

Gently Paul closed the young woman's eyes and covered her with the sheet. As he did, a pair of bandage scissors fell from her bed onto the floor beside his shoe. He looked at Quinn, Miju, and the guard. They were arguing with the old man and weren't paying attention to him. No one but Paul seemed to notice the shiny instrument lying in the dirt.

Miju turned and walked from the building. "I'm going to the latrine."

The woman's father dropped to his knees and called to Paul, tears streaming down his face. "Help her! Do something!"

Quinn shoved the man against the bed with his foot. "Quiet! There is nothing we can do."

"There must be something."

Quinn struck the old man, who cowered against the wall as the guard pulled his rifle off his shoulder and stood at Quinn's side.

"I said be silent. Your daughter's dead. You'll be joining her soon." The absence of empathy no longer shocked Paul.

Occupied with the old man, Quinn didn't see Paul reach down, grab the bandage scissors, and slip them into his pocket. He stood. By the time Quinn turned back to him, Paul had begun walking toward the old man.

Quinn grabbed Paul's arm. "Where are you going?"

"To check his symptoms. That's what you brought me here for."

"You've seen enough. Come, there's more." Quinn pulled Paul from the hut, shoving him down a path on the other side of the building. The guard followed close behind. Miju caught up a moment later.

As they moved along the winding path, Paul felt he was being watched. Rustling noises in the brush drew his attention, and he spotted a face peering through the greenery. It quickly disappeared only to reappear a moment later. Curious onlookers were following them from a distance—children. He shuddered at the horrors they must see each day.

"Turn here." Quinn pointed to his right. Paul took the path, and the stench worsened. Walking over a low hill, he stopped at the brink as a chill swept over him, and he turned away, fighting the urge to vomit. He held his hand over his nose as he looked again. In the ravine below, a hundred bodies lay in varying stages of decomposition, appearing to have been thrown there from the hilltop.

"What is this?" Paul had to ask.

"These have died from the disease. There are too many to bury, so they were brought here."

Paul noticed two men shoveling dirt into the mass grave. "They'll never finish."

"It's all they have to do," Quinn clarified. "Their relatives are—Don't move!"

Paul froze.

"To your left." Quinn spoke in a low voice.

Paul turned his head slowly. A black mamba, with its deadly gray head hovering nearly fifteen centimeters above the tall grass, had focused its eyes on the guard behind him.

"Don't move a muscle," Quinn warned the guard. "He'll attack if you do."

The snake hissed and moved its head from side to side. When the guard flinched and pulled up his rifle to aim, the snake disappeared into the grass.

"Run!" Quinn sprinted toward the village. Miju followed, with the guard bringing up the rear. Paul darted in the opposite direction, down the hill toward the huge burial ground.

A shot followed by the guard's screams stopped him in his tracks. Paul looked back. A second shot—then a third. Paul grabbed an abandoned shovel from beside the grave site and struggled back up the hill. When he rounded the first corner of the path, he saw the guard writhing on the ground in agony, holding his leg.

Paul knelt beside him and laid down the shovel. "Let me see."

The guard screamed. "It bit me!"

Paul tore his pant leg—two puncture wounds dripped blood. He pulled off the guard's belt and applied a tourniquet above the bite. "Hold this. I have to check the others."

Paul grabbed the shovel, stood, and moved past him to find a second man—a villager he hadn't seen before—only a few meters away, lying motionless on the ground. The bite wound on the side of the man's neck prompted Paul to check his pulse. He was already dead.

When Paul turned, Quinn and Miju were firing their pistols into the grass, but the snake was too fast and the vegetation provided camouflage.

As Paul approached them, the mamba slithered behind Quinn, raising its head above the tall grass every few seconds. Quinn couldn't see it since his back was turned.

"He's behind you!" Paul yelled. Quinn turned, but the mamba dropped into the grass.

Paul ran behind Quinn and held the shovel over his head to strike the deadly serpent. He heard the click, click of a pistol dry firing. Quinn had run out of ammo. The mamba raised its head, and Paul swung. The shovel swooped millimeters from Quinn's face and hit the ground in front of him, severely injuring the mamba. Quinn backed away, ejected his clip, and grabbed another from his belt. Paul swung the shovel and struck the ground, missing the huge flopping snake. It hissed and struck at him but hit the shovel blade instead of Paul's leg. Paul swung once more, and this time a direct blow severed the mamba's head from its body.

Paul fell to his knees, exhausted. He clutched his side, unable to catch a full breath. When he looked up, the dead mamba's hideous head faced him, only a meter away. Its piercing eyes were fixed on him, and its pitch-black mouth opened and closed as if still trying to strike, even in death.

Quinn finished reloading his pistol and fired a single shot through the serpent's head. Paul fell backward as the dirt pelted his face.

Quinn bent and picked up the remainder of the snake. It was twice as long as Quinn was tall, making it over three and a half meters in length.

Paul pushed himself to his feet with the shovel and walked past Quinn and Miju to the fallen guard. He rolled him onto his back.

"Can you hear me?" There was no response. Paul checked his pupils—they were constricted.

"Are you having trouble breathing?"

The guard nodded.

Miju gathered up the rifle and removed the guard's weapons and ammo from his belt and the holster from his leg.

Paul tilted the guard's head back to open his airway, but there was nothing more he could do. He held the man's hand as he convulsed and then stopped breathing.

Paul rose and faced Quinn. "I'm sorry."

Quinn nodded. "The good men die." A moment later, as if nothing had happened, he said, "It's time to return to the village."

On the path back, the reaction of the man to the snakebite reminded Paul of the symptoms of the illness the villagers were experiencing. It didn't make sense. The villagers behaved as if poisoned, but if it wasn't snake venom, what—?

"Come, Doctor. You're lagging."

Paul stopped. The experiments he had done with his research grant . . . the reactions they were encountering, the complications and . . . that was it. It made sense.

"Quinn."

Quinn stopped and turned. "What?"

"This plague. It's not from disease. It's not an illness at all. That's why it didn't make sense. This is poison, and you're responsible."

Quinn studied him without speaking, then moved closer. "What are you saying? That this may not be an epidemic, my wise physician friend?"

"Don't avoid my question. I understand enough about infectious diseases to know this doesn't fit. And snakes didn't bite all these people."

Quinn shrugged his shoulders. "It may not be snakes or poison, or it may be both."

"How did you—?" As he was speaking, Paul felt a tug on his shirt. He turned to see the old man from the hut grasping his sleeve.

"Help me, healer, please. My daughter's gone. I'm alone." Paul grimaced, and the elderly man seemed to sense that it hurt Paul to pull on his shirt. He let go, stepped back, and bowed.

"No, do not bow to him!" Quinn's face contorted in rage. "Why would you do this? Why would you dishonor me? I am the hand of God. This man is nothing." He gestured toward Paul. "And you dare bow to him?"

Paul grabbed the man's arm and lifted him. "He didn't mean—"

"Silence!" Quinn held up his hand to cut Paul off and pulled the man into the clearing. "Bow to me."

The man looked at Paul.

"Don't look at him! He can't help you!" Quinn grabbed Paul and shoved him into the jeep. "Tie his left hand and his legs."

Miju climbed in from the opposite side and bound Paul to the seat frame with zip ties.

"Stand in front of me, old man," Quinn said. The man did as he was told. "The one you've bowed to will kill you now."

Paul turned. "What did you say?"

"You'll shoot him, or Leza will die." Quinn drew his pistol and dropped out the clip. "There is one bullet in the chamber. You have a single shot."

"I can't. I won't kill a man in cold blood."

"Then Leza dies when we get to camp."

"If you kill her, you have nothing to bargain with. You'll lose my cooperation forever."

"You have no idea what I am capable of. I will bring your entire family here if I must to get what I need." Quinn grabbed Paul's right hand, placed the gun in it, and held his wrist with both of his hands so Paul could only point it forward.

"Have mercy," the old man begged. "I have nothing. I just want to live."

"Then bow to me!" Quinn demanded.

"Don't do this, Quinn. You can't be God's right hand and kill old men and children for no reason."

"I can be whatever I want. I decide who lives and who dies. I'm the one they'll bow to. I'm their lord."

"You are not my lord!" The old man's sudden boldness surprised even Paul. "You're not the hand of God, you devil. I'll never bow to you." He looked at Paul, his chin held high. "Pull the trigger, healer. You're a man of faith. Let me die at your hand, and the spirits will forgive you. They already have." The old man's expression suddenly changed. "You . . . you've seen the Dark One."

Miju interrupted. "What? Who saw the Dark One? Old man, who saw the Dark One?"

"That's enough!" Quinn yelled as he clamped Paul's hand more tightly and aimed the gun at the man's chest. "You've done this to yourself!" He placed his finger on top of Paul's and pulled the trigger.

"No!" Paul shouted at the deafening noise as a fine red mist appeared in the air behind the old man. He dropped to the ground.

Paul fought to free himself from his bindings so that he could shove the gun into Quinn's face. He couldn't break loose, and Quinn easily twisted the empty pistol from his grasp.

"Tie him up."

Miju forced Paul's free hand to the seat frame and secured it.

"Did you see the Dark One? The Ghost of Africa?" Quinn demanded.

Paul struggled to break loose. "You're a murderer."

Quinn grabbed Paul by his shirt and pulled him forward, straining him against his bindings. "Answer my question! Have you forgotten Leza? For your insolence, she will not eat for two days."

"You'll kill her."

"You will kill her. I warned you. Now tell me—have you seen the Dark One?"

"You're insane."

Miju stared at Paul in disbelief. "You did. You saw the Dark One. The old man said it."

"Silence, Miju." Quinn rolled the old man's body out of the way with his foot. "Now you know how it feels to kill," he said.

"I didn't kill anyone," Paul insisted.

"Really? Did you not hold the gun to his chest? Did you not pull back the hammer? Did you not think about shooting him to save your Leza?"

"I didn't shoot him."

"If you didn't shoot him, Leza must die. That was the deal. So think about your answer. Did you shoot the old man?"

Paul didn't speak.

"Answer me!"

"Yes. I shot him."

"Say it again."

"I said 'I shot him.'"

"Yes, you did. I saw you do it. Miju saw it. And so did everyone in this village."

Paul glanced at the people glaring at them from a safe distance.

Miju roughly pulled the hood over Paul's head and cinched it. Within seconds, the jeep pulled out of the village, and they began their long trip back to the compound.

General Bradley Jemison pushed the door closed in his Washington, DC, office and locked it. He walked to the windows that overlooked the US Capitol building and scanned the street below before closing the blinds.

After logging onto his computer, he brought up the site he needed and then unlocked a file drawer in his desk. Removing a tray holding a stapler, pens, and note pads, he lifted the false bottom of the drawer and pulled out a single manila envelope. Inspecting the seal's integrity before he opened it, he removed the contents: a stack of documents prepared for him by someone he'd never meet.

He spread them on his desk and studied the details for three hours to make certain he understood the request and its implications. Pulling a cell phone from his pocket, he unlocked it and dialed an encryption algorithm. Once he had clearance, he logged into a secure virtual private network that allowed him access to call anywhere in the world without revealing his identity or location. Linking through several isolated networks in different countries ensured that it would take hours to trace the origin of an Internet or Voice over IP connection.

The general's VPN originated in Chicago and routed through Cairo, Singapore, and finally New York City.

"Hello, Commander. I am your contact, the general. I've reviewed your documents and find them to be in order. I have no questions. You're hereby cleared to commence Project Enigma, but understand—you have no coverage, no backup, no assurance, and this mission is highly classified. You're entering through Uganda air space into the Congo, then you're on your own. You have the right to proceed or decline, Commander. I must know now."

Jemison waited for the man's response, then ended the call and turned off the VPN. He placed the documents in the shredder and watched them disappear into the receptacle below in tiny paper squares. He returned the tray to the drawer and secured the desk. After logging off and shutting down the computer, he opened the blinds, turned off the lights, and left the building.

CHAPTER ELEVEN

Absentmindedly, Jessica stirred her now-soggy cereal as she sat at the breakfast bar. Part of her attention was focused on CNN, the other on Special Agents David Kensing and Andrea Cummings. She didn't like the safe house, even if it was for her own protection—and protection from what? Keeping her in the dark seemed unnecessary, and being watched twenty-four hours a day for three weeks had made her claustrophobic.

The TV monitor caught her attention when a photo of a child in Sudan, suffering under the violent upsurge, appeared on the screen. Jessica reached for the remote and turned up the volume.

The news coverage, sympathetic to her father's plight, focused on corruption in North Sudan. The story portrayed her father as a hero, assisting the US government in preventing needless deaths from chemical weapons and providing medical care for the poor in Africa before his abduction. Jessica did her best to comprehend what they were saying about her father.

The nation had been rocked by the White House's acknowledgment of top secret chemical warfare research when a news probe had come too close to unveiling the truth. Damage control was offered as an excuse for the president's press release, but new fears kindled among the general public as images of chemical warfare paraded across the news day after day. The media was not about to allow this political firestorm to die.

As Jessica watched, a special report presented a description of the growing tensions between North and South Sudan and the South's determination to remain seceded from the North. North Sudan, reluctant to relinquish control of oil reservoirs discovered in South Sudan, was reestablishing battle lines that had once been drawn over prejudices. Bloodshed in the South had neared genocide during that war. Because of the oil, they were paying for peace with their lives once again.

Images on the television changed from photos of mass graves and burning villages to those of Joseph Kony and Jason Quinn, leaders of the LRA, depicted as violent, brutal killers and enslavers of the youth of Africa. The reporter went on to say that reliable sources indicated the LRA had abducted Paul Branson, but his whereabouts were still unknown. He was presumed dead.

Desperation clenched Jessica's heart, and she shoved her bowl across the counter. It slid off the edge and smashed on the floor, slinging milk and Cheerios around the kitchen.

Jumping up, she ran to the bedroom, slammed the door, and stared out the window at the skyline. "Oh God, where is my dad? Did he really leave me? If he did, I have to live with that, and I don't know how." She grabbed a tissue and dried her eyes, but the tears continued.

Suddenly her cell phone rang, interrupting her thoughts. The blocked ID caused her to take a deep breath. She knew she should take the phone to Agent Cummings before answering, but she couldn't help herself.

"Hello? Yes, this is Jessica. Who's this?" She blanched at the response, hung up, and rushed to the living room.

"What's wrong?" Agent Cummings asked.

Jessica whispered, "He's outside the door."

Agent Kensing heard her and took position beside the door with his back to the wall and his pistol drawn.

Agent Cummings looked at the cell phone in Jessica's hand and pulled her to the side. "Who just called? Who's at the door?"

"Charles Manning. He said he needs to talk to me alone and that I needed to get away from you."

Cummings looked confused.

"The other researcher in the photo with my dad? Remember? He's outside."

Agent Cummings stepped between her and the door. "I remember." She paused. "Jessica, Charles Manning is dead. He was under investigation for conspiracy when he was found dead in his apartment two weeks ago. We need to get you out of here—now." Cummings pulled her handgun from its holster and pushed Jessica down the hallway and into the bedroom. From there she had a clear shot to the front door. Unclipping the radio from her belt, she spoke quietly. "Homestead is compromised. Repeat, we have been compromised. Request immediate extraction. Hostiles on-site. Imminent danger."

A voice crackled on the radio. "Ten four. Backup on its way." Agent Cummings clipped the radio back onto her belt and turned to Jessica.

"Whoever killed Manning knows you're in protective custody, and they're trying to get you to open the door. They're here to take you."

Known for her nerves of steel, Jessica also had her mother's faith. But when Agent Cummings suggested someone was there to kidnap her, a cold chill ran up her spine. She turned to look at Agent Kensing guarding the door down the hall.

Agent Cummings glanced at her. "You must understand that your father is valuable for what he learned from the research he performed."

"But why is this even happening?" Jessica asked.

"There's something no one but the government and your father knows about, and it involves chemical warfare. If it falls into the wrong hands, people will die—many people." Agent Cummings paused.

"Somebody wants this information bad enough to kidnap your father and kill Manning to find it."

Jessica's mind raced.

"Your dad never told you because he couldn't. Besides, he probably thought it was behind him—ancient history. But Manning was found dead, your dad's been kidnapped, and now they're here for you."

"Why me?"

Agent Cummings turned to her again. "To get to your father."

"He's alive then?"

"We think he's alive, otherwise why would they want you?" She pushed Jessica down beside the bed. "Stay low."

Cummings called to Kensing. "Can we get her out?"

Jessica peeked over the edge of the bed. Kensing leaned over to look through the peephole. At that moment, two bullets punched through the steel door and exploded out his back. He slumped to the floor.

Jessica screamed as Cummings groaned, "Oh God . . . Teflon bullets." She ran to the bedroom doorway and fired four shots down the hall into the front door, then crouched behind a dresser with her pistol trained on the entrance to the apartment. "Stay down, Jessica."

Three more shots from the outer corridor shattered the locks on the door and a glass table in the breakfast nook. The metal casing of the door lock tumbled across the floor as it creaked open a crack. Cummings leaned out to take aim when four rapid shots slammed her against the wall. She fell lifeless to the floor next to Jessica.

Jessica grabbed the agent's gun and sprinted across the hallway to the kitchen. As she ducked behind the counter, a man burst through the front door into the living room, crunching across the broken glass and hurrying down the hallway to the bedroom.

Jessica's hand shook with every heartbeat as she turned toward him, aimed, and fired three shots. One hit his shoulder as he dove for cover. A second assailant rushed into the apartment and headed straight for Jessica from the other side of the kitchen island. She aimed and pulled the trigger but was out of ammo. Dropping the gun and bolting for the front door, she felt the second man close on her heels. He chased her down and tackled her to the floor.

With his arm around her neck, he attempted to put a damp cloth over her face, but Jessica snatched it from his hand, balled her fist, and struck his nose. The crunch sickened her, but it didn't slow her down. Her self-defense training, something her father had insisted on, was making a difference. She kicked his right leg, then punched his throat, forcing him to let go as he grabbed his neck, struggling for air.

Jessica jumped to her feet and ran for the front door again, but the first man dove for her legs and tripped her. She saw that he had the cloth in his hand as she turned toward him. A punch in the face knocked her back and dazed her. The room spun as she tried to collect her thoughts. Suddenly the damp cloth was covering her nose and mouth. As she felt herself losing consciousness, she dug her fingernails deep into her assailant's arms. It was the last thing she remembered.

Paul drifted in and out of . . . he wasn't sure where. His skin burned, but he shivered. A delicate hand touched his shoulder, and he opened his eyes to find he was back in his own hut. He turned as Adanna placed a cool cloth on his forehead.

"What happened?" he asked.

"You passed out in the jeep on the way back to the compound." She paused for a moment. "Is Nicki your wife?"

Paul sighed. "She was."

Adanna continued dabbing his brow.

"She died of cancer. I guess I was dreaming—or remembering."

"I'm sorry. I didn't mean—"

"It's okay."

"You've been talking in your sleep. You mentioned her."

"She fought cancer to stay with me, but God had different plans."

"What do you mean?"

"Sometimes we think we know how a plan is supposed to work, but then we're surprised when we don't have it figured out at all. There's a reason for her death. I don't know what it is, but I don't have to."

Adanna nodded but didn't say anything.

Paul broke the silence. "How did I get here?"

"When you passed out, they brought you to the room, and Hanna looked after you. She was here until an hour ago."

Paul looked at the fresh dressing covering the wound on his chest. "How long have I been back?"

"Since this afternoon. Hanna took care of you. She was worried about you."

Paul smiled. "Have you known her a long time?"

Adanna nodded. "She's a friend. We attended the same school many years ago, before she went off to medical school in Entebbe." Adanna's voice lowered. "There's something you need to know, Dr. Paul . . . That's what Leza calls you. Is that okay?"

Paul perked up. "Yes, of course. How's my little girl?"

"Not good. She's getting weaker each day." Adanna paused. "But she's a fighter. Hanna and I have been looking after her. She's in the hut next to mine so I can keep an eye on her."

"Can you tell her I love her?" Paul swallowed the lump in his throat.

"I will. She'll be glad to hear you're okay." Adanna smiled.

"Adanna, why are you here? Why would Quinn let you take care of me?"

Adanna walked to the window and cautiously peered at the clearing below. "He wouldn't. Quinn left the compound with Miju. They'll return any time, but I wanted to check on you."

"Thank you for that, but it's too risky. You should go."

"I needed to talk to you." She lowered her voice. "You must escape."

"What do you mean?"

"Something's happened. Something has changed in Quinn. Up to two weeks ago he was loving and kind to me. I know he's ruthless, even a murderer. But this is different. Now, if Quinn knew I was here, he might kill me even though I carry his baby." Adanna glanced out the window in both directions and walked back to Paul's bed.

"Quinn is obsessed with something. And he's . . . he's evil."

Paul fidgeted. "Do you know what happened in Botan?"

"Miju told me Quinn made you kill a man."

"He forced me to hold the gun while he pulled the trigger."

"You have nothing to feel guilty about."

"Because I wanted to save Leza, I thought about pulling the trigger myself."

"But you didn't."

Paul leaned his head back.

Adanna continued, "In the past two weeks, Quinn's heart has become much darker. I'm afraid of him now. And I'm afraid for you."

"Did the guard see you come in here?"

"Cijen is the guard right now, and he likes you."

That put Paul's mind at ease.

"But the guard will change in a half hour, and Quinn could return any time. You need to understand—deep down in his heart there is no light, only darkness. He hates you for who you are. He wants you dead, but he needs you alive even more. I don't know what for, but he needs you alive."

Adanna's choice of words surprised Paul. Quinn hated him for who he was? Why? What threat was he to Quinn?

"You have the respect of the villages of Sudan. They know you, they love you, and they would do anything for you. They hate Quinn. You heal—he kills." Adanna paused as she heard noises outside. Then she turned back to him.

"You saved me twice when Quinn could do nothing. You saved Quinn by killing the black mamba when he couldn't, according to

Miju." She paused. "And now he knows you saw the Dark One, and he hates you even more."

Paul knew of Quinn's irrational hate, but the word "psychotic" began to seem a better description.

"The men in the camp talk about you." Adanna smiled, obviously taking in Paul's puzzled expression. "They wonder why the spirits have spared you so many times. They wonder where your power comes from. Some think perhaps you are The Chosen—our deliverer. And since Leza arrived in the compound calling you Abdu, many believe you are."

"What does it mean, 'The Chosen'?"

"When the panther spares a life in the village, it's for a purpose. In the villagers' eyes, you've been chosen for something—something important. They understand that, but Quinn does not. A man can't make himself chosen. To try would be to invite death from the Dark One."

"I'm just a man."

"You're a man who has survived the Ghost of Africa, the black mamba, and being shot—several times."

Paul sighed. "What do I do now?"

"Quinn's planning a horrible offense against some of the villages of South Sudan, including your village—Leza's village. It's why the people of Botan are dying and dead."

Fear welled up inside Paul. He'd accused Quinn of being responsible for the deaths of the villagers. Now he knew it was true.

"What's he using, Adanna? He told me he wants me for the knowledge I have from a government research project. But the chemicals we used in that study are impossible to obtain—from anywhere. There is no way I could be of benefit to him."

"Well, the village of Botan was a failed experiment. They used chemicals. I saw the trucks being loaded. He wanted to make it look like an epidemic had struck, to frighten outsiders away. That's very important to his plan—for it to look like an illness. His scheme will not work if people die too quickly. That's why he took you to Botan. He wanted to see if you would figure out the truth or if you believed an epidemic caused the illness." Adanna paused. "He didn't like your conclusion. And Quinn's men are talking now. Four hundred people died in two . . ." She choked up for a moment.

Paul's mind darted from one possibility to another as her words sank in. "He's poisoning them with something, Adanna. Do you have any idea what it is or where he got it?"

"Quinn comes and goes as he pleases. Sometimes he's gone for days at a time, so it could have come from anywhere. I don't know what he's using, but the warehouse on the edge of the compound is where the secret things happen. Only a few men are permitted to enter. I don't know what they're doing, but the men at this camp who have been ill worked in that warehouse. A few days ago, one of them had a seizure and died. He was quickly buried."

Paul pondered what Adanna was saying.

"Quinn and his inner circle of men have been talking about nothing else. They speak in secret, but I hear some of what they say. They've planned to kidnap you for months now, not just to save me."

"You need to get out of here, Adanna."

"He's going to kill you and Leza when the plan is finished and he doesn't need you anymore. He'll never let you go." Adanna's voice shook. "It's you who must find a way out. You have a chance if you can break free from here. Do they check on you during the night?"

"I don't know. I don't think so."

"If they don't, and you escaped, they wouldn't find out until morning." Adanna's eyes filled with tears.

"Why are you staying with him?" Paul asked.

"There's no escape for me. He'll hunt me wherever I go, especially since I carry his baby. I would never be safe. You can go to America where he can't reach you. I cannot."

"You can't stay."

"I can't leave."

Paul raised his head and looked around the room. The wheels in his head started spinning.

As if she'd heard his thoughts, Adanna warned him, "There is no way to run right now. The guards are everywhere, and Cijen is outside the door. At night there may be a chance to get out through the fence behind the compound."

"I won't leave without Leza. If I do, she'll die."

"You must. There's no hope of both of you making it out alive. She'll slow you down too much." Adanna sat on the edge of the bed.

"How can I get out? Is there a way?"

"I don't know. We're in a fortress with two rows of fences surrounding the compound. There's one gate in and out—only one—with guards on both sides. And you don't have much time."

"What if I can make it to the plane on the edge of the compound?"

"Can you fly?"

"Yes."

Adanna thought for a moment. "You would have to get past the guards. There's an inner and outer gate, and the guards are heavily armed."

"How much time do I have?"

"A week, maybe less. They're planning to attack the villages soon." Adanna stood. "I must go." She reached for Paul's zip-tied hand and squeezed it.

He squeezed back. "Thank you."

"Don't thank me. I'm the reason you were taken from your people in the first place."

"There's a lot more to it than that. Like you said, Quinn would have come for me eventually."

"But it's my burden. You saved my life. I want to help save yours." Adanna leaned down to Paul's ear. "I've buried a pistol under Quinn's hut. No one would ever look for it there, but it won't be easy to find. It's under a small smooth stone near the northeast support post."

Adanna straightened and walked toward the door, paused, and turned. "I won't see you again, Dr. Paul. Remember me."

A lump rose in Paul's throat. "I'll remember you, Adanna. Thank you."

When she left the room, he pushed himself to the edge of the bed. He forced his hips to his zip-tied hand and pressed his fingers against his pocket—the bandage scissors he'd found were still there.

CHAPTER TWELVE

It seemed that night would never come. Paul waited for the guard to bring his food, watch him eat, and retie him to the bed. Finally he left.

Paul waited a full five minutes to make sure the man didn't return. The howling wind made it difficult to hear anything outside, but he finally decided he couldn't delay any longer. He arched his back, twisted his body, and lifted his right hip as he slid his leg toward the foot of the bed. Stretching his fingers while pushing his pelvis against his right hand, he reached into his pocket, grabbed the scissors, and eased them out.

Raising his head and focusing on his hand, Paul carefully turned the scissor blades toward the zip tie and slid the cold steel past his wrist. Wedging the nylon band between the blades, he squeezed as hard as he could. The awkward position made it difficult to cut through, but when he took a firmer grip on the scissors and squeezed again, the blades snapped the tie. One hand was free.

Paul then slid the pointed tip of the scissors into the lock of the zip tie on his left wrist and pried up enough to pull it loose without cutting it. He did the same with the ties on his ankles.

Carefully he walked to the door and listened. It sounded as if a storm might be brewing. The bamboo walls and tin roof groaned in the wind as he made his way to the window on the far side of the hut. He stood back from it to remain in the shadows and gazed toward the courtyard outside. The only guards he could spot were too far away to hear him between gusts.

He leaned out of the window just far enough to see and turned toward the back of the building; the chain-link fence two hundred meters away stood at least five meters high with coiled barbed wire looped through the top, reminding Paul of a concentration camp. The height of his hut, resting on three-meter stilts and nestled in a group of trees, made escape almost impossible. Almost.

Paul pulled against the bamboo wall as the breeze whistled through the trees outside. There was no way he could break through, not quietly. Looking around the room, he could find nothing to use to climb down from the window, but a squeak in the plank floor along the back wall drew his attention.

Two boards moved when he stepped on them. He pulled at them, thankful for the noise from the brewing storm that covered the creaking they made when he lifted the edges. If just two of them would pull loose, he could fit through. Wedging his fingers into a thin gap, Paul worked one of the planks up and down until he loosened the nail securing it to the beam. The scissors in his pocket made a useful tool. Placing the handles around the nail and compressing them like pliers, he pulled the nail out.

He manipulated the other board until it also worked free, then lowered his head through the opening. It was dark under the hut, but the support stilts were visible, and one was close enough to reach. He was nervous, but he knew he could do it.

Paul turned his body upright and carefully eased himself through the opening, grabbed the wooden support, and slid to the ground. The feeling of being out of the hut unattended was exhilarating, but he knew it would be short-lived if he wasn't careful.

Squatting at the base of the pole, he surveyed his surroundings. No one stood guard nearby except the man on his front porch at the top of the stairs. Paul scanned the area to gain his bearings. From what he could remember from his walks across the compound with Miju, he needed to circle around the clearing to the right and make his way to the warehouse on the opposite side.

Dense greenery under the hut made Paul wonder what deadly insects or reptiles surrounded him. He pushed those thoughts aside. Carefully scanning for guards before leaving the cover of his own building, he hurried to the one on his right and crouched beneath it. He paused to be certain no one had spotted him. This hut wasn't as high off the ground as his, only one and a half meters, but the space afforded him enough room to move if he bent at the waist. At least the foliage around the buildings was dense. That provided some cover.

Cigarette smoke. The odor, carried by the breeze, stopped Paul in his tracks. His eyes searched every direction, and then he spotted them. Two guards were walking toward him, smoking and talking. A German shepherd trotted between them.

Paul froze. He knew if he moved, the dog would likely see him. He was glad he was downwind so the canine couldn't pick up his scent. The men stopped long enough to drop their cigarette butts on the ground, crush them under their boots, then continue on their patrol. The dog followed alongside.

When Paul was certain the men had moved far enough away, he darted from the cover of the structure to that of the next one, trying not to step on anything that would draw attention. He stayed away from the back of the huts to keep from being spotted by guards along the fence. Moving under the dwellings was more difficult than being out in the open, but safer. He looked back—so far, so good.

Paul made his way to the other side of the compound and squatted next to one of the barracks. His legs wobbled on weak, underused muscles. He crawled the last few meters from the brush to the tree line in front of the forbidden building he'd seen before—the warehouse, according to Adanna.

Armed men guarded the front entrance and all four corners of the structure. Paul analyzed his next step. To move closer, he would need a diversion.

Men's voices coming from somewhere past the trees behind him drew his attention. Two of them had stopped to sit and talk by a fire burning in a fifty-five-gallon drum. Paul scooted through the tall grass, squatted under the closest hut, and watched. His heart pounded as he waited for them to move, or stop talking, or . . . something.

They continued to chat, so Paul scanned the area for a way out. A jeep was parked with the hood open as if someone had been working on the engine. He crawled to the edge of the vehicle and pulled himself under it. He waited. No one seemed to have noticed him.

With his scissors, he gnawed a small cut in the fuel line, and gasoline began to dribble onto the ground. He crawled back to the hut, careful not to be seen, and collected a handful of dry grass from the base of one of the support posts and wove it into a stick.

When the two men finally stood and walked away from the fire, Paul took a deep breath. *Time to do this.*

He looked in all directions. He heard more men nearby, but there was no one visible. He walked quickly and warily to the fire, lit the bundle of dry grass, threw it under the jeep, and hurried back to the cover of the tall brush. Seconds later the jeep was engulfed in flames, drawing the attention of the guards at the warehouse.

At the edge of the clearing Paul waited, but the guards didn't budge. Instead, they stared at the fire and shouted at each other. He looked back just as the jeep's gas tank exploded, spewing flames into the air.

Finally the guards left their posts and ran toward the inferno. Paul gathered his nerve and sprinted from the tall grass to the back of the building. When he looked, everyone was occupied by the blaze. Out of sight of the guards, he stepped to the edge of the cinder block foundation, grabbed the windowsill with his fingers, and with strength he didn't know he still had, pulled himself up and peeked inside. One bulb lit the warehouse room. It appeared to be empty of guards.

Paul dragged his body through the window and crumpled onto the wood floor. His aching chest burned, but he didn't move, wondering if he was truly alone inside. He expected a rifle to be pointed at him at any moment—but no one came.

Straining his eyes to see beyond the shadows, Paul realized he was in a large storage area with a small, enclosed office built against one wall. A chemical analysis console perched next to a microscope, and what appeared to be a distilling unit occupied a corner of the room.

Several walls were lined with shelves holding dozens of five-gallon containers, which got Paul's attention. He stood, walked to the shelves, and tapped on one—it sounded full. He moved slowly, not wanting to alert anyone by knocking something over. On the opposite side of the building, he stopped when he saw the blue fifty-five gallon drums. With his knuckles, he quietly thudded each one. They sounded full too, and each sported a bright orange international hazmat placard.

Paul moved closer and inspected the labels. Listed in three languages, including English, were the words, "WARNING: SOMAN COMPOUND. EXTREMELY HAZARDOUS. UNAUTHORIZED TRANSPORT FORBIDDEN." Below the placards, the only thing he could make out were four letters in the address: "IRAQ."

Paul stared at the containers as reality settled in. Standing in front of him were barrels of a toxic nerve agent similar to sarin. An internationally illegal substance, Soman had been classified by the United Nations as a chemical weapon of mass destruction. Except for small quantities used for research purposes—like his government research program—its presence remained banned from every country on earth. Paul was one of only a handful of individuals to ever deal with such an ominous substance.

He had studied Soman extensively from 1993 to 1995, after the Chemical Weapons Convention had outlawed sarin. His research had focused on developing potential antidotes and neutralizing the compounds dispersed in aerosol form. It made sense. Soman could produce the symptoms he had seen in the villages.

How did you get this, Quinn?

Voices approaching the building pulled Paul back to reality. He made his way to the window and saw that one of the guards had reestablished his position on the corner three meters away. Paul had no place to go as he heard the door unlock. His muscles tightened. He quickly glanced around the room and ran back to the barrels. The door swung open as he crouched behind one of them. Moments later, he recognized Quinn's and Miju's voices as they entered.

"Find out who was working on that jeep," Quinn growled in Arabic. "They know better than to leave the battery connected when they work on the engine. It was a perfectly good jeep, and the fire could have gotten out of control in this wind."

"I'll take care of it," Miju assured him.

"And the next time the guards leave their posts, I'll shoot them myself. It's not their job to put out a fire. It's their job to protect this building."

"Understood."

The door closed.

"We are on the verge of obtaining everything we've worked for for so many years, Miju. We must not fail now."

"Where do we stand if we can't get Branson to cooperate?"

"This formula is our only problem, and we knew it would be. No matter what we do, it kills too fast or too slow, then dissipates too quickly. It's no good to us if we can't control it. It must be slow and long . . . and painful enough for people to stay away. We must instill fear—permanent fear—so that no one returns."

Paul heard Quinn pacing, then stop at the window.

"What about him, Quinn?" Miju pressed.

"I'll force him to write it down for us tomorrow. He'll give us everything we need, or else we'll kill Leza in front of him . . . slowly."

"Branson knows that if you kill her, you have nothing else to hold over him. The motivation is gone. That's why he keeps dragging his feet."

"Remember, I said . . . slowly. No man can watch someone he loves be tortured, especially a little girl."

"She's sick. What if she doesn't last long enough to get what we need out of him?"

Quinn laughed. "I have something Branson knows nothing about—it's the perfect incentive. I'll save it for the time it's needed. We're on top of this. Nothing can stand in our way. We own the land, access to the oil, and the mineral rights . . . unless the villages exercise their option in time. But they can't if they're dead. It's a good plan, Miju. Stop worrying."

Paul's mind spun as he attempted to imagine what Quinn was talking about, thankful for the time he'd spent learning Arabic. What other incentive? And how could Quinn be so callous about killing a little girl? Nausea swept over him. He'd never felt so powerless even while his anger burned. He wanted to strike out, but here he was, crouched behind a barrel, hiding from the most dangerous man in Africa.

Just then voices approached from the clearing, drifting through the window. But . . . whose? Paul listened carefully. One of them sounded familiar, but he couldn't place it.

"It appears Jarrod finally made it." Quinn's sarcasm wasn't lost on Paul.

"Why did you bring him onto our team? Who needs him?" Miju made no attempt to disguise his contempt.

"As an ex-marine, he brings us up-to-date technology and first-hand experience. He's trained by the best, he can teach our men what they need to know, and he can prevent problems before they happen. Without him, we never would have pinned Branson down when he flew into Sudan. He's been feeding us information and keeping Branson's brother-in-law out of the way for months. It's worth giving him a piece of the action."

Jarrod? Jim's boss? No. No way.

"A piece of the action could be worth millions. I don't see any possible way he's worth millions."

"Don't worry, my friend. There will be plenty to go around. Get behind this, Miju. We must show a united front."

The door opened and several men speaking Dinka entered the warehouse. Quinn stopped their conversation.

"Excuse me, gentlemen," he said in English, "but the common language among us is English. For the benefit of our friends from the North and the West, we'll speak in Satan's tongue."

The men laughed.

"And let me give a proper introduction to our American friend. This is Jarrod Vincent, and he will be part of our implementation team."

Jarrod was a friend, Jim's colleague. *What had happened?* Something close to hatred began to burn in Paul. *Did Jim know about this? Was Jim in trouble? If Jarrod had done anything to harm him . . .*

Quinn continued, "Jarrod's an expert in hand-to-hand combat, assault weapons, and doing what it takes to get the job done—whatever it takes. He's been flying in to train our men for two weeks in Aketi, two hundred kilometers from here, but most of you have not yet met him. He's an essential member of our team, trained by the United States military."

"Thank you, Quinn. It's good to be part of the venture. I'm looking forward to this and our future campaigns together. Ooh rah, gentlemen." His deep voice with a trace of a Chicago accent echoed again, "Ooh rah!"

Paul desperately wanted to look with his own eyes, but he dared not risk being seen. He just couldn't believe it, but it was Jarrod for sure—the voice, the accent, the military history . . . *How far did Quinn's network reach?*

Quinn's voice drew Paul back from his thoughts. "So, gentlemen, we are on track to move the product to each location on the same night. There'll be no place for the villagers to go. They'll die in their homes, along the roads, in the latrines." The men cheered at Quinn's sick joke. "We'll finally take what's ours—South Sudan: its mango trees, its countryside and traditions, and, oh yes, its oil. Five days, men. We will have control of the land that bears the rights to the oil below, and no one will be alive to oppose us. Let me show you on the map the route we'll take."

Paul listened as Quinn led the group into the office. There must be something he could do to stop this. Burn down the warehouse? What? He'd never been more frustrated. This was happening. There must be something . . . something he could do.

Quinn continued speaking, and with the door open, Paul heard every word. "We'll distribute the barrels here at each point marked in red. It'll take several hours, but by morning, when the villagers go to the wells, they'll gather poison for their children to drink. Within hours, they'll be stumbling about, oblivious to their plight.

"Within days, their real troubles will begin, and they will have worsening symptoms including seizures, vomiting, weakness, and, of course, death. In weeks, the outpouring of sympathy for the people of Sudan will encompass the entire world. But no one will come, out of fear, except, perhaps, for a handful of dedicated physicians. Their loss of life will be even more tragic. This will make Ebola look like a common cold. Once a physician or two dies, no one will venture here for years. Ten months from now, we will own the entire region and control its oil. I assured the North that we would supply them with all they want before we sell the rest to the world." Paul heard Quinn strolling around the men and hoped he wouldn't start walking around the warehouse and possibly spot him.

"I will own South Sudan—at least the parts that are important. I will make you all governors rich beyond your dreams."

Jarrod cleared his throat. "Begging your pardon, sir, but have you obtained what you need from Paul Branson? From what I understand, unless you have those changes in the formula, the people will die in two days like they did in Botan."

"It is true that if we don't stabilize this formula in the next few days, we can't deploy it at all. The Soman must be controlled and the epidemic believable. Most importantly, it has to stay in the water table to poison it for years. You're correct. Branson's information is the key. Extracting the formula from the doctor is a challenge, but he will be highly motivated very soon. The girl will die in front of him if he refuses. If she dies before we have what we need, I have a contingency plan that is not open for discussion."

"Give me a chance. All I need is five minutes in the room with him, and he'll tell you everything you want to know," Jarrod boasted arrogantly.

"Don't worry about the details. I'll manage them, my marine friend."

"Ex-marine. And I just want you to know I can extract information from anybody."

"You'll have your chance—only if I say so." Paul noticed a rising challenge in Quinn's voice. "You will not approach him or ask him a single question unless I tell you to. Is that understood? I don't want him knowing you're involved."

Jarrod backed down. "Understood."

The men talked for another few minutes and then left the building in a noisy clamor. The bolt clanked, locking the door. Paul waited behind the barrel for a full minute before moving to the window to watch them leave. A guard still stood by the outside corner three meters away.

Paul turned and glanced at the barrels as his heart sank. How could he ever hope to stop this? He tried to swallow, but the lump in his throat stuck there. He held the key, and Quinn would kill Leza to get it.

The glow of a light in the small office caught his attention. He slowly pushed the door open and walked inside. The bulb shone on a wall map outlining the South Sudanese villages and surrounding regions of Matta, Wiroh, Lanyi, Buagyi, and Witto with a pump symbol indicating the locations of the wells. Each one had a date and its GPS coordinates scribbled beside it.

Quinn had it figured out. The water wells were the points of entry for the Soman chemicals. Paul knew that every well supplied clean water to one thousand villagers. Five wells per village were circled. That would mean five thousand people from the regions surrounding each village would be using the wells. And if all five wells in each of the five villages were poisoned, twenty-five thousand lives were in jeopardy. Each well was over thirty meters deep, with hand pumps to pull the water from the supply below.

Five wells per village were circled . . . five villages on the map were marked. Paul's heart sank. *If I give them the formula, the water won't be drinkable for years.*

"No, Quinn," he whispered. "You wouldn't . . ." But Quinn had already set the stage by starting an earlier small-scale attack on Botan that had all the markings of a plague except for a too-rapid onset and spread. The slightly ill villagers in Witto must have been poisoned with too little. Both were extremes, just like Quinn had said. Too fast or too slow didn't work. It would have to be slow, painful, and lasting to carry the right message.

The Soman had only a faint, fruity aroma, which no one would notice among the mango blossoms. Quinn would get away with genocide by taking over newly discovered oil fields under those villages with no evidence of his heinous act. No one would move into his territory or, if they did, they would die from the mysterious illness that plagued the region.

Quinn's experimenting had concentrated on accomplishing his plan by finding the best dose of Soman for adding to water, but he hadn't figured out how to bind it to the molecules to make it stay in an area long enough to kill its intended victims while leaving the appearance of a contagious epidemic instead of mass genocide. He'd been able to kill a village quickly, but by the next day, the chemical was no longer a threat. He needed the effect to last longer—years longer.

The formula to make this horror a reality was in Paul's head. Quinn knew it from putting the details together and realizing that Paul's abilities as a doctor went far beyond medicine to his past experience in research. Manning must have told Quinn what Paul had stumbled upon—the formula to keep Soman lethal in a water supply for years. Paul had shared the finding with only one person in the DOD, resulting in the sealing of the documents and termination of the program. Manning never had access, but he must have assumed he could figure it out.

Paul left the little office, his mind spinning with thoughts of how he could stop this insanity. He walked back to the window and carefully peered over the sill.

How am I going to get back to my hut?

Before he could come up with the answer, the dead bolt on the door clanked again. He ducked behind some barrels. Moments later he heard the door relock, but then all was silent.

After a minute of waiting, Paul peeked around the barrels—there was no one there. He waited a little longer, but still no sounds or voices echoed through the warehouse. He slowly stood and made his way to the window again—and stopped when the icy barrel of a rifle jabbed into his back.

CHAPTER THIRTEEN

"Step back from the window."

Paul recognized the voice. "Cij . . . it's me. Dr. Paul."

"I know this. What are you doing in here? Do you want to be killed?"

Paul turned to face him. "Does Quinn know I'm here?"

"If he did, you'd be too dead to ask. You're lucky I saw you crawl through the window instead of one of the other men."

"Okay. I know what I did was risky, but I had to do it. Now I need to get back to my hut. Can you help me?"

"You're not trying to escape?"

"No, I'm not. Well, not tonight at least."

Cijen studied his face.

Paul thought carefully about what he would say next. "Cij, if I don't escape from here in the next day or two, they're going to kill Leza . . . and me."

"How do you know?"

"I just do."

Cijen reached his arm out the window and waved the all clear signal to a guard outside. He walked back past Paul to the far corner of the warehouse. "Follow me." He laid his rifle on a shelf and grabbed the handles of a large crate. "Stand to the side."

Paul moved to his left as Cijen lifted the edge of the crate, which Paul saw was hinged to the floor, exposing a hole and a ladder that plunged into the darkness below. Cijen rested the crate on its side, then picked up his rifle and slung it across his back. "After you, Dr. Paul."

Climbing into a dark pit in the middle of the Congo wouldn't have been Paul's first choice of action, but it seemed better than what waited for him outside. "Okay. So I go first. I see."

He placed his left foot on the top rung of a ladder attached to the wall and lowered his right foot into the abyss. There—it landed solidly on the next rung. He grabbed the top of the ladder and inched down. Each time he extended his leg into the hole, he took a step of faith. Finally he reached the bottom. "Cij?" He could see only shadows and a few tiny LED lights.

Cijen climbed down after him, reached for the wall, and flipped on a light switch. Paul's eyes widened. He stood in the center of a subterranean room crammed with ammo, medical supplies, and lab equipment. In the corner of the room, an airplane instrument cluster lay disassembled. He walked to it.

"That's from Quinn's airplane. He replaced the old instruments with new digital navigation gauges. I helped install them. I'm good with electronics. In case of an invasion, he always keeps his plane gassed and ready to fly."

Paul stared at the shelves. There was enough ammunition to fight a war.

Cijen snapped him back to reality. "Here is how you get back to your hut. Take that tunnel." He pointed to a locked cage door covering the entrance to a dark dirt shaft. "It leads to another ladder. If you climb to the top and open the hatch, it comes out on the other side of the clearing, under Quinn's hut."

"Quinn's hut? I don't really want to be crawling around under there."

"This is Quinn's escape tunnel. Where else would it come out?"

Paul suddenly remembered that Adanna had buried the pistol there for him. "Okay. I come out under Quinn's hut. Good plan."

"Once you open the hatch, look toward the guard gate. When you face that direction, Leza's hut will be to the right. Follow that around to the fence line and the tall grass. Your hut is just past it, but you will need to walk straight through the clearing. The guards positioned in the treetops can't see directly under them. And watch for the guard on the porch. He will be facing the direction you're coming from."

Paul thought for a moment. "The guards are heavy where Leza is too, aren't they?"

"Yes, because Quinn's house is next to it."

"Cij, I appreciate your help. I don't know what—"

Cijen held up his hand and pointed to the room above. They heard the metal locks on the warehouse door moving. Cijen thrust the rifle and flashlight at Paul, switched off the ceiling light, and scurried up the ladder.

With a loaded assault rifle in his hand, Paul tucked the flashlight under one arm and stood at the base of the ladder running his fingers over the cold steel of the trigger. *What if—?* The crate above made a creaking noise as Cijen pulled it closed just before the warehouse door opened. He inched his way back down the ladder, being careful not to make a sound while Paul shone the flashlight beam on the rungs.

When Cijen reached for the rifle, Paul hesitated. Cijen stretched out his palm and motioned for him to hand it over.

Paul eyed him for just a second, then placed the rifle and flashlight in Cijen's hands.

When Cijen turned off the flashlight, darkness engulfed them again. Footsteps creaked on the floorboards above. Paul's scalp tingled from dust sifting onto his head when someone walked directly over where he stood. He felt a sneeze coming and covered his face with his arm, frantically rubbing his nose with his other hand until the urge left him.

Cijen turned on the flashlight but held his hand over the end so it only emitted a tiny beam. Paul squinted his eyes and nodded, indicating that he was okay.

Cijen moved to the cage door and stopped as if thinking about his next move. He set his rifle against the wall, pulled out a wad of keys, and carefully unlocked the door. It clanked—he didn't move. The walking on the floorboards above them stopped.

Muffled voices filtered down.

Slowly Cijen opened the metal mesh door. It groaned, but the voices in the warehouse above continued as if they hadn't heard it. Cijen motioned for Paul to walk through the gate as he grabbed his rifle.

Paul entered the tunnel, but Cijen gripped his arm and spoke so quietly he could barely hear him. "If you're caught, I can't help you."

Paul nodded and took a step into the narrow shaft as Cijen pushed the flashlight into his hand. Paul aimed it down the dark path with a sense of foreboding. A rustling on the floor grabbed his attention, and as he shone the light toward his feet, he saw a sea of glistening brown cockroaches scurrying deeper into the tunnel.

Suddenly the crate over the hatch moved a little. They both looked up.

Cijen stepped into the tunnel with Paul and pulled the rusty metal gate closed behind him. As if in slow motion, he pushed his key into the lock and waited. When the hinged crate covering the opening flopped down onto the wooden floor above, Cijen used the noise to mask the turning of his key in the dead bolt, locking them both in the tunnel.

Paul covered the flashlight so that only a tiny beacon of light escaped between his fingers and took the lead down the dank corridor. When he looked back, he saw the faint light from the warehouse above pierce the darkness through the open hatch.

"Cij?" a man's voice called down. Paul and Cijen stopped.

A second man's voice said, "I thought I saw him come into the warehouse. He waved out the window at me. I must have missed him leaving."

Cijen tapped Paul's shoulder, indicating that he should keep moving. Paul did so, feeling his way along the damp, rough walls. When he rounded the curve in the tunnel, an eerie muffled quietness surrounded them. He could barely hear his own footsteps. Looking back, he couldn't see anything since the bend in the path blocked his vision.

When suddenly the tunnel brightened as the lights in the room behind them were turned on, fear gripped Paul. He concentrated on controlling his breathing. He and Cijen listened in silent dread, waiting anxiously for the clank of the dead bolt on the cage door. They would be trapped like rats without enough time to reach the end of the tunnel. Paul stretched his hand into the darkness, moved ahead a few centimeters, then moved a few more, unable to see what lay ahead in the inky blackness. The light from the room was too dim to help. Cijen hunched close to Paul with his hand on his back as they slowly made their way down the tunnel.

When Paul took another step, his hand struck something hard. He snatched it back.

"What? What's wrong?" Cijen whispered.

"It's nothing." Paul spoke so softly he wondered if Cijen could hear him. "It's the ladder or something—took me by surprise."

He wished he knew what he was getting into. Could there be a trigger wire strung up to prevent intruders from entering or leaving the tunnel? He reached his hand out. The first rung of the ladder was covered with slime. He drew his hand back and smelled it. Moss—moldy moss. He stepped onto the lower rung, then climbed to a grate at the top. He pushed several times, but it wouldn't budge.

"Push hard. It's heavy," Cijen whispered.

Paul did so, the effort making his newly healed wounds hurt and his feet slide on the slippery rungs. He took a deep breath and replanted his feet, but the pain in his chest burned. He pushed with all his strength, and the lid finally lifted. He carefully poked his head through the opening. No one was close. He moved the grate far enough aside to squeeze through.

"Cij."

"Yes?"

"I need a boost."

He felt Cijen grab his shoe and push him far enough to crawl out. Cijen pulled himself through next. They were met with brisk winds and the smell of burning rubber and grass. Cijen looked at Paul and whispered, "The jeep. Was that your doing?"

Paul shrugged and spoke quietly. "What jeep?"

Cij allowed a slow grin to spread across his face. "Nice. Now let's get out of here."

Paul turned to Cijen. "If you get caught, Quinn will kill you. Why are you helping me?"

"You've seen the Dark One. You're The Chosen."

Paul nodded. "Thank you. You saved my life."

They squatted and surveyed their surroundings in the two-meter-high crawl space. The guards out front weren't very close—about twenty meters away. Paul and Cijen carefully moved the grate back to cover the opening.

Paul listened for sounds from the hut above him. He heard walking and floorboards creaking, but no voices. From the cover of the crawl space he studied the guards for several minutes and noticed they walked a simple pattern around Quinn's hut.

"You need to get out of here, Cij."

"Please don't let them find you, Dr. Paul. They'll hurt Leza to punish you."

"I know."

Cijen patted Paul on the back and moved to the edge of the crawl space. When the time was right he stood, slung the rifle over his shoulder, and strolled away.

Paul made his way to the northeast support post that Adanna had told him about and felt along the ground. He located the polished rock and dug down a few centimeters. The pistol, wrapped in a cloth, was a Glock 19.

Paul tucked it into his belt and waited for the guards to clear the alley between Quinn's hut and Leza's. Finally he saw his chance. He stifled another sneeze as he dove under the small wooden building seconds before the soldiers rounded the corner. He held his breath as they passed within centimeters of where he squatted. They paused briefly.

"I thought I saw something," one of them said in Arabic.

"You're always seeing something," the other guard responded as he continued walking. The first man poked his rifle into the brush at the foot of the hut where Paul huddled. Paul knew that the slightest movement would be his ruin. He refused to move, even when the rifle barrel came within a few centimeters of his position.

Finally the guard left to resume his surveillance routine with his comrade. Paul breathed for the first time in what seemed like minutes. He didn't want to move but knew he had to. He summoned his courage and stepped out, hurrying from building to building, making his way to the other side of the compound.

As he approached the tree line near his prison room, something caught his eye—the airstrip. He moved closer. A metal lean-to covering a small plane was visible through the trees. He could almost see—

"Hey! You there! Don't move!"

Paul didn't look or turn around. Instead, he ducked into the grass and bolted for the nearest building—the soldier barrack. As he ran, the guard shouted for help.

Paul darted behind a tree, crawled on the ground, and hid beside a boulder. He held his throbbing ribs to catch his breath.

"He's here! Over here!" A shot rang out. "Come on! He's over here!"

Paul recognized Cijen's voice. *What is he doing? Is he turning on me?* Paul cringed, waiting for them to surround him. Another shot rang out.

They should be on top of him in seconds. Instead, they were moving farther away.

He leaned over to glimpse around the boulder. They were sprinting in the opposite direction, where Cijen stood with his rifle pointed into the brush. Cijen yelled to the other men, "He went in there. I think I may have winged him. He's a villager."

As the men stormed through the tall grass, the wind gusts nearly forced Paul to the ground. Gathering his remaining energy, he ran behind the cover of the shrubbery to his hut. When he reached it, he circled around back to avoid the guard and huddled beneath it to catch his breath. His legs cramped, his muscles ached, and his lungs burned. But he was still alive.

The commotion Cijen had created kept the soldiers occupied, but the guard on his front porch was still on duty—watching. The guard finally walked to the bottom of the stairs just as the warm gusts of wind yielded a torrent of rain.

Paul studied the guard from the cover of the crawl space. He was facing away from Paul but had raised his rifle into position. Paul's lungs couldn't keep up with him. He slowed his breathing in an attempt not to pant, but his heart raced, and he needed air. He pulled the pistol from his belt and aimed it at the guard.

Please don't make me shoot you, he thought. The guard looked up at the pouring rain, abruptly slung the rifle strap over his back, and hurried up the stairs to the cover of the porch.

Paul breathed a sigh of relief and hid the pistol under a rock at the base of the support pole. He noticed that the smells of the burning jeep and the grass were gone, the rain having cleansed the air. He pulled himself up to the wooden floorboards the best he could, but his legs were sore and his stamina had evaporated. When his foot hit a nail that projected from the support pole, he used it to push himself the remaining twenty-five centimeters to the top.

Once Paul reached the beams, he pulled with his arms and dragged himself inside, where he lay motionless on the floor. There was nothing else he could do—not for a few minutes, anyway. He didn't have the strength.

Outside, Quinn's voice echoed as he stormed across the courtyard barking orders to his men. After a few minutes, Paul gathered enough energy to sit up. He pulled off his boots and crawled to the window. Keeping low, he peeked over the sill. The men's voices moved farther away as flashlights in the distance searched the tall grass.

"I know I saw him!" Cijen's voice drew the men away from Paul's hut. Many of them had simply abandoned the search due to the weather. Paul slumped to the floor, crawled back to the opening in the floorboards, and carefully replaced them.

Pulling his aching body to the bed, he tied himself to the metal frame with the zip ties. He twisted the one he'd cut to make it appear as if it had broken, but hooked it onto his wrist.

He lay back on the paper-thin mattress and stared at the ceiling. It felt good to relax while he thought through all he now knew.

As the shouting outside grew more and more distant, he imagined Leza struggling to get through each day with her little body hurting and her energy vanishing while Quinn withheld her food and used her as a pawn to obtain what he wanted. Paul had to get her out of there. If he left without her, she would be dead in a matter of hours. Quinn would see to that.

There seemed to be only one answer—escape with Leza and get her to a hospital, contact the authorities about Quinn's scheme, and hope they would believe him. Paul's brain whirled with details as a plan of escape formed in his mind. But much depended on things he didn't know. How well was the airfield guarded? If they could make it to the plane, could they reach Juba? Somehow he would have to break into Leza's hut unnoticed. He had a gun, but was he willing to shoot a man? There were so many other lives at stake, not just Leza's. The thought of killing someone hung in the air as he pondered it. There must be another way. He would have to be willing to do whatever it took if he was going to warn the villages.

The quiet outside meant the search had ended. Paul had Cijen to thank for that. Right now, he needed to rest and formulate his plan. As he lay on his back in the sticky Congo heat, he closed his eyes and schemed.

◆ ◆ ◆

When Jim entered the hangar, his neck hair bristled. Something was wrong. Every light in the building was out, even the desk lamp in the office. Jarrod always left that one on. Jim opened the door to the small cubicle and switched on the lights. The desktop was neat and clean. Not a paper to be found. He opened the top drawer of the file cabinet, then the next. Nothing seemed out of place there.

Walking to the metal box on the wall, Jim slid the latch, opened it, and threw the hangar and warehouse breakers on. As the rooms burst with light, the silent orderliness disturbed him. The wings of his plane reached practically from wall to wall since the hangar had been built for smaller aircraft. Slowly Jim walked onto the varnished concrete floor. What was missing? What was wrong with this picture?

"Jarrod?" No response. Jim called again. Still nothing.

Jim suddenly noticed that Jarrod's toolbox was gone. So was his footlocker, but the utility closet where Jarrod kept his flight gear was still padlocked.

Jim noticed the microphone tethered to the console, picked it up, and keyed the control tower.

"This is Captain Jim. Did Jarrod Vincent fly out today? He should be back if he did. It's late."

The question was followed by a pause, then the control tower responded. "Jarrod flew out two days ago. Said he'd be gone for a week. Left you in charge."

"Me? In charge?"

"Sounds like you don't know much about it, Cap'n. Everything okay?"

"I've been working on some other things and haven't been here for a few days. I knew nothing about this." Jim thought for a moment. "Listen, guys, don't worry about it. I'll do some checking and get to the bottom of it. I'm sure it's a misunderstanding. You never know what's on that guy's mind."

"Ten four, Cap'n. Let us know if you need anything. You had us scared for a minute there."

Jim looked around the hangar again as he collected his thoughts. He stopped when he spotted the bolt cutters in his own toolbox. Retrieving them, he snapped the lock off Jarrod's utility closet. Jim stared at an empty three-by-three-meter cubicle. He glanced around the room once more and noticed that several of the maps were missing from the wall.

Jim paced around his Cessna turboprop. This didn't add up. The last conversation he'd had with Jarrod was about the delay in Juba that had kept Jim from being there for Paul. Jarrod hadn't seemed to care, which was unlike him. Or was it?

Jim pulled the records of the flight plans they were required to log. There was nothing listed for Jarrod. He walked outside and checked the hangars one by one. Jarrod's SR22 was gone.

"Okay, Jim. Your best friend's missing, the FBI says your niece was kidnapped, and now Jarrod Vincent is mysteriously AWOL," he said out loud as if speaking to someone in front of him.

Quickening his pace back to his hangar, Jim continued his conversation. "I don't know what all this means, but I've had just about enough. I don't know where you are, Paul and Jessica, but I'm coming. I'll do whatever I can to find you. And if Jarrod had anything to do with this—God help him."

CHAPTER FOURTEEN

Paul sat across from Miju in the dingy corner of the three-room clinic. Outside the door, Cijen stood guard in the courtyard. Paul looked up from his writing to find Miju staring at him.

"I'm trying to work on this formula, but you're making it difficult to concentrate." Paul waited for a response, but Miju only glanced out the door, then stood and walked behind him.

"Miju, I said that—"

"Baba?"

Paul started to stand, but Miju pushed him down as Quinn glared from the doorway, gripping the little girl's arm.

"I wanted you to see she's fine and to remind you what's at stake, Dr. Branson."

Leza's legs wobbled as she struggled to keep her balance.

"Leza, are you okay?"

"I don't feel good." She started to cry.

Paul tried again to stand, but Miju forced him back into the chair.

"Stay down." Miju kept his hands firmly on Paul's shoulders.

Paul took a deep breath to calm himself and smiled. "I'm sorry I can't help you right now, sweet girl. We'll be leaving here soon. I'll be done with my work in a day or two, and then we'll go home. Mr. Quinn promised."

"Okay, Baba. Do you promise too?"

"I promise too."

"Very touching. Now she must go." Quinn pulled Leza out the door and shoved her toward Cijen, causing her to fall on her knees. "Take her to her hut."

"Come, Leza. I will take you." Cijen didn't grab her. He picked her up and nodded subtly to Paul. Relieved that Cijen was carrying her, Paul turned back to his work and tried to concentrate on the formula.

Quinn leaned over Paul. "I need that by tomorrow, or she'll pay with her life. Am I understood?"

Paul ignored the comment. His blood boiled as he stared at the paper on the desk. "If anything happens to that little girl, I will kill you. Do you understand me?"

Quinn moved within centimeters of Paul's face. "Look at me."

Paul looked up.

"Because I don't want the bleeding from your face to deter you from working, I'll let that threat go . . . for now. But hear me, Doctor . . . I need that formula by tomorrow, or she'll die. You're in no position to threaten me."

"It's not enough time. I need more time. This is a difficult formula."

"You have had too much time already. I should have demanded this from you by now. Tomorrow, or she dies. Do you understand?"

"Yeah, I got it."

Quinn walked to the door, but stopped and turned to Paul. "First thing in the morning, Branson. I don't want anything standing in the way of your devotion to the task."

"I said I got it."

"Good." Quinn turned to Miju. "Take him to his hut, but don't tie him tonight. I want him to rest and work on the formula. He's not going anywhere without his darling Leza." Quinn glared back at Paul. "But to be on the safe side, place a second guard at his hut."

Miju nodded. "Understood."

Quinn left the building and crossed the courtyard. Paul gazed in the direction of Leza's hut, wondering if his newly devised plan would still work. It would be dark soon.

Cijen carried Leza to her room and gently sat her on the hard bed. He took a bottle of water and washed her scuffed knees. Then he stroked her hair, and it suddenly seemed familiar. Picking up a tattered brush with very few bristles left from the table, he gently worked the kinks out of her dirty short brown hair. It looked as if no one had done it for quite some time. He recalled doing this before, but not for Leza. He closed his eyes and remembered. His little sister had sat on the chair in their house as he brushed her hair in the morning sun. She'd had a beautiful smile and a giggle full of life. He missed her, she—

"Mr. Cijen, are you going to hurt Baba?"

He sat on the bed beside her. "No, I would never hurt him. Don't worry."

"He doesn't look good. He's all skinny now, and when he smiles, it isn't a real smile."

"He's very busy, and he's been hurt. But he's doing better and getting stronger each day."

Leza lay back and curled into a ball. "Mr. Cijen . . ."

"Yes?"

"Am I going to die?"

He swallowed hard. "I don't think so. Why?"

"I think I am. I don't feel good, and Babatunde gave me medicine in the village to make me better. But since I've been here, I haven't had any." Leza paused, and Cijen tried to think of what to say. "It's okay if I die, because I'll get to see Mama."

"Your mother is dead?"

Her eyes filled with tears. "The men who came to take me from my house—Mr. Quinn's men—they killed her."

Cijen stood. "Are you sure, Leza?"

"Yes. I closed my eyes and it was dark, but I heard them. I heard her die."

A flood of memories struck him. His parents screaming. His sister . . .

"Please, Mr. Cijen. Don't tell Baba about Mama. It would make him too sad. I don't want him to be more sad."

Cijen hugged her. "I'm so sorry. I won't say anything, I promise. You're going to be okay, though." He gave her an extra squeeze. "I have to go now. I'll turn out your light. Try to sleep."

Leza gave him a weak smile. "Okay, Mr. Cijen. G'night."

Cijen turned the light out and left the hut. Standing on the front porch, he took a deep breath and tried to calm his growing rage. He looked at the stars and thought of his little sister—and how she'd died. He'd just finished brushing her hair that morning when he heard his father calling him from outside, where he was struggling to carry the fish he had caught already, even though it was still morning.

Cijen remembered running out of his hut, only to see his father's smile turn to a look of horror. Cijen had whipped around to gain his first glimpse of Jason Quinn. When one of Quinn's men grabbed Cijen on that bright, sunny morning, his father tried to stop him. When another of Quinn's men entered the hut, causing his sister's screams, Quinn's response was something Cijen had blocked from his mind—until now.

How could he have forgotten the horror of that day? How could he have forgiven the man who took his family from him?

The guard told Paul to get to work on what Quinn needed and then left the room, locking the door from the outside. Paul looked out the window at the dark night sky. Men's voices drifted through the bamboo wall from the porch outside his door.

He turned off the light and tiptoed to the back of the hut and moved the first board a centimeter to the side, but a soldier stood underneath the hut with a rifle strapped to his shoulder. Paul would have to wait. He silently made his way back to the bed to give things outside a chance to settle down. He lay down and, still exhausted from his jaunt through the compound the night before, fell asleep.

Jessica woke up on a cot in a small room. Her head spun, and a wave of nausea swept over her. Dehydrated and weak, she sat up and tried to remember—how had she gotten here? Panic gripped her, but she pushed it down.

Where am I?

Swinging her legs off the edge of the bed, she tried to think.

Concentrate.

Pieces of memory began to surface. Vaguely she recalled the horror of the attack in the safe house and then traveling—the never-ending traveling.

Muffled voices filtering through an air vent caught her attention. When she stood, she stumbled and grabbed the footboard of the bed for support. After a moment, she gained her bearings and crossed the room to move closer to the vent, but it was near the ceiling, and she couldn't understand what they were saying. She looked out the window at the moon high in the sky. It must be the middle of the night. She listened again. The name Branson came up, but they could be referring to her father, not her.

On the other side of the room, the glow of the moon pressed through the sheer curtains covering a window. Jessica eased her way back to the foot of the bed and braced herself. The dizziness was worse when she moved. Reaching for the window while still holding onto the bed, she parted the curtains with her hand. Her heart sank. Bars on the window kept her prisoner.

She gazed out at the moonlit lake surrounded by rolling hills and trees. A building to the left blocked her view, but when she turned to the right, a streetlamp illuminated the road sign below it. It read, "Kampala, 3 km."

"Kampala?" Jessica whispered and leaned back from the window. "Victoria . . . Lake Victoria." She'd been there before with her father. Kampala was about thirty-five kilometers north of Entebbe.

"Uganda?" she said under her breath.

The voices grew louder. Jessica carefully slid her bed closer to the wall where the air vent was located and stood on the mattress. The dizziness hit her again, and she almost fell. Leaning against the wall and listening, she could hear the men speaking in English of a kidnapping. Were they talking about her? They used the name Branson again, but they were talking about the Congo.

Congo? Daddy, are you in the Congo?

The voices stopped, and Jessica heard chairs moving, then footsteps. She slid from the bed and eased it back to where it had been as the door swung open and a man burst into the room.

"Hello, Ms. Branson. Are you enjoying your stay?" His sarcasm was undisguised.

Jessica clutched the bedpost, staring at the tall black man. "Who are you? What am I doing here?"

The man walked past her and took a seat on the edge of her bed while Jessica stood at the foot. "My name is Baraka. Your father works with us. You are here to make sure he continues to do so. It's that simple."

Jessica faced him. "You drugged me and kidnapped me from New York City and brought me to Uganda. You killed American federal agents. The United States will be looking for you."

Baraka grinned. "No doubt. That's one advantage of owning a private jet, a private yacht, a private villa . . . Shall I go on?"

"Don't take me or my father for fools, Mr. Baraka."

"Baraka. Just Baraka. And I wouldn't think of it."

Jessica felt woozy, but she didn't let on. "What do you want from me?"

"Nothing at all, Jessica. Just relax and don't fight this."

"Ms. Branson to you. And don't fight what?"

Baraka smirked arrogantly. "Very well, Ms. Branson. Don't fight being here. Consider yourself insurance. Very expensive insurance."

"Insurance?"

"If your father doesn't cooperate, we will remind him of his beautiful daughter."

Jessica felt the blood drain from her face. "Cooperate?"

"As I said, it's simple. If he does what we say, you live, although it might be nice to keep you for a while. You're quite lovely. We'll see." Baraka rose and walked to the foot of the bed where Jessica stood.

She backed away, but the wall stopped her. "Don't touch me." Goose bumps formed on her delicate skin. Baraka's wandering eyes betrayed his intentions. She held her ground, but when he stroked her cheek with the back of his hand, she punched him on the jaw with her fist.

Baraka grunted. "That will cost you." He slapped her face with his open hand, knocking her to the floor.

He turned on his heel, opened the door, and walked into the hallway. As he did, Jessica heard him say to someone she couldn't see, "We leave at dawn."

The obnoxious clank of the dead bolt once again woke Paul from his slumber. The lights burst on. He opened his eyes and sat straight up in bed, squinting from the brightness.

"What are you doing? You're supposed to be working! That's why you were untied tonight!"

Paul was confused. He stared at his untied arms and legs. Then all at once he remembered. He fell asleep! This was the night he was going to—

"Get up and get to work, you fool. Quinn will have your head if you don't finish this tonight. Mine too!"

Paul hopped out of bed. "You are so right. Thank you for waking me. Just needed a nap. You saved my life!" He went to shake the guard's hand, but the man snatched it from Paul's grasp.

"Just get to work."

Paul sat on the bed and picked up his pad and pencil. "Thanks again. I got this," he called as the guard left the room and bolted the door.

Paul fought growing panic and hurried to peek through the gap in the boards at the ground below. The guard under his hut faced the front of the building with his back toward him.

Carefully Paul lifted the first board and listened. At first he heard nothing. Then there were voices—men's voices from the porch. The guards were yelling at each other about something. Paul looked down at the guard under the hut again. He was still standing about two meters away with his back to Paul. The light now shone through the open hole. The guard would eventually notice, but for now he just shouted at the men on the porch above to be quiet. They didn't respond.

Slowly Paul lifted the second board, creating an opening he could poke his head through. Suddenly it slipped from his hands, and he watched it fall through the opening. When it dropped, he heard it rattle as it hit the support post. Paul crouched in frozen disbelief.

The sentry's footsteps approached the beam of light now projecting onto the ground below. Paul's heart was in his throat. The dark figure appeared directly beneath the opening, looking up with wide eyes. Without hesitation, Paul stood and dropped straight through the hole onto him, knocking him down before he could cry out.

Paul's fighter instincts kicked into action as he wrapped his arm around the dazed sentry's neck, flipped him onto his stomach, and squeezed him in a headlock from behind. The man dug his nails into Paul's arm, almost causing him to cry out in pain, but he pulled harder against the man's windpipe. A sickening crackle in the front of the guard's neck nauseated Paul, but he held on until the squirming stopped. With a fractured larynx, suffocation comes quickly.

Paul crawled off the man and listened for the guards on the porch. Their voices grew louder, still arguing. He looked at the lifeless form on the ground, and it struck him—he'd killed a man. With his bare hands, he'd killed a man. He had no time to dwell on it. It was time for action, and he had a plan.

Paul lifted the dead sentry's arm and checked his watch—it was 4:20 a.m. He pulled the black watch off and slipped it on his own wrist. He had just over an hour before sunrise. He dragged the body two or three meters to the tall grass behind the hut to hide it from the guards on the porch. Scanning the fence, he saw no other sentries nearby.

Paul removed the dead man's Glock, rifle, and camo shirt, and put the shirt on. It was a tight fit, but it would do. He tucked it in, cinched the belt and holster around his waist, and checked the Glock for ammo.

The guards on the porch sounded as if they might come to blows soon. Paul retrieved Adanna's pistol from under the rock where he had left it the night before and tucked it into the back of his belt. He brushed the dirt from the barrel of the rifle as he looked it over. The full thirty-five-round ammo clip added quite a bit of weight.

Paul had no delusions of shooting his way out of camp. He'd be full of holes before he made it twenty meters. The Sudanese army attack on the day he was shot proved that. Rubbing his hands in the moist soil and wiping them on his face, he dulled his fair skin. Then he shinnied up the support pole far enough to put the floorboards back in place so the light wouldn't draw attention.

Slinging the rifle over his shoulder, Paul left the shelter of the tall grass, circled to the right to avoid the arguing guards on the porch, and made his way slowly across the clearing. It would attract attention if he ran, so he took his time. Once he was close enough to Leza's hut, he ducked behind nearby buildings. The structures cast long shadows in the moonlight, and Paul used them to his advantage, edging closer and closer to Leza's hut. Huddling in the tall grass behind it, he waited for the guards to pass.

The moment they did, Paul darted to the hut and squeezed into the one-and-a-half-meter-high space underneath it. Something crawled onto his neck, but he brushed it off without looking. A ray of light from the room above filtered into his cramped, damp surroundings and caught his eye. He pulled himself to it and peeked into the room—the light was on, and Leza was curled up on her bed with her right foot hanging off. He saw no one else.

"Leza," Paul whispered with his mouth to the small opening in the floor. "Leza." He looked back through the hole as she swung her legs to the edge of the bed.

"Baba?" she called softly.

"Shhh. Down here." Paul stuck his finger through the hole and wiggled it. Leza dropped to the floor and peeked with one eye into the tiny opening. "It's me, little girl."

"Baba," she whispered back. "How did you find me?"

"I'll tell you, but I need you to come outside without anyone knowing. Can you do that?" He spoke softly, barely loud enough to be heard.

"I want to." She paused. "I'm not very strong, and I can't go out by myself. But my light is on because Marna, the woman taking care of me, went to the outhouse behind the hut. She's coming back any minute, and I can tell her I need to go to the toilet. She'll bring me out. She doesn't want me wetting the bed."

"Leza, I'm taking you away from here tonight. We're leaving."

"Baba . . . how?"

"I have a plan."

"Okay. I'll ask Marna. Shhh. Here she comes."

Paul quickly moved behind the outhouse and waited. A moment later, Marna appeared with Leza in her arms. Leaving Leza in the outhouse, Marna hurried back to the hut. Paul walked around and opened the door.

Leza smiled when she saw his camo shirt. "You're dressed like a soldier."

"Oh. Yeah. I borrowed this from one of the guys." Paul scooped her up.

"I didn't really have to go." Leza wrapped her arms around him.

He held her close and ducked behind the outhouse, hurriedly following a path that would keep the latrine between them and the hut until he could find cover. As soon as they were able, they hid behind the tall grass. Paul crouched on the ground to catch his breath. "What did you tell Marna that made her run back to the hut?"

"I told her I was going to throw up. She hates it when I throw up."

"You're a smart little girl."

Once he caught his breath, Paul took Leza in his arms and ran for cover under the next hut, then the next. Working his way to the edge of the compound, he forged through the grass, using it for cover while he held Leza's frail body close to his. Her thin arms were clasped tight around his neck.

"Where are we going, Baba?"

"You'll see."

Paul made his way through the trees down the narrow path from the compound to the airstrip—the only way to reach it. He hugged the edge of the trail until he arrived at the inner fence and gently set Leza on the ground a hundred meters from the gate. Two guards with assault rifles stood nearby.

Paul peered through the five-meter-high chain-link fence that separated them from a second fence twenty meters away. Coils of barbed wire on the ground reinforced the area between them. Forty meters beyond the second fence, a metal lean-to covered a small white aircraft. He recognized it as a Cessna 172.

"Good. I know that plane. I've flown those before. We need to dig below this fence so we can squeeze under it."

Paul looked to his left to see if they could move farther away from the treetop outpost, but realized that the guards would be able to see them from there. Surrounded by one-meter-high grass, Paul found a suitable stone and began to dig under the fence, trying not to make any noise that would alert the guards.

"Leza!" A voice in the distance called her name.

"Marna is looking for you now. She'll get help soon, and eventually they'll check my hut to make sure nothing's wrong. And . . ." Paul gave

Leza a look. "They won't like what they find." He turned his attention to the hole and dug harder. "I don't believe this."

"What's wrong?"

"Part of the fence goes underground." He found a sharper stone, but the farther he dug, the denser the ground became. He stopped for a moment to rest, then started again.

"Leza?" Marna's voice and several others echoed through the compound.

"This fence is buried so deep I can't find the bottom." Paul looked at the watch on his wrist. "We have thirty minutes until sunrise, that's it." He looked at the second fence beyond the first. "I'm not sure we'll make it in time."

"You won't make it at all."

Paul knew it wasn't Cijen's voice behind him this time.

CHAPTER FIFTEEN

Paul turned as floodlights along the fence illuminated the airstrip. The guard stood three meters from them with his rifle aimed at Paul's chest. Paul dropped the rock and pushed Leza behind him.

"Did you think changing your shirt and smearing mud on your face would fool anyone? Drop the rifle."

Paul slid the strap off his shoulder and lowered the weapon to the ground.

"Now the pistol. Take it from the holster with two fingers and drop it in front of you."

With his thumb and index finger, Paul grasped the pistol he had taken from the dead guard under his hut, lifted it from the holster, and dropped it on the ground. He hoped the man hadn't seen Adanna's pistol tucked in the back of his belt.

"I appreciate your attempt to escape. Quinn will reward me for this. Get on the ground and put your hands behind your head."

"Don't hurt her. It's me you want."

Paul knelt on the ground in front of the guard just as a shot rang out. The guard dropped to the ground beside him.

"What the—"

"On your feet!"

Paul turned toward the man barking the order as two other sentries from the airstrip ran up behind him.

"Cij?"

"Quiet. Let me talk," Cijen whispered as the others approached with their weapons drawn. "This is Quinn's prisoner," Cijen shouted. "He killed this man. Go. Find Quinn!"

"We can't abandon our post. We have to watch the airstrip."

"Fine. I'll go. But whatever you do, don't turn your back on him. Look what he's doing right now!"

As the guards turned to Paul, Cijen fired at one of them, killing him instantly. The second guard reached for his revolver, but before he could act, Paul shot him with Adanna's pistol. Leza screamed.

"It's okay," Paul said, hugging her. "Cijen is here. We're going to be fine." He turned to Cijen. "What's going on, Cij? You just put yourself in a lot of trouble."

"I don't belong here. I know that now." Cijen turned toward the compound. "We need to go—all of us. The shots will draw the men here, and it won't take long. Dr. Paul, if you have a plan, we should get to it."

Paul nodded. "The plane. Get me to the plane."

"You can fly? You're a pilot?"

"I can fly, Cij. Let's go."

Cijen took off running toward the gate as Paul scooped up Leza and hurried after him. "Cij, can you buy me a few minutes to get the plane ready?"

Cijen shot a hole through the lock on the inner gate, pushed it open, and ran to the outer gate. He fired, and the second lock exploded into fragments. The gate sprang open.

"Go. They can't see the airstrip until they come around that corner. I'll slow them down, but hurry!" Cijen waved Paul toward the plane and turned his attention to the path leading to the compound.

Paul ran for the aircraft carrying his precious bundle. He could hear men yelling in the distance, getting closer and closer as they rushed down the narrow airfield path. At any moment Quinn's guards would burst through, but he needed time. Just a couple of minutes would do.

"He's over there!" Paul heard Cijen yell as he reached the opposite side of the plane with Leza. "He ran that way!" Paul heard Cijen yelling again. "I'll guard the plane! Find him!"

From the corner of his eye, Paul saw Cijen running toward the Cessna.

"Come on, Cij!" Paul opened the passenger door, pulled the seat forward, laid Leza's tiny body in the backseat, and buckled her in.

"I love you, Baba."

Paul didn't slow down. "I love you too, little girl." He pushed the passenger seat back in place and untied the wing tethers that held the plane on the ground whenever a windy storm came through. He kicked the chocks from the wheels and crawled across the passenger seat so no one would spot him opening the pilot door. For the moment, he was out of their line of sight, but he knew it wouldn't be for long.

"Hurry, Dr. Paul!"

Paul switched on the ignition and pulled the headset into place. The engine slowly turned, building up speed as it prepared to fire. Once it did, it would draw everyone's full attention. Uncaring, Paul throttled up and turned toward the tree line.

He heard Cijen fire about twenty more rounds. Looking back, Paul saw at least fifteen guards a hundred meters away running toward the airfield. Cijen reloaded and turned a barrage of lead into the advancing men. They dove for cover.

Paul pulled the plane forward as Cijen ran toward him. When he was three meters away, he fell to the ground, grabbing his leg.

Paul throttled back the engine and was about to get out when Cijen waved frantically. "Go! Go! I'm okay!"

"I'm not leaving you! Get in!"

Cijen fired again into the onslaught of advancing men, then limped quickly to the plane. Paul shoved the copilot door open, grabbed Cijen's shirt, and dragged him into the passenger front seat. Paul hit full throttle and headed down the airfield before Cijen's door was closed. Cijen grabbed the handle, pulled it shut, and latched it.

Paul looked back. The guards crowded the runway behind them now. He yelled, "Put that on and buckle in, Cij!" He pointed toward the headset. Cijen let go of his leg long enough to fasten his seat belt and pull the headphones on.

"Can you hear me, Cij?" Paul spoke in a normal voice—with a little extra adrenaline.

Cijen nodded. "Yes, I hear you."

The sun's first peek over the distant mountains cast a faint glow across the green valley. Paul thanked God for the light on the horizon. As they roared down the field, several bullets hit the side of the plane behind their seats. Leza screamed.

Paul yelled back, not able to take his eyes off the field, "Are you okay, baby?"

Cijen twisted in his seat and reached back to Leza. "She's okay," he said through the headphones. "Now fly this stupid thing!"

Paul scanned the instruments. The short runway would make take-off a challenge. But if Quinn could do it, he could do it.

Several more bullets hit the top of the plane and the tail, then another came through the cockpit and splintered the window beside Paul. He kept his eyes on the horizon as the tree line approached. He needed more speed, more runway.

As they neared the trees, he rotated the nose off the ground. The plane climbed to four, eight, and then ten meters. Paul needed more. Cijen gripped the side of his seat with his left hand and the hole in his leg with his right.

The screaming engine strained to pull them over the trees. Paul banked left to miss the tallest ones. The landing gear skimmed the upper branches on the first few. Slowly they lifted over the forest. A thin blanket of early morning mist rose from the humid woodlands as they gained altitude.

Paul looked back at Leza. She had pulled a blanket from under the seat and lifted it far enough to peek over the edge at him. Her pale forehead was covered in sweat. He spoke loud enough for her to hear him over the engine. "I'm going to get you home. We'll find help soon, okay?"

She nodded and hugged the blanket.

Paul checked his gauges; they had a full fuel tank, and the altimeter read half a kilometer. He had started to relax when a motion in his peripheral vision seized his attention: the vapor trail of a rocket-propelled grenade approaching.

"Hang on!"

Paul banked hard right and pulled back on the stick. They entered a steep, spiraling pitch. If Leza screamed, he couldn't hear it over the engine. Cijen yelled at the top of his lungs. The missile whooshed past them, missing by a few meters.

Paul rolled the plane right side up and pulled out a quarter of a kilometer from the treetops. He trimmed the flaps and kept the engine at full throttle to regain altitude.

There was a moment of silence before Cijen blurted out, "Don't ever do that again!"

Paul reached back and patted Leza. She offered a weak smile, but her eyes were filled with tears.

As the aircraft continued to climb, Paul slowly relaxed once he knew they were out of missile range. He turned to Cij. "How's your leg?"

"It hurts."

"Tear your pants. Let me see."

Cijen tore the opening bigger. Paul could tell the bullet had entered from the back and come out the front. The bleeding was controlled, so he knew it hadn't hit an artery.

"See if there's a first aid kit in here."

Cijen scouted around until he found one under the back seat.

"Okay, Cij. Pack that with the gauze pads and wrap the elastic bandage around it. That will keep it from bleeding. We'll need to clean it out, but we can deal with that later."

Cij bandaged the wounds as instructed, then slumped back in his seat, exhausted.

"I'm glad you're with me, Cij. We would have died back there without you. What changed your mind?"

Cijen paused as if thinking. "My sister. I forgot my family somehow. There is much pain in remembering, but I remembered her." He smiled as if recalling a pleasant memory, but then his smile disappeared. "Quinn killed her. He murdered my whole family. My sister, my mother, my father . . . He made me believe I was special. But I wasn't special. I was an orphan—because he made me one." Cijen gazed out the window, but Paul was certain he was seeing something other than the scenery as he recalled his past.

Paul briefly surveyed the landscape below. "Cij, I'm sorry about your family, but you're part of mine now." Cij offered a small smile and a nod. "So let's figure out where we're going. Can you find a map? From the sunrise and the terrain, I have an idea for the direction, but I need to see where we're coming from in the Congo."

Cijen searched under his seat and Paul's. "Here. I found one." He opened it and spread it on his lap.

"How far is it to Juba?"

Cijen studied the map. "About four hundred fifty kilometers from where we took off."

Paul nodded. "I know this plane. It's a Cessna 172. It has a full fuel tank, and we are doing about one hundred thirty knots. We can be in

Juba in less than two hours." That gave Paul a reason to smile. "I just stole a terrorist's plane."

Paul turned to check Leza again. Her sweet face glowed in the early morning sun. She was sleeping peacefully. Paul reached back and pulled the blanket up to her neck. After several minutes, he turned to Cijen. "Take a nap. You need some rest."

Cijen didn't argue. He put his head back and stared out the window. Within minutes, he was snoring.

As Paul set the course for Juba, he recalled the first time he had taken Nicki flying. She was only seventeen. He'd had his pilot's license for a month. What he didn't realize was that she hated to fly. She screamed most of the trip.

As Paul remembered that day, he instinctively checked his gauges. The fuel was falling faster than expected. He tapped the gauge.

Cijen opened his eyes. "How long have I been sleeping?"

Paul checked the watch he'd taken from the guard under his hut. "About thirty minutes." He looked back at Leza—she was still asleep.

"Cij, once we're in Juba, we can tell the authorities what Quinn is planning. I also have to get Leza to a hospital. Juba has one of the best in South Sudan."

"Understood."

"But we may have a problem."

"What problem?"

"We left the airfield with a full tank, right?"

"Yes. Quinn always keeps it fully fueled. And I remember you checking it after we were airborne. It was full. Why?"

Paul fiddled with the gauges on the instrument cluster. "Because now the gauge reads a quarter tank. We're losing fuel. We should still have better than three-quarters of a tank. They must have hit our fuel line or tanks when they shot at us."

"But that would have made us explode."

Paul shook his head. "Not true, Cij. If the bullet doesn't ignite a spark when it hits, it just makes a hole—a hole that causes a fuel leak." He checked the setting on the engine fuel consumption from the flow meter. "It's dropping too quickly for the amount of fuel the engine is consuming. We're definitely leaking fuel. We aren't going to make it to Juba."

Cijen pulled out the map to look for closer airports. After about three minutes, Paul interrupted his search.

"We aren't going to make it to another airport. The gauge is dropping too fast, Cij."

The engine sputtered. "What was that?" Cijen grabbed his seat cushion.

Paul scanned the ground. "Okay. Look . . . I'll need to land soon. We'll find another way to get to Sudan."

"Where are we going to land, Dr. Paul?" Cijen asked. "There's nothing but trees."

"Look for an open spot."

Cijen searched desperately and then picked up the map and studied it. "I don't see anything unless you can land in water."

"Why? Do you see water?"

"Not yet, but the map shows a river just past that mountain range."

Paul eyed the peaks ahead. "Okay. Pray that we can clear that ridge. How far beyond it is the river?"

Cijen checked the map again. "Right on the other side. Not far. Maybe two kilometers."

Paul looked back at Leza sleeping. He wondered how he would find a hospital for her. The engine sputtered again. The gauge read empty. He checked the altitude—one kilometer. He had gained a little in the last few minutes.

"Cij, see what we have as far as supplies in the back. Any water or food?"

Cijen searched behind the seats. "Two bottles of water, that's all."

The engine sputtered again and then again. The third time it faltered and stopped.

"That's it." Paul turned off the ignition.

"We're almost to the ridge. Can we make it?" Cijen stared out the windshield, his body rigid.

"We'll make it. It'll be close, but we'll make it."

An eerie silence filled the little plane as they glided over the treetops by only fifteen meters. They dropped closer and closer to the lush green vegetation on the mountain's precipice as the plane lost altitude and the ridge loomed before them. The silent bird soared ten meters above the trees, then five.

"Hang on. We got this."

They slipped over the tree-covered ridge with only three meters to spare and floated into the valley below.

"There!" Cijen pointed to the river.

"I see it. Good work. Now we have to land this on a winding river."

Paul turned and looked at Leza. She stared at him.

"You okay, sweetie?"

She nodded with only her eyes showing over the edge of the blanket.

"We're going to have to land. We're out of fuel, but I'll take care of you. Okay?"

"Okay, Baba." Leza pulled herself into a fetal position and wrapped the blanket tighter.

"Got your seat belt on?"

"Yes." Leza's faint voice gripped Paul's heart. He could see tears in her eyes again.

"What's the name of that river, Cij?"

"Kibali. It's the Kibali River."

"Where does it go? Is there a waterfall we need to worry about, or does it open up into a bigger body of water?"

"Let me see." Cijen studied the map. "No waterfalls. It gets a little wider as it reaches Uganda, but here it's small."

"Well, it's big enough, and it will have to do." Paul banked right to approach the river from a better angle.

"Dr. Paul, how far did we get from Quinn? Do we have a head start?"

"Yes, we've been flying for an hour. That puts us almost two hundred kilometers ahead of him. In fact, he won't even know where to look for us."

"He may . . ." Cijen buried his face in his hands.

"What? What's the matter?"

"The plane. There's GPS on the plane—a homing device."

"Seriously?"

"Quinn installed it so we could find him if he ever crashed."

Paul shook his head. "When we land, we need to find it and turn it off."

"It can't be shut down even if the ignition is off. It's powered by its own battery and sends a signal for seven days after the power from the airplane is gone."

"Then we'll destroy it."

The quiet rush of wind over the wings would have been soothing if it wasn't so tragic. The ground and river approached quickly, and Paul turned to Leza once more. She lowered the blanket and gave him a weak smile. "I need you to sit up for me and buckle in real good, baby. Okay?"

Leza nodded and did as she was told. Cijen turned to help her.

"Okay. We have a problem, but we're going to get through this," Paul said. "The plane isn't made to land on water, so it's going to sink. We have to get out before it does, or not long after. I know that sounds scary, but we're together, and we can do this."

Paul looked at Leza and then at Cijen. They appeared petrified.

"We're going to make it, guys. Then we'll find someone willing to help us."

Cijen fumbled to fasten his seat belt as Leza spoke. "Are you scared, Baba?"

Paul smiled. "Yes, baby. I'm scared—just a little, though. We can do this. Quinn can't win. We'll be okay. I promise."

Paul tried to calm the fear welling up inside him. He'd never landed on water before, and the trees were coming fast. He maneuvered the aircraft to glide over the bubbling foam, banking to the left and right as he followed the liquid runway. The plane drifted silently over the surface as the trees rose above them on each side of the riverbank.

The landing gear skimmed the surface once and lifted off. The drag on the wheels pulled everyone forward. Paul drew back on the stick to raise the nose and lower the tail. If he could just keep the nose high enough to drag the tail . . .

He called to Leza, "Hang on, sweetie. Hang on tight." He braced for impact. "Let's do this."

Cijen pulled his seat belt tighter. Paul felt the glide path with his hands, making the tiniest adjustments by instinct.

The tail barely touched. But when it did, it slapped the belly of the plane into the river, spewing muddy water through bursting seams of groaning metal. Paul fought the forward momentum as it tried to take the nose over, but the current pulled them too close to the edge, where the left wing caught a tree trunk on the riverbank. The impact tore off the wing and flipped the tiny plane end over end before coming to rest upside down on the surface of the water.

The swirling current turned the aircraft sideways and carried it fifty meters into deeper waters. The twisted wreckage yawed and lifted its remaining wing into the air. For a moment, the little plane remained fixed and motionless, as if floating peacefully. Seconds later, it disappeared into the murky water of the Kibali River.

CHAPTER SIXTEEN

Miju watched the blip on the screen disappear sixty kilometers from the Ugandan border. He stared at the screen, but it never returned.

"How is that possible?" Quinn stormed around the barrels in the warehouse. "How can it just be gone?"

Miju stared at the blank monitor. "I don't know. We had a solid signal. It just—"

"And why in God's name did we have only two men guarding the airstrip? We knew Branson could fly a plane, yet it sat ready for him to use at his leisure." Quinn stood still for a moment and then cursed as he effortlessly punched a hole in a wooden crate. "How did he get out of his hut in the first place, overpower a guard, and take a child while escaping! Has he had military training? This is what I expect you to handle! This should never have happened!" He paced a little more. "I hold you responsible, Miju. You're better than this."

Miju didn't speak.

"And what if your men had managed to shoot him down with a shoulder-fired missile? What then? They fired a rocket at him, Miju!"

"They were never given orders not to shoot him. He was an escaping prisoner, for God's sake, Quinn. Of course they would try to stop him however they could, including shooting your plane out of the sky." Miju paused. Quinn's silence meant he agreed, but it was clear that he didn't like it. "I just don't understand how they missed," Miju added.

"You should be thankful they did, or it would be your head. If they had killed him, all would be lost. And if he makes it to the authorities, we are doomed just the same. He should have been stopped before he reached that plane!"

Quinn fumed, then turned to Miju again. "Could they have found the GPS locator and destroyed it? Is that why they dropped off the grid?"

Miju shook his head. "Hidden in the belly of the plane? Not likely."

"But Cijen helped me install it. He knows where it is."

"He also knows there's no way to reach it from inside the plane. In fact, that was his idea. They'd have to land first and find a way to destroy it. It's self-contained and fully self-powered with an encryption lock that requires your thumbprint. No. It's not possible for anyone but you to turn it off."

"Where were they when the signal vanished? Can you plot that?"

"Already have. Look, the marker was right here, then nothing. I can get you within two meters of the last known location."

Quinn leaned in close to the screen. "Why would they be there?"

"There's no mistake. I've plotted it twice. They're only eight kilometers from Adranga."

Quinn paced. "Something's wrong. Cijen knew nothing about Adranga. He's never been there. They wouldn't land in that area unless they were in trouble. That plane had enough fuel on board to fly to Sudan and back." He stopped, thought, and paced some more. "If we don't retrieve the information in Branson's head, we have to start over.

We need that formula, and we need it before Branson reaches anyone willing to listen to him. The one thing we have going for us is that no one is likely to believe him. He'll sound like a crazy American spouting conspiracy theories. But still, we have nothing without the formula and our secrecy."

"Well, his story may not sound so crazy. The news in America—and other places—is telling the world that he's been kidnapped and that he knows about WMDs, especially chemical forms."

Quinn leaned his palms on the table and stared at the computer screen again. After a long pause, he finally spoke. "Okay. What are the conditions where the signal disappeared? Is there a place they could have set down and retrieved the black box?"

Using the final GPS coordinates, Miju searched Google Earth images. "I see mountains, trees, and a small river. The forest is dense. No roads. No place to land."

"Then they crashed, Miju. They didn't land—they crashed in the trees. We shot holes in the fuel tanks or something, and they ran out and crashed."

Miju shook his head. "No. The GPS would still be working. It's made to withstand anything and keep sending a signal for a week. It's even fireproof. It would easily survive a crash. Even a bad one."

Quinn grimaced. "But if they crashed in the river, is the signal lost, or would it ping once it was submerged?"

Miju looked back at the images. "The water. That would kill the signal. But there is no pinger on that unit. Water-activated pingers are installed in commercial airliners, not small aircraft."

"Look at the images. Are there roads close enough to get us there? Can we reach the place the signal stopped transmitting?"

Miju studied the aerial photos. "There are dirt roads and narrow paths to within a few kilometers. We would have to hike in from there, unless the jeeps can get through. A four-wheel drive could get close."

"Send three vehicles, five men each. They can reach the area by tomorrow morning if they drive all night. You and I will catch up with them tomorrow night. First there is work to do here."

"Why not just fly into Adranga and find a car there?"

Quinn placed his palms on the table. "I no longer have a plane, Miju."

"That's not what I mean. We could have choppers here from Khartoum in hours and fly right to him."

"No. Even if I had a plane, or if we brought Jarrod's from the training camp, Adranga would draw too much attention. If we let our allies in Khartoum know that we need choppers this far inland, they'll assume we lost Branson. No, we have to be careful not to compromise our situation. We must do this quietly. They can't know we need them. They can't know we've failed—at anything."

Miju weighed his words carefully. "We should hurry, Quinn. If we don't find Branson, there's no plan. And if there's going to be a confrontation with the authorities, we need time to prepare. We should send ten men, not fifteen, to—"

"I've given you my orders. Carry them out. What's wrong with you, Miju?"

Miju paused to form his thoughts. "I don't want to drift off track. What are we going to do if we can't find Branson? We're in a bad place if he tells the authorities what we're trying to obtain from him. I'm just thinking about us—about our plans."

Quinn paced for a moment then turned to face Miju. "There's no plan if we don't find Branson in the next forty-eight hours. No formula means no plan. We've tried deploying it on our own and failed many times, even with Manning's help." Quinn paused. "We'll send Jarrod with the men to retrieve Branson. You and I will move forward as planned so we're ready if they find him in time to deploy. If they don't, we'll move the Soman barrels until we're able to regroup and find someone else to help figure out the formula. We have the chemicals. We have the equipment. We just need the recipe."

Miju thought of the insanity of it all. He kept calm. "We lost ten men last night, Quinn—eleven counting Cijen."

"Ten men? Branson killed ten of my men?"

"Between him and Cijen, yes, plus the guard under Branson's hut. He killed him with his bare hands."

Quinn stared at Miju. "We underestimated him. He's more capable than we believed. I respect him for what he's done. He's a brave man."

Miju stood. "What are you saying? That Branson is a worthy adversary? He permanently destroyed my knee and made a fool of me."

"I understand, Miju. But he cannot be allowed to interfere with our destiny. He must be stopped before he reaches the authorities."

Miju knew he shouldn't say anything more. If he uttered the wrong thing, Quinn would throw the blame at him again. They should be in the mode of damage control. Instead, Quinn wanted to attack, as if he hadn't lost control already.

Quinn stopped walking and faced Miju. "Cijen . . . his father fought me in front of him, so I cut off the old man's right hand." Quinn turned and stared out the window as if admiring the view. "Cijen tried to stop the bleeding, but there was too much. At first I suppose he hated me. But I showed him how to live, how to fight, and how to take what he wanted. He loved me for that." Quinn shook his head as if he didn't understand why Cijen would turn on him.

Miju didn't say a word. He concentrated on the computer screen, even though there was nothing new to see.

"I need Branson."

Miju stood and turned to leave. "I understand. I'll get the men ready."

"Miju . . . I need to know you're with me."

Miju stopped at the door without looking back. "I hate losing men, and some good ones died last night. That's all. I'm with you."

Quinn watched as Miju went out the door. He almost said something, but then fell silent, wondering about Miju's loyalty. He turned to the computer screen. "Are you dead, Branson, or hiding from me? I'll find you either way."

◆ ◆ ◆

Paul held his breath under the dark, swirling water. He opened his eyes, but only darkness surrounded him. The thick water burned his eyes. He forced himself to remain calm as he struggled to undo his three-point seat belt. He reached for Cijen's and unlatched it. Panicked, Cijen fought to get free, so Paul grabbed his arms and shoved him through the broken passenger window into the river current.

Paul reached into the rear compartment only to find Leza's seat empty. Frantically he swept his hands through the murky water but couldn't find her. He fought the urge to panic, and a memory flashed through his mind of the day he and Nicki had almost drowned together in the ocean surf.

He had struggled to keep afloat while she, injured on the coral, was unable to help. Her commanding words echoed in his head: "Paul, if you don't calm down, we're both going to die out here." She had tried to stay afloat, but her injured, bleeding leg prevented her from treading water as the tide pulled them out to sea.

"You have to do this for us. You have to swim for both of us."

Paul remembered his exhaustion. "I can't . . . out of air."

"Forget the air. You're here to save me. That's all you need to do . . . save me, or you'll never forgive yourself."

"I can't."

"Yes, you can." Her calm voice had reassured him. "Close your eyes. Control your breathing. You don't need as much oxygen as you think. Tell your body 'no' and calm your breathing. That's it. Now you're doing it."

Nicki's soothing voice now reached Paul in the dark, water-filled cockpit.

He stopped thrashing for Leza and pulled himself into the back of the plane. He slowly pushed the seat cushions and debris out of the compartment and reached up to the floor of the inverted aircraft. The pain in his ears intensified as the wreckage sank deeper.

When the plane hit the river bottom, the sudden jolt forced Paul down to the ceiling. Debris swirled around him as Nicki's voice gave him peace. When his air reserves disappeared, he didn't panic. As the final moments closed in, Leza floated into his lap from the tail of the plane. He grabbed her limp body. It was a miracle. He knew it was.

The current swept them toward the window as if an unseen force were pushing them out. He wrapped his arms around Leza as they were drawn through the narrow, jagged opening. His lungs burned, but he remembered Nicki's words and let the current carry them away from the tumbling pile of jagged steel.

Suddenly they exploded to the surface. Paul gasped, sucking in the sweet, humid air. He lifted Leza's head from the water—she wasn't breathing. With all of his strength, he swam for the shore ten meters away, but didn't fight the current as it swept them downstream. He continued swimming for the riverbank until he was close enough to grab a tree root. The water swirled and bubbled around him, forcing him to move from root to root until he reached one strong enough to use to pull them onto the bank.

He didn't have much time. For several minutes, Leza'd had no air. He checked her neck—a faint pulse. He pushed her body onto the damp ground, climbed up beside her, rolled her onto her stomach, and pushed against her back to compress her lungs. Water spurted from her mouth. He flipped her onto her back, pinched her nose, and breathed into her cold blue lips. She didn't move.

Paul started chest compressions. More water drained from Leza's nose, but she still didn't move. He pinched her nose and breathed again. No response, but her pulse was stronger. He pumped her chest.

"Come on, baby." He pinched her nose again and placed his lips on hers—and she blew dirty water into his face.

He almost fell over backward as Leza coughed and gagged and more water spewed out. She cried and wrapped her arms around him.

"Oh God." Paul held her close.

Abruptly she stopped crying, and her frightened eyes stared at something behind Paul. He turned. A crocodile was approaching, belly dragging on the ground. Massive legs moved it effortlessly through the underbrush, crawling toward them through the greenery three meters away. It stopped and uttered a throaty growl.

Paul scooped Leza into his arms and faced the croc as it opened its mouth, grunted, and smacked its jaws. Paul backed away, but the croc matched his movement, closing the distance with each step. As Paul picked up his pace, he slipped in the mud and fell back against a large boulder with Leza in his arms. He scrambled to regain his footing, but the wet, slippery ground refused to give him traction. He reached for Adanna's pistol in his belt—it was gone.

The croc snapped its jaws, alerting other crocs that this meal belonged to him. When it bulldozed through the shrubbery toward them, Paul had nowhere to go. He held Leza tight against his chest, closed his eyes, and waited for the end.

The shot made him jump, and his eyes popped open. A second shot hit just above the croc's snout. The monster lizard writhed, its enormous tail slinging leaves, bushes, and dirt as it thrashed about.

The third shot stopped all movement. Paul looked up. Cijen stood on a rock formation four meters away with a smoking Glock in his hand and a grin on his face.

"You are hungry, Dr. Paul?"

Paul shook his head in disbelief. "I don't know how I ever survived without you, my friend."

"Neither do I," Cijen said as he found his footing down the rocks. "A man must learn to run from the crocodile or ride it. And no one can ride it." He smiled again.

"Are there more of these things out here?"

"There are always more, Abdu. Are you okay, Leza?" Cijen asked as he brushed his hand over her head.

She nodded without speaking.

"You called me 'Abdu.' Why?"

"She calls you many things: Baba, Babatunde, Dr. Paul, but when I heard her call you Abdu, I knew who you were."

"I'm a man, Cijen. Just like you."

Cijen spoke as if he didn't hear him. "We must go, Dr. Paul. We are in croc and snake country. It's not safe here. The snakes hang from branches, so keep your eyes open. They will drop from above."

Paul stood with Leza still in his arms and noticed Cijen limping. "Your leg's bleeding again, Cij." He found a spot in the folds of the roots, checked for snakes, then set Leza down. "Let me look at that."

Cijen sat, and Paul carefully unwrapped the elastic bandage and examined the gaping wound on the front of his thigh. He felt the back of Cijen's leg. A smaller hole, the point of entry, bled a little. Paul tore off a wad of cloth from his own sleeve, twisted it into a knot, and pushed it into the wound. Cijen grimaced but didn't scream.

"You called me 'friend,'" Cijen said.

"Yeah, I did. You're one of the best friends I've ever had, Cij. You've saved my life and Leza's several times in the last few hours, and you saved my butt the night before. You are definitely my friend." Paul laughed, but Cijen didn't.

"I've never had one," Cijen responded.

Paul paused while redressing his wound. "What do you mean?"

Cijen shook his head. "A friend. I've never had a friend."

"You have one now. It's everyone else's loss that they didn't know you as a friend." Paul patted Cijen on his good leg. "Now—we are going to find some food and then transportation. But which way do we go?"

Cijen pulled a soggy map from his pocket.

"You brought the map?"

"Of course. I put it in my pocket before we reached the water."

"You're a genius, Cij. Can you tell where we are?"

They spread the map on the ground and looked for landmarks. "That mountain over there is this one on the map." Cijen pointed to the formation in the distance and then at the map.

"I think you're right. That would mean that the town, Adranga, would be this way." Paul pointed in the direction away from the mountain range. "How long do you think it will take to get there?"

"Maybe two hours with my bad leg."

Paul took off the camo shirt he'd stolen from the guard and made a sling with it to carry Leza but still have his arms free. He felt a little dizzy and stumbled but caught himself.

"Are you okay?"

Paul nodded. "Yeah, I think I'm just exhausted and thirsty . . . and hungry. I'm kind of weak, I guess."

"Do you want me to carry Leza?"

"No. Not with that leg, Cij. I'll be okay."

Paul sat again as he held Leza. "She would know what to do."

Cijen leaned against a tree across the path from him. "What do you mean? Who would know what to do?"

Paul looked at Leza in his arms and held her tight. What was he doing? How was he ever going to get this little girl to safety? If he hadn't returned to Africa, Leza would be living out her days with her mother in peace—even if they would have been shortened. With the trouble they were in, he wondered if this would have happened if he'd just stayed home.

"Dr. Paul?"

Paul looked up. "Sorry, Cij. Just had to rest for a minute. Let's go."

They walked for an hour through the dense undergrowth. Spotting a bluff in the distance, they traveled toward it to keep from walking in circles. Paul's damp shirt stuck to his skin, and the aching in his chest worsened from the weight of the papoose digging into his shoulder, but it was easier than walking with both arms holding Leza.

"Just out of curiosity, how many rounds do you have left in that pistol, Cij?"

They stopped walking. Cijen pulled the pistol from its holster, popped out the clip, and counted the rounds. "I have three left, with one in the chamber. Four altogether."

"Okay. I hope we don't need any, but the way this day has been . . . you know?"

"Yes. That's true."

They each took a deep breath and then set their sights on Adranga.

The morning sun poured in through Jessica's curtains. She pushed them aside and carefully peeked out. With no one in sight, she opened the window and pulled as hard as she could against the bars. The steel rods didn't budge.

Examining them from top to bottom for a weak link didn't help. There was none. The welded seams proved that this would not be the way out. Jessica slid the bed near the vent and pulled on the metal cover to remove it, hoping the small opening of the duct would afford her enough room to fit her slender body through. Jessica paused when she heard voices. As she listened quietly, the sounds faded. She pulled her upper body into the vent opening.

Wait . . . did the door just unlock?

She scrambled to pull herself into the vent, but a large hand gripped her ankle firmly and yanked her from the air duct, sending her flopping onto the mattress. She kicked at the man, but he grabbed her legs, dragged her to the floor, and held her down. Seconds later she felt the burn of a needle as it pushed through her jeans into her thigh. The rush of the injection entering her bloodstream made her head spin.

Baraka entered the room and stood over her. "Time to see your father."

As Jessica drifted off, she heard a woman's voice say, "We have a problem."

◆　◆　◆

"I've come to a conclusion, Miju. I'm afraid that my lovely wife did something very bad." Quinn snipped off the end of a cigar with a guillotine cutter, sniffed the length of the fresh-smelling tobacco, and placed it in his mouth. The two men sat on the steps of the warehouse.

"What do you mean?"

"One of the guards told me Adanna spoke with Branson while Cijen was guarding him. It was the day when Branson passed out on the trip back from Botan. It was also the day before the mysterious man wandered into the compound. You remember, the man we never found? The man Cijen said he saw in the tall grass but disappeared?"

Miju nodded, and Quinn continued. "Two days later, Branson escaped with Leza and Cijen." Quinn lit the cigar and took a few heavy, satisfying puffs.

"How could Adanna have helped him escape?" Miju wondered.

"I don't know, but her missing pistol concerns me. She says she misplaced it, but I don't believe her. When I asked her directly about meeting with Branson that day, she stumbled and didn't know what to say." Quinn took another puff, then another, and released the smoke slowly, as if it brought him pleasure. Finally he spoke.

"I want you to place a guard at her door. She's not to go anywhere until I figure this out. We'll take her with us to Mangai instead of leaving her here. I may be staying there for a while if we don't find Branson in time and need a place to lie low."

Miju was taken aback. "We don't allow our women to visit the compound in Mangai for good reason. We can't have them knowing about the girls we're trading. It would mean chaos. You've never allowed this before."

"She goes with us for a reason. If Adanna delivers a boy, I am blessed. If it is a girl, they both die."

Miju didn't know what to say.

"Hanna goes too. I expect casualties as in every battle, and we need 'Dr. Hanna.'" Quinn paused. "And someone else will be there."

Miju's puzzled expression seemed to amuse Quinn. "Someone else?"

"I believe I have the bases covered, although I never counted on Branson getting away from me. He's the first man to do so. But if we find him, Miju, we must have his loyalty. If Leza dies, or if he continues to resist, I've found someone who ensures his cooperation."

"Are you going to tell me?" Miju was losing patience.

Quinn placed his hand on Miju's shoulder. "I have Jessica Branson, our doctor's daughter. She's on her way to Mangai as we speak."

Miju's heart sank deep within him. He stared at Quinn a moment too long.

"What is it?" Quinn demanded.

"How did you do that? How did you perform an international kidnapping without even me knowing?"

"Stop pouting, Miju. I have contacts everywhere, and my network is expanding. This is the beginning, and everyone wants a piece. There are billions at stake."

Miju was beside himself. He didn't care about the quiet kidnapping of a doctor, the whereabouts of whom no one knew—no ransom, no trail, no risk—but becoming an international criminal hunted by the United States was different.

"What's the matter? It's a good plan."

"Where does it end?" Miju felt he had to ask.

"It ends with us having more money than God."

"But we don't even have Branson anymore, and you've kidnapped his daughter through a network I know nothing about. I'm part of this, and I should know. And what good is she to us now that Branson is missing?"

Quinn grabbed him by the collar. "What's going on, Miju?"

Miju recognized the look in Quinn's eyes he'd grown to hate. "I thought we were partners. Now you're bringing in people I don't know—like Jarrod Vincent—and using networks I've never heard of to kidnap people in the United States."

Quinn smirked and halfway released his grip on Miju's shirt. "So that's it? I never thought I would see this from you."

Miju tried to read the look on Quinn's face. "See what?"

"You're jealous." Quinn brushed the wrinkle from Miju's shirt. "I'm sorry, my friend. I never thought about the fact that I was leaving you in the dark."

Miju took a deep breath. "We have a network in the United States?"

Quinn nodded. "And it's growing. The wealthy always want to be wealthier, no matter the cost . . . or location. It doesn't make any difference if the product is drugs or people, there's always a buyer."

Miju attempted to take it all in. "What's next?"

"We find Branson."

Miju's head spun with the magnitude of what Quinn had done by bringing Jessica Branson overseas. He was in over his head and didn't realize it. Quinn was his own worst enemy, and Miju was his right hand.

"Go now. Secure Adanna and assign the guard."

"I'll take care of it." Miju turned and set off to do Quinn's bidding.

"You worry me sometimes, Miju," Quinn called after him. "But I think now I understand."

Miju left the building, but all he could think about was Quinn spinning out of control. If he'd developed a network that reached outside of Africa, he was involved with men who would kill them if anything went wrong. And things were going wrong.

As he walked toward Adanna's hut, Miju wondered what would happen if Paul Branson really was The Chosen. If he truly was Abdu, then nothing else mattered, except . . . Miju was on the wrong side.

Paul crouched in the bushes overlooking the small house. Cijen took a position a little closer.

"We're still five kilometers from Adranga, but there's a truck beside that building." Cijen pointed to it.

Paul nodded. "We need it if we're going to get Leza to a hospital. This is about as far as I can carry her. My strength is gone."

"Let's see if they'll be reasonable." Cijen handed Paul the pistol. "Come if I need you." He stood and walked toward the building. When he got close, a woman came out of the front door with a shotgun aimed at him. Cijen stopped, raised his hands, and spoke in Arabic. She didn't appear to understand. He tried Dinka, and that worked.

Cijen and the woman argued for a moment. Then Cijen turned, faced Paul, and motioned for him to come out, although he continued to hold his hands in the air.

Paul took a deep breath and looked at Leza in his arms. For her, he would do anything. When he stood, his knees buckled a little, but he got his footing. He walked toward the woman, who studied his every move as she held the shotgun on Cijen.

Paul felt suddenly dizzy and weak. He stumbled again and stopped. He didn't want to drop the precious bundle in his arms. His head spun, and he fell to his knees. He watched as the woman rushed forward. Then his world went black.

Hanna crossed the courtyard to Adanna's hut carrying a tray of food she had prepared. The man guarding the door seemed out of place to her, since Adanna had never required such measures before.

"I brought her some food. I would like to give it to her myself."

"I'm not allowed to let you in, Hanna . . . sorry. Miju left me with strict orders."

"Miju's not here, and I'm just a woman. What harm can I do?" Hanna spoke as gently as she could. "I won't tell anyone."

The guard fidgeted as he looked to his right and left. "Okay, but just for a second. Then you have to go."

"Thank you." Hanna smiled as she passed through the door he opened for her.

Adanna stood and rushed to meet Hanna. "How did you get in here?"

Hanna held up the tray. "I brought food." She placed it on the table, faced Adanna, and whispered, "Tell me, did you really help him escape?"

Adanna sat in the chair next to the table. Hanna did the same. "Yes. I'm sorry, but I did. I gave him my gun too, and Quinn knows. I don't know how, but he knows."

"Don't apologize. It's the best thing that could have happened. I'm so proud of you." Hanna felt herself blush and looked away.

"Hanna, are you okay?"

She nodded. "Yes, I'm just worried for you. Quinn and Miju are furious, and they're looking for him. They sent out a team to find him and Leza. I don't know what they'll do if they find Cijen."

"I know Quinn's suspicious. He wouldn't have placed me under guard otherwise."

"Yes, but they're taking us with them to the other camp . . . the one on the border near Sudan in Mangai."

"Taking who?"

"Taking us—you and me."

"Why would he do that? Quinn never takes the women to Mangai."

"I don't know, but we leave first thing in the morning. I wanted to tell you."

Adanna thought for a moment. "He's going to kill me, Hanna. As soon as the baby is born five months from now, he'll kill me. He doesn't want me out of his control until then. That's why he's taking me there."

Hanna wrapped her arms around her friend. "I know. But we will not let him do this thing."

CHAPTER SEVENTEEN

Paul slowly awakened in the dim room. He struggled to recall where he was. His head pounded, and it took him a moment to focus. He glanced down at Leza snuggled under his left arm, sleeping against his chest as they lay in a bed. Her body radiated heat. He felt her forehead. She had a fever.

"She insisted on sleeping with you."

Startled, Paul turned to the slender woman who spoke in Dinka; she was sitting in a bamboo chair across the room, gripping the shotgun across her lap. The long brown hair she wore in a ponytail told Paul she was probably of mixed race. She appeared to be in her forties.

Cijen's snoring drew Paul's attention to the floor where he lay sleeping, using a blanket for a pillow.

"You scared her," the woman added. "She worried you'd wake up and not find her. I tell her you just tired and hungry." The woman paused. "But I see the wound up here." She pointed to her own chest. "And scars on your hands." She rubbed her forearms.

Paul looked at his wrists where the zip ties had calloused his skin from being bound to the bed in his room night after night.

"You were shot in the chest. You were a prisoner." She gestured toward Cijen. "He was shot in his leg." She focused on Paul again. "You have escaped? No lies."

Paul looked at the sleeping Cijen. "What did he tell you?"

"Never mind what he said. I want to see if what you tell me is the same."

Paul thought for a moment. "I was a prisoner, and I escaped."

"A prisoner with a little girl? Strange."

Paul looked fondly at Leza and pulled the light blanket up to cover her. "She's like my own."

"I see your eyes—you're not a bad man. You don't lie."

Paul smiled. "I couldn't. Cijen already told you."

"How did you know he don't lie?"

Paul looked at his friend on the floor again. "He doesn't know how."

"I apologize for my language. I don't know Dinka much, and I know English less."

"You speak well."

"So you have escaped from somewhere. You are American, no?"

"Yes, ma'am."

"Escaped from prison?"

"No."

"From Kony?"

"Not Kony. Someone like him."

"Not . . . Quinn?"

Paul took a deep breath and stared at the weapon on the woman's lap. He sensed things had just gotten bad. "Yes. Quinn."

The woman stood, walked to the window, and pulled the frayed curtain to cover the opening. She turned back to Paul, gripping the shotgun firmly in her left hand. "When?"

"How long have I been asleep?"

"Since morning. Ten hours."

Paul noticed it was dark outside. He looked at the guard's watch on his wrist, thankful it was waterproof. "Eight o'clock?" He almost sat up but remembered Leza. "We left in an airplane at sunrise this morning. We crashed in the Kibali River and walked here."

The woman paced to the door and finally leaned the shotgun against the wall.

Paul broke the brief silence. "What's your name?"

"Toomi."

"I'm Paul, and this is Leza." Paul glanced at Leza, then at his friend lying on the floor. "That's Cijen. He used to be one of Quinn's men, but he escaped with us and helped us. We'd be dead if he hadn't."

Toomi couldn't seem to stand still for more than a few seconds. Her nerves got the better of her.

"What's wrong, Toomi?"

"If they find you, they will kill me."

Uneasiness came over Paul. Toomi must have seen it in his face. "Don't worry. I will not turn over a little girl—or the man who saved her—to the butcher of Sudan."

"We should go." Paul sat up.

"No. Not now." Toomi walked quickly to his bedside and put her hand on his shoulder as she focused on Leza. "It is not safe in the dark. And you must eat something. I made rice and beans. He had some already." She pointed to the snoring man on the floor. "And I cleaned his wound. The bullet goes through?"

"Yes, all the way. Toomi, we'll leave first thing in the morning. Any chance we could borrow your truck? We have a long drive to get her to a hospital." Paul gestured toward Leza.

"That truck is all I have—nothing more. There is no way of getting anywhere without it." Toomi walked back to the chair and sat, staring at Leza as she slept with her arm across Paul's chest.

Toomi shook her head and sobbed into her hands. Paul didn't speak.

"My little girl is gone three years. He took her and killed my husband."

"Toomi. I'm so sorry. I'm going to stop him. I will end Quinn."

"Many have tried. All are dead."

Leza's tiny voice drifted across Paul's chest. She mumbled two words in Dinka that Paul didn't quite catch, then she coughed and fell back to sleep. Paul patted her on her back gently. He looked at Toomi. She was standing now with her eyes fixed on Paul.

"You are The Chosen?"

"What? What did she say to you?"

"The panther? He saw you?"

"Yes, but—"

"How close was he?"

"A few centimeters."

"What is it he says?"

"I don't know. And everybody keeps—"

"He comes back."

Paul remembered that Orma had told him the same thing.

"If he did not tell you, he saved you for another time. He comes back." Toomi moved to the window and crossed her arms. Moments later she returned to the chair and dropped into it.

"Toomi, I'm sure there is more than one panther in Africa."

"So you do not believe what we believe, but know this: he returns to you—soon."

Paul felt a chill at the thought of facing the panther again. He took a deep breath and sighed. "Does the panther ever return to anyone?"

"One time long ago. He will return to you."

Paul couldn't argue. His respect for these people grew every day.

Toomi's expression revealed a new determination. "Take it."

Paul didn't understand.

"The truck—take it and bring it back when you can. If you cannot, it means you're dead."

"Toomi, I don't know what to say."

"It is what I can do. If you can end this man, then do that for us—for all of us."

"Thank you, Toomi. There's one more thing—do you have any weapons I can use? If you don't, I understand. You've done so much already."

"It is only my shotgun. You must have it."

"I can't take your only weapon."

"I will manage." Toomi stood and walked to Leza. "Do not move— she looks peaceful. I will get you food."

"Thank you. I'll repay you somehow."

"When Quinn is dead, it is enough."

Jarrod pulled off the main dirt road in the early morning light and drove ten more kilometers on a path barely wide enough for the jeeps to fit through. The tall grass scraped the sides of the vehicles as they plowed through the rugged terrain. Two kilometers from the river edge, they stopped to engage the four-wheel drive and begin the rocky journey to the riverbank.

As they neared the water, Jarrod motioned for them to stop. The jeeps came to a halt. He focused on the GPS finder in his palm. "This is the place." He jumped out and scanned the bubbling, muddy water of the Kibali River, then spread the map on the hood of the jeep and checked his GPS reading. "Right over there is where Quinn lost the signal. Looks like Branson landed in the water, guys. Team two, head west; team three, north; team one, we go east—downstream. Get your bulletproof vests on, and let's go, men. Find me that plane! And remember, these guys are armed."

The men pulled their vests on and split up.

"I want anything that looks like it doesn't belong," Jarrod called to them. "You see a broken twig, I want to know. Look for wreckage, pieces of airplane, clothing, a wing, a Kleenex—anything. It's here somewhere, and I want it."

Jarrod walked methodically—his eyes didn't miss a single detail. This was his arena. He loved the hunt more than the kill, although he enjoyed that too.

As he walked the riverbank, he spotted something. "Hold it, men." He examined a fresh gash on a tree trunk near the river's edge. "Okay, I'm looking for a wing. The whole airplane no longer exists. They lost something right here, and I'm betting it's the left wing since they came from that direction." Jarrod patted the gash with his hand and rubbed his fingers across the surface.

"Over here!" one of the men fifteen meters downstream shouted. Jarrod hurried to where he stood.

"Right there, sir. Under the water when the current washes from the other side. Wait—there!"

The white glow of the wingtip was barely visible under the surface. As the river sloshed over the edge of the wing, the tip projected a centimeter above the water line.

"Good. There's my wing. This shallow water can't be hiding the rest of the plane. It must be farther downstream. Keep moving. Keep looking." Jarrod pulled out his two-way radio. "Team two, circle back and make your way to us twenty meters inland. We're on the river."

The men walked cautiously, their hands on their weapons. Jarrod had no idea where the doctor and Cijen might be, or if they were even alive, but he knew they had guns, and he refused to give up his advantage. They moved along the bank, but the swirling, murky water offered no more clues.

The walkie-talkie crackled. "Team two here. Found something you need to see, sir."

Jarrod looked inland. "What's your position?"

"About a hundred meters behind you on your left."

Jarrod quickened his pace to reach the team. The men stood in a circle, staring at a dead croc. Jarrod examined the huge reptile and then addressed the men. "Must be four meters long. Three shots to the head right there." He pointed at the wounds and then looked up at the boulders. "The gunman fired from there."

Jarrod squatted. "Men's boots right here, pushing back against the rocks. The croc had him cornered." Jarrod pulled up the two-way radio again and called the men on team three. "We're looking for armed survivors. At least the two men lived through the crash."

Another crackle on the radio. "Team three here, sir. We have trampled bushes heading north. Ground's pretty soft. Two sets of footprints and some blood on the rocks."

"Understood. Hold your position. We're coming to you." Jarrod turned to his men. "We have a trail and a purpose, gentlemen. We have at least one injured person, maybe even the girl. They have a head start, but we know what we're doing. Team two, you men stay and keep looking for the plane. Go downstream about a kilometer and contact me the moment you find anything or anyone. Carry your AKs. There are more crocs out here. Team three, get in your jeep and circle around to the other side of these bluffs. We'll need the equipment if we find Branson. I'll forward our coordinates if we locate him. We could be looking for a body too. Let's get this done."

The sun cast its faint glow on one wall of the hut. Paul woke with a sleeping Leza under his arm. He looked down, but the floor was empty, with no sign of his friend Cijen. He checked his watch. "Five thirty. Good."

Paul was moving carefully away from Leza to keep from waking her when Cijen stepped through the doorway. "Morning, Cij. Where's Toomi?"

"I don't know. I haven't seen her."

"Well, she said we could use her truck."

Cijen looked out the door and then back at Paul. "I just went to the latrine. The truck is gone."

"What?" Paul hurried outside, his stomach tied in a knot. "We have to get out of here. It could be a trap."

He hurried back to the bed and scooped Leza into his arms. When he stepped outside again, he saw Toomi's truck speeding up to the house followed close behind by a jeep. Paul stood motionless as Toomi jumped out.

"Where are you going? I thought you said you needed my truck and some guns?"

A tall man hopped out of the jeep, a pistol holstered on his belt. His leather boots were well worn, and a sleeveless shirt stretched tight across his muscular chest.

"This is Doug," Toomi said. "He's a friend."

"Toomi says you need weapons."

The man's steady voice put Paul at ease. He glanced at Cijen. "We do, but we don't have any money."

"She said you're fighting Quinn. I want to help."

"I appreciate that very much." Paul looked over Doug's shoulder into the jeep. "What do you have?"

"A couple rifles and a few pistols with extra ammo. That's about it, but I think it will help." Doug opened the back of the jeep. "Take a look."

Paul recognized one of the weapons. "That's an assault rifle."

"AK forty-seven. Holds thirty-five rounds. Safety is right here."

Cijen looked at Paul. "It's the same as the one you used yesterday."

"You've shot one of these before?" Doug sounded surprised.

"Yeah." Paul picked it up and checked the clip.

"It's loaded. Everything I have is loaded, and the extra ammo is right here." Doug picked up an army-issue ammo case. "And this is a semiautomatic pistol." He checked the clip.

"I've used one like that for target practice," Paul said.

"Good. You're all set then." Doug turned to Cijen. "How about you?"

Cijen lifted a fifty-round semiautomatic Russian SKS assault rifle from the back of the jeep. "If you have extra ammo, this would be perfect. I trained with one like it."

Doug pulled another box from behind the backseat. "Here are two hundred rounds. Hope that will do."

"Thank you for this, Doug," Paul said. "Any chance you or any other men would consider coming with us? We could use the help."

"Give me a day. I'll gather some men. Come back through for us, and we'll go after Quinn with you."

"Thank you, Doug. That would be incredible. Any way we could get the word out that trouble is coming to Sudan?"

"I don't think so. Quinn has influence everywhere. Even the government is on his payroll. It would be suicide to report this to anyone." Doug paused. "We can fight him, though. And if the spirits are willing, we can win."

Paul nodded. "I understand." He turned to Toomi. "Thank you very much for the truck. Is there a hospital in Adranga?"

"No. The closest hospital is in Aru, to the east, near the Uganda border, but still in the Congo."

Paul faced Cijen. "Maybe we should just head for Juba in South Sudan. I don't know how we'll cross the border, and it would still be a long drive. We may get stopped by the border patrol."

Cijen pulled out the map again. "I know where to cross where there aren't guards. I've done it with Quinn, but it's all the way near Nabiapai. That would add an extra ten hours to the trip."

Paul kissed Leza's warm forehead. "She doesn't have that much time." Leza coughed hard. In fact, she couldn't seem to stop coughing. "I'm worried that she got water in her lungs yesterday and will need IV antibiotics soon. Aru it is."

Toomi ran her fingers through Leza's hair while she lay in Paul's arms. "She is a beautiful child. You take care of her."

"I'll do my best."

Paul climbed into the truck and sat Leza in the middle. Cijen settled in on the passenger side. When Leza lay down on Cijen's lap, he looked at Paul.

"Good job, Cij."

Paul turned to Toomi as he buckled in. "What will you do now?"

"I'll leave here for a while. You came this way—they'll come this way. So I can't be here."

"You sure you don't want to come with us?"

Toomi smiled. "No. My family is in Uganda. I'll go there until things settle down."

Paul nodded. "That sounds like a great plan. I hope you hear good things about us."

"Only that you are alive and he is dead. May the spirits be with you."

"Thank you again."

Doug reached through the window and shook Paul's hand. "I hope you men get him. I'll be rounding up the guys for a serious firefight from this end."

"I'll do my best. Thank you for your help, Doug."

Doug nodded and gave Paul a two-finger salute as he drove away.

When Paul was about a kilometer down the road, he heard the unmistakable sound of an RPG and glanced in the rearview mirror as a fireball engulfed Toomi's house. The powerful explosion rattled the doors of Paul's pickup seconds later. He slammed on his brakes, and he and Cijen both spun around in their seats to watch.

"Oh God . . . no!" Paul said, but just then Doug's jeep sped out of the smoke. "They made it out, Cij!" But no sooner had he said the words than a second RPG trailed through the inferno and exploded into Doug's jeep, throwing the flaming wreckage into the air and slamming it to the ground.

"Go, Dr. Paul! Drive!"

Paul turned around in his seat and stomped on the gas. He stared in the rearview mirror, waiting for the next RPG to appear from the smoldering carnage and chase them down, but it didn't come.

"They killed them, Dr. Paul."

Leza started to cry, and Cijen patted her on the back. "It will be okay. Just stay down. I'll protect you."

She sobbed.

Paul focused on the road and shifted gears. "How did they find us so fast?"

"I don't know, Dr. Paul. I don't know."

The Black Hawk pilot, nicknamed Murdock, used the intercom to call his commander, Major Gage, in the back of the chopper. A seasoned pilot, Murdock had flown thousands of hours behind enemy lines, often retrieving other soldiers at the peril of his own life.

"Boss, I have command on the line for you, sir."

Gage, a highly accomplished US Army Special Forces commander, gave Murdock the thumbs-up signal. "Put him through."

"Gage, this is the general. I understand you have a problem. What's your status?"

Gage looked around the chopper at his men. "General, we have not yet engaged Enigma. Our intel was incomplete. He was not where he was supposed to be. Although the LRA has a presence in the area, our man is not there and hasn't been for weeks. At this point we're not sure where to look."

There was a moment of silence on the general's end. "I don't have to tell you how important this is, Gage?"

"No, sir."

"Tell me how you intend to proceed."

"Sir, although we don't have a twenty on the package at this time, we believe we can have coordinates within twenty-four."

"Well, son . . . this mission is now a White House mandate. I don't need to explain that to you, do I? I realize you're too young to remember Watergate or the Cuban Missile Crisis, but the press is having a field day with the chemical warfare angle. It's a feeding frenzy with only one way to stop it. It's critical that you find our man, Gage. Find him and take the risk of chemical warfare off the board. Find it, contain it, neutralize it—and place it in our control again. Understood?"

"Yes, sir. Understood."

"On top of that, Gage, you may have less than twenty-four hours to locate and acquire before it's too late. Our intel indicates a countdown is already underway in Sudan based on the activity of troops in the North. Something big is going down. And if these issues are all connected, the LRA is planning to use chemical weapons, and we need to stop it before it becomes a global, international, US freakin' nightmare. Do I make myself clear, Gage? Enigma is the key. Do you copy?"

Gage nodded as if General Jemison stood in front of him. "Yes, sir."

"One more thing, Gage. Enigma's daughter was abducted from an FBI safe house in upstate New York. She hasn't been found, but the federal agents assigned to protect her are dead—assassinated."

Gage paused for a moment. "Sir, are we looking for the girl as well?"

"I can't give you that order, Commander. But you know how this works. Keep your eyes open, and for God's sake and the president's, bring her back."

"Copy that, sir."

"Good luck, son."

The radio went silent, and Gage gave the six men on his team the signal. He held up two fingers, then four. They understood.

As the morning sun cast long shadows across the runway, Jim throttled up and lifted off the Kajjansi airfield bound for Mundri. He wouldn't be checking in to get his passport stamped this time. He'd take his chances. That way no one would know he was coming, and no one could stop him.

Jim banked the plane over Lake Victoria and headed for Sudan, flying at two kilometers. He would drop to half a klick when he neared the border. He turned and scanned the arsenal of weapons he had strapped in the cargo bay. If he was forced down again, he was a goner.

But with Paul and Jessica missing and Jarrod on the loose, Jim couldn't just sit around and wait for bad news. It was time for action, and he had a plan.

CHAPTER EIGHTEEN

Jessica woke to the sound of an airplane engine and looked out the window. The brown grass and dried shrubbery far below rushed past with no rivers or lakes in sight. She had flown enough with her dad to know they were cruising at a ceiling of a little over a kilometer—lower than normal.

Stretching her weak, stiff neck, she glanced around the small overhead-wing aircraft. The man in the copilot seat in front of her spoke to the pilot. She recognized him—the guy at the house in Uganda. Yes, the tall African man. Jessica unconsciously rubbed her leg where they had injected her.

A tap on her shoulder startled her. She turned to see a pretty, middle-aged black woman leaning forward from the seat behind her. She wore traditional South African garb with a brightly colored scarf wrapped neatly around her hair. She handed a water bottle to Jessica. "It will help you feel better."

Jessica didn't have any reason to trust her, but thirst won over caution, and she drank half the bottle.

"Thank you." She handed it back to the woman.

"No, it's for you."

Jessica finished the bottle, but still felt a little dehydrated.

"My name is Gina."

Jessica didn't reply, but she recognized the woman's South African accent. As Jessica glanced around the plane, the spotless upholstery, burled wood trim, and smell of new leather told her this must have been a recent purchase. The individual seats were arranged in rows with two on the right and one on the left. A narrow aisle, barely wide enough to pass through, separated them.

"You don't trust me. I understand. This is a difficult business, and I'll do all I can to help you. I'm sure your father will cooperate, and the two of you will go home together." Gina smiled pleasantly.

"Where are we going now? Where's my father?"

Gina unbuckled her seat belt, walked to the tall man in the copilot seat, and spoke quietly to him. He shook his head. She returned to sit in the seat next to Jessica.

"I'm sorry, the answer will have to wait. My boss doesn't want me discussing it with you at this point."

For a moment Jessica gathered her thoughts and didn't speak, then she said, "I appreciate the water. Thank you for trying to assure me that everything will be okay."

Gina smiled again. "You're quite welcome."

"But I know my father. He won't cooperate—not with murderers or thugs, and certainly not with terrorists."

"Terrorists? I'm sorry you don't trust us."

"If you want me to trust you, tell me what's going on. What's my father doing here? Where are we going?"

Gina wore her polite smile as if it were painted on. "There are things you can't know yet. All will be clear in time."

Jessica looked out the window and noticed the landscape turning slowly from flat brown grass to green shrubbery and lush overgrowth. She knew they must be getting closer to a place where rain was more plentiful. The Congo perhaps? After a few minutes, she turned back to the woman. "Who are you, Gina? What is it you do?"

Gina reflected a moment before replying. "I provide a specialized service to an elite group of clients. I'm somewhat of a personnel director. I find the exact type of girl someone wants and then deliver her."

"You're a human trafficker." In general, Jessica tended to not mince words, and the last few days had made her bolder than ever.

Gina stopped smiling and narrowed her eyes. "I supply the most beautiful women in the world to the richest of men. I'm a matchmaker, not a trafficker." She spit out the word.

"What about the women you kidnap and oppress? Do they consider you a matchmaker?"

"I'm a liaison for women who don't even know they want to be liberated."

"Liberated from what?"

"From drudgery, from poverty, even from themselves. They don't know what they want until I show them."

"Is that why you're kidnapping me—to set me free? Because I liked my life before you showed up. I didn't need saving."

Gina reached for her own water bottle and took a drink. "Your situation is a bit more complicated than most, my dear. Normally my employer—your father's employer—is straightforward in the girls he . . . brokers. Your future—your fate—is in your father's hands."

"What did you mean, 'my father's employer'?"

"That's complicated as well and beyond my ability to explain. But you will see that the man I work for is unique. He gets what he wants."

Jessica looked at the tall man in the front Gina had spoken to.

Gina must have noticed. "No, not him, dear. You'll meet him soon enough."

Jessica gazed out at the horizon before turning back to Gina. "He's better than you."

"What do you mean? Who is better than me? My employer?"

"No. My father. He's better than you. He won't do what you say, so you might as well make your plans for me now. Just keep in mind that I'll die before I allow you to sell me to the highest bidder."

"Being sold to the highest bidder will be your fate, my beautiful young friend. That is, if your father refuses. Believe that. I will see to it." Gina stood and returned to her own seat.

Jessica rested her head back and gazed out the window. She closed her eyes and, after a few minutes, started to drift off to sleep.

Moments later, Gina tapped her on the leg. "I'm sorry, dear. I need you to wear this." She handed Jessica a black hood. "It's just a precaution, but I'm afraid it's necessary."

"Just tell me, Gina. Are we going where my father is?"

Gina paused for a moment, as if admiring Jessica's beauty. "I can honestly say your father has never been where we're going."

The man in the seat in front of Jessica turned and gave Gina an angry look. She changed her tone. "Now put the hood on and stop stalling."

Jessica took the black cloth bag and glanced out at the now lush green landscape before pulling it over her head. The plane began its descent.

Frantically Paul swerved down the narrow road as he kept looking in the rearview mirror every few seconds. "Okay, Cij—one more time. Where do I need to make the next turn? I don't know where I'm going, but for the past ten minutes, all you've done is mumble about how Toomi and Doug were killed and we weren't. You look at that map, but you aren't helping me. Where do I turn? You say go straight, but what does that mean? I have to turn somewhere, right?"

Cijen held up the wrinkled map. "Up ahead, that road on the right. Take it. It's small, but we can make it."

Paul swallowed his fear. "I'm sorry, Cij. I'm tired of running and being hunted like a dog by a madman, but that doesn't give me an excuse to snap at you."

"It's okay, Dr. Paul. There, take that path. The small one."

Paul steered the truck onto the shoulder, over an embankment, and through the tall grass.

Cijen studied the map. "If we follow the river, we can get to Aru."

"We don't have a lot of time."

"We'll make it. We don't have to cross any borders." Cijen looked at the road ahead and then at the map. "Before we reach the river, turn left down a path along the water. There is a bridge to the east where we can cross."

"Where are the guys who killed Toomi and Doug, Cij? Why aren't they following us? They must have seen us drive away. All they had to do was point and shoot."

"I don't know. There, turn left."

Paul turned onto the rough road. The massive roots from the river-bank trees intertwined across the path and slowed him down.

Leza cried whenever the truck bounced, but Cijen patted her with his left hand and held the map with his right. "Soon we'll come to a bridge. The road on the other side of the Kibali will get us to Aru in about three hours."

Paul felt Leza's forehead again. "She's still running a fever."

"I'm okay, Baba." She forced a weak smile.

"Cij, we have two very big problems right now. One, we need to get her to the hospital right away and . . . two, we need to get in front of these guys chasing us. If we fail to do either of those . . ."

Cijen checked the map again. "I understand. Up ahead, turn right over that bridge."

Paul turned and suddenly had an overwhelming feeling of apprehension. He stopped the truck.

"What's wrong? Why aren't you crossing?"

"It doesn't feel right." Paul looked out the back window. "They should be closer to us by now."

"Not if they were delayed at Toomi's house. Maybe they went to Adranga like I said."

"They're smarter than that. Quinn has Jarrod Vincent, an ex-marine with black ops training, working for him. I would bet you money he's with them, and we need to think like he thinks."

"How does he think?"

"Outside the box."

"What does that mean?"

"He's always a step ahead, somehow. He could be preparing an ambush."

Paul stepped out of the truck, reached behind the seat for the AK-47, walked to the river, and looked upstream. There was no one in sight—not a sound. He climbed back behind the wheel.

"Okay, maybe I'm just paranoid."

"You're what?"

"I mean I guess I'm worried about things that aren't really there." Paul pulled the truck onto the creaking boards of the rickety bridge and slowly drove across the narrow wooden structure. The old planks bent under the weight of the pickup. Paul drove slowly but steadily.

"Keep looking. They could be anywhere."

When they reached the opposite side of the bridge, Paul sped up a little.

"This road's not too bad, Cij. We can make better time on this. Is there any water left in—"

As he spoke, a jeep blazed out of the tall grass in front of him. Paul swerved around it, forcing it back into the underbrush. Moments later the jeep was behind them. Another one followed. Paul stepped on the gas, but he could barely stay ahead of the pursuers.

"Cij—shoot the driver. If they fire an RPG like the one they used at the house, we're dead."

Cijen unbuckled his seat belt and quickly moved Leza to the floor, setting her down as gently as he could. "It's going to be okay. Stay down, Leza."

Leza curled up on the floor.

"You'll be fine, sweetie." Paul's heart melted for her.

Cijen seemed to know what to do. He turned, broke out the back window with the butt of his rifle, and fired several three-round bursts into the jeep. It veered to the side. He fired directly into the driver's side of the windshield. The jeep turned sharply and flipped, slinging glass and its inhabitants into the air, then slid on its side before plowing into a tree.

The second jeep careened around the first as a man in the back stood, leaned against the roll bar, and aimed his rifle at Cijen.

Cijen fired into the vehicle, and when the man ducked behind the cab, Cij took the opportunity to scurry through the window into the pickup bed.

"There's a third jeep back there!" he yelled at Paul, who began to swerve the truck from side to side.

The man in the passenger seat of the jeep closest to them leaned out and fired at the pickup's tires. The bullets hit the tailgate and bumper. Cijen didn't give him a second chance. When he leaned out again, Cijen killed him with a single shot. He fell from the jeep and tumbled to the side of the road.

Cijen took aim and fired at one of the men when he stood to shoot over the roll bar of the jeep. From the backward lurching of the man's body, Paul realized his bulletproof vest had prevented the shot from doing more than forcing him back.

When the man stood again, Cijen was ready. He fired two shots into the man's head, snapping it back and causing him to trigger his automatic weapon onto the floor of his own vehicle. An explosion inside the jeep forced it off the ground in a ball of fire, turning it end over end in an inferno of wreckage, sending billowing flames and shrapnel in every direction. Skidding sideways, it rolled before coming to rest on its wheels. Paul's truck had gained enough distance to keep them from the explosion, but Cijen felt the heat.

The last jeep veered to the left to avoid the wreckage, but struck the back of the flaming jeep with its right fender, rolling the vehicle upside down in the tall grass.

When they reached the bend in the road, Cijen climbed back into the cab. "I'm not sure about that last jeep. I can't tell if it's permanently disabled or just overturned. I don't know what made the middle jeep blow up, unless they had explosives on board."

"Yeah, that got a little warm back there. Sorry, Cij. But even if the third jeep is still usable, they have to push it upright and make it run. That's bought us some time."

Cijen pulled the map out of his pocket. The truck no longer had a back window, and the windshield had several holes punched through it, causing the wind to flap the map as Cijen held it, but he managed.

"I think we should make Aru by nightfall," Cijen said. "I'll guide you. We'll get Leza to the hospital and find a place to hide until morning."

Paul nodded but didn't say anything.

"What is it, Dr. Paul?"

"I was just thinking. They didn't fire an RPG at us from the house, but they could have. And they didn't shoot at me here in the driver's seat. Based on the bullet holes in this truck, not one shot came close to me. They shot at you and at the tires, Cij."

"So what?"

"So . . . they have orders not to kill me. They're trying to capture me."

◆ ◆ ◆

Gage studied the intel on the computer screen in front of him as the Black Hawk sat silently atop the rocky bluff of Mount Odo.

Jake called to Gage, "What did you find, boss?" Lieutenant Jake was second in command and a specialist in hand-to-hand combat and munitions. He continued to inspect every block of explosive to ensure that all would detonate with precision, then double-checked the equipment before stowing it again.

As Jake walked over, Gage moved the laptop so they could both see the screen. "Look at this—the satellite and infrared images point to the same conclusion. Fifty-five minutes after a sunrise takeoff from this area of the Congo, a small plane crashed in the Kibali River two hundred kilometers away. If this is our guy and he survived the crash, he had to deal with crocodile- and snake-infested waters."

Gage sat back. "It looked at first like we may have lost him to the elements. I have an infrared image that puts the fuselage right here. It must have submerged after that since it's gone on the next pass, ninety minutes later. But this is where it gets interesting." Gage pulled up the next screen as Solo, sniper specialist A-team, joined the men.

Gage continued, "An hour after the crash, two figures walk from the riverbank carrying a third—possibly a child or a small woman. They trudge through the jungle to this structure. Must have taken a couple of hours through that terrain. It looks like a house. We've been looking for one guy, but maybe he had help. If he did, this could be our man."

Jake knew Gage well enough to know he was just getting started.

Gage pulled up the next IR satellite images. "Take a look."

Jake and Solo scanned the images. "What's happening here, boss?" Jake asked. "There must be a dozen guys combing that riverbank. When did this happen?"

Gage pointed to the time stamp. "Fifteen figures arrived on the scene eighteen hours after the crash, fourteen hours after we see those three people walking through the jungle. Depending on the roads, it could have taken them that long to drive from the same place where the plane took off. In any event, they appear to be searching for some-thing—maybe survivors."

Gage clicked on the next image. "Stay with me, men; it's about to get even more interesting."

Bart, chopper pilot two, sniper/sharpshooter, and fifty-cal special-ist, peered over Jake's shoulder to get a look at the computer screen as Gage explained what they were seeing.

"Five guys stay behind and comb the riverbank for about three kilometers downstream. They're carrying rifles—all of them. Five men track the three survivors on foot to that hut. Five more take this vehicle around the butte and meet up over here near the same structure."

Hawkeye, a sniper/sharpshooter and RPG and fifty-cal expert, con-tinued to check his gear as Gage spoke, but it was clear that he was paying attention.

Kid was the last man on the team and had held the position of sniper first class for three years in a row. At six foot four, it was easy for him to look over the other men's shoulders to see the screen.

Gage clicked to the next image. "Following an explosion that leaves two bodies on the ground and destroys the building and a vehicle, this pickup truck hauls down the road, crosses the Kibali right here on this little bridge, and three minutes later, three jeeps pursue it like their lives depended on it. And that's all we have. For now."

Jake patted Gage on the back. "Did we just catch a break, boss?"

Gage grinned as he looked at the men surrounding him. "Let's just hope it's him and that he outran them. The doc may have given us what we needed to find him. Without this, we were lost. Now we have something—something real."

"*De oppresso liber*, Chief!" Jake shouted.

Gage called to his pilot, who was busy securing gear in the chopper, "Fire it up, Murdock. It's time to go!"

◆　◆　◆

Hunger pangs jabbed at Jessica's ribs. She sat up on the cot and looked around the room. Cinder block walls surrounded her, and a single bulb suspended by a wire from the three-meter-high ceiling provided the only light other than what filtered in from the window near the roof. She couldn't tell what time it was, but it was still light outside. A steel door with a sliding metal plate near the bottom secured her in the small cell.

This fortified compound Gina had brought her to was a prison.

Jessica collected her thoughts as weakness and exhaustion begged her to lie back down. But she needed to explore her surroundings. She walked to the heavy metal door and listened. Muffled talking in the hallway was too far away to be understood and probably wasn't English anyway.

Footsteps approached and stopped at her cell. The metal plate near the bottom of the door slid open. A man's hand reached in with a sloppy food tray and dropped it on the floor. The metal door plate slammed shut immediately.

Jessica picked up the tray and smelled the mixture of rice and beans. "You've probably eaten worse, and you need energy," she said out loud. Scooping some up with her fingers, she took a bite. It tasted—not so bad, so she ate the rest, and then listened at the door while she examined the hinges and lock.

Next she walked around the room and studied each crack in the wall. Escaping and helping her father seemed more and more impossible as the reinforced concrete and metal-barred window loomed imposingly before her.

Jessica jumped involuntarily when the bolt on the door clanked. She hurried to sit on the bed. A tall, muscular man wearing army fatigues and a beret walked in. His massive arms pushed the door closed, and he sauntered to the cot and stood over her. She immediately recognized him from pictures on the news. Jason Quinn.

Quinn's eyes bore into hers, but Jessica didn't look away. He reached out his hand and brushed the stray hair from her face with his finger. His muscles rippled, and his body odor made her cringe, but she didn't budge.

"Amazing." He studied her. "You have his eyes." He stroked her face. "But I think you have your mother's mouth."

"Don't touch me." Jessica pulled away from him.

"I see—a spirited one. That comes from your father too."

"How do you know him—my father?" Jessica glanced longer than she meant to at Quinn's scar-covered arms.

He paced slowly. "I'm Quinn, and you are here because of your father."

"Yes. As insurance, I'm told."

"Very good. You understand. Your father and I were partners working on a dream." Quinn stopped, and his voice turned harsh. "But your father decided he wanted it for himself. He escaped with my plans."

"Escaped? That seems like a strange word for a partner."

"Indeed. Nevertheless, your father needs a strong incentive to cooperate. You provide that. If he gives me what I need, you go home to your luxury apartment in New York. If he refuses, I'll take you for my pleasure." Quinn stepped closer. "At this moment, I hope he refuses. You're beautiful. I'll take you until I tire of you, then I'll sell you. The market for attractive young American women is quite profitable—thriving, in fact."

Jessica swung her fist at his jaw, but he grabbed her arm effortlessly. Spitting in his face earned Jessica a slap across her brow, forcing her against the wall. She glared, refusing to cry.

Quinn walked to the door, where he stopped and turned. He spoke sternly but quietly. "You will learn that I get what I want. Sooner or later, I get whatever I want." He pounded twice on the door, and a guard opened it. "You would do well to cooperate."

"Let me see him." Jessica kept her face expressionless.

"In due time."

"Where are you keeping him?"

Quinn turned away from Jessica. "That, my dear, is part of the problem. I'm not keeping him anywhere at the moment."

"You don't know where he is."

"I will find him, and you will serve me soon, one way or another. Do not cross me."

Once Quinn left and slammed the door behind him, Jessica dropped to her knees on the filthy concrete floor. "Where are you, Daddy?" she whispered.

Jim welcomed the sight of Mundri airfield more than he ever had. He couldn't believe it had only been a few weeks since he dropped Paul off on the same soil.

He taxied to the end of the runway and pulled the Cessna turbo-prop nose first into a newly hewn nook in the far right corner of the field. The moment he shut the engine down, men from the village quickly covered his plane with branches they'd cut from nearby mango trees, per Emeka's instructions.

Jim opened the cockpit door and climbed down to greet his friend Buru. Jim shook his hand. "This is perfect, Buru—just what I asked for. Thank God for shortwave radios, right?"

"I don't understand why you requested this, Jim. We've never hidden your plane before."

"I'm not supposed to be here. This plane does not have a registered flight plan. It's just missing—like me. I don't want anyone spotting it from the air."

Buru gave a quick nod and a knowing smile. "I understand."

"Have you heard anything at all?"

"Chima and the other village chiefs have met with one of the military officials. They believe that Quinn plans to attack the villages. The South Sudanese army is supposed to keep us posted on any warning signs, but Dr. Paul is still missing."

"His daughter's missing too now, Buru. She was kidnapped from New York."

Buru looked at Jim with determination on his face. "Okay. We're here for you. Whatever you need, we'll do."

Jim smiled. "I'm glad to hear that. We're going to be busy."

CHAPTER NINETEEN

"There's something you should see, Gage." Murdock looked up from his laptop. "I found them, sir. We're not after a truck with three vehicles chasing it anymore."

Gage walked from the chopper, bent over Murdock's shoulder, and studied the satellite images on the screen. His eyes lit up. "When is this?"

"Zero seven hundred today. On the satellite images there are three vehicles chasing this truck. There's gunfire, the first vehicle rolls and slings bodies. The second one gets close to the truck, but then—boom!—it explodes. Debris from the explosion forces the last jeep upside down about twenty meters into the tall grass."

Murdock leaned back from the images. "Must have been explosives on board the middle jeep for a fireball that size."

Jake stepped up to look. "C4. Must've been C4 for that crater."

Murdock nodded. "Next sat pass ninety minutes later, the jeep in the grass is gone. I would guess it was just overturned and needed to be flipped up on its wheels."

Gage stood. "Okay, ladies. We're back in business. Our mission is to find that pickup truck chased by a single jeep. Trace the sat images as far as we can and use infrared to corroborate. It appears our missing doctor is alive, but we need to locate him in the next fifteen hours, or—according to their speed and tenacity—these guys will catch up with him."

The men went to work on their tasks.

Gage looked at the images again, and under his breath he said, "You're still alive, Doc—and we're coming."

He stood up straight and shouted, "Hooah, ladies!"

"Hooah!" they responded in unison.

Jessica was still kneeling when Gina walked in.

"You don't look comfortable huddled on the floor. Why don't you sleep on the bed?"

"I wasn't huddled on the floor. I was kneeling." Jessica didn't like looking up at Gina, so she stood. "What do you want? You circle like a vulture. Quinn already made his disgusting intentions clear, which means you don't get me for a while. So why don't you go annoy someone else?"

"Understand, you insolent child, that Quinn will do as he says. Once he tires of you, he'll sell you. That is where I come in." Gina sighed. "I can see you're not going to embrace your situation easily. Pity. Eventually you'll cooperate, one way or another."

"I'd die first."

"I'll decide if, when, and how you die." Gina's smugness was infuriating. "You need to be more concerned about your father's situation with Quinn. If he cooperates, then none of this is necessary."

"My father won't work with that—that beast."

"You underestimate what a father will do for his daughter."

"You underestimate what my father will do when he finds out you've kidnapped his daughter."

Gina stared at Jessica for a moment and then slapped her. "This disrespect ends now. You will speak to me as you should or regret it."

Jessica planted her fist in Gina's left eye, taking her by such surprise that she fell backward over the cot, breaking off one of its wooden legs. She scrambled to her feet and punched Jessica in the stomach. Jessica responded with a sharp jab to Gina's throat the way she'd been taught in self-defense class.

Gina bent over to catch her breath. She was in no position to notice when Jessica grabbed the broken leg from the cot. Jessica swung it, striking Gina on the back hard enough to throw her against the wall. When Gina turned toward her, Jessica struck again, this time hitting her in the face, gashing her right eyebrow and cheek. As Gina tried to regain her footing, Jessica took advantage of her position one more time, striking her on the back of the head and knocking her out.

Abruptly the truck headlights landed on pavement. It seemed as if they were gliding on glass after hours of bouncing on pothole-covered dirt roads. Blacktop streets and concrete buildings were a welcome sight, even if the asphalt was weatherworn and the buildings falling apart.

"They can't track us on paved roads like they can on dirt, Cij. Let's find the hospital. That's the first order of business—getting Leza some help." Paul laid his hand on her side. She was in a deep sleep, and her skin radiated heat.

Cijen scoured the map with the weak beam of his fading flashlight. "Turn left at the next intersection, then take the second right. It should be on that street about three blocks down."

Paul took the turns, but as he approached the small hospital, an unwelcome thought came to mind. He pulled over and stopped before arriving at the building.

"What's wrong?"

"What if Quinn's men are already here?"

"How could that be possible?"

"I don't know, but what if they arrest me? It would delay Leza's care."

"Why would they arrest you? You have a right to be here."

"If Quinn owns the people of this town, they'll be looking for me. There may even be a reward on my head." Paul paused and stared at the hospital half a block away.

"That would not surprise me, Dr. Paul. Quinn has done that before."

Paul leaned out his window to scan the front of the building. "Do you think there are guards inside?"

"Guards are everywhere because of the LRA. It's impossible to tell who's on Quinn's side and who isn't until you confront them. Why don't I take Leza in? I speak the language better, and I look like I belong. They won't ask me for papers."

"We both need to go. I have to tell the doctor what's going on with her so he knows what to do and what to expect. That way she'll get the right care. But you may need to translate for me if I don't speak his dialect."

"What do we do next?"

Paul was in action mode and paused for only a moment. "We roll. God help us." He pulled the truck onto a side street beside the hospital, then turned down an alley to hide it. He shut down the engine and opened his door. Reaching across the cab, he took Leza from Cijen's arms and stepped out carefully, cradling the limp bundle against him.

As they walked to the main street and approached the small hospital lobby, the security guard inside got up from his chair and opened the door. He held up his hand to stop them. "You speak English?"

Paul nodded. "Yes, sir."

"Who are you?" The guard would not let them pass.

"I'm a doctor, and I have a little girl who's very sick. She needs medical care and IV fluids right away."

"Your papers, please." The guard held out his hand expectantly to both of them.

"I don't have my passport with me. But this little girl needs help right away. Can you please let us in?"

The guard stepped back and placed his hand on his pistol. "If you are an American, you should have papers. Who are you?"

"Yes, I'm an American," Paul said. "Do I look like a threat to you? Why are you being so defensive?"

"Your shirt is covered with blood, he has blood on his leg, and she is unconscious. You're in trouble. I need to know what kind of trouble, right now."

Cijen spoke up. "Get the doctor and we'll be on our way."

"You're not going anywhere." The guard stood his ground as a second security guard joined him from a room nearby.

"We're here because this child is running a high fever and may have pneumonia."

"How did you get here? You have no identification. Who are you, and what are you doing here? Put the girl down and hold your hands over your head."

"No." Paul didn't budge.

"What did you say?" The guard took a step closer.

"I want you to get the doctor, then we'll talk."

"You will do as I tell you, or—"

"Or what? You'll shoot a little girl?" Paul shouted, "Doctor! Is there a doctor here?"

"Keep your voice down, and put the girl on the chair," the guard demanded.

Paul looked him in the eye. "Listen to me. I'm not a criminal. I'm not looking for trouble. My name is Dr. Paul Branson, and I need help for this child. She has cancer, she's dehydrated, and she probably has pneumonia. That's the only reason I'm here. Now get the doctor, for God's sake!"

As the guard glared at Paul, an African man dressed in a lab coat stepped from the trauma bay. "What's your name?" The doctor had a distinct Ugandan accent.

"Paul Branson. I'm a doctor from—"

"I know who you are." The doctor stepped between the guards and Paul but addressed the guards. "I know this man, and he's no threat to you. Calm down and holster your weapons."

"We can't do that. He has no passport and no identification."

The doctor stood his ground. "I'm telling you, this is a colleague. It's okay." He turned to face Paul. "I'm Dr. Davis. Come with me." He pushed Paul toward the back of the trauma area and down the hallway, ignoring the guards. Reluctantly they holstered their weapons. Cijen limped down the hall behind Paul.

When they neared a treatment area, the doctor ushered them inside and closed the door. "Are you crazy, Dr. Branson? Thank God you're alive, but you shouldn't be out in the open."

"How do you know my name?"

"You're all over the news. Everyone's looking for you, both good and bad. There's a bounty from Quinn for the equivalent of fifty thousand US dollars, and there's a reward from the United States for a similar amount. Thank God the guards apparently don't watch TV. The word on the street is you're dead. Obviously that's not true."

"No. Until yesterday morning I was Quinn's prisoner, but we escaped from his compound a few hours from here by air. This little girl, Leza, was under my care for cancer when Quinn abducted me from Matta, a village in South Sudan. He's trying to use her to coerce me to cooperate."

"Are you armed, Dr. Branson?"

"No. We brought no weapons inside the hospital."

The doctor looked as if he were sizing Paul up.

"Dr. Davis, if you can take care of Leza for a few days. We need to cross the border into Sudan. We couldn't attempt it with her. She's too ill and needs IV fluids, antibiotics, and a chest x-ray. We were trapped underwater yesterday for close to three minutes. She's been running a fever and coughing since. I'm afraid she may have pneumonia."

"Lay her on the stretcher." Dr. Davis motioned to the gurney next to him. Paul gently put Leza down on the clean sheets and tucked a pillow under her head.

As the doctor examined her, Paul continued, "Can you notify the authorities that there's going to be an attack on five targets in South Sudan in the next few days? They're the villages of Matta, Witto, Wiroh, Buagyi, and Lanyi. We believe the attack will be on the water supplies in an effort to poison the community."

Dr. Davis stopped examining Leza and looked at Paul. "Why can't you go to the authorities and tell them yourself?"

"I don't know who I can trust, and Quinn has informants everywhere. You saw what happened at your front door. I can't risk running into someone who knows who I am. It would keep me from stopping Quinn."

Dr. Davis turned his attention back to Leza. "She's very ill."

"I know. Please help her."

Davis opened the door a crack, peeked down the hallway, and then closed it again. "You're not safe here. Your captors will be looking for you, and this is one of the first places they'll come to see if either of you has been injured." He looked at Cijen's bloody pant leg. "For obvious reasons, apparently. Let me look at that." Dr. Davis took off the make-shift dressing, and they continued their conversation as he cleaned the wound and redressed it.

"If you take care of her, Dr. Davis, I'll return and pay you for everything," Paul assured him.

"I'm not worried about the money. You'll be dead in twenty-four hours anyway if you go after this man. Do you understand who he is? What he's capable of?"

"More than anyone."

Davis nodded as he stared at Paul. "I believe you might. But that won't stop him. He'll kill you, Branson."

"Not if God has anything to say about it," Paul responded as he saw a glimmer of compassion in the man's eyes. "Please take care of her for me."

Dr. Davis looked at Paul. "Of course I will. But I can't help you, for obvious reasons. Now go. Or they'll find you and kill us all."

"One more thing," Paul said. "She's been on chemo, and she's overdue. If I give you the specifics, can you get it for her?"

Davis handed Paul a piece of paper. "Write it down. I'm not promising, but I'll see what I can do."

Paul wrote down the information, then grabbed the doctor's hand and shook it. "Thank you."

"You're welcome. Now hurry. I'll take you out the back."

"Give me one second." Paul leaned down to Leza's ear. "I hope to come back for you. I never wanted it to end like this. So many called me Abdu, I started to believe it. I have to warn the villages that Quinn's coming. If I don't see you again, know this: I loved you as if you were my own little girl."

Paul kissed her forehead as his single tear ran down her cheek. He stood, faced the doctor, and collected himself. "Okay. Let's go."

Dr. Davis opened the door and poked out his head. No one lurked in the hallway. He walked down the corridor with Paul and Cijen following him. Stopping at the nurse's station, he wrote orders on a chart. He turned to the nurse behind the desk, who couldn't take her eyes off Paul.

"Nurse, there's a little girl in room seven. Start her IV and sit with her until I return. I need to show these men out."

After walking down several dark halls, they arrived at a back door.

"The alley will turn to the right and take you to the street. I don't know how you got here. I don't want to know." Davis paused, then said, "For what it is worth, Branson, I believe what you've told me. I'll give you a head start of twenty-four hours and then notify the authorities of Quinn's plans. That will keep them from finding you here. But I can't promise they'll do anything."

"Please don't mention Leza to anyone. I don't want Quinn's men to know where she is or that she's even alive. Tell them I came for medical care, and you refused to treat me."

"Don't worry about that. Orphan children are dropped off here all the time. I'll make sure she blends in, and I'll warn the guards. I can change her name on the records too. That will keep snooping eyes from finding her."

Paul shook his hand again. "Thank you, Dr. Davis. Do what you can. I'll return for her. I swear I will."

"I pray that you can."

They left, walking down the dark alley toward the street and climbing into the truck. As Paul drove off, Cijen looked at the map with his flashlight. "Let's find a place to rest for tonight."

"Cij . . . have you noticed?"

Cijen looked up from the map to see men on street corners and shop owners staring at them as they drove. "That's strange, Dr. Paul."

"I guess going through the city in a truck riddled with bullet holes and no windows draws attention no matter where you are."

Cijen nodded. "We need to hide this thing—soon." He searched the map again. "According to this, the northwest side of the city is less populated. It looks more industrial, and it'll be close to the road we'll take in the morning. There are a few warehouses. We may be able to find a place to hide the truck and get some sleep at the same time."

"I'm starved, Cij."

"I am too. Let's find a place to stay, and then I'll walk to get us something to eat. You may be recognized."

They drove in silence for a few seconds before Cijen turned to him. "Dr. Paul, I have wanted to ask you . . . what happened to your wife?"

Paul hadn't seen that coming. He took a deep breath. His emotions were on overload already, but he did the best he could.

"She became sick with cancer, Cij. She fought very hard, but she died after thirteen months. She used to come to Africa with me."

Cijen stared at Paul. "I'm very sorry for this. You're a great man. You do good things. How could this happen to you?" Cijen shook his head. "You are Abdu."

Paul turned his attention back to the road. He hoped Cijen didn't see how much he still struggled with the question. "Being the right kind of person doesn't prevent you from enduring pain. I know there's a reason for Nicki dying. I don't know what the reason is, and I don't need to know. I just have to believe and trust there's a reason."

Cijen seemed to be thinking that through.

"Cij, I know my wife died as part of a bigger plan, but I may never know what that plan is. When she passed away, it was the worst thing that ever happened to me. But I realized that as part of the overall plan, it made sense even in the pain. That doesn't make it easy, though. I wonder every day if I've done the right thing coming back here. I just don't know. Look at the trouble I've caused. If I hadn't come back . . ."

"You're The Chosen."

"Cij, you call me The Chosen, but we are all chosen for something."

"Not as you have been chosen. It is you who fight it, Abdu."

"I don't, Cij. It's how I live my life now. I fear it's how I'll die."

Paul turned down a street that became darker and darker as they moved away from the lights of the city.

"There doesn't seem to be electricity here, Cij. It's dark."

"That's good. It'll be harder for them to find us. Go that way. The buildings look deserted. See if you can get to one of them at the end of the road—one where we can pull the truck inside."

"Should we keep going, Cij? We could travel on the back roads and maybe make some progress."

"No. We need rest, and a truck with headlights is a sitting duck in the middle of the jungle. We'll be ambushed for sure."

Paul knew Cijen was right. He steered around debris piles and crumbling equipment and pulled up to a two-story abandoned warehouse. A crooked garage door covered the entrance.

"I'll move it." Cijen slipped out of the truck and crawled between two broken boards. A moment later, he lifted part of the door. "Try to pull in."

Paul eased the truck forward under the framework that hung by only a few bolts, slowly making his way inside the bay. Cijen lowered the door, then gathered the rifles, handguns, and ammo from the truck. As they walked from the garage into the dark room, Paul stopped. He whispered, "Someone's here. Where's your flashlight?"

Cijen switched on the dim light, and a dozen eyes glistened in the corner of the room.

A woman spoke in Arabic. "Please don't shoot us."

Paul responded in the same language. "Who are you?"

"You speak English?" a man's voice questioned from the shadows. "Your accent—you sound American."

"Yes, I'm an American doctor." Paul switched to English. "We're looking for a place to spend the night. We mean you no harm. Are you armed?"

"No. We have no weapons. Please, there are children here."

Paul turned to Cijen, who still had his rifle trained on them. "You can put that down, Cij."

Cijen lowered his weapon.

The man walked toward Paul. "You have many guns for a man intending no harm."

"I'm sorry. We're just trying to survive. We pose no danger to you."

The man turned to the woman and children who sat on the floor and then back to Paul. "You can stay tonight if you like. We have some food we can share. It isn't much, but it's enough." The man looked Paul over. "You're running from someone?"

"Yes, we escaped from a prison compound in the Congo. We're weary and hungry. My injured friend and I appreciate your help."

The man appeared concerned. "Who do you run from?"

"From a compound in the jungle where we—"

"Not from where. From who?"

Paul hesitated. "Jason Quinn."

The man glanced at his wife. "He'll be searching for you."

"I know. We'll leave first thing in the morning."

The man's tone changed. "You will leave now."

"No," the woman protested. "They need food and sleep. We cannot turn them away."

"Think of the children, Mara. If they find him here, we will all die."

Paul spoke up. "I understand if you don't want us to stay, and I realize you were here first. But we need rest, food and water, and a place we can hide our truck. We're not leaving, but you're free to go."

The woman spoke up. "We'll stay with you." Then she turned to her husband, and they argued in Dinka, probably expecting Paul not to understand.

"They will get us killed!" the man said.

"They'll die if they leave tonight. Where is your heart?"

"Cij? I don't like this," Paul whispered to his friend.

"Don't worry. She'll win." Cijen smiled.

The man turned to Paul. "You may stay until morning, but you must leave at first light."

"Agreed." Paul sat on the floor.

Cij remained standing. "I'm going to check the street. I want to make sure we weren't followed."

Paul ate some rice and beans and drank a bottle of water. Mara held a little girl and slowly fed her something mushy from a wooden bowl.

Paul looked on as he thought about home and Jessica . . . and Nicki. She would be amazed to see him right now with a gun in his belt, a band of ammo across his shoulder, and an assault rifle strapped to his back. He wondered what she would say. She had saved him from throwing his life away on fighting, and now he sat in the heart of Africa, the land they both loved, the land they had dreamed about, fighting to survive.

"Thank you," Paul said to the woman. She smiled and turned back to the little girl, holding up a bite for her to eat.

The man walked to Paul and squatted next to him. "I'm sorry for asking you to leave, but my family is more important to me than anything in the world. You understand that, don't you?"

Paul nodded. "Yes, I do understand that."

The man patted him on the shoulder. "You need some rest. We will wake you at sunrise."

Cijen came back in and sat against the wall. "Everything looks quiet on the street. I'll take first watch and wake you in a few hours."

Paul nodded. "Thanks, Cij. I can barely keep my eyes open." He took off his weapons and ammo, rolled up his shirt, and stuffed it under his head for a pillow. In a matter of minutes he was asleep. An hour later, so was Cij.

At four o'clock in the morning, no one saw the dark figures in the shadows outside as they slowly surrounded the building.

CHAPTER TWENTY

Before he opened his eyes, Paul sensed something was wrong. He looked around the dark room and saw the shadow of a man silhouetted against the window. The figure was tall with broad shoulders, wearing something on his head.

"Don't move, Branson."

The man's head looked deformed. It took a moment for Paul to realize his captor was wearing night vision goggles. He heard Cijen moving in the dark on the floor beside him.

"That goes for you too, Mr. Cijen."

Paul sat up. He recognized the voice.

"I said don't move."

"Hello, Jarrod. I never would have figured you for a scumbag. Especially with your history as a marine."

"'Scumbag' is an ugly word. True, depending on your point of view, but ugly. I prefer 'entrepreneur,' if you don't mind, Paul. And the reason I'm not still a marine is because they didn't understand aggressive suppression of the enemy."

"You got kicked out?"

"In a manner of speaking. But they taught me a lot that I now use to my advantage. Not a bad deal when you look at the big picture."

"But you treated Jim and me as friends."

Jarrod grunted. "Yeah. All you need to know is what to say to people and you're in."

"Listen, Jarrod, it's me you want. Let Cij go, and I'll leave peacefully with you."

"You're in no position to bargain. We have our weapons trained on you and your traitor friend. You'll leave peacefully enough." Paul could see Jarrod moving his head from side to side as if searching the room. "Where is she?"

"Where's who?"

"The girl—the dying-of-cancer girl. Where is she?"

Paul looked toward the floor in the dark. "She . . . didn't make it." He lifted his head again. "Does that make you happy, Jarrod? Does it make you feel good to know you killed a little girl?"

"You killed her, Branson." Jarrod's harsh, emotionless voice pierced the darkness. "You killed her the minute you put her on that plane."

"She would have died if I'd left her in the compound."

"Enough. Dan, check the building. Make sure she isn't here somewhere."

One of the men on Jarrod's left walked through the vacant building. He returned a few minutes later. "All rooms empty. She's not here."

Jarrod shook his head. "Instead of leaving her in the compound, you fed her to the crocs in a murky river. And you have the nerve to call me a scumbag. If you'd given Quinn what he needed, you could've been part of this. She'd be alive, and you'd be rich. It's that simple."

"It's not that simple."

Two high-beam floodlights abruptly illuminated the room. Paul squinted as the men set them on the floor and removed their night vision goggles without lowering their weapons. As his eyes adjusted to the bright light, Paul saw that Jarrod stood with two men on his left and one on his right, each bearing an assault rifle and a semiautomatic sidearm.

Paul turned to Cijen.

"What did I say about moving, Branson?"

Paul looked back. "How did you find us?"

"It wasn't hard, really."

Paul scanned the room.

"If you're looking for the family who was here earlier, don't bother. They left not long after you boys fell asleep. We followed them down the street about a block, questioned them, and let them go. They said two armed men drove in here in a bullet-riddled pickup."

"After you talked to them, you didn't—"

"I came for you, Branson. Not them. They're fine. I even gave him enough to feed his kids. Turns out I'm a pretty nice guy." Jarrod's cocky smirk made Paul want to strangle him.

Cijen shook his head. "This is my fault, Dr. Paul. I fell asleep. I was supposed to be on watch."

"It's okay, Cij."

Jarrod interrupted. "Touching, gentlemen. But Quinn has a special place for you, Mr. Cijen. You won't like it." He turned back to Paul. "Now, Branson, get up nice and slow, and if you try anything, I'll shoot your buddy here. That clear enough for you?"

Paul stood, lifted the loaded pistol from his belt, and set it on the floor in front of him. Jarrod waved his gun at Paul's face, indicating for him to put his hands up. Paul raised them over his head.

"Search him," Jarrod ordered the guard on his right.

The man leaned his rifle against the wall and moved behind Paul to pat him down, kicking the pistol and ammo out of reach.

"Tie his hands behind him," Jarrod ordered.

The guard pulled Paul's hands down and zip-tied them behind his back.

"Now you, Mr. Cijen. Slow and easy."

Cijen moved to his feet, and the soldier searched him, removing a semiautomatic pistol from his leg holster and a knife from his belt. His rifle remained on the floor.

"Now, Dr. Branson, we have a long drive ahead of us. It's good that we're getting a predawn start." Jarrod paused. "You know, you surprised me. You put up a good fight." He smirked again. "And you almost made it. You killed eleven of my best men today. Nicely done."

The soldier on Jarrod's right gathered the weapons.

Cijen turned to Paul. "I'm sorry, Dr. Paul."

Paul recognized the look in Cijen's eyes and braced himself.

Suddenly Cijen rushed the man on Jarrod's left, grabbing the man's knife and driving it into his abdomen. He gripped the guard's pistol and shot the second man to the left of Jarrod in the head.

Paul followed his lead and snapped his head back, butting the guard behind him and driving his foot down the man's leg, crushing his ankle with his body weight. The man screamed in pain as Paul dove for Jarrod, knocking him to the floor as the guard behind Paul recovered enough to fire his pistol at Cijen, hitting him in the shoulder. Cijen spun to his right and grabbed his wound.

In an instant, Jarrod pushed Paul off, aimed his .357 Magnum at Cijen, and fired. Cijen's body lurched backward and crumpled to the floor.

Paul used his feet to sweep Jarrod's legs out from under him. When Jarrod landed on his back, Paul kicked the gun from his hand, then rushed for the door with his hands still bound behind him. The guard he had injured attempted to block him, but Paul's momentum carried him into the man, knocking them both to the floor. Paul quickly scrambled to his feet and continued toward the door. A single shot into the wall in front of him blew some concrete into the air and stopped Paul in his tracks. He didn't have to look. There was only one man left who could hold a gun.

"I see that killing eleven men is not enough for one day." Jarrod spat blood on the floor. "You managed to end two more lives and cripple another. I'll take credit for Cijen's death. But this ends now. You know I'm not allowed to kill you, but I can shoot you in the leg. Is that what you want?"

Paul didn't respond. He didn't move as the guard he'd knocked down slowly stood and glared at him. Finally Paul turned and faced his friend on the floor. A pool of blood had emerged from beneath Cijen's body. Paul choked back tears as he looked at Cijen's lifeless eyes. He'd saved Paul. He'd saved Leza. Now Paul stood helplessly beside his friend who had breathed his last.

"Cut me loose." Paul wasn't asking.

"I beg your pardon?" Jarrod gave a smug chuckle.

"I said cut me loose. I want to close his eyes."

Jarrod paused, then grabbed the jacket from one of the dead guards and threw it over Cijen's face.

"Now you don't have to bother."

Paul turned to Jarrod. "He was a good friend, a true man, not like the coward who just shot him. I promise I will watch you die."

"Bold words from an unarmed prisoner, Branson."

"They weren't just words. It was my vow."

Gage adjusted the headset and listened.

"Hello, Gage. It's the general here. What do we have?"

"Sir, we've located our target. He escaped from a compound in the Congo, which alerted us to his whereabouts and allowed us to track him to the city of Aru. We lost contact when his vehicle disappeared late last night. We do have a lead though, sir."

"What do you mean? What lead?"

"Well, sir, his vehicle hasn't surfaced, but this morning we picked up a visual on sat imaging of the missing jeep from yesterday. It's definitely the same vehicle that was in pursuit. We have roof markings that gave us a positive ID. Although Branson may be dead, these guys followed the truck to this location and then left. If they didn't have Branson, where would they be going? I think this is our ticket, sir."

"This is a special ops mission, Gage. I need hard evidence."

Gage adjusted his headset. "General, with one more satellite pass we'll find that jeep. The last image we have shows it leaving Aru and heading northwest toward the Sudan border. It's our only hope at this point. If we can find it, it will lead us to the target. I'll have those images in twenty minutes with your approval, sir."

"The satellite is yours, Gage. We need to find the doctor before they get what they want from him. This is a White House mandate."

Gage paused. "Yes, sir. Copy that, sir."

"Find our man, Gage. The president is breathing down my neck, and I don't like it. Is that understood?"

"Yes, sir. Understood, General."

Gage put the headset down as the men gathered around him. "Let's pack it up and be ready to fly as soon as we have our images. It's time to find our man."

Jessica's cell door clanked open, and Quinn walked in. Obviously agitated, he approached her bed as she lay tied to the frame.

"You've wounded Gina badly."

"Not bad enough."

"Did you think you would escape? Did you think you would help your father?"

"That woman disgusts me. Keep her away from me. I beat her because of who she is. Not to escape."

Quinn balled up his fists and shouted, "You are so much like your father!" He walked away from the bed several paces, then slowly turned and faced Jessica again. He spoke angrily but calmly. "You're not in a position to make demands. One way or another you will pay for what you did to Gina. If you have left permanent scars on her face, I'll do the same to you. I don't care if it brings less money for you."

Jessica didn't speak. She knew better.

"For the rest of your life, I will determine the consequences of your actions."

As Quinn walked out, Jessica prayed for strength.

Jim sat in the shade of a great mango tree with Chima.

"Chief, when I spoke with Buru, he told me that you and the other leaders met to discuss Quinn, the man who apparently kidnapped Paul. Is that right?"

Chima nodded. "This is true. I informed Buru that Commander Toru of the South Sudanese military explained to us that he feels there is reason to believe Quinn is going to attack the villages with chemicals he may have stolen from a shipment on a sunken freighter. If he can kill all of us, he can access the oil beneath us. He has bought land in this region, but he can't drill unless the villages give their permission. He's an outlaw. We won't give our permission, and Quinn knows that. For his plan to work, we must die."

"Well, that's where I'm afraid this may get complicated, and I need to explain something. Paul may not have been taken at random. He has knowledge of chemicals that could be used for such a purpose—chemical warfare, to be specific. At least I think so based on research he was involved in for the US government a number of years ago. If that's the case, I think we should be ready for trouble in each village twenty-four hours a day. We'll post guards and lookouts so we'll know what's coming. Arm the men and move the women to safety in Mundri. We could ask for permission from the South Sudanese army to use the barracks near the airfield—you know, the abandoned ones they used until five years ago."

"Dr. Paul had a similar plan before he was abducted, wanting to move the women and children."

"I think it's still a good plan. Let's start the evacuation as soon as possible and set up sentries at the entrances of the villages. Do we have a time frame for a potential attack?"

"I'm afraid not. We were told that it could be any day based on the time that has passed since they kidnapped Dr. Paul."

"So we need to be ready, Chief. You with me?"

"Yes. It's a good plan, and Buru will be our key man. He knows who can fight, who can shoot, and who we can trust."

"Good. Let's get moving, Chief."

The men climbed into a jeep and set off to find Buru.

Six hours after leaving the abandoned building in Aru, Jarrod's jeep pulled into the LRA's Mangai compound. As they approached the entrance, Paul noted that wooden guard outposts dotted the borders of the encampment every twenty meters. The same kind of double fence surrounded the compound as the one where he'd been imprisoned in the Congo. An empty flagpole bordered by stones and gravel stood in the center of the clearing, giving the appearance of an old armory or small military base.

The jeep pulled up to a two-story cinder block warehouse at least three times the size of the one at the other compound. Exhausted, Paul's knees ached as he stepped down from the jeep. He was sore all over and had never felt so defeated. Still, cooperating with Quinn was the last thing on his mind. The relief of not having Leza's life in the balance calmed him. Quinn might resort to torture, but if Paul could hold out, he might be able to stop this madness.

Quinn and Miju stepped out of the warehouse and approached him with a swagger of confidence. "Welcome to your final destination, Dr. Branson." Quinn stressed the word "final." "I hope you enjoyed your outing—and my plane." Quinn's words dripped with sarcasm. "You've cost me precious money and time and caused a great deal of trouble. You're responsible for robbing me of the pleasure of killing Cijen myself, and you're also the cause of the death of an innocent little girl. I'll spare you no longer." He walked to Paul and punched him in the stomach. Paul doubled over from the pain and struggled for air.

"I'm done playing games. Give me the formula, Branson, or I'll hurt someone you love—right now."

Paul glanced up at him. "You've overplayed your hand, Quinn. Since Jarrod has obviously filled you in, you must realize by now that you've eliminated my motivation. Leza's dead, and I have no reason to give you what you want."

"I had a feeling you might say that. I feel sorry for you, Branson. God always places me one step ahead of you. It seems almost unfair."

"You don't even know who God is."

Quinn's face glowed with arrogance. "He is the one who gives me power. Remember what 'the LRA' stands for? The Lord's Resistance Army."

"And you believe that your lord is actually God and that He's up there serving you?"

"You tell me. The advantage is always mine. Is He serving you? I think not. Look at yourself. What more could go wrong?"

"We do not serve the same God, Quinn."

"Agreed." Quinn turned to Miju. "Bring her."

Paul looked at the warehouse. His blood ran cold in his veins. "No . . ." How could they have found Leza? It was impossible. Then he heard what he'd never expected. Jessica's fussing and kicking as she was forced out of the building brought Paul to the ground on his knees. "Oh God . . ."

"Daddy?"

Jessica tried to pull free from the guards, but they wouldn't let her go. Quinn signaled for them to release her. She ran to her father and dropped to the ground in front of him. "Daddy—"

"I'm sorry, Jessica. How in God's name did they bring you into this?"

"Into what?"

"Quinn's a madman who needs a chemical formula that's buried in my head."

"Formula for what?"

"A formula to kill people—tens of thousands of people."

"Don't do it, Daddy."

"If I don't tell them, they'll kill you, or worse. I can't let that happen."

Jessica wrapped her arms around her father's neck and put her lips next to his ear. She whispered, "They're going to kill us anyway, Daddy. Don't give it to them."

"Enough!" Quinn tore Jessica from her father and threw her at the guards. "Lock her up!"

"Be strong, Daddy!" Jessica yelled the words until she was too far inside the building to be heard.

Quinn waited until all was quiet. "I need the formula now." He squatted in front of Paul and spoke with eerie calmness. "Branson, this is my dream you're playing with. So please understand me: I'm not threatening to kill Jessica. I am promising a fate for your beautiful daughter that will be much, much worse than dying . . . for years . . . and years . . . and years. She'll beg for death, and it will elude her. She'll pray for help, and God—yours and mine—will abandon her. She'll curse this day and hate you for the rest of her life. You need to believe me, because I'll do it. Now, what will it be, Dr. Branson? If there are supplies I need to obtain for this formula, we don't have much time. So tell me."

Paul looked into Quinn's eyes. He couldn't imagine allowing his daughter to go through what Quinn had promised. "How do I know you'll let her go?"

"You don't. I could give you my word, but I can't be trusted."

Paul's scrambled mind searched for an answer. As he prayed silently for wisdom, he knew in his heart what he must do.

"I'll do it—the formula and my life for hers."

Quinn seemed to be having trouble containing his enjoyment of the moment as a toothy grin crossed his lips for the first time since Paul had known him.

"If you go back on this, Quinn, may the Dark One destroy you," Paul said. "May he choose between you and me. My God is real. Yours doesn't exist."

Quinn's smile vanished. "Enough of this. What supplies do you need?"

"You have everything already. You just don't know how to combine it. Or should I say—bind it."

Quinn signaled his men to lift Paul to his feet. "Bring him." Quinn walked toward the warehouse, and Paul followed, a guard latched onto each arm. He stopped as he watched two of Quinn's men dragging Adanna toward the huts near the back of the compound.

Quinn turned. "You thought I wouldn't know she helped you, Branson? You used her gun to kill my guard. She was with you in the hut the day before you escaped. It wasn't hard to figure out."

"What are you going to do with her?"

Quinn smirked. "It's your fault she's here. Her soul is one more for you to bear. How would your dead wife feel about you now? Oh, wait—you can ask her yourself, very soon."

As they walked to the warehouse in silence, Paul pondered all that could have been and wondered where he'd gone wrong. Just twenty-four hours earlier, his chances of stopping Quinn had seemed so promising. He'd even begun to think he might actually be The Chosen—Abdu— God's choice for delivering his people from evil. Now he had his answer.

Buru handed the sentry their last rifle. "Do not leave this post. Guard it with your life. Everyone is depending on you."

Jim crawled behind the steering wheel as Buru climbed in the other side of the jeep. "Looks like we're all set," Jim said. "The women and children will be transported to Mundri, and our men are guarding the villages. I don't know what we can do to protect ourselves from chemical warfare, if that's what's coming. But we're as ready as we can be."

Buru nodded. "I wish I could do more. Dr. Paul is a good friend. This is wrong what he's going through." He was silent as Jim pulled onto the road to Matta. "But he will be back. He is Abdu."

Jim swerved to miss some potholes, then turned to his friend. "I hope you're right, Buru. I hope you're right."

The silence resumed briefly, but Jim knew Buru wasn't done. "Jim, is it possible that Dr. Paul is Abdu, and that the God he speaks of called him to this task, instead of our spirits?"

Jim stifled a grin. "Yes, but why do you ask?"

Buru shook his head as he looked out at the flatlands, then back at Jim. "I have prayed and believed in the spirits all my life, and still I receive no answers. Dr. Paul prays to his God, but there is something different in him—something powerful that I can't explain. That's why the panther came to him instead of one of us. I saw it. Can you tell me more about this God of his?"

Jim nodded. "I can, Buru. I'm glad you asked."

Jessica sat in the corner of her room, thinking. Before she realized it, darkness had set in. It must have been five or six hours since she'd been torn away from her father. She listened—noises in the hallway—there were men outside her room. The door opened. Quinn entered and squatted beside her.

"You'll be pleased to know your father has given me the information I need. This delay, all of these problems, the death of a little girl, never had to happen. It's his fault you're here instead of living your life of luxury in New York."

Jessica's fears welled inside her. She controlled her expression and refused to cry.

"Attacking Gina intensified your problems. You and your father have been nothing but trouble from the start. You don't understand how life works outside your own little world filled with riches and skyscrapers. Manning had the same problem, but he wanted more—of everything. Unfortunately, he couldn't deliver where your father could."

"You know nothing about our world," Jessica said. "My father gave up a wealthy practice to offer medical care to poor, dying people here in Africa—your world, the world where you plunder and rape and kill your own people. Don't talk like you care, you disgusting hypocrite."

Quinn stood, grabbed Jessica's hair, and pulled her from the floor. "Shut your mouth, or I may break my promise to your father." He shoved her against the wall. "You and I will be taking a ride tonight."

"Why? Where?"

"You'll see when we get there."

"But if he gave you what you need, why are you taking me?"

"Until I see it with my own eyes, I will not believe it. There is no deal if the formula doesn't work, and your father knows that. Come."

"I want to see my dad first."

Quinn paused at the door of the cell. "I'll do this because it pleases me for your father to see you, knowing he may never see you again. Say your good-byes. Your father's life is over. He will not go free."

Jessica stared at Quinn. "He traded his life for mine."

"Yes, he did."

Quinn's hand engulfed Jessica's entire upper arm as he pulled her from the room and walked her down the corridor. When they exited the building, she saw that the compound was bustling with workers. Trucks lined the main road from the warehouse to the gate. Several were loaded with blue drums and nothing more while others carried men.

Quinn dragged Jessica to the clearing where her father knelt on the ground, his hands bound behind him to a flagpole that seemed out of place in the center. Jessica struggled to pull away from Quinn, and he threw her in Paul's direction.

Jessica dropped to her knees in front of her father and gently wrapped her arms around him. "Daddy, I love you."

Paul controlled his emotions, but his tears for his daughter couldn't be stifled. "Jessica, I love you. I'm sorry you have to be here."

She hugged him tenderly. "It's okay, Daddy. Quinn said you gave him the formula. You shouldn't—"

Paul whispered, "Everyone will know it's a terrorist act. If you get free from here, you have to warn the villages, otherwise people will die from the well water in forty-eight hours. I couldn't trade the lives of thousands for yours. I love you, Jess, but I couldn't." Tears streamed down his face.

Jessica held her father gently and whispered with her lips touching his ear, "Daddy, you did the right thing, and I'm proud of you. Please don't be upset." She paused. "Quinn is taking me with him tonight."

Paul turned to Quinn. "You promised to let her go."

"I must see with my own eyes that the formula works, or there is no deal."

"You're a—"

"Shhh, Daddy, don't." Jessica's eyes filled with tears.

Paul saw in her face that she understood she would never see him again.

"I thought I could do it, Jess. I thought I could save us." This would be the last road for his sweet daughter. If Quinn took her with him, he'd never let her go once the formula failed. All the dreams they'd shared were gone. It was over. They'd ended on the bloody gravel in front of a flagless pole.

Quinn broke in. "It's done. Tomorrow will begin a new era for Sudan."

Jessica kissed her father's cheek as Quinn grabbed her by the arm, pulled her away, and pushed her into the back of one of the personnel carriers. He pulled himself into his jeep at the front of the caravan, and they moved out, truck after truck.

Paul's eyes widened when he looked at the last vehicle. Hanna stared at him from the back with tears streaming down her face. Paul watched her until they were out of sight and the quiet of the compound returned. Losing it all hadn't been the plan. Nothing could be done now. He looked at the guard standing over him. The man gave him a half-toothed grin and spat in his face. Paul crumpled to the ground and no longer hoped—for anything.

"Major, take a look."

Gage walked to Murdock's computer and studied the screen. "Interesting."

"And here, sir." Murdock clicked to the next screen.

Gage scanned the images of Paul strapped to a flagpole inside of a compound. He studied them and stood proudly. "Suit up, ladies. Fire up that bird, Murdock. Let's do this now!"

CHAPTER TWENTY-ONE

The gravel cut Paul's knees as he knelt in front of the flagpole. Only faint light from the nearby warehouse penetrated the darkness. Blood dripped on the ground from somewhere on his head. His body was cramped, and he couldn't think, and a pounding headache made rest impossible. He changed position, but the bindings on his wrists holding him to the pole tore his flesh.

"Don't make me live longer than I have to," Paul said out loud.

"What are you doing?"

Paul glanced up. "Who are you?"

"Rulu. I said what are you doing?"

Paul looked at the ground again. "I'm watching myself bleed."

"Do it quieter."

Paul closed his eyes and imagined Nicki calling his name, her voice carried by the warm breeze wafting through the mango grove.

"I messed up," Paul whispered. "I don't know what I should have done to stop Quinn. People will die tonight, and Jessica will suffer an even worse fate." He fought for a full breath. "Oh God."

"I told you to be quiet!"

Paul looked up. "Quinn put you in charge of me. You know what that means, right?"

"I said quiet!" Rulu raised the butt of his gun to strike him.

"Your only chance of living more than a few hours is if I'm alive when Quinn gets back. Now point that at somebody who cares or shoot me. I'll talk if I want to."

Rulu cursed and turned his back to Paul.

Paul looked at the sky. "I don't know if I should even have come back to Africa considering all that's happened. I don't understand." He paused to collect his thoughts. "Even if it was just to save Leza, it was worth it, I guess." He coughed and spat blood on the ground. "Stop Quinn, God. If I'm Abdu, stop Quinn."

Paul stared at the heavens. "There are millions of stars tonight." When he lowered his gaze, he saw Rulu squatting in front of him, his face just centimeters away.

"If you're Abdu, why hasn't God heard you?"

"Rulu, get away from—"

Rulu dropped his rifle, grabbed Paul by the neck, and pulled him to his feet. "Does this hurt?" He squeezed Paul's throat harder. "I'll tell Quinn you escaped and that I killed you." He tightened his grasp more.

Paul struggled to free himself, but the bindings were too tight.

"I want to see the fear of death in your eyes." Rulu's voice had turned gravelly and deep.

Paul focused on Rulu's hate-filled face and squirmed. He ran out of air, and panic struck, but he refused to show this man fear. His strength weakened and his vision dimmed, and then he heard a sickening thud as something warm and wet splattered his face. Rulu dropped to the ground.

Paul inhaled through his painful throat and glanced at Rulu's mangled, bloody face. He scanned the floodlight-illuminated outposts along the fence. As he watched, seven of the perimeter guards fell silently to the ground. A noise from behind caused Paul to turn, but a gloved hand clamped over his mouth before he could see anything. He braced, waiting for the snap of his neck.

"Dr. Paul Branson?" The man's deep American whisper took Paul by surprise. He nodded once.

"I'm Gage, sir. Commander of the United States Special Forces Team Seven."

Paul couldn't move. Was he hallucinating? A wave of emotion swept over him, but he pushed it down.

"Sir, I need you to answer two questions. This is extremely important. I'm going to move my hand from your mouth and ask you to answer quietly. If you understand, nod."

Paul did as he was told. Gage moved his hand enough for Paul to speak.

"Sir, I need to know the name of your first pet."

"A dog, Slinky." Paul's raspy voice made it difficult to speak quietly, but he managed.

"One more question, sir. Your youngest sister's first name is Joanne. What is her middle name?"

"Joanne is my oldest sister, not my youngest. And her first name is Leah, but she's always gone by her middle name, Joanne."

"Very good, sir." Gage took his hand away completely and moved in front of Paul where he could see him. "We're here to take you home, Dr. Branson."

Paul's knees buckled, and Gage lowered him to the ground. "Thank you."

"You all right, sir?"

Paul looked at him again. "Are you actually here?"

"Yes, sir. We're here." Gage pulled his knife and cut the ties. Paul rubbed his swollen wrists and wiped Rulu's blood from his face.

Stumbling to his feet, Paul whispered to Gage, "There are men in the warehouse between us and the front gate, another few in the cell block to our left. I don't know how many in the other buildings, but there's the remnant of a small army here."

As Gage repeated what Paul said, the headset taped to his forehead picked up everything, and he relayed it to his men. He added, "The package is with me. Repeat—I have Enigma."

Stunned, Paul asked, "How did you find me?"

"It wasn't easy, sir. I'll explain later. We have to go."

"Thank you for coming for me. I—gave up."

"The entire country of the United States is here for you, sir." Gage surveyed the immediate area. "We need to move. Are you hurt, Doctor?"

"I'm okay. I can walk." Paul paused, then added, "There's a woman being held prisoner here. She's Quinn's wife."

Gage shook his head. "I'm sorry, sir. We're here for you. We can't extract a citizen from the region."

"I understand. I hope she'll be okay. They took her somewhere to the back of the compound."

Gage nodded. "There's very little chance we'll get near her. I'm sorry. On my heels. Copy, sir?"

"Copy."

Gage scanned the terrain around the mango trees and moved toward the front of the compound to the edge of the cell block, then turned to face the main gate. He led Paul behind a jeep, leaving the cover of the trees to maneuver past the warehouse. He spoke quietly. "Enigma and I are on the move."

The moment Gage finished speaking, a guard stepped out of the warehouse, spotted them, and yelled something in Arabic. In an instant, Gage drew his silenced FN Five-seveN semiautomatic pistol and fired one shot, quietly killing the guard.

"Heads up, guys. We're engaged." Gage holstered his pistol.

Five men exited the building and fired at the jeep where Paul and Gage were taking cover. One by one they dropped to the ground as silenced sniper bullets found their mark on each man.

Paul searched the border of the compound with his eyes. "Where are the snipers?"

"The mango grove." Gage turned his attention to the warehouse. "Jake, set the charges." He focused on Paul again. "We're a long way from the front gate, and we've lost the element of surprise. We're not going to be able to leave the way I came in. Where do they keep the vehicles?"

Paul pointed. "They were working on the trucks over there by that building today." He took a jagged breath.

Gage glanced at him. "Still with me, Doc?"

"Never been better."

"One more thing, Doc. No more pointing. If anyone's watching us, we don't want to give up any information. Copy, sir?"

"Yes. Understood."

"Very good, sir."

Another hail of gunfire focused on them. One shot came dangerously near Paul, and glass from the windshield of the jeep fractured into a thousand spiderweb cracks.

Gage spoke. "We're under fire. Jake, hold the C4 and cover us."

Within seconds, five shots echoed from behind the warehouse, killing the men who were shooting at Paul and Gage. One Special Forces team member took a position in front of them while another circled behind.

The roar of an engine preceded a pickup truck as it broke through the tall grass behind the jeep. Rounds whistled past their heads, and Paul felt a sting on his neck. He instinctively grabbed the wound.

One SF soldier returned fire into the vehicle with his M4, taking out the driver and two men in the truck bed. It veered to the right and careened past them.

Gage pushed Paul to the ground and stood over him as his eyes searched every angle, every potential point of attack. "You okay, Doc?"

"I'm good—just a scratch." Paul watched as the snipers in the mango trees dropped every man who ventured from the warehouse.

Gage turned toward the cinder block building. "Jake, how's the C4 coming?" He paused as he waited for the answer. "Copy that." He turned to Paul. "We need to get you out of here, sir."

Gage turned to a building one of the SF men had entered to check for hostiles. "Bart, catch up with us. Heading north." Bart ran from the building and joined them as Gage was still speaking.

Gage faced Paul. "Where's the garage?"

Paul looked around the huge compound to gain his bearings and remembered Gage's instructions not to point. "It's directly to my left. Nine o'clock. I saw it briefly. It's just past those low huts with the green tin roofs. They were working on a personnel transport earlier."

Gage nodded. "Got it. Let's go. Hawkeye, you're with Bart and me."

Hawkeye surfaced from the other side of the jeep.

A barrage of gunfire from the warehouse streaked red-hot metal into the mango trees.

Gage tapped Paul on the shoulder. "Our Black Hawk spotted three vehicles, pickup trucks, approaching from the bamboo grove at your two o'clock. They have a fifty-cal mounted in the truck bed, so keep your head down and stay close to me."

Gage called to the other men. "Hawkeye, move to the rear with Bart. Take the first shot you can."

"Copy that," Hawkeye responded.

Gage grabbed Paul's arm. "I need to move you, sir. Right now. Follow me." Paul crouched as Gage turned toward the garage. "Kid, we're headed to your left to the cinder block building on the east edge of the compound." Gage and Paul sprinted toward the structure. Gunfire from the warehouse struck the ground near them, sending clumps of dirt into the air as Gage forced Paul to the ground behind a fallen tree before taking cover beside him.

"Kid, it's too hot to move. Jake—you in position? Talk to me. We're taking fire. Need to light that building up." Gage listened. "We're never going to make it to the garage with the warehouse intact. Too many men firing from the windows." Gage turned to one of the SF soldiers behind them. "They're almost to your position, Hawkeye."

Hawkeye nodded. Paul watched as he quickly checked his equipment, focused on the tall grass, and flipped down his bipod to stabilize his fifty-caliber rifle. In a matter of seconds he was on his belly, locked and loaded.

The first vehicle burst through the shrubbery thirty meters away. "Look alive, men!" Hawkeye yelled and unleashed a large-caliber assault of lead into the first truck. It exploded into flames as the second truck, following closely, careened into the burning wreckage. Hawkeye fired into the tumbling, flaming debris as both trucks rolled to a stop.

The third truck, bearing its own fifty-caliber machine gun, burst into the clearing, firing into the mango grove. Hawkeye and Bart emptied their weapons into the cab until the driver slumped over the wheel.

Hawkeye snatched his gear from the ground and dove for cover as the driverless truck blazed its own path. Gage shoved Paul out of the way as the truck slammed into the fallen tree.

Gage leaned down to him. "I'm going to try to move you again. I need you to—"

Gunfire exploded close to the wreckage near them. Machine gun slugs caused the ground to erupt.

"Jake. Where's our detonation?" Gage asked as he stood over Paul. "We're pinned down." The gunfire splintered fragments of metal from the nearby trucks. "Jake, let's go. Make it hot. Do it now!"

Paul spoke up. "Gage, there are toxic chemicals in blue barrels in that building."

Gage repeated the information to Jake, then turned to Paul. "Sorry, Doc. No blue barrels inside."

Gage listened for Jake's confirmation, then shouted, "Fire in the hole! Get down!" He turned to Paul. "Cover your ears, Doc!"

Even with his hands over his ears, the initial explosion from the C4 briefly deafened Paul as the roof of the warehouse lifted six meters. The explosive concussion blew out chunks of wall in a ball of fire, then sucked the flames back into the building from the backdraft. The ground under Paul trembled.

The roof crashed onto the inferno as a deafening eruption from the ignited accelerant launched eleven-kilogram concrete blocks into the air. Fragments of metal showered the surrounding jungle. Wood and bricks rained on the men as they took cover under the overturned vehicles.

Gage glanced toward the back of the compound, then turned to Paul. "Murdock in the chopper says there are thirty or forty men gathering at the front gate to block our exit. He can also see there are no vehicles in that garage we're heading toward. Are there any vehicles left here at all? A caravan pulled out earlier—was that everything?"

Paul looked toward the back of the compound. "I don't know."

Gage spoke as if the chopper pilot were standing in front of him. "Murdock, do you see anything else from where you are? Any options?" Gage listened for a response. "Check it out, Jake." Gage turned to Paul. "Murdock spotted vehicles next to the blue-roofed building near the back perimeter. That's our goal. Kid, hold your position in the trees. Solo, drop out and head for high ground. We'll need coverage when we go deep. Murdock—what's your position?"

Paul couldn't hear Murdock's response, and Gage's expression told him nothing.

"Copy that. Hold it there." Gage turned as Jake caught up with them.

Jake reached for Paul's hand. "Good to meet you, Doctor. I'm Jake." Paul shook his hand vigorously. "Good to meet you too, Jake."

Gage nodded. "Let's go, men." He headed toward the back of the compound, moving from building to building with the others close behind. He stopped after forty-five meters and addressed Paul. "Solo says we're clear to the perimeter building by the back wall, but there are guards inside."

Gage flipped down his night vision binoculars and scanned the concrete structure near the wall. "Murdock, I need a Somalia scenario." Gage waited, then replied, "Copy that."

He turned to Jake. "Take point. Fifty meters."

Jake immediately ran ahead while Paul, Gage, and the other men took cover at the edge of a barrack.

Gage leaned toward Paul. "Jake is thirty meters from the perimeter building. Armed men on high alert surround it. There's something inside worth guarding. He's moving closer. We'll do the same." Gage motioned toward the building as Paul stayed close.

Several men attempted to hide behind the cinder block structure, but one by one they fell prey to Kid's deadly aim.

"Jake's reporting a large, fully enclosed jeep inside the building, but it's heavily guarded." He turned his attention to the chopper. "Murdock—you close?" Gage paused. "Copy that. Engage."

Seconds later the Black Hawk appeared and hovered above the trees as if studying the compound. It turned its searchlights onto the guard gate, sending men scrambling to escape its powerful beacon.

The deep rumble of the chopper blades created widespread confusion. Without Quinn or Miju to lead them, the men descended into chaos.

The deadly thunder of the Black Hawk's fifty-caliber machine guns firing into the cinder blocks forced men to dive for cover. Dirt filled the air, and boards splintered as Murdock wreaked havoc on the building below.

When Murdock paused, Jake sprinted for the entrance, shooting his way through the dangling remnants of the garage door. An explosion of automatic gunfire lit up the room inside, then it fell silent again.

Paul took a sharp breath and turned to Gage.

"Jake, report." Nothing.

Paul stared at the building—waiting.

"Jake?" Gage called again.

Murdock opened fire on the forces below as they focused on the chopper. The fifty-caliber turret prevented anyone from getting close.

Suddenly a large jeep exploded through the dangling warehouse doors and raced toward Gage. Jake was at the wheel.

Gage fired at the men trying to stop the jeep, while Bart and Solo ran from their position to catch up. Several rounds hit near them as they struggled to gain their footing. Gunfire pounded Bart, forcing his body back with each blow, his bulletproof vest preventing the slugs from getting through.

Sparks pinged from the sides of the jeep as Jake sped through a cloud of ricocheting bullets and skidded to a stop in front of Solo. Before Solo could enter the jeep, Paul watched his body lurch forward and fall to the ground. Bart grabbed Solo's shirt and shoved him in, then dove on top of him.

Jake stepped on the gas and blazed another hundred meters where he slid, wheels locked, just past Gage and Paul. When gunfire pinned them down, Murdock moved the chopper into position and unloaded a circular pattern of coverage around the jeep, giving them a chance to run.

"Let's go!" Gage pushed Paul through the door Bart had opened. Paul looked back just in time to see Gage shot in the vest. He dropped to the ground but pushed himself up and ran. When a second round hit him, he tumbled and sprawled on the ground. This time, he didn't move.

Jake jumped out and covered Gage with his body while Murdock fired into the approaching men. With Murdock laying a trail of high-caliber rounds, Jake dragged Gage to the door of the jeep, and Paul pulled him inside. Automatic rounds pinged off the hood while Jake jumped back in, throttled up, and steered the jeep toward the front gate.

Paul turned Gage onto his back. A bullet had entered through the back of his neck and exited through his forehead. Paul checked for a pulse. When Jake glanced back, Paul shook his head.

Jake radioed the chopper. "We're en route to the extraction point, Murdock. Gage is down. Repeat: commander is down."

Paul noticed Solo holding his left shoulder with his right hand. Blood oozed between his fingers. Paul nodded at him and said, "I'll check that as soon as I can and get you bandaged up."

Solo nodded. "Yes, sir. Just a scratch."

The Black Hawk lifted and turned from the trees to the guard gate. The rapidly firing fifty-caliber machine gun spewed hot lead into the entrance, destroying everything in its path. A few of Quinn's men escaped, scattering into the woods, and Murdock launched a single missile into the fence to clear a path for Jake.

The jeep bounced as it sped through the gunfire, over the rubble, and between burning vehicles and debris. Jake stopped barely a kilometer down the road and picked up Kid. When they met up with the chopper ten minutes later, Murdock came out to meet them.

"Tell me," he said anxiously.

Jake responded, "We have Enigma, but Gage is dead. Let's get in the air."

Seconds later they were airborne with headphones in place.

Everyone was silent for a moment, then Paul took a deep breath. "Jake, as if this isn't bad enough, there's more going on here than my abduction. The commander of the LRA is Jason Quinn—I'm sure you've heard of him."

Paul wondered if anyone was listening at first. He saw that Jake was watching Solo and Bart zip Gage into a body bag. Then Jake turned to Paul.

"Go on, sir," he said in a subdued voice.

"Quinn has my daughter. He used her to force me to give him a formula he needed to poison the village well systems." Paul coughed, and Jake handed him a water bottle. Paul took a long drink and cleared his throat.

"Jake, I owe you men my life." All of them now turned their attention to him. "But I have to stop Quinn and save Jessica. He's on his way to five villages in Sudan to poison their water supplies with enough Soman chemicals to kill twenty-five thousand people. He wants to take over their land for the oil rights." Paul paused to give that a chance to sink in.

Jake spoke up. "The White House sent us to find and extract you, hopefully before you could give Quinn the formula he needs from your research. We already knew about the Soman."

Paul sighed. "I supplied him with a false formula, one to make certain he's caught and to minimize the loss of life—possibly prevent it. I'd hoped to warn the villages before the activated Soman became lethal—two days from now—thinking I could buy time and save Jessica. But even if it doesn't work for two days, once it's in the wells, it's impossible to stop. He was determined to poison the wells even without my help. My hope was to slow him down. If he succeeds, the land will be uninhabitable for a decade. If we can stop him, no one else dies."

A solemn pause followed.

"What Quinn is going to do to my daughter is unfathomable, but what will happen to the men, women, and children is beyond heinous."

Jake sat beside Paul. "Some of us are fathers too, Doc." He paused. "So what happens if he pulls this off? What's next?"

"My plan was to warn people not to drink the water so no one dies, but that's only a short fix. If the land is abandoned, the balance between

North and South Sudan will be destabilized and throw the country into civil war. The North is experienced at fighting that battle. Inhabitants of South Sudan will be relocated, possibly to camps. With you men, we may have a chance to stop Quinn before this happens."

Jake nodded. "And if Quinn doesn't take over the oil, someone else will, leaving it unstable and in the hands of people the US can't trust." He paused. "And your daughter, Jessica—you sure she's with Quinn?"

"I spoke with her before they left the compound," Paul assured him. "Can you alert the authorities that Quinn is on his way to poison the wells so someone can stop him?"

Jake took a deep breath. "There are two problems with that, sir. We don't have permission from any government to be here, so we aren't here. Being discovered on a military mission in Sudan would be an act of war or, at the very least, an international incident the White House can't endure, especially if this goes sideways. Our orders are to rescue you." Jake hesitated. "But there's another problem."

Paul already knew what he was going to say.

"They'll kill your daughter for certain if we contact the authorities. There would be no way to protect her."

"There's a chance the authorities have been contacted already."

"What do you mean, Doc?"

"When I left a little girl in the hospital, one of the doctors there promised to contact officials. But I don't know if he did, and I can't have any way of knowing if he contacted someone who's not on Quinn's payroll."

Jake thought for a moment. "Is there an antidote for exposure to Soman?"

"There is, but it would have to be administered within seconds of exposure, or it would be useless. And for this level of contamination, it would take more than anyone has stockpiled—as far as I know. There's no time." Paul cast a knowing glance at Jake.

"Don't even think it, Doc. You're considering sacrificing your daughter and going to the authorities. And if you did, you figure thousands could be saved—except that isn't true. First, we have only a few hours. Along the channels that we'd be required to follow, warning the authorities would take days. And even if we could give them a heads-up, and even if they would listen, and even if they had enough men to get to those wells, what are the chances they could do all of that in the next few hours? It's impossible. And according to what you're saying, the area will be polluted for years and uninhabitable. Even if we stop the villagers from drinking the poisoned water, it doesn't solve the big picture for Sudan or the US. It gives Quinn what he wants either way. The political fallout would be incalculable."

Paul looked at the men. "What's the answer? I need to make it right. How do I do that?" They all turned to Jake and waited.

Jake thought for a moment. "There's only one option that accomplishes the true mission and gets your daughter back." He turned to his team. "Gentlemen, it appears we're not done. In order for us to be a part of this, we'll go off-line. You know what that means. We will have to declare a certain jeopardy situation."

The men nodded but said nothing. Paul didn't understand. "Certain jeopardy?"

Jake explained. "It means making a decision in the field because something has come to our attention requiring us to change our mission objectives. It must be a compelling reason—that US interests will be in certain jeopardy unless we act. That's clearly the case here." He paused. "It also means we'll be on our own—no support, no coming back if we fail."

Paul felt the eyes of the men on him. "I know this is a lot to ask."

"Doc, you don't know us. Our work doesn't end just because you're no longer a prisoner—it's not over until we resolve the imminent international threat. Then we take you home. But to be honest with you, the chances of surviving this are not good—for any of us."

Paul looked around the circle of men. He'd never seen such unself-ish devotion. "I don't know what to say."

"Understand that certain jeopardy takes priority over everything. It becomes the new mission."

"Meaning?"

"Meaning that you may die with the rest of us, Doc."

Paul took one more look around. "It would be an honor to fight beside you or die with you."

Jake turned back to his fellow soldiers. "I respect every opinion. One man says no—we go. We've already lost the commander." He looked at his small, powerful, dedicated army as they sat in the chopper in a small circle, armed from head to toe. They were many kilometers from the compound, but in the distance an occasional explosion still lit the night sky.

Jake continued, "Our mission would require us to defeat Quinn by turning this chopper around, reaching the villages, stopping him before he poisons the wells, or warning the villagers if it's too late. If he suc-ceeds, the damage he'll cause will be catastrophic, and if we fail, the loss of life will be immeasurable. At the very least, a permanent evacuation would be necessary, and the villages will be lost. We have six hours."

Paul watched as the men hung on Jake's every word.

Solo weighed in first. "I say stay and fight. I have my good arm. That's all I need. Failure is not an option."

Bart was next. "Count me in. Failure is not an option."

Murdock chimed in. "I'm in, men. I'll fly you to Hell if that's where you say to go. Failure is not an option."

Kid spoke up. "I will not go home without helping these people." He looked at his fellow soldiers. "Failure is not an option. *De oppresso liber.*"

Jake and the other men repeated in unison, "*De oppresso liber.*"

Jake turned to Paul. "It's done. Let's go get your daughter and stop a psycho."

"Thank you." It was all Paul could say.

"We have work to do, men," Jake said.

Within minutes, the Black Hawk headed for Sudan and Quinn's convoy.

Jake keyed the radio and called command. "This is Black Team Seven—changing our call sign from Enigma to Dark Harbor, command from Gage to Jake." As soon as he placed the call, he turned off radio communication with the base.

Paul adjusted his headset. "What did that mean?"

"Command now knows our team is off-line. The code I gave didn't say we have you yet—a little concealment of the truth." Jake cocked his head briefly, but then added, "It also informed them we lost our commander and have declared a certain jeopardy situation." Jake handed Paul a protein bar and another bottle of water. "You need your strength, Doc. Eat."

"Thank you."

Jake leaned his head against the bulkhead for a moment's rest before the next battle.

As Kid started an IV on him, Paul's mind drifted to Jessica and what she might be going through. "We're flying into a black hole," Paul mumbled.

Jake lifted his head and looked at Paul. "Yeah, but we'll fly out too."

"A lot of people have died already. That's on me."

"This isn't on you. None of it's you. This is on psycho boy. Every death is on Quinn."

Paul settled into the seat. He knew that before dawn, either he or Quinn would be dead. As the Black Hawk flew into the dark night sky, he could not shake the feeling that the one to die might be him.

CHAPTER
TWENTY-TWO

The swerving of the truck on the rough road slammed Jessica into the bulkhead so hard her arm felt bruised. She glanced across the narrow aisle at her captor whose dark eyes, illuminated by the occasional beam of headlights from the truck behind them, remained fixed on Jessica.

"It's rude to stare, Gina."

The crooked smile Jessica had grown to despise coursed across Gina's lips. "My revenge for what you did will be sweet."

The truck hit another pothole, causing Jessica to push herself back onto the seat with her feet.

"Don't worry, I won't mar your pretty face. It's my property now, and I need you to bring a good price." Gina's sarcasm had an evil twist. "Quinn wanted me to ride with him, but I told him I needed to be alone. So . . . here I am."

Jessica tugged at the zip tie that secured her to the seat. "I'm not your property. My father gave Quinn what he wanted. He promised to let me go."

Gina's grin disappeared. "And you believed him?" She shook her head. "Foolish child," she grunted.

Jessica glanced into the darkness interrupted only by the bouncing headlights behind them, wishing this nightmare was over. Her joints hurt and her muscles ached, but when she shifted in the seat to find a better position, a dark, shiny object appeared in Gina's right hand.

"It took thirty-five stitches to fix the damage you caused when you clubbed me. These scars on my face will never fade, and neither will the markings I carve into you. I'll never be beautiful again, all because of—"

"You were ugly even without the scars."

Gina's mouth dropped open. "What did you say?"

"I said you're ugly inside—and disgusting. What you look like on the outside doesn't matter."

Gina trembled as she stood and grabbed the roof support with her left hand. The flickering lights shone on her contorted features, and Jessica saw a face she barely recognized. Gina's knife snapped open. The ten-centimeter blade glistened even in the dark.

"You'll pay for what you did to me. You'll never—"

"You're a coward too."

Gina looked at Jessica with disbelief on her face and moved closer. "Enough . . . !"

Jessica lurched forward as far as she could and head-butted Gina. Stunned, Gina stumbled backward. Before she could regain her balance, Jessica stretched against her ties and kicked Gina with all her strength, slamming her staggering body over the tailgate. When Gina tumbled onto the road, the truck behind them ran over her, finishing what Jessica had started.

The pounding of the Black Hawk's massive blades somehow comforted Paul. As Jake checked Paul's IV bag and drew some fluid into a syringe, he said, "This should give you a little boost, Doc." He held the bottle so Paul could read it.

"Solu-Medrol."

"You need this for the degree of inflammation in your body right now. It will add a little energy too."

Paul nodded and leaned back. "Agreed. I could use a little energy right now."

Jake pushed the syringe into the IV line slowly. "Don't worry, Doc. We're all trained medics."

Paul nodded his approval. "How's Solo's shoulder? I'd be glad to take a look at it and do what I can."

"He's fine. I cleaned the wound and wrapped him good. I don't know how bad the bones and joint are damaged. It's a through-and-through wound, and I'm sure he'll need surgery. But like he said, he has one good arm, and he can still use his left for support. He's an incredible sniper—one of the best." Jake gave Paul a quick nod. "Get some rest, Doc."

Paul marveled at his situation. An hour earlier he'd been tied to a flagpole while a man tried to strangle him. Now he sat in an assault chopper, surrounded by computer screens, technical equipment, weapons he didn't even recognize, and a team of US Army Special Forces willing to die for him.

Jake's voice broke Paul from his trance. "Are you allergic to any medications?"

"No. Why?"

"I'm going to add a little Rocephin antibiotic to the IV." Jake held the bottle for Paul to read again. "Those cuts on your arms and legs are going to get infected. I'll give you a gram."

"Perfect. Thank you." Paul thought for a moment. "Jake, I don't know what to say. The thought of Gage in a body bag—"

"Gage did what he came to do. He gave his life to save others. That's what we do. Sometimes we succeed—other times we don't. When we don't, we die trying." Jake paused and looked away. "Gage would never forgive me if I turned my back on this mission. He expected me to carry on with or without him. That's why I'm second in command." He stood. "I need to check our coordinates. Try to rest a little if you can. We still have a lot to do."

Paul dozed in and out of thoughts of Nicki. He remembered her struggle with chemo. It gave him strength somehow too. Paul remembered sitting beside her, holding her hand as the rain pattered lightly against the window.

"You know I have to go, right?" She'd turned to him as if she'd wanted to make certain he was listening. "God's calling me, and I need a new body. This one . . . it's just no good anymore. You have to let me go, Paul."

She was stronger than Paul. With every ounce of strength he could muster, he'd smiled at her that day.

"Okay. When He comes, you go. I want your pain to stop more than anything in the world."

They embraced, and as he remembered that moment, Paul knew he would have to draw on the strength that Nicki had shown him he had.

Jake's strong voice brought him back to reality again. "Hate to bring this up right now, but I need to know—how tough is your daughter? Can she handle herself, or is she going to fall apart if bullets start flying?"

"She's tough as nails and doesn't understand the concept of falling apart. If she gets a chance to fight, she'll fight. It wouldn't surprise me if she's already slugged Quinn by now." Paul grinned as he thought of Jessica's spunk. "I wish I had a picture to show you what she looks like, Jake. You wouldn't believe it."

"No need. Take a look." Jake tapped a few computer keys, and a dozen pictures of Jessica popped onto the screen with various dates and events printed below each one.

"What? Where did you get these? She isn't part of your mission."

"'Wasn't' would be a better word—at least not officially." Jake turned to Paul as he scanned the images. "You're right. She's beautiful, Doc. Your wife must have been too."

Paul smiled and nodded again. "Yeah. She's just like her mom." Paul paused. "You married, Jake?"

"No, sir. Haven't found the right girl yet. I will someday, though."

"In that case, I'll introduce you to her properly."

"I'd like that. Let's make it happen."

"You got it."

"Tell me, Doc—how many wells are we dealing with, and what kind of security is in place in the villages?"

Paul thought back to the map on the wall. "There are five wells in each of the five villages Quinn will attack. He plans to poison them all. Each well supplies water to around a thousand people, so twenty-five thousand lives are at stake if all the wells are poisoned. They plan to accomplish that before dawn."

"Are the villages that big? It doesn't look like a thousand people even live there."

"The wells serve a large region. People travel from all around to get clean water and carry it home in five-gallon cans every single day."

Jake nodded and looked at his watch. He tapped the back of Murdock's seat. "What's our ETA?"

Murdock checked his computer screen and GPS. "Fifteen."

Jake leaned down to Paul. "Okay, Doc, here's the plan. I need you to identify the bad guys and let our team move in. You need to stay in the background and pretend you're not even there."

"But Quinn will kill Jessica unless we get to him first. He has her for a reason, Jake. He held a child with cancer at gunpoint to draw me out of hiding, then starved her to force me to cooperate."

Jake nodded. "I understand your concern. But stick to the plan. We'll improvise depending on what we find, but our first priority is to get your daughter back and stop the well contamination."

"Jake, the first priority is to stop the poisoning. We can always go from village to village and warn them not to drink from the wells, but if the wells are poisoned, the land will be rendered unusable for a decade. Quinn already owns the land and all the rights as long as the villagers, who have the mineral first rights according to the treaty, don't get in his way. It's the long-term poisoning that makes the difference." Paul swallowed the lump in his throat. "First we stop the deployment of Soman, then we find Jessica."

Jake nodded. "We'll get her back, Doc. It's what we do."

Miju spread the map across the hood of the jeep and held his flashlight so the men could read it. Jarrod drew a circle around each well with a black marker as he spoke.

"You'll travel in teams of four men to each well, just like you've trained. Your call letters are Mission Eagle, teams one through five. You know how to take the covers off the wells and insert the nozzles. You've practiced this a hundred times. It will be no different in the field. The chemicals take ten minutes per well to run in. Don't touch the liquid—don't breathe the fumes. Just pour it in wearing your respirators and gloves, load the empty barrels onto the trucks, and rendezvous back here at zero five hundred. That gives you four hours. Once you've returned, we'll head for Matta. We have women and children to load up before they drink the poison. Matta will be the final stop before returning to the compound. We'll treat those wells last. Understood?"

One by one, each man indicated that he knew what to do.

"Any questions?"

No one responded.

"You have your assignments, coordinates, and orders. Don't engage unless you're forced to do so."

The men saluted Jarrod and headed for their vehicles.

Watching the teams load into five separate transport trucks and get ready to drive toward the villages should have been exciting for Miju. Instead, he felt conflicted about Branson, this operation, and how everything was being handled.

Jarrod folded the map. "What's going on, Miju? Something's got you all twisted up."

Miju didn't trust Jarrod. "Nothing." He thought about what to say. "I just like to be prepared in case—"

"Prepared for what?" Miju didn't expect Quinn's booming voice. He turned as the big man strutted into the clearing.

"For anything. We can't afford to take chances tonight. We're hiding in the foothills with ten trucks and three jeeps waiting for the Soman transports to poison the wells and meet us back here. Then we can drive to Matta to gather up the young women and children. It's a good place to hide, and it's a perfect location to stage this operation, but if someone finds us, we'll be sitting ducks. There's no exit route. Nowhere to go."

"We're not taking chances. No one knows we're here, Miju. These people are so ignorant I almost feel guilty killing them." Quinn laughed, but Miju didn't see the humor. "Besides, why do you think I brought sixty of my best men with us? You never know when the South Sudanese army might show up. I can't fight them off myself, so I have a small army of my own."

Miju changed the subject. "What are you planning to do with the doctor's daughter? Why did you bring her with us?"

"I've told you before—I'll keep her alive and use her as I please, Miju. Then I'll sell her. It's that simple. Jessica will pay for killing Gina. I would not have touched Jessica until our project was complete, but now that Gina's dead . . . I may take my revenge tonight." Quinn grinned at Jarrod and slapped him on the back. "Right, my American marine?"

"Ex-marine."

"Where is she now?" Miju pressed.

Quinn's aggravation with him erupted. "Why are you asking so many questions? You sound like a woman. She's tied to the seat in the back of my jeep. I told you. She's not going anywhere." Quinn turned to Jarrod. "Contact the compound. Have one of the warehouse guards check on the doctor. I don't know if I fully trust Rulu, and I want Branson to see his precious daughter suffer for my pleasure, though it's not *exactly* what I promised him."

When Jarrod unclipped the sat phone from his belt, the lights on the side caught Miju's eye. They blinked orange then red, then orange and red again in a cycle.

"How long has it been doing that?" Miju asked, shocked at the pattern.

Quinn looked where Miju pointed and grabbed the phone from Jarrod. "The panic signal. There's trouble at the compound." Quinn dialed the number as he spoke and held the phone to his ear. "It isn't ringing. The call isn't going through."

Quinn shoved the phone into Jarrod's hands. "When did those lights come on? How the—"

"I don't know," Jarrod interrupted, then dialed in his codes and the number. After a short beep, the line went dead. He tried again with the same response.

Quinn snatched the sat phone from Jarrod and threw it to Miju. "Call the Congo warehouse. See if they know what's going on at the Mangai compound."

Miju punched in the codes. Moments later he spoke with the gate sentry in the Congo compound where Paul had been held captive. He hung up and turned to Quinn. "This is not good. They can't get in touch with anyone at Mangai. They received a distress signal an hour ago and have been trying to reach us ever since." He glared briefly at Jarrod, judging him for missing the call. "They're evacuating. They're abandoning that compound."

Miju hurried to the jeep, pulled up the shortwave radio, and keyed the Mangai compound and then the warehouse. No response. "We've been hit."

"How could Mangai be hit without us knowing? That's impossible!" Quinn insisted.

"I'll tell you what's impossible—the sat phones and shortwave radio are dead at the same time and the warning lights are on. That can't be a coincidence," Miju fired back, "especially with the distress signal Mangai sent to the Congo compound an hour ago."

"He's right," Jarrod admitted. "It's a breach. We've been attacked."

"Branson," Miju mumbled. He hadn't meant to say it out loud.

Quinn grabbed Miju's arm. "How could it be Branson? He's one man, chained to a flagpole in the middle of nowhere. How could he possibly be responsible?"

"It's him. He's doing this. I don't know how, but—"

"Listen to yourself, Miju. You sound crazy! There's no way he could be involved."

"He's Abdu, Quinn, and—"

Miju didn't see Quinn's fist. The bones in his nose cracked as he tumbled backward onto the ground.

"You're out of your mind, Miju. He's just a man with no power." Quinn turned to Jarrod. "Miju's right about one thing. If anyone attacks us here, we're too boxed in. We have to move our operation to Matta—quickly—where we can defend ourselves in the village with the mountains behind us. It'll give us a strategic advantage. Get the men back into the trucks and contact the Mission Eagle teams. Tell them to watch for trouble and meet us in Matta instead of here when they're finished with the wells. Whoever's coming won't expect that. And, Jarrod, we must use Mungavi Crossing to get there. It will take us longer, but the rainy season made the other roads impassable. We'll have to pass our teams to get there, so let them know."

Miju took a moment to gain his bearings. He pushed his nose from right to left—it crunched into place with excruciating pain. He spat blood on the ground and rose to his feet. Unable to breathe through his swollen nose, he watched as Quinn barked orders at the men. But Miju saw the truth now: Branson was Abdu, and Quinn had lost control. He was a man obsessed, and Miju couldn't pretend he didn't see it. Jason Quinn would never be Abdu. Miju wiped his bloody face with his shirt.

Jarrod unclipped his walkie-talkie from its holster and held it to his mouth. "All drivers, fire your engines and load up. Time to move out."

One by one each driver confirmed as the other men climbed into the backs of the personnel carrier trucks. In a matter of minutes the dirt highway blazed with headlights as they prepared to leave for Matta.

Jarrod changed channels. "Mission Eagle teams, do you copy?" He held the radio ready to speak as soon as they responded.

"Eagle One, copy."

"Eagle Two, here."

Each Mission Eagle team checked in.

"Change of plans. Quinn's convoy will be coming up behind you. Pull over and allow us to pass—we need to get to Matta immediately. After completing your missions, rendezvous in Matta. Repeat, rendezvous in Matta at zero five hundred, and keep your eyes open. We may have unwanted company tonight. Use force if you have to."

Jarrod nodded to Quinn. "We're still in control. No one can stop the teams regardless of what's happened at the compound."

"It's too late to rob me of my victory." Quinn stormed off to his jeep. "We must be ready for who's coming, Jarrod. Get us to Matta where we can fight."

Miju cursed and spat blood on the ground again. "Are you forgetting we don't want to be discovered? Matta is the exact place he'll go, and we'll lose our advantage of being an invisible force. This needs to look like an epidemic, not a hostile takeover, remember?"

Quinn threw up his hands. "Whoever is attacking us will not expect to find us there, because it's not Branson. And the people in the village who see us will be dead in a matter of days. What is the difference?"

Miju stood in the clearing and watched Quinn as he drove off. He knew what he had to do. If Branson was Abdu, fighting him meant fighting God. The oil, money, and mission had seemed so important to him at one time, but now . . . as Miju watched the caravan pull out, he was certain that he was on the wrong side.

Jessica pulled against her restraints—a futile attempt. Firmly tied to the seat of the jeep, she craned her neck and squinted to get a glimpse of her dark surroundings, but all she could see were the lights from the trucks, and all she could hear was the noise of running engines.

Sweat poured down Jessica's back, and she still tasted blood from when Quinn had hit her hours earlier. She thought of what he'd told her: that her dad would remain chained to the pole until they returned from their deadly rampage and that he'd then be forced to watch as Quinn "punished" her for killing Gina. Jessica knew what that meant and couldn't imagine the horror of her father being forced to watch.

Jessica jumped when Quinn abruptly climbed behind the wheel. His driver ran to meet him. "I'm here, boss. I can drive."

"Do I look like I want you to drive?"

"Uh . . . no, boss. But—"

"I'm driving. We're moving the operation to Matta. Grab a ride with someone else."

"Yes, boss. I'll see you in—"

Before the driver finished speaking, Quinn started the engine, threw the jeep into gear, and stepped on the gas. Gravel flew as they pulled out from the path and onto the main road to join the other trucks. The caravan tore down the dirt highway in a cloud of dust. Quinn remained silent, his eyes fixed on the road ahead.

The Black Hawk hovered near Witto in quiet mode, although above the plains of Africa, a helicopter is hard to hide. Hugging the rock face of Mount Odo helped to provide camouflage. Kid donned the night vision scope and leaned out of the eerie black monster suspended in the night sky.

Jake addressed the men. "We've intercepted messages tonight from a man Doc knows as Jarrod Vincent. He refers to himself in his communications as 'JV' and Matta as the rendezvous location after the other villages have been poisoned. They likely plan to poison Matta last, but it's hard to say. The product we're dealing with is Soman, better known to us in the military as GD."

The men looked at each other briefly. This was part of the job.

Jake continued, "Dr. Branson is the expert in GD research, so I've asked him to brief us on this chemical weapon."

Paul took the floor. "This nerve agent is a chemical weapon of mass destruction for several reasons: it's resilient, it can bind and combine with other compounds, and it can create new forms of weaponry based on the manner in which it's dispersed and the binders used to deliver the payload. If it gets into the air, it's deadly. If it touches your skin, it's deadly. If you drink it, it's deadly faster."

The men hung on every word.

"Soman, depending upon its delivery, can cause crippling paralysis or outright seizure disorders and death. At times it may mimic dysentery or dementia, but if you encounter someone having seizures, it's too late to help them—they're already dead."

The men continued to listen intently as Paul spoke.

"You must take precautions in managing exposure or finding yourselves in close proximity to this chemical. It is one hundred percent unforgiving. That means if you're exposed and unprotected, you'll die." Paul turned to Jake.

Jake added a few details. "If necessary, this stuff can be torched, but the fumes are deadly. If we rupture a container, we'll wear respirators and cordon it off until authorities can clean it up. Any questions?"

Kid spoke first. "What if we have to blow a truck? We'll kill everyone within a hundred kilometers, won't we?"

"If it's airborne, yes. For that reason, we can't explode any barrels or set them on fire. If we have an explosion, it's a deal killer, unless we use napalm. We have the best snipers in the Special Forces. Precision will carry us through," Jake added.

Paul looked at Jake. "Do we have napalm?"

Jake shook his head to indicate they didn't. "Hopefully that won't be necessary." He turned to the men. "Doc informed me that Chief Chima can probably contact the authorities and get hazmat teams sent from Juba to pick up the sealed containers once we've neutralized the forces. He has some influence with the military. Also, we're hoping that the doctor Paul spoke to in the Congo hospital has contacted authorities as he promised. Unfortunately we won't know until we're in the thick of it."

"Understood. Can we contact this chief and warn him now?" Bart asked.

"We've tried, but Chima is in Matta. There's no way to reach him other than shortwave radio, and they're not responding. It's possible Quinn is monitoring communications if he's already there. But we don't know that. Chima's village is one of those that will be attacked tonight. We need to get there, but it's last on our list. We have to catch up with the chemical trucks first."

Jake turned to Paul. "Won't the people in the villages be surprised that trucks are entering during the night?"

Paul shook his head. "Trucks pass through all the time from Juba to the west. Night traffic is common since it's cooler than daytime."

Kid leaned out of the door again and saw the first truck approaching the wells. As the truck rounded the bend a kilometer from the village square, it suddenly stopped.

Kid had the best vantage point with his night vision scope. "Bad news, guys. They've spotted us."

Jake leaned out. "Murdock. You got a fix on that truck?"

Then, as if in slow motion, Paul saw the RPG streaking toward them. "There!"

"Hang on!" Murdock ordered as the Black Hawk soared up, banked hard left, and deployed chaff countermeasures consisting of a cloud of metal fragments and shavings. Jake's lifeline kept him from being thrown through the open door as the metal decoy fragments sprayed into the air. The missile headed into the chaff, missing the underbelly of the chopper by a few meters. Murdock banked right and pelted the truck with fifty-caliber machine gun bursts, shooting out the engine. The four men inside scattered toward the foothills.

From the sniper chair, Solo zeroed in on the moving targets and dropped them one by one—a single shot for each man. He turned to Jake. "The first Mission Eagle team has been eliminated."

Briefly the chopper hung motionless in the night sky.

"They were expecting us," Jake surmised. "So much for the element of surprise."

"You ready to pull out, boss?" Murdock asked.

"No, hold on." Jake focused his night scope on different spots around the area. "There are villagers out there with bows and arrows—and a couple of rifles. They're approaching the truck now. A few are looking this way."

Paul pointed toward the edge of the clearing. "This is good. Let me tell those men to guard the barrels."

"Do it fast, Doc," Jake ordered.

"Take me down."

Murdock dropped the chopper to a half meter off the ground and hovered. Paul jumped out with Jake and Bart and approached the men.

Before they reached them, Paul called out, "I'm Dr. Branson. I need your help."

The men looked at each other, and several dropped to their knees. Paul shouted at them, "Stand up!"

"You are Abdu."

"I don't care. You don't bow to me. What are you men doing out here in the middle of the night with weapons?"

"Chief Chima has ordered this for all the villages. They are expecting an attack sometime soon and want us to be ready. We've been keeping watch for five days. The women and children have been moved to Mundri."

"How did you know trouble was coming?"

"Chima told us he was warned by a military commander, someone he trusts as much as you."

Paul breathed a sigh of relief. They were preparing for the worst. Somehow, they were getting ready for Quinn.

"Chima was right. Now I need you to guard those blue barrels." Paul pointed. "Don't touch them or breathe any fumes. Keep everyone back twenty meters. It can kill you if you get too close and expose your skin to a drop or inhale the fumes. Can you do that? Can you guard them?"

"We can do this, Abdu."

Paul thanked the speaker. "We must hurry to the other villages. I'm counting on you."

"You can trust us. We will do this. But the other villages are preparing as well."

"Good. Stay alert, men."

As Paul and Jake walked back to the chopper, Paul called back, "Don't leave the barrels."

They climbed aboard, and the chopper lifted off to the next location.

"Do you know everyone around these parts, Doc?"

Paul smiled. "I've never seen superstition spread so fast. They're calling me Abdu, as if I'm someone who's supposed to save them—" Before he finished the sentence, Paul saw the correlation for the first time. He looked at Jake, who simply stared.

"Well, if the shoe fits . . ."

Paul shook his head. "I'm not that guy."

"Begging your pardon. You seem to be exactly that guy."

As the chopper rose over the trees and approached Lanyi, they saw that the truck carrying the Soman had already arrived.

Kid assessed the situation with his night scope. "We have a problem, Jake. The first barrel is beside the well, and men from the village are approaching Quinn's guys with clubs and spears. They're gonna get themselves killed. And if that stuff spills . . . The men in the truck don't seem to see them yet."

Jake, seated behind Kid, flipped down his night vision goggles and adjusted the settings. It made the five hundred meters look like two with the twist of a knob. "They haven't attached the nozzle to the well or the barrel yet. They're getting ready to, though." He paused briefly. "Take him, Solo."

A single shot dropped the man beside the barrel.

"Use the fifty-cal," Jake added.

"Copy that." Murdock fired the fifty-caliber turret into the engine block and the undercarriage. Parts flew from the truck, and the tires exploded into fragments. Sparks scattered everywhere the vehicle was struck. Seconds later, an RPG launcher jutted from the back of the truck aimed at the chopper.

Solo quickly eliminated the man holding the weapon. Only two men were accounted for from the truck.

"The other truck had four men. Do you think there are more than those two guys?" Jake scanned the vehicle. "The men from the village are pointing at us. Some are moving toward the truck still. This isn't good."

Murdock crackled on the radio. "Civilians approaching on the right, Jake."

"Take us down, Murdock. But keep your eye on that truck. Solo and Bart, look for any movement in that vehicle. If you have a clean shot, take it, but don't hit the barrels," Jake ordered.

"Copy that," the men confirmed.

The villagers backed away as the Black Hawk descended, but several of them approached the chopper, shining their flashlights with their rifles under their arms.

Paul hopped out when the helicopter was hovering less than a meter from the ground and waved at the men. "It's Dr. Paul. Don't shoot."

As Jake jumped down behind him, Paul suddenly heard a voice he recognized.

"Paul. Is that you?"

A figure approached in the darkness.

"Jim?"

Jim wrapped his arms around his brother-in-law. "I can't believe it. Where have you been? You're so thin!"

"There's too much to explain, and we're running out of time."

"Is Jess with you?"

Paul shook his head. "No. I don't know where she is—other than with Quinn, the guy causing all of this. But what are you doing here, Jim?"

"I had to do something, so I met up with Buru and Chima, and we realized we had to protect the villages. A military commander named Toru warned them that Quinn might try something with stolen chemicals. To make things worse, Jarrod Vincent is missing, and I think he could be involved somehow."

Paul nodded. "He is. He trained these guys to poison the wells with a substance used as a chemical weapon." Paul looked at the men standing with his brother-in-law. "You're on the ball, Jim, and we still need your help. We're moving on to Buagyi, Wiroh, and finally Matta, which is where Quinn is probably headed. But we're running short on time. I don't think we can stop all three trucks before it's too late. The chemicals are in blue barrels in each truck. Keep folks away from them."

"What chemicals?"

"Soman, a WMD banned by the international community. It's what I worked on in my research days. We gotta roll, Jim. I'll see you soon." Paul gave Jim a little punch on the shoulder and turned toward the chopper.

"You may be able to take all three trucks at once since the side roads are closed," Jim shouted over the chopper noise.

Paul stopped and turned back with Jake right behind him. "What do you mean?"

"You can hit all of them, the trucks headed for Buagyi, Wiroh, and Matta, at Mungavi Crossing—if they haven't already been there. All three trucks have to pass through that location, since the roads are deep in mud, before branching off on the other side. If Quinn is in Matta, he had to caravan through there too."

Paul turned to Jake. "He's right. I'll show you on the map. That's our chance."

Paul turned as a bullet whistled past his head and struck one of the villagers, hitting him in the arm. They all dropped to the ground and watched the truck. Paul could see no movement until the driver hopped out and ran toward them with a package clutched against him, only to be silently dropped by Solo. A small explosion followed.

Jake's voice came over the com line to Solo and Bart. "Suicide bomb. Bummer. Nice shot, guys."

Paul peered above the grass to see if he could spot the other man. Several more bullets struck the ground around him, and he ducked back down. Jake stood up straight and fired a single bullet into the back of the truck. A man Paul hadn't even seen fell over the edge.

Paul nodded. "That's truck number two. Three to go."

As Paul stood, Jim looked at him, horrified. "You don't even seem fazed by what just happened here! You're holding an assault rifle, and you have an FN Five-seven strapped to your leg."

"I'm fazed. I'm grieved. I'm just—different now," Paul said.

Jim shook his head. "What have they done to you?"

Paul looked his brother-in-law in the eye. "Everything they could. But . . . not everything they wanted." He added, "I have to go. My final stop will be in Matta, but I'll be there before you can make it by jeep. Come as soon as you secure this site. No matter what, Matta is going to need your help." Paul turned to the chopper as Jim called to him.

"Paul. They think you're Abdu. The people—they believe you're The Chosen."

Paul shrugged as he continued walking. "I can't seem to convince them otherwise. Superstitions are hard to break."

"Maybe that's because it's true," Jim added. "Godspeed."

Paul and Jake boarded the chopper, which rose and banked toward the south. Jake turned to Paul. "Where's Mungavi Crossing?"

Paul pulled up the map on the computer monitor and pointed to a location. "The last three trucks will have to come through this spot.

There's no other way because of the flooding. Mungavi Crossing is high ground where the roads branch off and head to the other villages."

Jake looked over the map. "So we ambush all of them there."

"If we don't, we won't have time to stop them—especially since we just lost ten minutes. If we get there before they do, we have a chance."

Jake studied the screen. "Murdock, can you get us to these coordinates in the next five minutes?" Jake tapped the location on the monitor, and the latitude and longitude appeared on Murdock's map overlay screen.

Murdock scanned the results. "Affirmative, boss."

Jake clapped Hawkeye on the shoulder. "We need boots on the ground to surprise them—you and me. We can't risk them making a run for it. Kid, you handle the fifty-cal. Solo and Bart, you stay on sniper. Copy?"

"Copy, boss," they responded.

Hawkeye prepared for a ground offensive and moved to the door of the chopper with his gear, inspecting his scope, checking his ammo, and attaching the rappelling lines.

As they approached the intercept point, the Black Hawk dropped low to the ground and waited, facing the crossroads.

Jake turned to Paul. "If we missed them or they went another way, we're wasting our time sitting here. I need you to be sure."

Paul looked at the map on the screen and remembered the last rainy season he'd been through. The mud was so deep on the back roads that trucks were stuck in a half meter of muck for weeks. Men couldn't even cross on foot safely without sinking in the mire.

"We didn't miss them, Jake. Those roads are impassible. If anything, they tried to go that way and had to turn back. They'll come through here. They have to."

Jake nodded. "I trust you, Doc."

Seconds later, the trucks turned the bend and approached the crossing. Murdock announced, "Three trucks matching expected descriptions half a klick away and moving."

Jake gave Paul a nod. "Nice. That's what I'm talking about."

The chopper lifted away so quickly no one could have seen the two men dropping into the grass.

Murdock hovered in their new location, facing the three trucks as they approached. When they reached the crossing, the vehicles stopped about twenty meters apart, two hundred meters from the Black Hawk.

Paul watched Jake and Hawkeye through his night vision goggles as they flanked the trucks. One of the guards on the back of the first vehicle aimed a shoulder-fired missile at the chopper. In a breath, the man dropped silently, a casualty of Hawkeye's deadly aim.

Kid fired the fifty-caliber into the engine block and cab of the second truck. Three men ran from the back of the vehicle, but the driver never had a chance. Kid spewed hot lead from the huge machine gun into the first truck's undercarriage and radiator in a sea of sparks and flying debris. He avoided the gas tank and kept low to miss the fuel lines. The men rushed out of the vehicles and fired at the chopper, but they were no match for the skills and accuracy of Jake, Hawkeye, and Solo.

The RPG streaked from the third truck so quickly that Murdock didn't see it until the alarm sounded, causing him to thrust his Black Hawk into the sky full throttle, deploy the chaff, and bank hard right. Even so, the missile missed by only a few meters as the final truck sped away.

Murdock turned the chopper toward the last of the men running for the hills and sprayed a white-hot trail from the nose guns. The dirt flew as the men dropped, one by one, lifeless to the ground. So far that night, the Black Hawk team had disabled four trucks and eliminated sixteen of Quinn's men without spilling a single molecule of the deadly Soman. But one truck remained.

Murdock dropped to the surface and Hawkeye and Jake climbed aboard. They left in hot pursuit of the third truck, which had taken the branch road through the trees toward Matta.

"They'll have another shoulder-fired missile aimed at us if we approach from behind, Murdock. We're running out of luck avoiding lethal contact with one of those," Jake warned.

"Agreed, boss. I'm out of chaff countermeasures too. They'll have a better chance of hitting us next time."

Paul's voice came across the com line. "Murdock, can you get past them around Mount Odo and come in from the other side? There's low ground at the base of the mountain as the road approaches Matta. They wouldn't see us till they were on top of us. The downside is that there isn't room to maneuver."

Murdock looked at the map. "The other downside is that Odo is huge. It will take us ten minutes to circle around. We may miss them."

Paul pulled up the map on the computer screen. "Look. Right here. We'd be sitting ducks if they got the drop on us. But if they come over that ridge and we're waiting with a fifty-caliber turret to hose them down, we got 'em. It's a risk, but they'll be looking for us in the air behind them, not near the ground in front. The driver will see us first, but he's not going to be holding a weapon—at least not a missile."

Jake nodded. "That's crazy enough to work. Let's go, Murdock. Get this thing high enough to avoid a missile or RPG and take us around the mountain. We have to get to the other side and stop that truck."

As the moon cast a faint glow on the Imatong Mountains and the sheer rock face of Odo towered above them, the Black Hawk hovered a meter from the ground in the middle of the road, bordered by trees on both sides. There were no lights—no markings—only the thumping of idling chopper blades that would be covered by the sound of a racing truck engine.

"Did we miss them? Are we too late?" Paul asked.

Jake shook his head. "I don't think so. We made that in seven minutes. We must be ahead of them."

Paul stared into the darkness. No headlights, no movement. Nothing.

Jake's voice came over the intercom. "We're at risk, men. But it's our best shot at stopping this. We need to end it here and now. This is the epitome of being one step ahead—if we really are one step ahead."

"Engine approaching." Murdock's voice crackled through the com line. "Single engine." He added, "Lights—headlights approaching, one hundred meters."

Jake sat on the left sniper seat of the chopper while Solo sat on the right. They simultaneously chambered their weapons—M134 machine guns. As the truck lights approached the ridge ahead, Jake addressed the men.

"We need the element of surprise, surgical accuracy in our munitions, and the complete refusal to fail. Hooah, ladies."

They responded, "Hooah!"

The moment the transport truck came over the ridge, its headlights landed on the Black Hawk a hundred meters in front of it. Before the truck's rear-facing tail gunner carrying the shoulder-fired missile could turn forward, Solo took him out with a single bullet.

"Fire on the engine and tires, Murdock. Now!" Jake ordered.

The gunfire from the Black Hawk took out the engine block and tires and tore the doors from the sides of the vehicle. The truck skidded to a halt sideways in the road as the tires erupted beneath it.

"Jake?" Paul spoke quietly as he stared at the truck in the silence that followed.

Jake turned. "What's wrong?"

"Those barrels should have kept the truck from skidding sideways. They're too heavy to let it slide like that."

Jake's orders were rapid and precise: "Fire at every man exiting that vehicle." He unstrapped and turned to Hawkeye. "Get ready. It's you and me." Jake hung out of the left door of the chopper as he spoke to his pilot. "Set it down, Murdock. We need to check out that vehicle. Doc's right. Something's wrong with this. Let's go, Hawkeye."

Before the chopper touched the ground, Jake and Hawkeye were out, approaching the truck so fast no one inside had a chance to react. Hawkeye fired a single shot into the vehicle as Jake did the same from the opposite side. Hawkeye then grabbed the driver, pulled him from the truck, and disarmed him. He dragged him back to the chopper and threw him on the ground as Paul jumped out to meet them.

"We do have a problem, Doc," Jake said.

Paul nodded. "The truck's empty, isn't it?"

Hawkeye answered as he held his weapon to the driver's head, "There's no GD in that truck. Not a single freakin' barrel."

Jake turned to the driver. "Is there another truck with chemicals on it?"

The man didn't answer. Paul asked in Arabic, but he still refused to respond.

"We know that Quinn will be waiting in Matta for us," Jake said. "How many men will be there, and is there another truck? You have three seconds. One, two, three." Jake fired his pistol into the man's left thigh.

Paul jumped at the unexpected shot, but then surprised himself by pulling his FN Five-seveN from its holster on his leg and pointing it at the man's right thigh.

Paul spoke in Arabic. "I'll be straight with you, man. I'm not Special Forces, but my daughter is in Matta with your boss, Quinn. Since he'll be dead in a few hours, you need to talk to me. Just to make sure you know I'm not bluffing, I'm a doctor, and I know where your femoral artery is."

Paul shot the man in the right thigh. He screamed in pain.

"It's about five centimeters to the right of that. Now tell me . . ." Paul moved the pistol five centimeters to the right and pressed it against the man's leg. "How many guys are meeting us, and for God's sake, is there another truck with chemicals? Tell me right now—or die."

The man gripped his leg and spoke in English. "Sixty men armed with assault rifles are waiting in Matta with Quinn. They are ready to fight. The other truck with the barrels, it's with Quinn in Matta too. It never left his convoy. We are a decoy in case anyone tried to follow us—as you did."

Paul nodded. "Does Quinn know we're on our way?"

The man grinned at Paul. "They radioed us that trouble was coming. Quinn and his men, they know someone is coming—but not you, Abdu."

"How do you know who I am?"

"Everyone knows but Quinn. I've seen you in the compound many times from a distance. I was there when they kidnapped you in Matta. Don't shoot me. I tell the truth."

Paul turned to Jake. "Quinn's already there. I was hoping . . ."

Jake nodded in agreement with Paul's sentiment, then turned to his own men. "Time to meet the man responsible."

"What about this guy?" Hawkeye continued to hold his weapon on the driver.

Jake squatted next to the man. "Put a tourniquet on that and get yourself to the highway. Hitch a ride to Lui. It's eight kilometers that way. Don't do anything stupid." Jake stood. "Stand down, Hawkeye." Hawkeye holstered his weapon. "Check the truck. Make sure there's no way he can communicate with anyone. We gotta roll."

In less than a minute they were in the air again, on their way to Matta.

After a brief silence, Jake moved next to Paul. "It was a good plan, Doc—catching them all at the crossing."

"Thanks, but we just wasted twenty minutes chasing nobody. I should have seen that coming."

"But we got intel that we're going to use. And by the way . . . you ever consider a career in the Special Forces?"

Paul smiled. "Just getting my daughter back will be good enough for me."

Jake nodded. "I have to be honest with you. The next step is going to be the most difficult. Those guys in the trucks were ready for us. According to the man we just talked to, Quinn is expecting someone to attack him in Matta. We stopped the trucks for Wiroh, Buagyi, Witto, and Lanyi. It may be too late for Matta, but we accomplished something already. From what that driver said, we have the element of surprise. Quinn doesn't know it's you who's gunning for him. Time to end this and find Jessica."

Paul knew Jake was right. It was time to finish this, once and for all.

CHAPTER
TWENTY-THREE

Quinn drove to the edge of Matta, parked his jeep, and checked Jessica's bindings. Then he stormed off without a word.

Jessica watched him until he was out of sight, then twisted her arms under the zip ties and wiggled to free herself. It was no use. She heard a noise and turned to see a young woman step from the tall grass and hurry to the jeep.

"Don't be frightened," the woman whispered. "Where did Quinn go?"

"He just left. I don't know where he went. Who are you?"

"My name is Hanna, and I don't have much time. I know your father."

"How?"

"I removed a bullet from his chest and took care of him."

"He was shot? My dad was shot?"

"Yes, very bad. But he was braver than any man I've ever met. He saved Adanna, Quinn's wife, twice. And then he told me how to save him too. He's different from other men."

"What are you doing here, Hanna? These men are evil. I don't know who you are, but how could you be involved with this?"

Hanna paused. "I was in my final semester of medical school when Quinn abducted me from my apartment along with some other girls. When he discovered I was almost a doctor, he assigned me to removing bullets from his men when they'd been shot. I guess I did a good a job because I became valuable to him. I've always wanted to leave, but if I did, he'd find me and kill me."

"I'm sorry, Hanna."

"I wanted to come to you sooner, but Quinn would not allow it."

"Hanna, if I can't get away, they're going to rape me tonight. Quinn may even kill me." Jessica turned and studied Hanna's face. "You know that, right?"

"That's why I came. We must get you out of here." As she spoke, Hanna reached into her bag and pulled out a small pair of surgical scissors. She began to cut the ties with them.

"I've been with Quinn and his men for two years. But when your father came into camp, everything changed. I could see from the beginning he had such compassion for Quinn's wife. He wanted to help her. Many could see it . . . except for Quinn."

Hanna cut through the first and second ankle ties.

"But what he has done to Abdu, keeping him a prisoner, is unforgivable. He will answer to God for it. I will be silent no longer."

"Who's Abdu?"

"The Chosen, the man God has selected to deliver His people . . . your father."

Jessica's mind spun. "You believe in God?"

Hanna answered without looking up from her task. "I believe in God, but not the one Quinn follows. There is no such God."

Jessica didn't know what to ask. She had so many questions. "Does anyone else here believe in God?"

"Very few. They believe the spirits control everything, not God."

Hanna feverishly sawed at the zip tie on Jessica's left wrist, but her delicate scissors were dulling. "My people know—even many of Quinn's men know—your father is Abdu."

Jessica found her voice. "Then why is he in the center of the compound we left hours ago, strapped to the flagpole with one of Quinn's men guarding him? He's dying back there. They beat him and tied him to a pole, then left him to die."

Hanna put her head down and sobbed.

Jessica stared at her for a moment. "You knew that, right?"

Hanna collected herself. "Yes, and I'm sorry. I'm just very . . . I don't know. I'm so sorry for what they've done." She shook her head and wiped the tears from her eyes. "Your father is different. He treated me like I was worth something. No man has ever treated me that way. And I just . . ."

"You what?"

Snap! The left wrist was free—one zip tie to go. The surgical scissors were barely usable on the final plastic band. Still, Hanna sawed desperately to free Jessica from the tie.

"Please don't make me say it, Jessica."

"Okay, Hanna. Just hurry."

"What are you telling me?" Quinn demanded of Jarrod. Miju knew the tone, and it frightened him.

"I'm telling you that the trucks have dropped off the map. All five were there, on course, and then I got a mayday call from Eagle Five, and the line went dead." Jarrod checked his radio again. "Come in, Mission Eagle teams, come in." No response.

"First the compound in Mangai was attacked, forcing us to come to Matta, then the Soman disappeared. Miju! Where are my trucks?" Quinn kicked the side of the jeep so hard the door dented.

"I don't know. Jarrod was in charge of them."

"I don't care! You're my right hand. This is *our* purpose. Our mission."

Miju looked Quinn in the eye. "You don't want to hear what I have to say."

Quinn grabbed Miju by the collar. "We can't reach the warehouse, we've lost contact with the compound and the Mission Eagle teams. Someone has taken control from us, and this can only be a planned attack. We have to stop reacting and act on what we know. Who could pull off an invasion at this level? It can't be Branson—he's dead. If the compound was hit, he's dead."

"What if he—"

"It can't be him, Miju! Let it go, and let's figure out who's coming after us. Who knew what we were doing, and who'd have the resources to stop us?"

One of Quinn's men ran from the village clearing dragging Chief Chima. He stopped in front of Quinn.

"What is it? Can't you see we're busy?"

"Your orders—we can't carry them out, sir."

"What do you mean?"

"You told us to load the women and children into the trucks, and there aren't any. But the village chief and elders are here. This is the chief. One of the elders, Buru, is in the clearing under guard."

"They're hiding the women in the fields. Look for them and make the chief talk," Quinn ordered.

Chima stepped toward Quinn. "Abdu will come for you."

Quinn drew his weapon and held it against Chima's forehead. "Say it again."

Chima was silent.

"I thought not." Quinn holstered his weapon. "Get him out of my sight."

"Yes, sir." The man grabbed Chima and headed toward the center of the village.

Quinn turned his back on Jarrod and Miju, shook his head, and mumbled obscenities. When Jarrod spoke, Quinn moved to squarely face him.

"I don't know about all this 'Abdu' and 'Ghost of Africa' bull. But you brought me here for my military expertise, and so far I have a pretty good track record. So here it is: to attack the compound, warehouse, and trucks on the same night at the same time requires an army and strategic planning with the ability to combine efforts with a central command. There's probably only one man coordinating this. Does that tell you who it may be?"

Quinn's attitude suddenly changed as he pondered the possibilities. His face lit up. "Commander Toru, of course—the ambassador of the South Sudan–American alliance. He is in charge of troops and has been questioning our oil agreement terms for two months. The motive to attack us, the desire for control and power over the oil, is evident in his actions."

"He's your number one man then. If he has unlimited troops, and we are outnumbered and outgunned, we need to reconsider our current position," Jarrod insisted.

"What does that mean?" Quinn responded defensively.

"We need to get out of here and regroup immediately," Jarrod responded.

Quinn stared at him, then at Miju. "Admit defeat? Run? That's what you suggest?" Quinn looked as if he'd suddenly had an epiphany. "If Toru is behind this, they're already here. They've taken the women and children. They're a step ahead, but *we* need to be a step ahead!"

Miju wondered what madness was yet to come.

Quinn turned to the tree line. "They planned an ambush, but we came to Matta sooner than expected." He addressed Jarrod and Miju. "Gather the trucks. We'll fight right now for our freedom in the village Branson loved. When we're done, we'll destroy it along with everything he held dear." He turned to Miju. "Get the girl. If the compound was attacked and Branson's dead, there's no need to wait."

"You were just talking about launching a defense, now you want the girl?"

"Do as I say, Miju. I have reasons for what I do. She must pay for her sins."

As Miju turned to retrieve Jessica from the jeep, his stomach twisted. He walked as a man going to slaughter. *Pay for her sins?* When he reached the jeep, Hanna was gnawing away at the final zip tie with a broken pair of surgical scissors.

"What are you doing?" Miju grabbed Hanna's arm and dragged her from the vehicle. "Are you insane? Quinn will kill you if you cut her loose! What were you thinking?"

Hanna backed away then suddenly stepped forward. "Miju, you and I have worked together for years. You know me."

"What does that have to do with anything?"

"I'm asking you for this."

Miju stared at her.

"You need to let her go. You can't let Quinn rape and kill her. She's done nothing wrong. My God, what are we doing, Miju?"

Miju turned his back on her, but he knew that what she was saying was true.

Hanna forced her way between him and the jeep and pointed to Jessica. "Let her go right now and stop this. I've had enough. She's the daughter of Abdu. Are our hearts that hardened?"

Miju could barely think. His mind spun with the reality of what Hanna was saying. He knew this was wrong—all of it was wrong. The fact that he had not seen it for so many years was bad enough. How could he have been part of such evil?

"Answer me," Hanna insisted.

Jessica turned to face him. "Miju . . . That's your name, right? Listen—you're not the kind of man Quinn is. I see it in your eyes. You don't like what he's doing. I don't want to die tonight, and you don't have to kill me. You can let me go."

Miju pulled out his knife and cut the remaining tie, but he wouldn't let Jessica get up from her seat.

"Look at me." Jessica spoke softly. Miju turned to her, and their eyes met. "You don't want to kill me . . . I know you don't. So let me go. Quinn is the madman, not you."

Miju couldn't take his eyes off her. It wasn't her beauty that captivated him—it was the truth she spoke. He was unable to move, unable to turn from her.

Hanna grabbed his arm. "Please . . . do not do this thing. Let her see her father again. He is innocent. He is Abdu. He has the power to—"

"Her father is coming," Miju mumbled.

Hanna gasped and covered her mouth with her hand.

"What do you mean he's coming?" Jessica asked.

Miju looked at her. "I . . . don't know how, but he is. I can feel it."

Quinn's voice barked from the clearing. "Miju! I told you to bring her to me, not chat with her."

"Miju, please," Hanna begged. "I love . . . I just . . . Oh God."

"He's close, Hanna. Branson will be here soon," Miju assured her. As he spoke, he grabbed Jessica by the arm to take her to Quinn. He knew in his heart that everything she spoke was the truth. He pulled her close to him as they walked and quietly said, "Wait for a sign, then run. I'll protect you."

◆ ◆ ◆

"There are men everywhere, Jake, but I can't spot—Wait. There."

Jake focused his night goggles where Paul pointed. "What am I looking at?"

"The man sitting on the left by the campfire is Chima. He's the chief of this village and very powerful in the region. To his left is Buru. He's not only one of the elders, he's one of the chief hunters for the village, and a friend. The guard behind them must be keeping them there, because they don't appear to be tied up, and they wouldn't be sitting around voluntarily. The hut to their right, our left, belongs to Chima."

Paul peered through the night goggles. "The truck with the chemicals—it's to the right. The blue barrels are visible inside. I'll bet they wanted to take the women and children before they poisoned the rest of the village." Paul continued to search with the goggles. When he spotted Miju holding Jessica's arm, his heart went to his throat. "No."

"Take is easy, Doc. I see her. It's gonna be okay."

Paul focused on Jessica's face, and his rage boiled.

Jake touched his shoulder. "Stand down. Slow your breathing and trust me—do it."

Paul closed his eyes and took a deep breath. As he opened them, he saw Quinn slap Jessica, knocking her to the ground.

"Jake . . ."

"Wait. It's just you and me. Solo, Bart, Hawkeye, and Kid aren't in position. We're not ready. Please wait."

Paul hung his head as he spoke. "I can't do this. I can't watch him torture her."

"Doc, hang on. We will do this, just give us time." Jake grabbed Paul's shoulder again. "You go out there now, we all die, including Jessica."

Solo's voice crackled in Paul's earpiece. "I'm in position. Clear view from here."

Jake whispered his response. "Copy that. You out there, Kid?" They waited a moment for Kid to answer.

"Kid here—almost in position."

"Bart in position on the south perimeter. Locked and loaded."

"Hawkeye here. I'm ready, boss."

Paul watched as Jessica knelt on the ground in front of Quinn while Miju seemed to be arguing with him.

"Looks like they're having a little disagreement," Jake said as he looked through his binoculars.

Paul focused on Quinn and Miju again. "They're arguing about something."

Kid's voice crackled on the com line. "Kid in place. Good position. Who are the players?"

Paul whispered into the microphone, "Our targets include the man with the fatigues wearing a red kerchief around his neck. His name is Miju, and he's Quinn's right hand. The guy next to him is Jarrod, a US citizen and mercenary ex-marine. He's as bad as he looks." Paul swallowed hard. "The man wearing fatigues and a beret is Quinn, and the girl on the ground next to him is my . . . my daughter, Jessica." Silence filled the com line for a moment. "The two men sitting by the fire are leaders in this village. They're on our side. Scattered around the compound are other men from the village, and according to my brother-in-law, Jim, some armed men and villagers are hiding near the entrance. Maybe they're watching this, but I can't see them."

As Paul finished, Jake spoke. "They're going to make a move on her, Solo."

Jarrod pulled Jessica to her feet and dragged her toward a nearby hut.

"I have the solution," Solo's voice whispered.

"Take the shot," Jake responded without hesitation.

The silent slug hit Jarrod's head, and he stumbled forward. Jessica bolted for the tall grass as Jarrod fell lifeless to the ground. Quinn darted after her as Miju dove for Quinn's legs, tripping him to the ground. Miju jumped to his feet and leapt over Quinn, chasing Jessica into the brush.

Gunfire echoed as Quinn's men fired wildly into the surrounding trees. They dropped to the ground one by one as Kid, Bart, Hawkeye, and Solo hit their marks.

Paul watched through night vision goggles as Quinn scrambled to his feet. A sniper bullet struck his left shoulder. He ran for the grass as a second bullet grazed his back, tearing his shirt. Quinn suddenly fell, grabbed his left calf, and rolled behind Chima's hut. Seconds later he limped into the tall grass out of sight of everyone. Hawkeye took a shot, but another man ran into the path of his bullet.

"I can't believe it. I counted three hits on Quinn, and he still ran off." Paul dropped his goggles on the ground.

"The grass is obstructing my view!" Solo's voice crackled. "He's no longer in my line of sight."

A guard standing beside Buru placed his pistol against Buru's head. Jake took him out. Buru grabbed the man's knife from the sheath on his belt and skillfully fought the men near him.

"I have to go after her, Jake." Paul knelt. "They'll kill her if they catch her."

"You'll never make it across the clearing, Doc."

"I have to." With a silent prayer, Paul jumped up, darted from the grass, and sprinted into the hot zone. He heard Jake's orders.

"Cover Doc. He's going for Jessica."

As Paul darted across the clearing, it seemed he was running in slow motion. Man after man dropped to the ground as Jake, Kid,

Bart, Hawkeye, and Solo blazed a path for him. Some of Quinn's men dropped their rifles and surrendered as others fought a foe they couldn't see, dropping silently one by one.

Paul's lungs burned and his heart raced as he neared the grassy coverage on the other side of the clearing and plunged into the bush. Bullets whistled past him as he ran blindly through the coarse blades, ignoring the abrasive stalks. The trodden grass told him he was following someone, and he prayed the footprints were Jessica's. He found a path, jumped over some boulders, and scurried under a rock ledge overhanging the old riverbed. When he burst into the clearing on the other side, Quinn was waiting.

Paul stopped. As the first morning light cast a glow across the mountains, Quinn stood with his bleeding left arm around Jessica's neck. She stopped squirming as her eyes fixed on her father.

"Daddy?"

Out of breath, Paul gasped for air. "Hi, baby. I'm not dead."

"How is this possible, Branson? Who are you that you can do this?"

"I had help."

"You've destroyed everything, but the gunfire in the village behind you is my men killing your beloved villagers, and I will come back and finish this after you're dead."

"Actually, Quinn, the gunfire is your men blindly firing at my men and dying or surrendering."

"Your men? What do you mean your men?"

"The Army Special Forces of the United States of America."

Quinn shook his head as Paul watched his anger burn. "Then before you die," he said and raised his pistol to Jessica's head, "watch your daughter beg for—"

A bullet sliced through the tall grass and pierced Quinn's right shoulder. He dropped the gun and released Jessica, grabbing his wound with his left hand. He stumbled and fell as Miju stepped into the clearing, his rifle trained on Quinn's chest.

"Miju?" Quinn's eyes grew wide.

Miju moved closer to Quinn. "I trusted you, killed for you, and followed you anywhere you wanted to go. But this is wrong. He's Abdu, whether you believe it or not. It's over, Quinn. I tried to tell you, but you wouldn't listen."

Jessica hurried to her father's side just as a black panther dropped from the rocky overhang to the ground in front of Paul. Its deep, horrible growl caused Jessica to grip her father's arm and gasp as the huge cat fixed its gaze on him. Miju held his rifle on Quinn as if he couldn't move.

"Get behind me, Jess." Paul's calm voice surprised even him.

"Is he going to kill us?"

"Not us." Paul pushed her behind him.

Paul remembered Buru's words: "You will know what to do, Abdu. You are The Chosen."

Slowly Paul knelt on one knee in front of the black beast. Jessica crouched behind him. He said out loud, "Give me strength." The peace he felt reminded him of where his journey had begun two months earlier. The panther's sleek, sinewy muscles rippled beneath its thick, coarse fur. It growled low and deep again. Its huge green eyes focused on Paul's as it had done before. Its hot breath burned his face.

Paul knew what to do. He stretched out his hand and rested it on the head of the Ghost of Africa.

"No!" Quinn gasped, wide-eyed. "This cannot be!"

Paul spoke only one word. "Now."

The panther grunted, stepped back from Paul, and turned to where Quinn sat on the ground three meters away.

"No! Get him away from me! Shoot him, Miju!" Quinn pushed with his legs and backed himself against the boulders. Black death stared him down and lowered its head—its icy eyes fixed on Quinn's quivering body.

Paul spoke calmly but forcefully. "Miju, step back from Quinn and drop the rifle." Miju slowly retreated, slipped the strap off his shoulder, and dropped the rifle to the ground.

"I should have killed you, Branson!" Quinn grabbed at the shrubs and pulled himself against the rock as the cat crouched. "Miju, for God's sake, help me!"

"For God's sake, I will not." Miju stood like a statue.

The panther shrieked. "Close your eyes," Paul warned Jessica as she buried her head in his back.

Quinn grabbed for the pistol on the ground, but the cat leapt toward him. Quinn struggled as quickly as he could into the tall grass behind him, but the panther was on his heels. The screams and thrashing that came from the thicket were over in a moment.

Jessica held onto her father tightly.

The black cat walked from the grass and faced Paul, its fangs dripping with Quinn's blood, its fur wet from the fight. Paul nodded at the beautiful, sleek creature before it turned and disappeared into the tall grass.

Jessica looked up. "Daddy, what just happened?"

"Quinn's dead. The panther is gone."

Paul turned to Miju.

Miju shook his head. "You're The Chosen. You're Abdu. You were this whole time. I fought you and tried to kill you—and I hated you."

"But today you saved my daughter's life."

Paul pressed the earpiece in his ear. "This is Paul. You guys safe?"

Jake's voice came across the headset loud and clear. "We're good. You okay, Doc? We've been listening to some of that."

"I'm fine. I have Jessica."

"We just got things under control out here. We're on our way to you. Stand firm."

Paul went into the thicket to look at Quinn's remains. "It's okay, he's dead. Quinn's dead, Jake."

Jake paused. "How about his buddy, Miju?"

Paul looked at Miju. "He's not going to be bothering anyone ever again. You don't need to find us, we're on our way out."

"Roger that. The compound is secure, but we need to get out of here. The sun's coming up, and the chief said a doctor in the Congo notified the South Sudanese army. They're on their way, and we are not supposed to be here. You know, plausible deniability?"

"Copy that. We're headed to you."

Miju faced Paul in silence. Neither of them spoke as Miju stripped off the rest of his weapons and dropped them to the ground. Then Paul took Jessica's hand and hurried through the tall grass, leaving Miju behind.

At the edge of the clearing they stopped. Jessica gasped. Quinn's lifeless men lay scattered on the battleground. She covered her mouth and pulled herself close to her father. Villagers gathered around them.

Paul walked to Chima and Buru. "My friends, I—"

Buru hugged Paul. "I thought I would never see you again. Jim and I talked, and we have much to share with you."

Paul shook Buru's hand warmly. "We'll talk more soon, Buru."

Chima bowed politely to Paul. "The spirits have spoken. They've brought you back to us. You were willing to be used in a way you did not desire. May the spirits be with you."

Paul looked around the clearing. "Chief, we need to talk about 'the spirits' real soon. In the meantime, get word to Orma that Leza is safe and that I will get her home as soon as I can."

Chima placed his hand on Paul's shoulder. "Orma is dead, Abdu. They killed her when they kidnapped Leza."

Paul shook his head and swallowed the lump in his throat. "I didn't know."

"She died protecting the child she loved. Just take care of Leza. It's enough."

"Does Leza know, Chief?"

"She knows."

Paul nodded. He watched as Hanna ran to Jessica and threw her arms around his daughter. Jessica hugged her back.

"I will miss you, Jessica," Hanna said. "I wish I could have known you longer."

Jessica gave her a squeeze. "You will, Hanna. I'll be back with my dad. I promise."

Hanna turned to Paul. He saw in her eyes something he had tried to ignore. He didn't want to admit it, but his heart jumped when he looked at her. She walked to him. "Thank you, Abdu, for saving us." She placed her hands on his shoulders, stood on her tiptoes, and kissed him on the cheek. He remembered being kissed like that before. He pulled her close and felt the warmth of her cheek against his. He wrapped his arms around her and held her for a long time. She didn't seem to mind. He kissed her forehead.

"Thank you for everything, Hanna. What are your plans?"

"I'll check on Adanna. They said the compound was struck tonight. Was that you?"

"It was. I think she's okay if she was in the back of the compound."

"I'll find her and let you know. But . . . I'm going to finish medical school and get my diploma. I want to work as you do, helping others everywhere."

"I'll do whatever I can to make that happen. Just let me know." As their eyes met, Paul realized he was still holding her hands. He pulled on them, and she moved closer. He wrapped his arms around her one more time. "Hanna . . ."

"It's okay. I know." She looked at him—her lips only centimeters from his. She nodded. "I know."

The noise of the chopper and the swirling dust interrupted them and forced them to cover their eyes as it landed in the clearing. Paul grabbed Jessica. The villagers backed away as Paul and Jessica rushed aboard the chopper, followed by Solo, Kid, Bart, Hawkeye, and Jake.

When the Black Hawk lifted from the ground, Paul turned and waved to Buru, Chima, and Hanna. Buru saluted Paul as Hanna waved, tears streaming down her face. Paul watched her until she was out of sight.

In a matter of seconds, Murdock was racing for the border, flying as low as he dared to avoid radar. They didn't need an encounter with North Sudanese gunships.

Paul put on his headset. "Thank you, Jake. You saved my daughter."

"It looked a lot like you saved her, Doc. What happened in the thicket with Quinn?"

Paul shook his head in disbelief. "It's a long story, but I promise to tell you later."

"I look forward to it."

Paul moved next to Jessica, sat, and wrapped one arm around her. "Jake, this is my daughter, Jessica."

Jessica smiled. "Hi, Jake. It's good to meet you." She extended her hand.

"Yes, ma'am. Good to meet you too."

While Jake and Jessica talked, Paul moved to the other side of the chopper, took off his headphones, and looked out the window as the sun peeked over the distant mountains.

Moments later he heard Jake laugh for the first time—at something Jessica said. Paul leaned across the aisle to get Jake's attention as he put his headphones back on.

"Hey, I have one more favor to ask."

Dr. Davis pulled the curtain back to examine Leza. "How's my favorite patient today?"

Leza smiled. "I'm feeling much better. Thank you."

The doctor looked through some tests he had performed the night before. "Your lab work looks very good, Leza. I'm quite pleased. If this keeps up, you will be out of that bed soon. The IV antibiotics have your pneumonia clearing up, and we hope to get your chemo restarted. Your doctor friend left me very detailed instructions on what you need."

Leza's smile waned a little. "Dr. Davis, have you heard from Baba? I mean Dr. Paul?"

Dr. Davis closed the chart and sat on the edge of the bed. "Well, it hasn't even been two days yet. Let's give him some time."

Leza looked down at her hands. "He isn't coming back, is he?"

"Well, I don't know. He certainly seemed to want to. And he said he would if he could. We'll hope for the best. But if he doesn't, we'll find a good place for you to live. I promise."

Leza gave him another weak smile. "I'll keep praying and hoping."

As she spoke, the walls and ceiling began to shake, and a thunderous roar vibrated the windows. A nurse ran into the cubicle.

"Dr. Davis, there's something happening. Come quickly!"

Davis turned to Leza. "It'll be okay. I'll be right back."

She pulled her covers up to her eyes.

As Davis hurried to the lobby, sand and debris hit the glass doors in a whirlwind. When the dust cloud settled, a soldier in military gear appeared in the entrance fully armed, followed by two more soldiers who walked past the first and stood on each side of the doorway. The hospital security guards placed their hands on their weapons but quickly thought better of it and backed away.

Davis stepped toward the lead soldier. "What's going on here? This is a hospital, not a military outpost."

As the doctor spoke, Paul stepped in from the dust wearing military fatigues, a pistol on his belt, and an FN Five-seveN strapped to his right thigh.

"Hello, Dr. Davis. I promised I'd be back."

Davis's mouth hung open for a moment as he gathered his thoughts.

Paul added, "Sorry for the chopper in the street. Those things are a pain to park."

Davis laughed. "I don't believe it. Where is your friend with the injured leg?"

"He gave his life for the cause." Paul paused. "But we're here to take Leza home. We need to hurry. Can you bring me to her?"

Davis smiled. "Come with me."

Paul followed him down a long hallway to the cubicle where Leza lay on a comfy bed. Paul looked around the corner as she leaned out to see him.

"Oh, Babatunde. I knew you'd come back."

Paul rushed to her bedside and wrapped his arms around her. She cried as he held her close and kissed her cheek.

"I missed you, little girl."

"I missed you too."

Davis interrupted. "You'll need some fresh IV bags to take with you, Dr. Branson. Leza was severely dehydrated, and you were right, she has pneumonia—right lower lobe. There are antibiotics in the IV bags." He turned to the nurse. "Bring four extra antibiotic bags and some IV tubing. Hurry!" He looked back at Paul and Leza. It warmed his heart to see them together.

As Paul carried Leza to the lobby with the extra IV bags and antibiotics, he turned to Davis. "I can't thank you enough for all you've done, Doctor, but I intend to seriously try."

Davis touched Leza's face. "You were my best patient ever."

Leza reached across with one arm and hugged Dr. Davis. "And you're my second favorite doctor ever."

Dr. Davis laughed. "Well, considering who's number one, I'm honored."

Paul nodded. "Thanks again for everything." He walked out the door followed by the three men in military gear and boarded the chopper. Moments later, it lifted off, scattering debris once again. Within seconds it rose high in the sky.

Dr. Davis walked outside and watched as the chopper disappeared over the mountain range into Uganda. He smiled as one of his nurses walked up beside him.

"Who was that man, Doctor?"

Davis smiled. "What man?"

EPILOGUE

Jessica scooped scrambled eggs onto the plate, buttered the toast, and poured a cup of coffee. She opened the door of the apartment—the newspaper waited on the mat as usual. She picked it up and placed it on the tray next to the coffee.

Life was different than she had ever expected. She walked past the TV. Today was not a day to care about CNN. She had talked to enough reporters and done enough interviews in the past few weeks to last her a lifetime.

The morning light welcomed her to the balcony overlooking the skyscrapers of Manhattan. She was just like her dad—she loved this city.

As Jessica sat, the scent of the magnolia bush growing in the pot in the corner of the patio reached her. It had been her mother's favorite, and its fragrance reminded Jessica of her every day.

Jessica placed the tray on the table beside her and sat in the chair to enjoy the view. She looked back at the tray. "Nuts." She shook her head. "I forgot the creamer."

"That's okay, baby. Sometimes I like it black." Paul gave her a big grin.

"How are you feeling today, Daddy?"

"I'm good. Gaining weight and getting stronger every day."

"Okay, but that doesn't mean you belong on an airplane headed back to Africa just yet. I know you need to go back, but give yourself time to heal. I don't care if Uncle Jim does have everything planned for you already." Jessica gave Paul the smile that always seemed to melt him.

"You are your mother's daughter. You have me wrapped around your finger."

Jessica shrugged her shoulders. "Can't help it. I love my dad." She looked at the computer on Paul's lap. "What are you doing?"

Paul sheepishly closed the screen. "Just a little research."

Jessica took his hand. "I'm serious. You can't go back yet."

"I know, but I'm finding out things that would shock you. Gina was only a tiny part of an organization involved in human trafficking that reaches into Egypt and Ethiopia. It's big business—big business that preys on young women and children all over the world."

Jessica shook her head in disbelief. "You're a wonderful man, Daddy. I just don't want to lose you."

"If they planned to sell you, they're doing it to other girls. That needs to stop," Paul insisted. "And Jim agrees. But I'll give myself time. I promise."

"Thank you." Jessica paused, squeezed her dad's hand, and then smirked. She was tired of waiting for her father to say what she sensed had been on his mind.

"What?" Paul asked.

"Have you heard from her?"

"Her?" Paul pretended he didn't understand.

"You know exactly who I'm talking about—Hanna. Have you heard from Hanna?"

Paul squirmed a little. "Yes. Adanna is okay. She stayed in her hut at the back of the compound until the soldiers arrived and rescued her. She's fine."

Jessica took a sip of coffee. "That's not what I was asking, but . . . okay." She rested her head back. "I know you'll always love Mom."

Paul gave her a reassuring smile. "Yeah. I always will." He set his coffee on the table. "And how about you? What's Jake up to?"

Jessica blushed and smiled. "He's coming here to New York in a week for four days. He got a furlough to come stateside. We're going to see a play or two, go out to dinner, and walk through Central Park to Loeb Boathouse for lunch one day. I also want to take him to Café Lalo, Sushisamba, Isabella's, Bond Forty-Five, and . . . everywhere. He's never been here before."

Paul nodded his approval. "Does he need a place to stay?"

"Well . . ." Jessica looked at her dad sheepishly. "I figured you would want him to stay with us in the guest room, so I sort of invited him to." She batted her eyelashes in an exaggerated plea and giggled.

Paul laughed. "You were right. I'd love for him to stay here."

Jessica leaned over and kissed Paul on the cheek. "Thank you, Daddy. I'm glad you approve of him."

Paul chuckled a little. "Approve? Yes, I think you could easily say that." Paul marveled at his little girl, all grown up. "Hey, you want to take a walk with me after we eat?"

Jessica looked at her watch. "Oh yes. Yes, I do."

As Paul and Jessica entered the waiting area, the little girl left her nurse and practically ran Paul over. He leaned down, and Leza wrapped her arms around his neck as he stood and lifted her into the air.

"How is my Leza today?"

"I'm good. I'm learning all kinds of stuff, and I really like my tutor, Mrs. Kelly. And the chemo isn't so bad. I'm happy here, Baba, but when can I come home?"

Paul grinned and kissed her forehead. "I have some news for you."

"Really?" Leza's face lit up.

"I talked to my lawyer this morning. Chima has helped us open a few doors back in Africa, and Sudan is going to allow me to file my petition to adopt you. Not only that, but since you are undergoing treatments here in New York, they're giving me custody of you until the adoption takes place. A year from now, if all goes as planned, you will officially be my daughter, but you can live with me starting now—today."

Leza smiled and threw her arms around Paul's neck again. "Can I call you 'Daddy' yet?"

"Oh, I wish you would, sweetie."

Jessica stroked Leza's short hair. "And you can call me 'Sis' if you want. We already have your bedroom fixed up. It's beautiful! Do you like Tinkerbell? Or is your favorite Rapunzel, like in *Tangled*, or Anna and Elsa like in the movie *Frozen*?"

Leza stared at Jessica, bewildered.

Jessica laughed. "We have a lot of catching up to do, don't we?"

Leza giggled as she let go of Paul's neck, reached over, and wrapped her arms around Jessica. She whispered something to Jessica that Paul couldn't hear.

As Paul stood admiring his new family, he was amazed at how fortunate he was to be surrounded by those who loved him and lived for everything he did. Even though he knew he would never stop missing Nicki, as he watched his two daughters smiling about something Jessica had whispered into Leza's ear, he knew he was the most blessed man on earth.

Whatever was to come, it would be an adventure with these two for sure. Nothing was going to hold him back from what might lie ahead.

ABOUT THE AUTHOR

Photo © 2015 Magen Davis

Don Brobst was born in New Jersey and educated in Chicago. He currently lives in Birmingham, Alabama, where he is a practicing physician, a member of the American College of Occupational and Environmental Medicine, and the medical director of the state of Alabama.

The father of three grown children and grandfather of five, Brobst divides his time between his practice, family, writing, and trips to Africa. He is dedicated to giving medical care in the African bush, as well as in Egypt and Ethiopia.

For more information, visit www.donbrobst.com.

WITHDRAWN

WITHDRAWN